VENGEANCE

VENGEANCE

A NOVEL

NEWT GINGRICH

AND PETE EARLEY

CENTER
STREET

New York Nashville

Center Street
Hachette Book Group
1290 Avenue of the Americas, New York, NY 10104
centerstreet.com
twitter.com/centerstreet

Originally published in hardcover and ebook by Center Street in October 2017
First Trade Paperback Edition: October 2018

Center Street is a division of Hachette Book Group, Inc. The Center Street name and logo are trademarks of Hachette Book Group, Inc.

The publisher is not responsible for websites (or their content) that are not owned by the publisher.

Library of Congress Control Number: 2017478119

ISBN: 978-1-4789-2304-6 (hardcover), 978-1-4789-2305-3 (ebook), 978-1-5460-8326-9 (signed edition), 978-1-5460-8325-2 (B&N signed edition), 978-1-4789-2303-9 (trade paperback)

Printed in the United States of America

LSC-C

10 9 8 7 6 5 4 3 2 1

We dedicate this novel to our wives, Callista Gingrich and Patti Luzi-Earley, for their love, wisdom, and unconditional support.

"Men never do evil so completely and cheerfully as when they do it from religious conviction."

—Blaise Pascal, *Pensées*

CONTENTS

CAST OF CHARACTERS

Ebio Kattan, Al Arabic TV correspondent

Esther, Mossad officer

Falcon, radical Islamic terrorist

Hakim "the Destroyer" Farouk, bomb maker

Khalid, General Intelligence Directorate, Saudi Arabia

Major Brooke Grant, U.S. Marine Corps

Mohammad Al-Kader, radical Islamist Imam

Nuruddin Ayaanie "Rudy" Adeogo, Minneapolis congressman

Omar Nader, Islamic Nations spokesman

Payton Grainger, CIA director

Umoja Owiti, billionaire African businessman

VENGEANCE

PART ONE

—m—

THE FALCON DRAWS BLOOD

"We should forgive our enemies, but not before they are hanged."
        —Heinrich Heine, German poet

CHAPTER ONE

6:00 a.m. Saturday
New Jersey Turnpike

Mass murder was traveling south on this beautiful April morning.

Hakim Farouk, known to his fellow radical Islamic brothers as *the Destroyer*, locked the speed on the twenty-four-foot rental truck at exactly five miles above the posted speed limit. It was enough to prevent impatient drivers traveling behind him from becoming annoyed, yet not so fast as to attract the notice of a New Jersey state police trooper.

Two days before this morning, he'd painted the truck pale green, which was the shade of the delivery vehicles owned by Coswell's Catering. It was the most elite wedding service in Washington, D.C., having been awarded the "Gold Medallion Award" for fine food catering each of its seventy-one years in operation. Its gold logo had been stenciled on the truck's outside to make it an exact duplicate, but his cargo had nothing to do with Brie en croute and peppercorn beef tenderloin appetizers or Chef Andre Chevalier Laurent's famed slow-roasted pork loin in honey sauce.

Farouk hated the United States. He hated everything about it. He hated the smell outside the Queens apartment where he was staying when he awoke each day before sunrise to say his morning prayer. He hated the stale taste of the overpriced coffee that he purchased in a neighborhood shop called Good Eats and the babbling old homeless woman who he passed each morning sitting on a park bench guarding a grocery cart stuffed with overflowing green plastic garbage bags.

He hated the brick and carved stone churches with crosses atop their spires that he passed, the giggling schoolchildren chasing one another behind tall chain-link fences in their neighborhood school playground and the teenage boys with odd haircuts who brushed by him on skateboards. He especially hated the Sons of Zion, whom he encountered at the nearby subway stop with their black Hasidic hats and tzitzits dangling from their white prayer shawls. He hated, too, the women who waited for the subway platform, dressed like whores with their arms and legs exposed. He hated the Manhattan commuters in business suits speaking on their cell phones—always speaking on their phones—and the hoodie-wearing young African Americans with earbuds. He hated America's president, every one of its politicians, its Hollywood movie stars, its crowded major cities, its small towns, and its endless suburbs filled with cul-de-sacs edged by carefully cut lawns and cookie-cutter houses. He hated its universities, its fast-food chains, and its Home Depots, Staples, and Walmarts. There was nothing about America that Farouk liked, admired, or envied. *Who did these Americans think they were? Such arrogance!* Always chanting "We're number one" on television. Always bragging about being the world's only "superpower." *What ignorance!*

One morning he'd asked a woman seated next to him in a crowded café if she had ever heard of the Umayyad Caliphate. She had asked if it was a new type of cappuccino. He'd simply nodded, not wishing to waste his time explaining that it was an Islamic form of government that had reigned over an estimated 62 million people—nearly 30 percent of the world's population—between the years 661 and 750, covering an area of 5.1 million square miles, making it one of the largest empires in history in both area and proportion of the world's population. It was the second of four major Islamic caliphates established after the death of Mohammad, spanning some 1,200 years. *What was the United States in comparison?* Had any serious scholar ever called America the "cradle of civilization"?

He would teach these Americans how insignificant they were. He would cause them to cower. He would show them they were not safe. He would do this in a few short hours by which time he would be long gone from this soulless cesspool called the United States of America.

He'd purchased an airline ticket the night before that would transport him from Philadelphia International Airport to London, England, the first leg of several more stops all designed to conceal his whereabouts. If everything went according to his schedule, he would soon be resting comfortably on an international flight when the bomb that he was now transporting was detonated.

Farouk was not a big man. In his midthirties, he was slender with delicate hands, a soft voice, and a calm demeanor that reminded one of a scholarly professor, not a violent jihadist.

Farouk's life depended on his ability to blend into the crowd and live as a ghost.

He checked his watch as he entered the ramp into the Walt Whitman Service Area, some nineteen miles northeast of Philadelphia. Stepping from the truck, he strolled casually across the blacktop parking lot toward the rest area's sandstone building. As he neared its portico, a uniformed New Jersey state trooper came outside, holding a cup of steaming coffee in his right hand. Farouk averted his eyes, but the officer stopped him.

"Just saw you pull in and couldn't help but notice you got New Hampshire plates," the trooper said in a friendly tone. "I grew up in D.C. and didn't know Coswell's Catering operated that far north."

Thinking it was better to admit ignorance than risk giving a wrong answer, Farouk replied, "Wouldn't know. I don't work for Coswell's Catering. My boss runs a custom paint shop in Brooklyn." He nodded toward the truck. "They must've scored a good deal buying the truck and having us paint it before delivery."

"That green's an odd color. I'll admit that," the state trooper replied, taking a big gulp of coffee. "That's partly why I noticed you drive in. 'Course, no one I know can afford Coswell's Catering, but everyone has heard about them."

Farouk shrugged. "I'm just a driver."

"What's your native country?"

"Kabul in Afghanistan," he lied. "Such a beautiful city until those bastards ruined it. The Taliban is destroying everything."

"I agree," the trooper said, taking another sip. He started to walk away but stopped. "I like your hat but you might want to take it off when you get to D.C." He nodded at the official New York Giants baseball cap on Farouk's head. "Washington fans are loyal to their Redskins, or as some folks say, 'Washington's team.' And they hate the Giants."

Farouk, who was wearing the cap so his contact inside the service pavilion could identify him and to help shield his face from security cameras, said, "Thanks for the tip."

The trooper hesitated again. "You should ask the folks at Coswell's to give you a sample."

"Great idea!" Farouk smiled as he turned away from the trooper and entered the building's double doorway. He ignored a brass wall plaque that explained the turnpike service stop was named after Walt Whitman, an American poet who'd spent the last decade of his life in nearby Camden, New Jersey. Once inside the lobby, he looked through a wall of windows at the departing highway trooper. As soon as the officer left the parking lot, Farouk hurried outside to the fake Coswell's Catering truck.

Not using Washington, D.C., plates had been an amateur's mistake. He'd rushed and been sloppy. Retrieving a screwdriver from the truck's glove compartment, he removed the New Hampshire plates, which he tucked inside the light jacket he was wearing. Pressing them against his ribs, Farouk scanned the parking lot.

Walt Whitman was one of the smaller rest stops along the turnpike, but a constant stream of cars and trucks was entering and departing on this Saturday. He noticed a Honda minivan with D.C. license plates. Five elementary schoolchildren bolted from it while two women stepped from its front seats.

"Slow down, Danny," one woman hollered after a boy darting through the parked cars.

"*Havetogotothebathroom!*" he called back over his shoulder.

"Wait for your older brother."

The second mother shouted: "Meet us in Cinnabon for breakfast."

As soon as they entered the service center, Farouk moved quickly to their van, dropped to his knees, and exchanged his license tags for theirs. Hurrying back to his truck, he attached the D.C. plates.

Now satisfied, Farouk entered the building, going directly into a self-serve cafeteria, where he bought coffee and a Danish. He took a seat in a booth near the front windows, casually placing the keys to the rental truck on the plastic red tray that he'd used to tote his coffee and pastry.

He'd finished about half of his drink and eaten none of the Danish when a young man wearing a server's uniform approached his table.

"If you're finished, I'll take this tray for you," he volunteered.

The young man had sent a selfie earlier that morning to a disposable cell phone that Farouk was using so the jihadist could recognize him.

"I don't care for the Danish or more coffee," Farouk replied, "so please take the tray."

The young man did but returned seconds later.

"Sir," he said politely, "you left your keys on the tray." He offered him a key ring.

"Oh, how careless of me."

Taking the keys, Farouk exited the service pavilion and found a blue Honda Civic with a New Jersey license tag parked exactly where he'd been told it would be in a morning text message.

Farouk had satisfactorily completed his task. He'd delivered the bomb inside the truck to the parking lot and to the young man who was seeking martyrdom. They'd exchanged vehicle keys when the youth had picked up the red tray and switched his car keys for the truck keys.

Farouk felt proud as he drove the Civic south toward the Philadelphia airport. The bomb was meant for a specific target selected by an international terrorist known only as the Falcon. He had issued a fatwa against Major Brooke Grant. Today was her wedding day. It was supposed to be one of the happiest days of her life. Instead it would be her last.

CHAPTER TWO

S o it is true?"

"Yes, Madame President, we have three independent and reliable sources."

President Sally Allworth folded her arms across her chest as she stood in front of her Oval Office desk and considered the gravity of what CIA director Payton Grainger had told her.

She'd known when Grainger had arrived unexpectedly on a Saturday morning without waiting for his boss, the director of national intelligence, to return from an overseas trip that he'd come bearing bad news.

"The Chinese were supposed to be keeping North Korea in check," Mallory Harper, the White House chief of staff and President Allworth's most trusted advisor, volunteered from where she was standing some three feet from the president.

"I'm not certain Beijing is even aware," Grainger replied. "If it is, it doesn't want to acknowledge it or get involved. The Chinese will be of no help to us."

"How could they not be aware that their next door neighbor has sold a nuclear bomb to a terrorist?" Harper replied in an incredulous voice.

"Our sources tell us it was the Iranians who provided the expertise that Pyongyang needed to make a nuclear bomb," Grainger said. "Not China."

"Iran," Harper hissed, "they've been a thorn in our side for way too long."

"Not just our side," President Allworth added, "the entire world's. They're the biggest backer of terrorism against the West and the primary cause of instability in the Middle East. Now you're telling me that Iran has helped a mentally unstable, half-pint, puffed up, spoiled little man-child sell a nuclear bomb to our enemies?"

"The intelligence we've gathered strongly suggests the 'outstanding leader' knows it will be targeted against us," Grainger said. "Meanwhile, he's getting help from the Iranians to make an intercontinental missile-delivery device strong enough to hit our shores."

"That misfit runt will spark another world war—even if it means his own destruction," Harper added.

"Let's focus on the immediate problem," the president said. "We're not going to allow a terrorist to detonate a smuggled nuclear bomb in one of our cities."

"There is a high probability the Falcon is the terrorist who has bought the bomb," Director Grainger said as he studied the president's face.

As with all her recent predecessors, Allworth seemed to have aged at a much faster pace than others during her past five years in the White House. When she'd launched her unlikely campaign at age fifty-six, she'd invited journalists to jog three miles with her before dawn each morning in whatever city she was visiting. It guaranteed a local newspaper and Internet photo and showed her vitality. But as president, she'd had few moments to jog.

President Allworth had come to politics later than most. After the sudden death of her husband, a popular Pennsylvania senator, she'd served the remainder of his term and then had shocked everyone by entering the presidential race. Her victory had stunned pundits and swept her into the Oval Office on a wave of anti-Washington, anti-incumbent sentiment. But thanks to an obstinate Congress and serial domestic and international crises, she'd been kept from delivering on most of her heartfelt campaign promises.

To Grainger, she now looked worn-out.

"Okay, let's get everyone assembled ASAP to discuss our options.

When does Stephen get back from London?" Allworth asked, referring to Grainger's boss, the director of national intelligence.

"His flight is scheduled to land at three-fifteen this afternoon," Chief of Staff Harper replied.

"Let's schedule a four o'clock National Security Council meeting here," Allworth ordered.

"I can provide a more thorough briefing by then," Grainger assured them as he excused himself from the Oval Office.

Addressing her chief of staff, President Allworth said, "Mallory, notify the vice president first about this meeting so he doesn't get his nose further bent out of joint about us not including him."

Harper smirked. Neither she nor the president cared for Vice President Wyatt Bowie Austin. Their contempt was one of Washington's most gossiped "secrets."

"Your chairman of the joint chiefs isn't going to be happy about an emergency meeting," Harper said.

"Oh my, I totally forgot!" the president replied. "What time did the invitation say?"

"Major Brooke Grant's wedding is scheduled to begin at two thirty."

The president thought for a moment. "Her parents were murdered during the nine-eleven attacks, so General Grant will be walking her down the aisle. How long does a wedding ceremony last nowadays?"

"It depends on how religious the bride and groom are. My nephew's ceremony lasted less than ten minutes because he and his bride wanted to spend more time partying with their friends than saying their vows. Major Grant is not getting married in a church, so I suspect the formal ceremony will be rather short."

"If I'm going to drag the chairman of the joint chiefs of staff away from his niece's wedding, the least I can do is make an appearance at the ceremony."

Harper frowned. "The Secret Service is going to make a fuss with this short notice."

"Of course it will. But this might be just the thing I need to lift my spirits before the four o'clock meeting."

"I'll see to it," Harper said, turning to leave.

"Mallory," President Allworth said, "screenwriters and novelists have been concocting plots about terrorists getting their hands on a nuclear bomb since nine-eleven, but I never thought this would happen under my watch. We can't let the Falcon destroy one of our cities. We just can't have that."

CHAPTER THREE

Geraldine Grant was nervously waiting at the front door of her home.

The security team stationed at the front gate to protect the chairman of the joint chiefs of staff had called her moments earlier about an unexpected visitor.

"I'm Cindy Gural," a fortyish-looking woman wearing a U.S. Park Police uniform announced as she came up the front steps, extending her hand toward Geraldine. "I've come to speak to Major Brooke Grant."

"Yes, yes," Geraldine answered impatiently. "The guards said it was important and it better be because today she's getting married and we've got to be leaving lickety-split. Should have been gone ten minutes ago."

"Yes, ma'am, I know she's getting married because I'm helping provide security at her wedding. Earning a bit of extra off-duty pay. But I promise I'll take only a couple minutes. Just long enough to deliver this packet." Officer Gural lifted a thick manila envelope in her left hand as if it were a shield between her and the formidable wife of a four-star Army general who was visibly unhappy about the morning interruption.

"Five minutes tops, you hear?" Geraldine lectured. "Not six, not seven." Without waiting for a reply, Geraldine called out, "Brooke, a Park Police officer is here."

Wearing worn denim jeans and a red Washington Nationals baseball jersey, Major Brooke Grant appeared at the top of the steps inside the two-story brick Colonial where she had lived as a teenager after her parents' murders.

"Auntie," Brooke said as she began descending the stairs, "I can't find my mother's necklace. I put it out last night in a special place where I wouldn't forget it and now I've forgotten where."

Shaking her head as if to say, *What's wrong with you?* Geraldine replied, "Girl, I've never seen you this scatterbrained but I suspect weddings do that. Now, I just told this officer she's got you for only five minutes. Five minutes! Your uncle just got a phone call and now he's decided he wants to ride with us downtown rather than waiting. We all need to get a move on."

"Why's he coming with us?" Brooke asked. "We're going to do makeup and hair and he doesn't wear makeup and he has no hair."

"Ask him yourself. He's being all mysterious," Geraldine snapped. "I'll go find your mama's necklace."

Speaking to Officer Gural, Brooke said, "When you called, it took me a moment but I remembered as soon as you mentioned Mary Margaret Delaney—the suicide on the George Washington Parkway."

"That's what the medical examiner says happened, but I don't think she killed herself and you promised to look into it if I ever came up with anything suspicious."

"I'd like to help," Brooke said in a hurried voice, "but I'm not on a joint terrorism task force anymore, so I don't have any jurisdiction."

"Major, I know it's your wedding day, but I had to share this information with someone." She handed the manila envelope to Brooke. "Maybe after your honeymoon you can give it a glance. My conscience won't be clear unless I do this. Please take it."

Brooke accepted the thick envelope but before she could respond to Officer Gural, Aunt Geraldine appeared at the top of the steps. "I've found your mother's necklace in your bedroom right where you left it." Peering down from the top step, she said, "Officer, are you still here? Your time is up, missy. We've got to get moving."

"I'm sorry I had to bring this by today," Gural said.

"Okay," Geraldine announced as she descended the stairs, "now you said what you needed to say. Out the door with you." Exchanging a pearl necklace for the package in Brooke's hands, Geraldine added, "Whatever's in this envelope can wait." She placed it on a side table next to the front door.

"Don't worry," Brooke said reassuringly to Gural as she was leaving. "I won't forget it."

Shutting the front door behind Officer Gural, Geraldine said, "Your mother and daddy would have been so proud of you. Oh gosh, I'm going to start crying and we're not even at the ceremony. It's just, when I think of them and how they were murdered—" She stopped speaking and used a tissue to wipe her eyes. "I still remember the day when you first came to live with your uncle and me. My oh my, and now here we are, you getting all married."

She leaned forward and hugged Brooke, who was fumbling with the necklace's gold clasp behind her neck.

"Help, Auntie, please," she whispered.

"What's going on here?" General Frank Grant asked as he joined them from the family room. "Little Miss Jennifer has beaten me in four straight games of some dang computer game called Drawful."

"Five games!" bragged a fifteen-year-old girl who followed him into the foyer. "He's a lousy artist and I'm not a little girl."

"Don't be so hard on him," Geraldine playfully scolded.

"After this wedding and the adoption papers go through," General Grant said to the teenager, "you will be my niece's daughter and at that point, I will expect you to allow me to win on occasion."

Jennifer broke into a grin. "Can I call you Uncle Frank once I'm adopted or do I still need to call you General?"

"Well, now, that's something I'll need time to thoughtfully consider," he replied jokingly.

"Oh stop this nonsense," Geraldine said. Looking lovingly at Brooke, the older woman continued. "You know the general and I have thought of you as our daughter since the day you stepped foot into our house. And after you get married and adopt Jennifer, I'll not have her calling him anything but 'Gramps' and me 'Grandma.' Now let's get moving."

"Maybe I'll have you call me 'General Grandpa,'" he said teasingly to Jennifer.

Changing subjects, Brooke asked General Grant, "Why are you coming with us? You know it's just us girls getting ready and the ceremony doesn't begin until two thirty."

"Girls only," Jennifer interjected.

"Don't you worry about me interfering with a bunch of cackling hens," the general replied.

"You know, that's really offensive," Brooke said.

"He's just being ornery," Geraldine replied. "Getting under your skin. He's all full of himself today."

"I wish it was just onerous," Brooke replied in a serious voice.

Everyone smiled, but her jab was based on a long-standing feud between her and the general when it came to gender roles. As the stern father of three sons, General Grant had expected his boys to join the military, which each of them had. But he'd not expected his niece to do the same. He didn't think women belonged in the military services, although he never shared that view publicly. Even worse, she had entered the Navy as a Marine just to spite him. All of his sons had joined the Army, following in his footsteps.

No one questioned the love between Brooke and her uncle, but he had been completely flummoxed when she'd first arrived as a teenager after her parents' murder in the Twin Towers. Brooke had been deposited on her aunt Geraldine and uncle Frank's doorstep as an angry, shell-shocked, and a very stubborn teen who'd immediately rebelled at her uncle's strict rules. She still did. After she'd joined the U.S. Marine Corps against his wishes, he'd pulled strings to keep her out of harm's way by having her assigned to easy military attaché jobs in Paris and London. But his plan hadn't worked. In the past three years, she'd helped stop a terrorist bombing in London and later outside a Somali mosque. She'd rescued an American ambassador and U.S. Marines being held hostage in Mogadishu. And after returning to the States, she'd saved President Allworth from a suicide-bent attacker and unmasked a traitor working inside the White House.

After all of those life-threatening events, you might have thought her uncle would stop trying to shield his thirty-one-year-old niece, but he hadn't and their latest argument had been their most bitter. After bracing himself with two scotches, General Grant had told Brooke two nights ago that he'd wanted her to call off her wedding.

"Are you drunk, crazy, or both?" she'd replied.

"Brooke, I just can't see how this marriage is going to work. He's an Indian from Montana. You have nothing in common."

"The correct term is Native American and I'm an African American. That makes us both minorities."

"I can't visualize you crouched outside a teepee raising babies."

She was so upset by his racism and sexism that she had stormed out of his study. As always, Aunt Geraldine had chided her husband and the general had apologized and begged forgiveness the next morning.

Like always, she had given in, excusing his awful words as whisky blabber. Still, deep down, she knew he was opposed to her marrying a Crow Indian named Walks Many Miles.

This morning, the general was all smiles. Reaching out and taking Brooke by the hand, he said, "What happened to that little girl who used to crawl onto my lap when your parents visited us and ask me to read Winnie the Pooh?"

She leaned into him and kissed his cheek. "I was only five back then, but you'll always be my Pooh Bear."

"Who's Winnie the Pooh?" Jennifer asked.

Aunt Geraldine shook her head in disappointment. "Trouble with this generation is they don't know nothing about nothing."

But there was another explanation for why Jennifer was unaware of Winnie the Pooh. She'd sustained a traumatic brain injury that had caused her to forget much of her childhood, and she still had trouble retaining information.

"Pooh's a character from a children's book," Brooke explained.

Aunt Geraldine, a deeply religious woman, chose that moment to deliver a sermon. "It would be better today if children read Winnie the Pooh and the Holy Bible than all those books about vampires and wizards."

"Shouldn't we be leaving?" Brooke asked.

As they left the house for the waiting limousine, Brooke asked, "Uncle Frank, who called you this morning? Aunt Geraldine mentioned you received an important call."

A mischievous grin swept across the sixty-seven-year-old general's face. "Oh, you'll find out soon enough."

CHAPTER FOUR

New Jersey state trooper Justin Ambrose was parked in his squad car near the southern exit of the sixth busiest toll road in the nation when he spotted a pale green Coswell's Catering truck. More than four hours had passed since he'd begun his shift with a cup of coffee at the Walt Whitman service area. That's where he'd spoken to the NFL-cap-wearing, Afghanistan-born driver of what appeared to be this very same freshly painted truck.

Why had it taken him so long to complete what should have been a thirty-five-minute turnpike drive?

As the truck neared, Officer Ambrose noticed it was bearing D.C. license tags—unlike the one he'd seen earlier. As it passed his squad car, Ambrose focused on the driver's face. There was no New York Giants hat and this Arab looked much younger. Clearly, he concluded, this was a different Coswell's Catering truck that was being delivered to Washington, D.C.

Inside the truck, Salman Basra checked the vehicle's side mirrors. He didn't relax until he had put a mile between himself and the parked state trooper. Unlike Hakim "the Destroyer" Farouk, who had delivered the bomb in the truck's cargo area, Salman Basra did not hate America. He had always felt alienated from it, however, even though he'd been born in Jersey City. As he had become older, he'd come to believe his birthplace was representative of his own predicament. Jersey City was considered part of the greater New York metropolitan area even though it was the second most populous city in the Garden State. Basra was a native-born U.S. citizen, yet he considered himself a Pakistani even though he had visited his father's native country only three times. His mother was a Saudi, but he'd never been there and she had cut off all contact with her Saudi relatives.

Basra's parents had never intended to live in America permanently but they were happy to have their son born here and guaranteed American citizenship. For them, Jersey City was a means to an end, a way for them to reap the nation's prosperity and get their only son a good education before they returned to Karachi to reunite with relatives. Because neither parent intended to become citizens, they had lived in the United States as if they were still residing in Pakistan. Neither was Americanized, nor did they wish to assimilate.

It could be argued that his parents didn't fully understand the impact that their actions had on their impressionable son. At age twenty-two, Basra had formed an overly romantic image of everyday life in Karachi that was based entirely on the fun-filled family vacations. Pakistan was full of color and was exotic and exhilarating. Life in Jersey City was gray and muted.

His father rose early each morning to commute into Brooklyn, where he co-owned a three-aisle bodega with another Pakistani, returning late each night exhausted before beginning the same routine the next morning and the next, seven days a week. Basra's mother provided childcare in their apartment for infants. Although Basra had dreamed of becoming an artist, his father had insisted he study accounting at a local community college, a subject that he found tedious. His shyness and awkwardness had made it difficult for him to make friends in a largely commuter college, and like many males his age, he had isolated himself in his bedroom where he'd played Internet combat games with strangers known only by their macho online nicknames.

It was through the Internet that Basra had learned about sex, a taboo subject in his parents' home. In the safety of his bedroom, he would click from one free porno site to another, ignoring the pop-up ads telling him that a woman who lived within a mile of his house was available. Basra always felt guilty after his voyeur experiences because he knew his Muslim parents would disapprove, but each night he was drawn back to the same Web pages, unable to avoid their siren calls.

It was those sexual fantasies that had played a role in him becoming a jihadist. Although religious, his parents did not pray the required five times a day nor read the Holy Quran.

One night during strong feelings of mental flagellation, Basra had stumbled upon a YouTube video made by a Minneapolis-born Somali American who'd changed his birth name for an Arab one. Abdul Hafeez had joined Al-Shabaab in Africa and in a series of professional quality videos had boasted about how he was answering Allah's call for the creation of a pure Islamic state. The videos showed him firing an AK-47 in Somalia and in one gruesome posting, Hafeez had chopped off the hands of a captured American diplomat. The videos mimicked the combat games Basra enjoyed but these videos were real and laced with radical Islamic propaganda.

"Those who believe fight in the cause of Allah," Hafeez boasted on the videos, reciting the Quran 4:76. Gasping for breath between firing off rounds, he would recite Hadith (authentic) teachings:

"No one who enters Paradise wants to leave it even if they are given the world and everything in it, with the exception of the Shaheed (martyr). He wants to leave Paradise, come back to this world, and be killed in the sake of Allah again."

When Basra discovered that Abdul Hafeez had been killed by a U.S. Marine, he was sad for days. And then Basra had learned another jarring bit of news. Abdul Hafeez's older brother was a member of Congress, a revelation that had outraged most Americans.

Basra had soon found a new Arab mentor, and this one lived only four hours away in suburban Maryland outside Washington, D.C. The cleric Mohammad Al-Kader was much older than Abdul Hafeez, having fought with the Mujahedeen against the Soviets in the early 1980s. But in his Internet teachings, the Imam was even more persuasive. He couldn't be challenged when it came to reciting passages from the Quran and the Hadith, and he called for a complete, worldwide adherence to Sharia law rather than man-made rules and governments.

Basra had become so mesmerized by Al-Kader's teachings that he had driven to the Great Mosque of Allah in Maryland to speak personally with the Imam.

Shortly after their meeting, Basra had been contacted via the Internet by followers of the notorious jihadist known only as "the Falcon." At first, Basra had been tested with minor assignments, such as forwarding messages or purchasing U.S. goods for mailing to Pakistan. After three months, more serious demands had been made, and a month ago, Salman Basra had been asked if he felt worthy of becoming a martyr.

Today was his day for glory.

As he crossed the Delaware Memorial Bridge, the disposable phone that he'd purchased received a text.

Delivery at 1430 exactly. The text included an address. When he typed it into his GPS, it showed he was ahead of schedule and would arrive at his target much too early. Still, he continued driving at a steady pace until he reached the Maryland suburbs, where he pulled into a gas station to wait. He read the Quran to pass time and ready himself mentally. What would his parents, aunts, uncles, and cousins think? He had not come into this world to live a meaningless life running a bodega simply to earn earthly goods. He had been born to serve Allah.

"*Allahu Akbar*," he whispered. "*Allahu Akbar.*"

CHAPTER FIVE

Major Brooke Grant's choice of a wedding venue went completely opposite her understated tastes. She'd chosen a castle.

At the turn of the twentieth century, Washington's most magnificent houses were constructed around Dupont Circle, one of more than thirty traffic circles in the city. Originally Dupont Circle had been called Pacific Circle but Congress renamed it in 1882 to honor Samuel Francis Du Pont, a rear admiral during the Civil War (Union, of course) and a descendant of the famed Du Pont family, one of the richest in America.

The Du Pont families had wanted something grander than a mere statue of the admiral, so they had the one Congress had erected carted off to Wilmington, Delaware, for display. An ornate marble fountain designed by the same architects responsible for the Lincoln Memorial took its place.

Massachusetts Avenue, one of eight major roads that fed into Dupont Circle, eventually contained so many mansions the area became known as "Millionaires' Row." When the Great Depression hit, many of them were sold to foreign governments for use as embassies and the area was renamed "Embassy Row."

Brooke's wedding was being held inside the Heurich House Mansion, just south of Dupont Circle along New Hampshire Avenue. The thirty-one-room brownstone Victorian had been one of the city's most imposing homes when it was constructed in 1892 by Christian

Heurich, a German-born immigrant who'd been orphaned at age fourteen and had spent a decade working in Europe brewing beer before arriving in the United States. By age fifty-two, he had become one of Washington's wealthiest citizens by selling alcohol. At its peak, the Christian Heurich Brewing Company produced a half-million barrels of beer a year and was the second largest employer in the city after the federal government. He'd erected his brewery along the banks of the Potomac River on land where the John F. Kennedy Center for Performing Arts later would be constructed.

Heurich's grand house became known as the "Brewmaster's Castle" because the four-story home resembled a German fortress, complete with a corner watchtower topped by a cone-shaped dome. The house was credited as being the city's first "fireproof" building because it was constructed almost entirely of steel, concrete, and brownstone. When the last of Heurich's heirs died, the city's historical society had converted it into a museum available for rent on special occasions.

Although Brooke preferred denim jeans, T-shirts, and Nikes to Zac Posen designer outfits and spiked heels, the castle had first enthralled her when she was an impressionable teen attending a family friend's wedding. Her uncle had argued that she should be married at the Fort McNair Officers Club while her aunt had insisted on a ceremony inside the local Baptist church that she attended. Brooke had overruled them both.

The Brewmaster's Castle reminded her of fairy tales and her unlikely love affair with Walks Many Miles was the stuff of such fantasies. They'd met in Mogadishu as Marines sent to open an embassy there and together they had survived a brutal Al-Shabaab campaign to kill them and hundreds of others.

Brooke had asked Jennifer to be her maid of honor along with two bridesmaids who were friends from her days as a cadet at the U.S. Naval Academy. Miles had recruited Brooke's three cousins—the sons of Aunt Geraldine and General Grant—as groomsmen after explaining that he and Brooke would need to be wed a second time in a Crow ceremony in Montana, which she had yet to visit.

Brooke and her attendants, along with Aunt Geraldine, were getting their hair and makeup done professionally at the front of the mansion when Brooke's phone rang.

"I know I can't see you until the big reveal," Miles said, "but a call would be okay, right?"

"You getting cold feet?"

"Never. I'll gladly trade this tuxedo for BDUs in a heartbeat if you'd let me," he replied, referring to battle dress uniforms, the Marines' name for camouflaged fatigues.

"Not a chance. Oh, when I was stationed in London on the dip circuit, I was informed by a rather stuffy English diplomat that only lower-class people referred to them as *tuxedos*. He called them dinner jackets."

"Then I doubt he'd approve of my cowboy boots," Miles replied, chuckling. "Have you told your aunt and uncle you're wearing a matching pair?"

"Not yet," she whispered. Then in a voice loud enough for everyone around her to overhear, she added, "Wait until you see Jennifer. She's so beautiful!"

The teen, standing a few feet away, beamed.

"Good-bye, soon-to-be Mrs. Walks Many Miles," he said, hanging up before she could remind him that she had no intention of taking his last name.

At 2:20 p.m., the wedding coordinator entered the room and announced it was time for Aunt Geraldine and the bridesmaids to walk down a long hallway to a one-story brick addition that had been added at the back of the grand old house to accommodate larger events.

Brooke's phone rang again. The wedding coordinator frowned and shot her a stern look.

"I have something to tell you," General Grant declared when Brooke answered.

"What's wrong?"

"My morning phone call before we left the house?"

"The mysterious one?"

"The president just made a surprise appearance. She's sitting in the front row."

CHAPTER SIX

Heurich House was clearly marked on Google Maps.
Despite this, Salman Basra was having trouble reaching it. The reason: D.C. police officers.

Normally, a motorist would turn south from Dupont Circle directly onto New Hampshire Avenue, which Heurich House faced. But that thoroughfare was blocked off. His only choice was the next exit: 19th Street.

The French-born American civil engineer Pierre Charles L'Enfant had laid out the capital in a grid. All north–south bound streets were numbered. All east–west bound streets were given letters in alphabetical order. But there were exceptions and New Hampshire Avenue happened to be one of them. It cut diagonally between 19th and 20th Streets, creating a triangle-shaped block with the Heurich Mansion based at its southwesternmost corner. The base of this triangle was a single block named Sunderland Place.

Sunderland Place would take him directly to the side and rear of the Heurich Mansion, putting him within fifteen yards of the actual wedding service. But it was a one-way street going the wrong way for Basra, and, even more problematic, two police cars were blocking its entrance from 19th Street. Uncertain what to do, Basra circled the neighborhood several times, hoping to find an alternative way to enter Sunderland Place. Meanwhile, the ceremony began.

Feeling a sense of panic, he returned to 19th Street, stopped his truck in the middle of the street, flipped on its emergency blinkers, got out of the truck cab, and approached one of the D.C. officers blocking the Sunderland Place entrance.

"Got a delivery to the wedding," he said. "Extra desserts and I'm already late. Can you move those cars and let me through?"

The officer nodded toward two men wearing dark suits, sunglasses, and telltale earpieces.

"Talk to Secret Service," the officer replied, "special security because the president's here."

The U.S. president! Basra had no idea. He glanced at the two agents standing some fifteen feet away and then surveyed Sunderland Place. It had been cleared of all vehicles. It looked like an empty airport runway leading directly to his target. The only obstructions were the two police cars parked nose-to-nose across the street's entrance and several wooden sawhorse barricades strategically placed on the sidewalks.

Basra had no way of knowing how fortunate he was. Normally, the U.S. Secret Service would have had the D.C. government park large garbage trucks or city buses to barricade Sunderland Place's entrance. Waist-high concrete barriers would have been lowered onto the sidewalks.

But the president's last-minute decision to attend Brooke's wedding had caught everyone off guard. Most D.C. city offices were closed on Saturdays and communications between the Secret Service and D.C. sanitation and transportation departments had been faulty.

Basra was running out of time. He had no other choice. Returning to his truck cab, he waved causally at the police officer and two agents watching him and then spun the truck's steering wheel sharply and pushed down hard on its accelerator.

The truck's front wheels bounced as they hit the street curb and jumped onto the sidewalk, slipping in between the police cruisers blocking the street and the office building facing the street. Basra's truck easily smashed through the sawhorse barricades.

In a well-practiced move, one of the Secret Service agents reached inside his blazer and swung a Heckler & Koch MP5K submachine gun into sight. He fired a flurry of rounds at Basra just as the jihadist was turning his truck off the sidewalk onto Sunderland Place, having driven around the parked police cars.

Nine-millimeter rounds shattered the truck's glass side windows and punched through the driver's door. Basra was struck twice in his left leg but he managed to keep his right foot pressed against the accelerator as the truck sped toward the mansion and Brooke Grant's wedding ceremony.

The D.C. police officer also drew his sidearm and fired at the speeding truck's rear tires. The second Secret Service agent ran adjacent to the truck, firing his submachine gun. Another slug hit Basra's left shoulder, rendering it useless.

As if from nowhere, a black armored SUV appeared midway down the street, flying from its hiding place inside a parking garage. It slammed into Basra's truck, knocking the rental sideways and bringing it to a halt about twenty yards from Brooke Grant's venue.

The three hundred guests inside heard the collision and glanced through windows in the large room where the ceremony was under way. With his good right hand, a critically wounded Basra mumbled a final *Allahu Akbar* and punched a button attached to the steering wheel.

A blinding white light was followed by a deafening boom and shock wave. Next came a blast wind of negative pressure, which sucked items back toward its center. The devastation was immediate and cataclysmic.

Basra and the Coswell's Catering truck blew into pieces. The mansion's brownstone walls collapsed, including the castle's corner tower, although a few heavy brownstones that made up the portico and front wall remained erect. The others became jagged rock fragments that flew like bullets from the blast area. The explosion blew out windows in every building within a two-block area. Southbound cars traveling on 19th Street were overturned and shoved into storefronts. The Secret Service agents, the D.C. police officer chasing Basra, and the officers' colleagues stationed outside and inside the mansion were killed—as were every one of the three hundred guests seated inside the huge ceremony room.

In an instant, Sunderland Place became a rubbish heap, resembling large city refuse dumps covered with a mishmash of broken objects. While some corpses were badly mutilated by the flying debris, the human body proved to be incredibly elastic. Most wedding guests' bodies were still intact. They were lying burned and battered, mostly buried under jagged and bent steel, splintered shafts of wood, and chunks of concrete.

It was the most devastating bombing in the city's history.

CHAPTER SEVEN

Ten minutes earlier
Heurich House Mansion

The unexpected arrival of President Sally Allworth had flummoxed the normally unshakable wedding coordinator. Last-minute decisions had to be made quickly. Should the president be the last to be seated before the bridesmaids and groomsmen entered the room or should it be the mother of the bride, in Brooke's case, her aunt Geraldine? The president ended the confusion by insisting the wedding proceed as originally planned with no special changes because of her prominence.

President Sally Allworth had waited until the last possible minute to exit the White House grounds earlier that morning. She hadn't wanted the Washington press corps following her and disrupting Brooke's wedding.

Brooke had been unaware until her uncle had telephoned her about the president's arrival and had not known that Secret Service agents had used hand wands to check guests and had examined photo IDs.

This commotion had caused a few minutes' delay before Aunt Geraldine had been escorted into the ceremony wearing an embroidered floral trumpet gown that she had bought on sale at Lord & Taylor. She topped her gown with a black church hat decorated with a ruffled satin ribbon and coque feathers.

An imposing General Grant had stationed himself at the doorway waiting for Brooke and Jennifer to come down the hallway. He was wearing his U.S. Army dress blues with a chestful of ribbons designating his many military accomplishments. Everyone was waiting on the bride and her young maid of honor.

In a break from tradition, Brooke had invited Jennifer to walk alongside her when General Grant escorted them both down the aisle. Brooke had felt it important to show everyone that she considered Jennifer to be her daughter, even though she technically was still her legal ward.

White satin bows with a single pink rose decorated the ends of each row of padded folding chairs inside the venue, where an arch had been erected lined with light pink roses. The Baptist minister from Aunt Geraldine's church had agreed to perform the ceremony. He stood waiting, Bible open in his hands, flanked by Walks Many Miles and Brooke's three cousins.

Everyone waited and then waited a bit longer.

As Brooke and Jennifer were making their way from the bride's dressing room along the mansion's long hallway to the ceremony, Jennifer had whispered in a panicked voice: "I gotta pee."

"It's okay, honey," Brooke said. "Everyone will just have to wait on us."

"You'll have to help me with my dress." It buttoned down the back. Brooke, who was wearing a white Vera Wang V-neck dress with inverted pleats and linear appliques of corded lace that fanned outward from the waistline, said, "Let's find a ladies' room." She'd asked the now near-frantic wedding coordinator where the closest toilet was located.

"In the basement. It was the servants'. Please hurry!"

Brooke handed her wedding bouquet to the coordinator and took Jennifer's hand. Together they descended a narrow spiral staircase hidden behind a hallway door that appeared to be part of the corridor's wood paneling.

"This is like a secret passage," Jennifer gushed.

Just as Brooke was closing the bathroom door behind them, Salman Basra detonated the truck bomb.

Twenty minutes after the explosion, D.C. firefighter Jamal Simpson heard voices yelling from under what had been the mansion's center hallway. He tried to concentrate, but he couldn't be certain he was hearing human voices because of the ear-piercing sounds of fire and rescue vehicles rushing to the blast site from across the city and the suburbs.

Dropping to his knees, he lowered his right ear until it was only inches above the debris.

"Help!"

He definitely heard it. A woman's voice.

"We got survivors!" he hollered, waving his arms in the air.

Within seconds, he was surrounded by other first responders, who began digging with their bare hands through the wreckage of steel beams, bits of wood debris, and heavy rocks. With each removed piece, the woman's cries for help became clearer.

"Please, please hurry! My daughter's hurt!"

"How many are you?" Simpson asked.

"Me and my daughter!"

Within ten minutes, the rescuers had created a crack wide enough for Brooke Grant's face to appear.

The workers formed a bucket brigade, passing every piece of rubbish that could be lifted from one person to the next until the gap became large enough for Brooke to hoist Jennifer through.

"I think her leg is broken."

An EMT tugged Jennifer free from the opening and immediately placed her on a litter because the ruins around them made it impossible for any vehicle to drive any closer. Jennifer was not crying.

Brooke crawled through the hole next, emerging for the first time to see the butchery surrounding her. At first she couldn't wrap her mind around what she was seeing, and out of instinct, her brain chose to focus on Jennifer.

"How badly are you injured?" Simpson asked.

"Take me to my daughter!" Brooke demanded, ignoring his question.

With first responders on each side of her, she marched across the uneven piles of rubbish toward the team carrying Jennifer to a waiting ambulance on what appeared to be a war-torn 19th Street. Inside the vehicle, an EMT shined a light into Jennifer's eyes and peppered the teen with questions, but she didn't respond and kept her eyes staring straight ahead as if she were a zombie.

"Shock," the EMT explained. "We've got to get her to the hospital ASAP."

"I'm going," Brooke announced, stepping inside the ambulance. "Did you check her leg? It was pinned under rocks."

"It's not broken. We need to examine you too."

"Forget about me. Save my daughter."

Someone shut the ambulance's back doors.

"I don't know how you two survived," the EMT inside said.

"We were in a basement bathroom," Brooke explained as she sat next to Jennifer and held her hand. "It was like a foxhole. Only a few pieces of the ceiling collapsed."

The house's massive steel rafters under the heavy Italian marble flooring had proven to be an effective bomb shelter.

As the ambulance began slowly pulling away, Brooke glanced out the back windows. She saw officers removing limp and blood-covered bodies—all guests who she'd invited. She gasped at the horrific scene and in that instant instinctively understood this was the work of a suicide bomber sent by the Falcon to murder her.

"Where's my fiancé, my auntie and uncle? Where's the president? Where are the other survivors?" she blurted out in a panicked voice.

The EMT didn't answer. He was still checking Jennifer's vitals and looking for wounds.

"The others?" she insisted, her voice rising higher. "Where have they been taken?"

"There's only you two," he said quietly. "President Allworth is dead."

The enormity of the moment came to her like a heavy weight crushing down on her chest. She stared outside, still unsure that this had actually happened. *Everyone? How could this be?* Amid the carnage, an item caught her eye.

A lone cowboy boot. It matched the pair that she was still wearing.

CHAPTER EIGHT

Two hours after the wedding bombing
Manhattan, New York

Umoja Owiti needed out of New York.

Although he'd had nothing directly to do with the truck bombing, the African billionaire was afraid he might eventually fall under suspicion. This bombing was merely a prelude, a foreshadowing of what was to come next.

Owiti knew the North Koreans had sold a nuclear bomb to the Falcon because he had paid for it and arranged its delivery. He also knew the bomb was only one element in a grand plan of the mass destruction that he and the Falcon had been plotting for more than a year to put in place.

It was time for him to go. He ordered his private Gulfstream G550 luxury jet to be readied for departure and then rushed downstairs to where his armored Rolls-Royce Phantom was waiting to carry him to Teterboro Airport, just across the river in New Jersey. It was the most popular and nearest airport for wealthy Manhattan residents. As soon as his chauffeur turned onto the street, his entourage of bodyguards and personal assistants riding in armored SUVs fell into position.

Two beautiful flight attendants greeted him on the tarmac where his jet was waiting. When called upon, both women shared his bed in the private jet's custom master suite.

He hurried by them, going directly into his private cabin in the jet, where he switched on a bank of television screens so he could watch coverage of the wedding bombing's aftermath in Washington.

Had you not known Owiti was Africa's richest businessman, you would not have given him a second glance. Standing six feet tall with an ample belly spilling over his belt, he looked the part of any other New York businessman in an overly expensive tailored suit.

But Owiti wasn't like anyone else. Forbes estimated his personal wealth at $22 billion.

Everyone excused his eccentricities because of his wealth. The rich were different, after all. The fifty-five-year-old believed deodorants caused cancer, so he refused to use them. He resisted bathing because he didn't trust the purity of water, even in Manhattan. Instead, he splashed his face each morning with Roja Dov Amber Aoud Absolue Precieux cologne, a fragrance that announced his arrival before he entered a room.

For a man who was both well educated, having obtained degrees from both Oxford and the London School of Economics, and exceptionally rich, Owiti had an exaggerated fear of dentists. This explained why he'd never had a chipped front tooth repaired or his crooked lower teeth straightened. Only those closest to him were aware it was because of an inept Nairobi dentist who had so badly bungled a root canal in his mother's mouth that the poor woman had lived in constant pain for two decades before her death. That had marred her son. Later, he had used his vast wealth to track down the inept dentist. Police found the elderly man's corpse tossed from a car, minus all of his teeth, which appeared to have been jerked out of their sockets with a pair of pliers.

Another of the billionaire's oddities was Owiti's belief that sexual activity caused a chemical reaction in his brain that made him think faster than other men. Where others jogged or lifted weights, he routinely had sex two or more times a day.

Although Owiti already had amassed a fortune, he wanted more. He loved making money and he had no ethics when it came to getting as much of it as he could obtain. His mother, a beautiful and cunning Somali, and his father, a Maasi warrior, had produced a Machiavellian offspring who thrived in a world of moral weightlessness of his own creating.

In public, Owiti presented himself as an honest, peaceful, quiet, practicing Muslim. That was a well-crafted façade. Privately, he was petty, cruel, and vicious. Like many of the wealthy, his money was a sign to him that God favored him. That he was special.

His father had launched him at age fourteen by giving him part ownership in a failing diamond mine. Only months later, Allah had blessed him when an abundance of the valuable gems had been unearthed there. Through bribes and questionable legal and often violent means, he'd become sole owner by age eighteen. In the next decades, he'd parlayed that mine into a financial empire with holdings in uranium, telecommunications, the Internet, and publishing, as well as companies that built medical equipment and disposed of toxic wastes, and international shipping companies with operations that extended beyond Africa into Eastern Europe and China.

What was the point of having wealth if you couldn't show it off?

Owiti did without a hint of propriety. The 1903 Beaux Arts mansion off Central Park in Manhattan that he'd purchased for $84 million had not been grandiose enough, so he'd gutted the 15,000-square-foot dwelling and installed over-the-top finishes, including red Hermès leather wall coverings and marquetry dining room floors inspired by those in the Pavlovsk Palace in St. Petersburg, Russia, which happened to be the location of another of his palatial estates. In all, he owned ten houses in ten countries and each came with a different wife.

Owiti never acquired anything that could be purchased by someone else, so when he'd decided to buy his Gulfstream G550, he'd met personally with General Dynamic's designers to personalize his jet with a custom floor plan and extra fuel tanks that expanded the aircraft's range from 6,750 nautical miles to nearly 8,000, enough for him to travel nonstop from New Jersey to his private compound and airstrip outside El Wak, a bleak desert outpost of 16,000 impoverished Africans along the Somalia and Kenya borders. The remote village was so far removed from both nations' formal governments that neither ever interfered with him.

After his jet became airborne, Owiti entered his computer password and opened a program designed by a team of highly paid programmers on his staff. He sent a message via his own personal satellite addressed to "Sahib."

Sometimes it would require an hour for Sahib to respond, other times a half day, and on rare occasions two days. In those later instances, Owiti assumed Sahib—a code name for the Falcon—was burrowed deep in one of his remote hideouts in Pakistan within a series of natural caves in the Western Mountains covered year-round by snow.

This time it took only two hours for Sahib to reply: As-salamn Alaykum.

May Allah, blessed be his name, continue to show you his love and mercy, Owiti typed, adding, You have removed the great Satan's head.

Yes, Allah truly has blessed us, but it was not the head I sought.

Owiti was well aware of the Falcon's fatwa against Major Brooke Grant.

You will soon have another chance to end her life, Owiti replied.

Yes, when will my gift from the North Koreans be ready? the Falcon asked.

Bad storms in the Pacific are slowing delivery.

Our brother, Hakim Farouk, is already en route. Do not disappoint me by making him wait too long.

Have you chosen a date? I'm still transferring funds into the best accounts, but we must be careful not to draw attention.

Owiti was referring to the world financial markets. After the 9/11 attacks in 2001, gold prices had spiked, going from $215.50 to $287 an ounce in London trading. Oil prices had mushroomed, too, while the U.S. dollar had fallen sharply against the euro, British pound, and Japanese yen. Owiti expected to reap hundreds of millions of dollars when the Falcon's nuclear bomb was exploded inside the United States. The trick was making certain his investing did not leave tracks that showed he knew in advance about the pending Armageddon. They had agreed to split the profits fifty-fifty.

Fi Amanullah (may Allah protect you), Owiti wrote, ending their brief communication.

Owiti's chief butler in El Wak and the international head of his security team, Ammon Mostafa, greeted him at his private airfield outside town. There was no air traffic control tower because he was the only one who used the field. Only wandering goats posed any landing problems.

A custom Lamborghini SUV carried them from the airfield through the heavily guarded front gate of his walled compound. A driveway lined with palm trees led to the main house's oversized portico. Although in a hurry, Owiti paused in the foyer long enough for a buxom woman to remove his shoes and wash his feet. He walked barefoot across the black-and-white floor tiles, each of which contained seventy-five slightly raised diamonds, which he believed helped increase blood flow in his feet, and then waited for the servant to put silk slippers on them.

Continuing into the massive 80,000-square-foot house that included an underground parking garage and employees' quarters, Owiti ignored the cavernous room directly in its center. That main room featured a thirty-foot-tall running waterfall and larger-than-life statue of a Maasi warrior made of black opal, both under a dome where cutting-edge electronics could make it appear to be any time of the day. Instead, he went directly to the double door entrance of the master bedroom suite where his Kenyan wife was obediently standing, averting her eyes out of respect.

"Welcome home, my lord," she said softly.

"Go prepare yourself," he replied. "There is work I must do but you should be ready."

"Master," she said, without lifting her eyes, "I already have bathed and our bed is ready."

"Don't challenge me," he snapped.

"I do not mean to be disobedient, my lord. It is only my anticipation and eagerness that you are hearing in my voice."

"Go bathe again," he said dismissively.

It was still morning in El Wak but Owiti never paid attention to local time. The world operated on whatever time he wished it to be. Leaving the bedroom entrance, he walked along a circular hallway to a solid steel door that had been hand-painted to blend into the walnut wood paneling. Two biometric locks keyed to his handprint and right eye protected it. No one but Owiti was ever allowed inside.

The door opened into a theater room illuminated by the constant glow of flat-screen monitors. Owiti took the only seat in his private man cave, perched comfortably behind a massive computer console.

Owiti first checked the cameras located inside his Zurich, Switzerland, house where he found his wife still lounging in bed. She was his newest acquisition and he'd intentionally chosen a Nigerian girl half his age who came from a good family but was not especially well educated and certainly didn't speak the Swiss language. She had replaced his earlier Swiss wife, an Egyptian who had been married to Owiti for seven years and had been one of his favorites, before her sudden death. She had been confident, outgoing, and college-educated and had not only learned to speak French and German but also had become fond of snow skiing. Too fond. She and her Swiss instructor had been found dead on the mountain slopes with necks broken in the exact same spots. The police had called the deaths suspicious, but Owiti had been a half-world away and the layers of lawyers that he put between Swiss investigators and him had kept them from proving what everyone suspected—that his wife had paid the ultimate price for having an affair with her instructor. Whatever Owiti owned was his and no one else's.

After checking his Swiss house, he went through his other residences, which required a good half hour of scanning. The last camera shot that he put on the room's largest screen was the Manhattan home that he had just fled.

Of all his current wives, his New York one was now his favorite. Simone was French and fancied herself a poet. Owiti had obliged her by publishing her books and staging grand parties in SoHo each time a new one was finished. American critics were not especially kind, but

Simone claimed they were harsh because they didn't have an ear for French poetry.

"Modern French does not have a significant stress accent to highlight a specific syllable in a word," she'd explained to Owiti, "so the French metric line is generally not determined by the number of beats but by the number of syllables. Besides, they are Americans and what do Americans know of poetry or any culture really?"

He let the camera linger on her face for several moments.

Yes, he was going to miss New York.

CHAPTER NINE

Late Saturday night after the bombing
Cedar-Riverside neighborhood
Minneapolis, Minnesota

U.S. Representative Nuruddin Ayaanie "Rudy" Adeogo was about to speak when two young girls burst into the Brian Coyle Center's auditorium, sobbing loudly. Their hijabs and blouses were smeared with rotten eggs.

"Look what they did to us!" one shrieked.

"It's starting," an audience member yelled.

Security guards, who had been hired specifically for tonight's community meeting, hustled outside to see if the egg-throwers were still lurking near the center.

"We're Americans too!" one of the victims declared defiantly.

Holding a microphone in his hand, the only American Somali member of Congress tried to quiet his rattled constituents. Some two hundred of them had gathered tonight to ask how he planned to stop the violence they all knew would be aimed at Muslims because of the truck bombing and murder of President Sally Allworth.

"Please settle down," Representative Adeogo pleaded.

Minnesota's Fifth Congressional District was home to the largest community of Somali Americans in the nation. At last count more than a hundred thousand people. Their Cedar-Riverside neighborhood had been a haven for waves of immigrants flowing into Minneapolis since the mid-1800s, when scores of Scandinavians first began putting down roots. But while other immigrants had moved to other sections of the city, many Somali Americans had not. They remained entrenched in a triangle between Highways 35 and 94 on the west side of the Mississippi River.

"My brothers and sisters," Adeogo said, "this is another difficult time for us, but I have faith our fellow Americans will join forces in demanding an end to this prejudice and persecution. They know only a few Muslims are jihadists."

The forty-two-year-old, first-term Congressman didn't generally recite scripture. He wanted the public to recognize him as an American first and a Muslim second. But he suddenly felt the urge to recite a passage from the Holy Quran to calm his constituents crowded into the auditorium.

"Remember the Prophet, blessed be his name, was subjected to horrible insults and hate crimes yet he remained steadfast, patient, and tolerant. Hear His words. 'Good and evil deeds are not alike. Requite evil with good, and he who is your enemy will become your dearest friend. But none will attain this save those who endure with fortitude and are greatly favored by God.'"

As two women escorted the egg-smeared girls from the auditorium into a nearby restroom, Adeogo continued. "We need to speak out publicly and not be terrified. We must start calling these actions against us what they are: *Islamophobia*. We must remind our fellow Americans that racism, anti-Semitism, and Islamophobia are all fruits from the same tree of hate."

"What would you have us do?" someone hollered.

"Report every incident of Islamophobia that you, your family, or your friends encounter. It's important for me to have actual statistics—personal examples like what happened to these two young girls—when I meet with others in Congress about stopping this persecution."

"It's going to be worse this time," a woman declared loudly, "because these radicals murdered the president."

"That's right," a well-attired, thirtysomething man said loudly. Adeogo recognized him as a local community activist and someone who would probably be seeking election to Adeogo's House seat in the future. The activist said, "In just the last few hours since the bombings, there have been reports of five physical assaults in Minneapolis, forty-nine verbal threats, and fifty-six acts of vandalism. Nationally, there have been eight fatalities and nine arsons of Muslim-owned businesses that we know of and it will only get worse in the coming days."

"We need to arm ourselves," someone yelled.

"Patrol our neighborhoods," added another.

"No! No! No!" Adeogo exclaimed into the microphone, gesturing with his free hand for the group to be quiet. "We have the right to protect ourselves just as every other American, but we can't create an alternate police force or a vigilante squad. Words must be our weapons, not bullets."

Adeogo hesitated for everyone to become quiet and then added, "I was always proud that President Allworth refused to utter the words 'radical Islamic terrorists' because she knew our religion has nothing to do with these murders and criminals."

"Her vice president has used them and now he is in charge," the community activist yelled.

"And I will speak to him," Adeogo replied calmly. "My friends, we are not alone. We have three speakers here tonight who have come to defend us. Let's hear their words."

One by one, he introduced them. First up was Menachem Weis, the most prominent Jewish rabbi in Minneapolis, who urged the group to make the term *Islamophobia* as common as *anti-Semitism*. He pledged his synagogue would defend Muslims' right to celebrate their religion freely, just as he hoped they would acknowledge and respect Judaism. A female priest from a prominent Episcopal church spoke next about how ISIS brutalized women. Finally, a Roman Catholic priest read quotes that President George W. Bush had spoken at the Islamic Center of Washington after the 9/11 attacks.

"The face of terror is not the true faith of Islam. That's not what Islam is all about. Islam is peace. These terrorists don't represent peace. They represent evil and war.

"When we think of Islam, we think of a faith that brings comfort to

a billion people around the world. Billions of people find comfort and so-
lace and peace. And that's made brothers and sisters out of every race—
out of every race.

"America counts millions of Muslims amongst our citizens, and
Muslims make an incredibly valuable contribution to our country. Mus-
lims are doctors, lawyers, law professors, members of the military, en-
trepreneurs, shopkeepers, moms and dads. And they need to be treated
with respect. In our anger and emotion, our fellow Americans must treat
each other with respect."

"Respect!" Adeogo emphasized as he brought the meeting to a
close. "We deserve it and I will demand it. I will carry your words to
Washington, D.C."

Adeogo was instantly mobbed after the meeting ended. He remained at the front of the auditorium and patiently listened to each
constituent's personal comment or complaint. When the last voter
had gone, Adeogo's press secretary, Fatima Olol, came forward.

"We need to get you to the hotel," she said. "You're booked on the
earliest possible flight out in the morning and you look exhausted."

Adeogo glanced nervously around to see if anyone might have overheard her. "Don't say hotel."

"Oh, I forgot," she said, grimacing, her eyes also dancing around
the now nearly empty room.

William Randle, the director of Adeogo's Minnesota office, joined
them. "My car is running outside."

With 20 percent of Somali Americans in his district out of work
and many of the others living below poverty levels, Adeogo refused to
use limos when he came home to his district. Instead, he had his staff
chauffeur him around the city.

When the three of them were in Randle's car, Adeogo asked, "How
do you think it went tonight?"

"Everyone is terrified," Randle replied, "and they should be. People
are suspicious of all Muslims even more now."

"Let's not ignore the proverbial elephant in the room," Adeogo
replied. "Everyone in America knows my youngest brother was Abdul

Hafeez, the Al-Shabaab terrorist who was a devoted follower of the Falcon. That's not made it easy for Americans to trust any of us. If the only Muslim in Congress had a jihadist in his family, then every Muslim family must have one. Right?"

"Those of us who know your family understand," Randle said. "But there's no denying your brother's radicalism has done a lot of damage here in Minneapolis and everywhere in the country."

"Even in Congress, there are whispers," Olol said. "Thankfully, as soon as someone meets you, they quickly realize you are not your brother."

Hoping to put a more positive spin on their conversation, Randle said, "When that Catholic priest started quoting George Bush, I got worried. Our people blame him for starting the Iraq War."

"It was the rabbi who worried me the most," Olol offered. "Does he know Somalia doesn't recognize Israel as a country?"

"He was clever. That's why he talked about unity," Adeogo replied. "The Jews, immigrants, all of us are outsiders and easy targets. He communicated that well."

"Your suggestion about reporting every incident of Islamophobia," Randle said, "was taken directly from the OIN press kit." He was referring to the Organization of Islamic Nations, a sort of United Nations exclusively for Muslim countries. It had sent out emails instructing influential Muslims in the United States and abroad what to say about the Washington truck bombing.

"When the OIN makes recommendations that are well reasoned, I have no trouble backing it," Adeogo said.

"Even though all of us despise Omar Nader, its executive director?" Olol asked.

"With good reason," Randle quickly added. "He did everything he could to defeat you and ruin our campaign."

"He still wants to defeat you because he and the OIN can't control you," Olol added.

"The OIN was furious at me because of my demands that Arab nations do more to police themselves and fight radical jihadism. They accused me of encouraging anti-Muslim sentiments."

"I still believe Nader used *her* to control you," Olol answered.

No one in the car saw a need to identify *her* by name. Each of them knew Olol had been referring to Mary Margaret Delaney, a Washington lobbyist who had been found dead in her car, parked along the George Washington Parkway, outside Washington, D.C., shortly after the November presidential election. The coroner ruled it an apparent suicide. Nor did anyone riding in the car mention that Adeogo and Delaney had once had a passionate affair. His actions were why he was spending the night in a hotel rather than with his wife, Dheeh, and teenage daughter, Cassy, at their Cedar-Riverside apartment.

"Let's drop Fatima at her parents' house first," Randle said. "It's better if she is not seen anywhere near a hotel with you."

As soon as those words left his mouth, Randle regretted saying them, but neither Adeogo nor Olol complained. Instead, they rode in silence until Olol said, "You're a lucky man despite your brother's treason."

"Why are you saying that now?" Adeogo asked.

"Because you and your family could have been murdered along with the president if you had attended Major Grant's wedding. You were invited."

"Cassy wanted to attend because she is such a good friend with Jennifer and we thought about having our daughter stay with Major Grant so the two girls could be at the wedding, but Dheeh said it would be rude to have Cassy sleep over while Brooke and her family were preparing for the wedding ceremony. Besides, Dheeh wanted our daughter to be at the funeral this morning."

"It's ironic that your mother-in-law's funeral happened on the same day as the bombing. I'm not superstitious, but it really is as if she saved all of your lives," Olol noted.

Randle parked outside Olol's parents' house. After she had said good-bye and the two men were driving to the hotel, Adeogo asked Randle, "Have there been any whispers about Fatima and me?"

Keeping his eyes directed at the street, Randle replied, "No, sir, and I'm sorry if I offended you by mentioning we needed to drop her off first. I simply wanted to protect you."

"No, it was a smart suggestion. Olol is single and quite attractive. I don't need people gossiping about her behind my back."

Adeogo closed his eyes as Randle continued driving. It had been a long day and he was dreading the telephone call that he still needed to make to Major Brooke Grant. His marital problems with Dheeh seemed minor compared to her losses.

"It's an American cliché but perhaps because you are young, you haven't heard it," the congressman said with his eyes still closed. "If you threw all of your problems into a pile with everyone else's and you were required to choose, you would gladly take back your own."

CHAPTER TEN

Sunday, late afternoon
Champion Mental Hospital
Falls Church, Virginia

"What exactly are you telling me?" Major Brooke Grant demanded.

Dr. George Jacks, the hospital's chief psychiatrist and an expert on childhood trauma, seemed visibly uncomfortable as he rested his hands on top of Jennifer's thick medical file, the only item on his otherwise clutter-free desk.

"I'm not certain recovery is ever going to be possible in Jennifer's case," he repeated in a solemn voice.

According to the certificates and degrees mounted on his office wall, Dr. Jacks knew his stuff: Harvard College undergraduate, George Washington University School of Medicine, residency at Columbia University Medical Center, along with numerous prestigious psychiatric-related honors.

Brooke knew he was wrong.

What could this esteemed doctor have learned about Jennifer in the past twenty-four hours that entitled him to make such a dire declaration? All he'd done was read Jennifer's past medical records and conduct a brief physical examination during a time when the teen was clearly still traumatized by yesterday's bombing.

Brooke understood Jennifer, really knew her, better than he ever would. She knew how resilient Jennifer had been during other traumatic incidents and she felt certain Jennifer would fully recover.

"Based on what I have read and observed," Dr. Jacks continued, "Jennifer has withdrawn inward so deeply this time that we simply can't reach her. She is not catatonic but she has retreated into an inner imaginary world and bringing her back to reality may be impossible."

Since being pulled from the mansion's basement bathroom after the bomb blast, Jennifer had not acknowledged anyone who had spoken to her, including Brooke. The teen continued to look through them as if they were invisible. Brooke had first noticed Jennifer's disconnection when paramedics removed a sliver of glass from her arm and applied an alcohol-based disinfectant to cleanse the wound. She hadn't flinched. Her facial expression hadn't changed. It was as if she were a mannequin. At that point, Brooke had known what was happening was more than shock.

Before the blast, Jennifer's last-minute need to use the toilet had saved both of them in the basement. The thunderous blast wave that had destroyed everything in its path had swept above them, leaving them relatively untouched physically, but clearly not psychologically.

"Dr. Jacks," Brooke said, "you're underestimating Jennifer. She is very determined and she has been through a lot—"

"Yes," Dr. Jacks said, rudely interrupting her. "Major Grant, I have taken time to read her complete medical and psychiatric file. But—"

Now Brooke interrupted him. "If so, you'd realize this is not the first time she has retreated into an imaginary world for her own self-protection. When I first met her, she was living in a locked facility, mostly for elderly patients with Alzheimer's, where she had been mute for three years."

"I didn't say I was giving up on her," Dr. Jacks replied in an indignant voice. Like many physicians, he didn't appreciate having his diagnosis questioned. "I am simply telling you this is an incredibly tragic case and she may—"

"Doctor, Jennifer is not a case! Get that straight! She's a beautiful young girl!"

"Major Grant," he said in a stern voice, "I just told you that I have read how Jennifer suffered a traumatic brain injury in Cairo when she was sitting in the backseat of a parked car when a bomb under its hood exploded. I have read that the bomb killed her mother and brother sitting in the front seat. I have read how her father, a CIA operative, was poisoned in Germany—all of which happened before you met her."

"And that's my point," Brooke replied. "She recovered from that car bomb blast. She recovered from her father's murder."

"And maybe if those had been the only traumas this girl has overcome, I would be more optimistic. But, Major Grant, all of us in Washington and across the nation have read news accounts describing what Jennifer and you have been through more recently—how she and a Minnesota congressman's daughter were kidnapped by terrorists, beaten, and held captive until they both were rescued. She watched you get shot during that rescue attempt and she actually saved your life by strangling your attacker with the chain that he was using to keep her restrained. It's all in this file. I'm not trying to be heartless but what child can survive that kind of trauma without suffering permanent damage to their psyche?"

"My daughter, that's who! Jennifer didn't have a mental breakdown after that terrible kidnapping. Yes, she currently has retreated into some imaginary world for her own sanity, but she will come out of it."

Dr. Jacks ran his left hand over his chin, smoothing his salt-and-pepper beard. "Major Grant," the sixty-four-year-old psychiatrist replied, "we are on the same team here. I'm only trying to—"

"Are we?" Brooke interrupted. Her words were a sign of the sheer frustration and exhaustion that she now was feeling. "Because it doesn't seem to me that we are together. You must have hope that she will get better because without hope, she never will."

"There is hope but there is also false hope."

"No, there is only hope because you can't predict the future," Brooke answered. "No one can. Jennifer is resilient. Now, what is your treatment plan?"

In the next several minutes, Dr. Jacks recited several medications that he had prescribed and then he surprised Brooke.

"My goal is to release her as quickly as possible from our hospital into a more relaxed treatment environment where she can feel safe."

"Whoa! She's coming home with me."

Dr. Jacks shot her a skeptical look. "My colleagues and I are against that." Thumping his finger on Jennifer's file, he continued. "Your daughter is attending a private school where she enjoys horseback riding, according to her records. Am I correct?"

"Legally, I am her guardian, but the plan was for me and my husband—" Brooke stopped. She needed a second after thinking about Walks Many Miles to get her emotions in check. "Yes, Jennifer enjoys riding horses. She's always been fascinated with unicorns and I believe she feels a connection with animals."

"A few miles from here is a wonderful residential facility near a small town called Clifton. It's in Virginia and it's a farm whose emphasis is equine-assisted therapy. Are you familiar with horse therapy?"

Brooke shook her head.

"Jennifer was able to become stable with medication after her traumatic brain injury. That was a physical injury to her brain, which happened during the car bombing in Cairo and with psychotherapy and time, she overcame her PTSD. The fact that she did not have any debilitating mental issues after her kidnapping incident suggests to us that her current condition is a choice that she is making, perhaps without even fully realizing it."

"A choice?"

"Actually, quite a logical one. If you touch a hot plate, you jerk your hand back because you don't want to be burned again. Jennifer has been burned and burned and burned again as a young girl, so she has withdrawn into a safe place, into her own imaginary world because reality is simply too hurtful and ugly. It's a form of disassociation. In addition to her mother and brother being killed, her father being poisoned, her own kidnapping, and now—when it appears that she is about to be adopted by two new parents—everyone she loves except you being murdered, well, that would be an overload for anyone, an overwhelming test of sanity."

"She's not alone. In addition to me, she still has her best friend at school, Cassy Adeogo, who wasn't able to attend the wedding because of her grandmother's funeral in Minneapolis."

Dr. Jacks jotted down Cassy Adeogo's name on a pad and said, "Major Grant, have you considered the idea that Jennifer may be blaming herself?"

"What? That's ridiculous. How's Jennifer responsible for any of this?"

"In reality, she isn't. But teenagers are extremely self-centered. They see the world revolving around them and Jennifer may believe God is punishing her for some reason or that she is cursed. If she loves someone, she might be putting him or her in grave danger. For that reason, she has pulled away, especially from you, because she doesn't want to be responsible for causing your injury or death. It is quite possible that she is trying to protect you by retreating."

"She doesn't need to protect me. I need to protect her!"

"That is your reality, Major, but it may not be hers."

"I don't see how horse therapy is going to change that."

"It could be a transitional step. A way back for her. All of us need love and one of the strongest bonds humans can make is with animals. Even people who can't engage in healthy personal relationships can obtain love through relationships with animals, who are nonjudgmental, loyal, and have no preconceived expectations or motives. We have found that horses are unexplainably skilled at reading humans, knowing in advance who is going to harm them or who is afraid of them and even which humans are suffering and hurt."

"But I love her. I can't believe you and your colleagues think sending Jennifer to live at this horse farm with complete strangers is better than having me take her home."

"This is not a judgment against you. As I just explained, one possible reason why Jennifer has retreated could be you. She doesn't want you to be hurt and she doesn't want to feel the pain that will come if you are hurt. Right now, the more that you are around her, we believe the less likely are her chances of recovering."

A crushed look swept across Brooke's face.

"I didn't intend to hurt your feelings," Dr. Jacks said sympathetically, "but Jennifer is my patient and I strongly recommend that she be discharged to the therapeutic horse farm and enter its equine therapy program. At some point in the future, after Jennifer has developed a therapeutic relationship with a horse, we can reintroduce her best friend, Cassy Adeogo, to her—all steps to coaxing her back to reality."

Brooke felt defeated but as she allowed Dr. Jacks's reasoning to settle in, she realized taking Jennifer home would be selfish. Jennifer wasn't the only one traumatized. With Brooke's parents dead for more than a decade, and now her aunt, uncle, and fiancé murdered, she realized that it was she who needed Jennifer—the only member of her family she had left—possibly more than the other way around. She really did think of Jennifer as her daughter, and being a mother meant thinking about the needs of your child more than of your own.

"Before I sign off on this, I'd like to see Jennifer."

Dr. Jacks led Brooke through a locked door and down a corridor to Jennifer's room. This was not like any hospital that Brooke had seen. The room contained a twin bed, a desk, and a chair. "We don't allow iPads and televisions or even radios in the rooms because we want our patients to socialize and interact with each other in the hall's main meeting area," Dr. Jacks whispered. "Unfortunately, we've not been able to coax Jennifer out of her room."

Jennifer was dressed in clothes that Brooke had brought from home earlier and was sitting on the edge of the bed staring blankly out a window.

Brooke entered, leaving Dr. Jacks in the hallway, and sat next to Jennifer. Kissing her forehead while wrapping an arm around the teen's shoulders, she said, "Hi, sweetie. How are you feeling today?" She moved her left hand onto Jennifer's right hand and joined her in staring outside. Her room looked out onto a manicured lawn, groomed shrubs, and flowerbeds surrounded by a tall white fence.

"April showers will bring May flowers," Brooke said cheerfully. "I can already see some yellow day lilies. Do you see them?"

Jennifer didn't reply.

"Honey," Brooke continued, raising her hand and gently running it through Jennifer's brown hair. "The doctors here want you to live on a ranch for a while and the best part is you would have your very own horse to ride all day, not just a few hours. Wouldn't you enjoy that, sweetie?"

Brooke focused on Jennifer's brown eyes, but the teen continued to stare through the window. "Imagine, having your own horse to ride each morning," Brooke continued, beginning to fight back tears. "Gosh, it sounds so much better than sticking around in this old hospital, don't you think?"

It was as if Brooke were talking to herself.

"I'm so, so sorry you got hurt," Brooke whispered. A tear slowly slipped down her cheek. "We're going to be happy again after you get better. I promise. But first I need you to come back from your imaginary world—the one with rainbows and unicorns you told me about after you were kidnapped. Please, please come back to me."

Brooke hugged Jennifer and kissed her twice on her cheek. The teen felt like a rag doll. "Please come back to me. Don't leave me alone here," Brooke said. "You're all I have now. I love you. Get better please."

Jennifer continued to look straight ahead, mute and unresponsive.

Dr. Jacks was waiting patiently in the hallway holding a clipboard with several consent papers to sign when Brooke exited the room. She began scribbling her name on each of the documents.

"I'll want to visit her at the farm," she said.

"When she is ready, but let's give her time to adjust to her new life there."

Brooke felt another dagger in her heart. "I heard what you said. How I'm a reminder of her pain, which doesn't make any sense to me."

"I'm sure it will only be a few months of separation."

"Months?" Brooke replied. She couldn't believe what he was telling her. Months? She glanced back into the barren hospital room at her catatonic daughter. She handed the clipboard to Dr. Jacks and walked briskly down the hallway and out of the hospital.

CHAPTER ELEVEN

Port of Tanjung Priok
North Jakarta, Indonesia

Hakim Farouk, aka "the Destroyer," took great pleasure and silent satisfaction knowing that it was his bomb that had killed U.S. president Sally Allworth and three hundred guests at a Washington, D.C., wedding. The survival of Major Brooke Grant and Jennifer was not something he could have foreseen nor controlled. For some reason, Allah had spared them but Allah had given him and the Falcon a great victory in the death of a sitting president and the chairman of the joint chiefs.

As the flight into North Jakarta circled above the city, he marveled at the sight of Indonesia's most advanced and busiest seaport below him. It was far more impressive than the Rason seaport in the Democratic People's Republic of Korea, where he'd gone to collect his bosses' ultimate prize—a nuclear bomb built by the North Koreans with technical assistance provided by Iran.

The Falcon had sent Farouk to oversee the purchase and the North Koreans had delivered a bomb to an airplane hangar near the seaport and watched the aircraft carrying it fly away. At least that is what they had thought they were seeing. What they didn't know was the bomb had not been on that private jet. Farouk had arranged for the carton carrying it to be switched with an identical one before it was loaded. In the circles in which the Falcon and Farouk traveled, no one trusted anyone and that included the North Koreans.

Instead of going by air, the bomb had been transported that same night to the Rason port where it had been hidden inside a Sea Trident

Inc. shipping container loaded aboard a cargo ship called the *Sea Voyager* for transport to Jakarta. The African billionaire Umoja Owiti owned both the Sea Trident Shipping Corporation and the *Sea Voyager*, which was part of his fleet.

The bomb was supposed to already be in Jakarta but was behind schedule because of storms.

Even though he had been traveling for thirty-six hours after delivering the truck bomb on Saturday morning, Farouk only stayed at his hotel long enough to drop off his luggage before hailing a cab to drive him to the Istiqlal Mosque, the largest in southeast Asia. As they approached it, the driver asked, "Which entrance?"

It was a sprawling religious compound with two domed buildings near Merdeka Square in downtown Jakarta.

"The one closest to where I can get a tour," Farouk replied.

Several mosque guides near where the taxi dropped him directed Farouk across a wide courtyard to a gathering spot alongside the main building. The mosque was a minimalist structure that had been heavily criticized after it was completed in 1978 because it did not reflect either Islamic nor Indonesian culture.

Along with fourteen other visitors, he waited until a slightly built Indonesian man in his early twenties wearing a white button-down shirt, white pants, sandals, and a white skullcap arrived and introduced himself.

"My name is Ahmad," he said, smiling. "I will be your tour guide. Let me begin by answering your first question, which will be what the word *Istiqlal* means. It's an Arabic word for 'independence' and it was chosen for our mosque's name to commemorate our national revolution and freedom from the Netherlands in 1948. Even though my country has the largest Muslim population in the world, there was no grand national mosque before this one."

As Ahmad began walking toward the mosque's main entrance, he explained that Indonesian president Sukarno had insisted the white marble building be constructed adjacent to the Jakarta Cathedral (Catholic) and Immanuel Church (Protestant) to symbolize religious harmony and tolerance.

"We call it 'pancasila,' which are the five philosophical principles of Indonesia," Ahmad proudly explained, raising a hand so that he could use his fingers to count. "Number one is the belief in the absoluteness of God. Number two is a belief in a just and civilized humanity. Three is national unity. Four is democracy, and the fifth is social justice. You will discover that Indonesian people believe numbers are important and symbolic."

The single minaret in the courtyard used to call worshippers to prayer each day was 66.66 meters tall, he explained, representing the 6,666 verses in the Quran. A dome that covered the main prayer room was 8 meters in diameter and could hold as many as 125,000 worshippers. The number eight symbolized August, the month of the Indonesian independence.

"Our mosque has seven entrances and all seven gates are named after *Al-Asmaul-Husna*, the different names that refer to God in Islam," Ahmad said. "The number seven also represents the Seven Heavens in Islamic cosmology."

Ahmad gave this tour so many times each day his thoughts often wandered while he was speaking robotically and it was during such moments that he studied the tourists listening to him. A youthful-looking white couple in their twenties wearing blue denim jeans and carrying backpacks struck him as being Eastern Europeans because of their shoes. As a tour guide, he'd learned shoes often provided the best clue to countries of origin. It was easy to identify the older talkative couple as Americans because of their shirts. One read BEST GRANDPA and the other BEST GRANDMA. They also were wearing brand-new white sneakers, which he assumed they had bought before leaving home. The rest of the tour was composed of men of different ages whom Ahmad assumed to be Muslims visiting for the first time. All but one of them appeared to be Indonesian. This left only a lone Arab-looking male and Ahmad couldn't tell where he was from based on his shoes, dress, or mannerisms.

The tour was scheduled to last twenty minutes, but the American couple kept asking questions, after explaining they were retired Idaho schoolteachers eager to learn about Indonesia and Islam.

"Are Muslims baptized?" Best Grandma asked. "That's how you become a Christian."

"No. But if I understand Christianity, the concept behind baptism is that your sins are forgiven once you accept your new faith. The same concept is true for us. When you come to Islam, your sins are forgiven because Allah knew that before Islam you were ignorant, but once you make your *shahada*, or commitment, then you are responsible for your sins."

"Shaha-what? What is that?" asked the woman, who had covered her white hair with a scarf out of respect.

"A personal declaration: *'There is no god but Allah, and Mohammad is the messenger of Allah.'* With that statement, you are dedicating your life to being a good Muslim and you are starting a walk down a long path of knowledge."

Happy to continue proselytizing, Ahmad said, "I've already talked about the importance of numbers. In Islam, we have five pillars of our faith. They are *shahada*, which is sincerely reciting the Muslim profession of faith; *salat*, performing the ritual prayers in the proper way five times each day; *zakat*, paying an alms tax to benefit the poor and the needy; *sawm*, fasting during the month of Ramadan; and *hajj*, making a pilgrimage to Mecca. I personally believe the first, second, third, and fourth are essential and we can do them anywhere we are."

He paused and then added, "If you wish to be a good Muslim, you must also accept the six articles of our faith too. They are a sincere belief in Allah and monotheism; a belief in the day of resurrection and angels; a belief in the Divine Books from Allah; a belief in all of the preceding prophets and Mohammad; a belief in the final day of Judgment; and finally a belief in divine preordainment and predestination."

The tour continued until the group had returned to where it had started. The elderly Americans tried to give Ahmad a cash tip, which he refused but suggested they donate to the mosque. It was when everyone else had gone that Hakim Farouk approached the young tour guide.

"*Assalamu alaykum*," he said, offering the traditional Islamic greeting. "Might you be free for coffee? I have a few questions."

Ahmad glanced at his watch and noticed his next tour was scheduled to begin in a few minutes, but no one was waiting to take it. "Why not? I know a place close by," he replied.

With Ahmad taking the lead, they exited the compound and took chairs at a nearby sidewalk coffee shop.

"Where are you from?" Ahmad asked.

"The Middle East," Farouk replied evasively as he stirred a tiny spoon in his cup.

"I can see that. But where? I always try to guess but I wasn't sure with you."

"Yemen."

"If you're from Yemen, I will have more questions for you than you will have for me. I have never left our island but I've read about the fighting in Yemen. Americans love to fight everywhere, don't they?"

"It's their lackeys, the Saudis who are bombing our schools, hospitals, and homes in Yemen. Muslims are murdering my people."

"Muslims should not kill other Muslims."

"We have been killing one another for centuries," Farouk replied casually. "Shiite. Sunni. It will not stop after the Americans are gone."

"In Indonesia, we coexist through mutual respect."

"Respect," Farouk repeated, letting that single word hang in the air. "When do you cross the line between respect and blasphemy? When is your acceptance so great that you forget who you are? If you are a devout Muslim, should you not correct the errors of your fellow believers?"

"I'm proud of my faith and openly talk about the beauty that it brings into my life, but I am not judgmental of other religions nor am I a radical," Ahmad explained. "I do not believe force can bring someone to the wisdom and beauty of Allah, and although I agree with many of the causes the jihadists espouse, I simply don't approve of their methods."

"How can you believe in a cause and not act? Aren't you obligated to join in the crusade for Allah?"

"None of the pillars of our faith require me to commit violence or to go to war with nonbelievers."

"Ah," said Farouk, "this depends on your interpretation of the Holy scriptures, does it not?"

"There's no reason for disharmony and bloodshed," the tour guide replied. He was becoming frustrated by Farouk's nagging questions.

"This is because the cause of Allah is a luxury for you," Farouk said. "You don't believe in violence because it is not your homes, hospitals, and schools being bombed. It's not your parents, your uncles and aunts, and your children who are being butchered in a war that you cannot escape."

"I would not fight," Ahmad insisted. "Allah means peace."

Farouk took out a cigarette. There was no rule in the Quran condemning tobacco because cigarettes hadn't been around in the seventh century but many devout Muslims avoided tobacco because they believed Mohammad's teachings about respecting your body required them to be nonsmokers. Given Farouk's strict religious beliefs, his coffee companion was surprised to see him light a cigarette and spend several quiet moments inhaling and exhaling.

"You smoke?" Ahmad said. "Yet you speak of piety."

"You claim piety but reject putting actions behind your words."

"Have you lost someone in Yemen?" Ahmad asked.

Farouk let the question linger between several exhales of smoke. It deserved a thoughtful reply even though he knew that he'd already said too much. From the moment that he had asked Ahmad to coffee, Farouk had understood he was sealing the tour guide's fate. Farouk could have walked away as just another easily forgotten tourist. Ahmad would never have known that he had encountered a murderer. But for reasons that even Farouk did not fully understand, he felt an inner need to share his religious beliefs on occasion and because of who he was and what he did, he could only tell it to strangers. Farouk was not having coffee with Ahmad to recruit him. Nor did he really care what the tour guide sitting across from him on the sidewalk café thought about Islam. What Farouk was doing was entirely selfish and was completely to meet his own needs. There were times when he needed to tell his personal story to keep it alive and remind himself of the deep pain that had led to his hatred of infidels. His own words would reinforce the decision he'd made to become a radical jihadist. They would recommit him to his course of actions. He would be able to look each morning into the mirror and admire the man whom he'd become—an unflinching and unmerciful sword of Allah.

"It was not the Saudis," Farouk finally said. "It was the Americans and one of their predator drones. A coward's way of killing. Like one of their video games."

Ahmad didn't interrupt.

"Do you know our capital city of Sana'a?" Farouk continued.

"Only what I've read."

"I was living there with my family—my wife, Ayeesha, and our two-year-old daughter, Leyia. They were everything to me. One day while I was away, the Americans fired a Hellfire drone missile at a car in which was a Houthis leader. The Americans believe the Houthis are proxy fighters for the Iranians who are Shiite and trying to destroy my country—so you see, in Yemen we have both the Saudi Sunnis and the Iranian Shiites killing the rest of us instead of all Muslims banding together to fight the infidels."

Farouk tapped the ashes from his cigarette. "The Houthis leader's car happened to be riding near our house when the Americans fired their missile. Had that car taken a different avenue, had the Americans waited ten seconds before firing, then my wife and daughter could have been spared. They were not. They were murdered."

"I'm sorry," Ahmad said.

"What does the word 'sorry' mean? You say this not for me, but for yourself to help you feel better. I am the one with no wife, no child."

"We have seven Imams at the mosque. You should seek guidance from one of them about your loss," Ahmad suggested.

"Tell me, my young friend, of the seven Imams—which is the wisest? Which is the most radical? Which is the most anti-West? Who is the most pro-West?"

"All of them consider politics as *dunya*. Their interests are in the spiritual, not the temporal world and its earthly concern and possessions."

"Then how can they answer my questions and advise me about the

losses that I have suffered in my temporal world if they have such little interest in it?"

Ahmad checked the time on his cell phone and said, "I should
be returning to the mosque. There is one more tour before *salat al-
maghrib*."

Farouk hadn't realized that the sunset prayer was only an hour away.

"Before you leave," he said, "let me ask you another question since
you were so helpful on the tour, especially answering questions by the
Americans. You were very helpful to them."

"I am always helpful to everyone who asks me questions about our
faith," Ahmad said, bristling because Farouk had singled out his help-
fulness to the older Americans.

"You mentioned the sixth belief of Islam is about divine decree.
Given what I have told you about my wife and daughter, how do you
interpret divine decree? Do you believe Allah wished them to be murdered by an American missile? That Allah wished me to suffer?"

"I know there are different interpretations," Ahmad replied, choosing his words with care. "I know that *Al-Jabiriyah* believe humans
have no control over their actions and everything is dictated by Allah,
as you have said. While *Al-Qadiriyyah* are of the opinion that humans
have complete control over their destinies, to the extent that Allah
does not even know what humans will choose to do. I believe the
Sunni view is in the middle of these two extremes. As you know, most
Muslims are Sunni and most Sunnis believe that Allah has knowledge
of everything that will be but that humans have freedom of choice."

"You have recited the options as if I were a teacher and you were a
student hoping to impress me and in doing so, you have hidden behind your religious instruction and not answered my question. What
do you believe? That is what I am asking *you*. Was your fate sealed
when you were born into a Muslim family or do you have free will?
Was our meeting here today at this café a happenstance or preor-
dained? Can you change your destiny?"

"I believe Allah knows all and sees all, but I have been given the
right to choose my actions."

"If you choose unwisely, then you will pay a price for your sins?"

"I would rather put it like this: because I choose wisely, I will be rewarded for my faithfulness."

Farouk looked at the tour guide and said, "I have enjoyed our conversation."

Standing, Ahmad earnestly replied, "I would urge you again to speak to an Imam about the death of your wife and child."

"Perhaps I will."

Drawing another cigarette to light, he remained seated and said, "I will let you depart with one last comment. Do you wonder if what I told you was all fiction, created for the sole purpose of engaging in a lively conversation? Or do you believe me? Do you believe my pain and my losses of Ayeesha and Leyia are real or imaginary?"

His comment struck Ahmad as being so strange that he didn't know how to respond. For a second, he said nothing and then, as he turned to leave, he said, "I do not know if what you said about your family is true or imaginary. Either way, you're a man who needs spiritual guidance." He quickened his pace back to the mosque and he did not think of Hakim Farouk again until just before midnight when he opened his apartment door and found Farouk standing outside.

"*Assalamu alaykum*," Ahmad said.

Farouk smiled and in a well-practiced move swung his right hand upward from his side and with a razor-sharp knife slashed Ahmad's throat.

In shock, Ahmad grabbed the gash as he collapsed onto both knees in front of his attacker. Blood gushed from the wound. Some squirted back into his mouth. A gurgling sound came from his throat and panic filled Ahmad's eyes.

An expert with his knife, Farouk had delivered a single cut that he knew would render a near painless death rather than having Ahmad drown in his own blood.

He bent down and spoke into Ahmad's ear. "Allah awarded you free will. That's what you told me. And you are condemned by the choices you have made. In your willingness to accommodate infidels, you and those like you have become mongrels and thorns in the throat of Islam."

The next morning, Farouk found a copy of the *Jakarta Tribune* outside his hotel door and the photos of two men staring up at him. One was Ahmad's, the other a prominent Imam from the mosque. The headline read:

IMAM MURDERED IN DOUBLE HATE CRIME ATTACKS.

Retreating into his hotel room, he sat with his coffee and read the front-page story. A deputy Imam at the mosque had been found dead in his apartment with a slashed throat. His body had been discovered when he did not appear to deliver the fifth prayer of the day. Police also discovered a twenty-four-year-old man who worked as a tour guide at the mosque murdered in the hallway outside his apartment. He, too, had been slashed across the throat. The killer, who had not been seen by any witnesses, remained at large but had left a handwritten note. In it, he claimed the murders were hate crimes against Muslims in retaliation for the assassination of President Sally Allworth in the United States and other attacks in Indonesia by Muslims against Christians. The newspaper speculated the murderer was a Christian zealot who was hoping to stir up trouble between non-Muslims and Muslims.

After Farouk finished reading the story, he smiled, folded the newspaper, and placed it neatly in the trash.

CHAPTER TWELVE

The White House
Washington, D.C.

Wyatt Bowie Austin didn't like waiting. It was early Monday morning and he was eager to launch his presidency but he understood that he needed to wait at least until after Wednesday before stepping into the spotlight. That was when his predecessor, Sally Allworth, would be laid to rest.

He had been given the oath of office within an hour after Saturday's truck explosion and that night, he had gone on national television to assure the nation that the Republic was in steady hands and those responsible for the reprehensive murder of Sally Allworth, along with the chairman of the joint chiefs of staff and other wedding guests would be hunted down and punished "like the cowards they are."

It was a matter of decorum now to allow the nation to mourn its fallen leader and pay her tribute. At the moment, Sally Allworth was lying in state in the U.S. Capitol Rotunda where her closed casket would remain until her nationally televised funeral. There had been some discussion in the media about what condition her body had been found in after the explosion. The White House had ignored all inquiries about that ghoulish topic, saying only that an autopsy had been performed for historical purposes and that Allworth had succumbed from impact trauma. The White House press secretary had announced her service would be held inside the Washington National Cathedral, which is where a memorial or funeral service for every president since 1893 had been held.

Despite Austin's self-imposed restraint, there was one task the native Texan could do and when he arrived this morning at the Oval Office, he immediately summoned White House chief of staff Mallory Harper.

Austin was not a politician who minced words.

"You—and I do mean *you* personally, Ms. Harper—did your best to make my vice presidency about as important as a one-cent postage stamp," he declared.

If he expected an argument from Harper, he was about to be sadly disappointed because what he was telling her was accurate. She didn't care for him and now he was her boss.

The two of them had next to nothing in common. She had been born into a wealthy Greenwich, Connecticut, family with deep roots. Her great-great-grandparents had been listed on Mrs. William B. Astor's famous *Four Hundred* list—a not-so-secret ranking of who mattered and who didn't in New York society during America's Gilded Age, and her bloodline remained as blue or bluer than most others of privilege.

The new president was a fifth-generation Texan, one in a long line of small-town sheriffs and Texas Rangers—an often-disagreeable lot who were as tough and mean as the men they arrested. His name, Wyatt, had been given in honor of the memory of Wyatt Earp, and his middle name, Bowie, had come from James Bowie, the famous "Bowie knife" Western fighter who'd perished at the Alamo.

Harper was liberal, secular, and a refined Ivy League graduate. Austin attended a state university and prided himself on being a common man with a well-honed "aw-shucks" campaign style and deeply held evangelical beliefs. His public speeches often were laced with biblical references and while East and West Coast elitists frequently made fun of him, he had found a way into the hearts of those faithful and hardworking voters who still believed God had and always would bless America.

It had been President Allworth's chief political strategist, Decker Lake, who had convinced her to add Austin to her upstart presidential campaign ticket against Mallory Harper's advice. Voters throughout the West and South loved him. He had served four terms as the Texas governor, executed more criminals than any previous elected official, and at age sixty-three, he still looked very much like the Texas cowboy he was, a rugged figure who was constantly compared by the Texas media to the Marlboro Man featured in old cigarette ads, although many of his younger constituents had no idea what that meant. He had a reputation for bluntness and for wearing cowboy boots embedded with the Texas flag.

But Americans understood he was someone who they could count on to do what he said, and for many, that was a refreshing change coming from Washington, D.C.

"Ms. Harper, we both know you would trot me out whenever you needed someone to chair an insignificant White House task force studying global warming, public education, or mental health reform. And y'all would send me to international conferences that were a waste of time. Let's not play games now. You liked keeping me on the bench and I hold you responsible for persuading President Allworth that's where I belonged."

President Austin paused to give Harper a chance to defend herself. She did. "Mr. President, I regret if you believe I have slighted you. It was never the president's nor my intention to minimize your importance to this administration." She knew it was a falsehood and so did he.

"They have a saying in Texas that no matter how a bird flies, eventually it has to come down for water, Ms. Harper."

"Sir, I've not heard that before and I'm not quite sure I understand what it means."

"It means that your days of flying high are finished."

She had always known that he didn't like her personally, but she had come to believe that she was irreplaceable, especially now that President Allworth was dead. Surely he realized that. She had been, after all, effective, although the habits that she'd brought with her from the corporate world, where she had been an Internet wunderkind, had clearly ruffled feathers on Capitol Hill.

It was the arrogance that she conveyed that upset most political veterans. She ignored the unwritten rules that governed Washington's

I'll scratch your back and you scratch mine playing field. She thought she could walk over someone such as Austin and he would accept the indignity rather than biting back when the opportunity came.

Now sitting before him in the Oval Office, Harper finally was beginning to understand that she had both underestimated him and overestimated her own power. As President Allworth's most trusted advisor, she had been intimately involved in discussions about how to thwart Russian and Chinese aggression against the United States and its allies. She and the president had brainstormed late into the night inside the Oval Office about methods to counter international terrorism. She'd dined at White House dinners with the world's most powerful leaders and she'd been profiled in the nation's most influential publications. She had become a celebrity in her own right, someone who was seen as being influential and powerful. She'd overseen the drafting of executive orders and had advised congressional leaders about legislation that had impacted the lives of millions of Americans. When necessary, she had rapped the knuckles of much older senators and House members—even the formidable ones—when they'd opposed the White House's agenda while rewarding those who'd fallen in line. Early on, Harper had been smart enough to realize the power that she had wielded had not come from her, but from her position and proximity to the president. As time passed, she had been seduced. Like the thin line that separates a social drinker from an alcoholic, Harper had sipped more and more until she had awoken one morning completely drunk on power. It was *her*. She was invaluable not only to a president but also to the entire nation. And now the new president was about to strip all of that away, everything that she had achieved.

"Mr. President," she said, carefully searching for just the right words, "it's true we've had our differences but we've also made major accomplishments here working together."

"We have?" he replied. "Ms. Harper, I'm not certain *we* have accomplished anything because there was never a *we*; there was only 'you.'"

"Sir," she replied, suppressing the feelings of injustice rising inside her, "if I may be so bold, this is no time for me to leave the White

House, not with our nation under attack and not with us not knowing that the Falcon has obtained a North Korean–made nuclear bomb."

"I understand, Ms. Harper, and I'm also fully aware of the crisis we are currently facing, having spent all day Sunday in briefings."

"Then you must know there is too much at stake for me to leave. You need me for stability, consistency, and a steady hand."

President Austin decided it was time to deliver the deathblow.

"I'd like your desk cleaned out by seven p.m. That should give you sufficient time to say your good-byes and surrender your White House credentials."

Harper felt her jaw tighten. She'd fired many underlings as an executive but she had never been fired.

"I will have the press office issue a release," he continued. "Something low-key since the nation is in mourning. You will be complimented for your loyal service to President Allworth. I see no need to make this more than what it is—a new president bringing in a new White House chief of staff."

"Mr. President, in addition to the Falcon's nuclear threat, there are important legislative projects I am overseeing on the Hill. You will need someone intimately familiar with them to help orient your new chief of staff for a smooth transition. If I may, I'd like to suggest—"

"Seven tonight," Austin said firmly. Her groveling made her even less attractive. "Good-bye, Ms. Harper."

The president didn't bother to stand or extend his hand when she stood to leave. Instead, he glanced at a huge stack of papers in front of him.

His dismissal was too much for her. When she reached the exit, she decided to lecture him. "There is a lesson that you need to learn from a fellow Texan who was a greater president than you ever will be," she declared, not hiding her contempt nor waiting for him to reply. "His name was President Lyndon Johnson and when he was asked why he kept FBI director J. Edgar Hoover in charge, Johnson replied, 'It's probably better having him inside the tent pissing out, than outside pissing in.'"

The new president looked up and in a calm voice replied, "Ms.

Harper, I would urge you to consider the bright side of your dismissal. It is better to be a has-been than a never was."

As soon as she was gone, President Austin had CIA director Payton Grainger brought into the Oval Office from a side room where he had been waiting.

"Have you learned anything new about Saturday's bombing?" he asked Grainger.

"We now have a hundred percent certainty about our initial findings," Grainger replied. "The bomb was composed of ammonium nitrate fertilizer, nitromethane, and diesel fuel, about half as much as what Oklahoma City bomber Timothy McVeigh used in Oklahoma City back in the nineties."

"Curious. Why only half as much?"

"We suspect the bomber didn't want to arouse suspicion when he, or someone who was helping him, was buying supplies. That's based on the assumption that it is more difficult for an Arab to buy a large quantity of fertilizer in the United States than it was for a white domestic terrorist living in Michigan."

"And have you changed your views about who is behind the bombing?"

"No, sir. It has all the earmarks of the Falcon and I continue to believe that his actual target was Major Brooke Grant."

"Yes, you mentioned that before—that the president was collateral damage?"

"President Allworth decided to attend the wedding at the last minute. It certainly wasn't on her daily schedule. I don't believe a suicide bomber could have known she would be there."

"I think you are right, but why hasn't the Falcon claimed credit if that's the case?"

"Oh, he will. Based on the psychological profiles we have prepared, he's waiting, probably until Wednesday before or after President Allworth's funeral to take maximum advantage of the national and international audience that will be watching."

"Spitting on her grave."

"Spitting on all of us, sir."

"Tell it to me straight Director Grainger—is there going to be anything coming out about this bombing that will embarrass your agency? Did your people miss some warning?"

"No, sir, obviously that is one of the first things I checked and we did not."

The president looked sad. "It won't matter, you know. Congress is going to find someone to blame. We can't have a U.S. president murdered in our nation's capital without someone taking a hit. If there was some red flag that was overlooked, some tip that was not fully investigated, you need to tell me now. I've already spoken to the FBI and Homeland Security and they claim their houses are in order. But we both know the CIA is judged differently. There's always going to be some half-baked, conspiracy theory ignoramus sitting in the Nevada desert in his boxers claiming you guys allowed this to happen because someone in our government wanted to get rid of President Allworth. It will only get worse if someone tries to hide information."

"Mr. President, I have personally reviewed all of our intel and there is nothing in any of our cables that would have warned us about the bomb. If someone missed something it was missed by another agency."

The new president admired Grainger. About to turn sixty, the CIA director had spent nearly three decades in Washington, rising through the ranks in the Navy and eventually earning a law degree from Harvard University before being tapped to run the spy agency during a time when morale and its credibility were at all-time lows. He'd turned both around.

Even from his sideline seat as vice president, Austin had been aware of the critical roles that Grainger had played in resolving dicey situations for President Allworth, including cutting back-door deals with corrupt foreign leaders and warlords. President Austin had decided the CIA director now sitting before him understood the world of *realpolitik*, which meant he would be open to bending or even breaking rules if it served a greater purpose.

"Director Grainger, I'm in a firing type mood, having just sent Ms. Harper packing."

The president studied Grainger for a reaction but the director was well-practiced at hiding his emotions and personal thoughts. Grainger would be a tough opponent playing Texas Hold'em, President Austin thought.

"I would be honored, sir, to continue serving you, but if you are asking for my resignation, I certainly will submit it. There will be no need to fire me."

"Grainger," the president replied, "I'm not looking for a change yet, especially if you're correct about this violent jihadist Falcon being responsible for Saturday's bombing and now having a nuclear bomb in his hands."

"Yes, sir, if he can destroy one of our major cities, he'll move one step closer to bringing all jihadist groups together with him as their undisputed leader, which is clearly his ultimate goal."

"I need your agency to hunt him down and kill the bastard before he can use that nuclear bomb." The president leaned forward at his desk and raised an index finger as he lectured Grainger, who was seated directly across from him. "Let me make myself clear. I don't want him arrested or captured or spending his life sitting in a cell in some Middle Eastern country or at GITMO. I want him dead. D-E-A-D like an armadillo smashed by a Mac truck with its entrails splattered across a Texas highway."

"I agree, sir, that would be a most welcome outcome."

"No, Director Grainger, that can be the *only* outcome. We got to find this nuclear bomb and we got to kill him, in that order."

"With all due respect, sir, if he were taken alive, he could provide critical information."

"Fine, take him alive if you can, but as soon as you've squeezed every bit of information from him, I want him executed. No trial, no jurisprudence, no bleeding heart liberal lawyers crying about how he is being abused. No Miranda rights. No public stage for him to preach hatred. DEAD. My question to you is, can you do that for me? Can you find this bomb and kill him?"

"Clearly we're doing our best to find the missing nuclear bomb and the Falcon and if capture isn't possible, then a drone strike or kill may be the best option."

The president frowned as he leaned back in his chair. "I don't think we're on the same page here. I don't need a bureaucrat running the CIA. There's a saying in Texas I learned as a youngster. A man without cojones lives on his knees. The same is true of a nation."

"The lawyer in me needs clarification, Mr. President. What exactly are you saying?"

"D-E-A-D. Can't make it clearer than that. You have a paramilitary branch in your agency."

"Yes, sir, the Special Activities Division—Special Operations Group."

"That's right, which makes for a rather depressing acronym—SAD-SOG. Now the reason why you have that SAD-SOG group is because the focus of your agency has changed."

"Yes, sir, during the Cold War it was recruiting Soviet assets. In the war against terrorism, we've come to depend more on our paramilitary teams."

"Do you remember what the Israelis did after a gang of Black September terrorists murdered eleven of their Olympic athletes at the 1972 summer games in Munich?" President Austin asked. Without waiting for Grainger to reply, he continued. "The Israelis tracked down each and every one of those Palestinian pricks who participated in those Olympic attacks and assassinated them. It didn't matter what rocks they crawled under or what country was giving them shelter or how many years it took. They tracked them down and they killed them. Do you know what the Israelis called the mission to hunt down those terrorists?"

"No, sir, I don't."

"Operation Wrath of God!" President Austin replied triumphantly. "That team didn't give a damn about anyone's civil rights. Just like your drone strikes. You find a target and kill it. Nice and simple. But the Israelis went beyond drones. They did whatever it took to find and kill their enemies and if that meant going after people, even family members, who knew where they were, that's what they did."

"Mr. President, the Israelis alienated several nations when they executed Palestinians who'd taken refuge on their sovereign land."

"Do I need to remind you of who we are? We are the most powerful nation in the world, a nation that prevents chaos and combats evil and oppression every single day. I want you to create our own Wrath of God team. I want a handful of the best of the best, and I want them to have whatever they need, whenever they need it, to do whatever is necessary. And I don't want them shackled by a bunch of rules and regulations."

"With all due respect, we live in a country of 'rules and regulations'—especially my agency. None of us is above the law."

The president flashed a sly smile. "You let me worry about those rules and regulations. We'll talk about that later, after you handpick me a team to hunt down and kill that bastard. In fact, let's call it the Kill That Bastard team. Yes, KTBs, will work fine. And I want you to keep your team off the grid, deep-cover, whatever you want to call it. The CIA will continue working with every other federal law enforcement and intelligence gathering agency, sharing information, et cetera, et cetera, et cetera, but this KTB team will report only to you and you will report only to me and no one else."

"Mr. President, it sounds as if you are proposing a secret assassination squad."

"That's exactly what I am proposing," Austin unabashedly replied. "Do I need to remind you the Falcon has a nuclear bomb and he intends to kill as many of our people as he possibly can? Are you in or do I need someone else to fill your shoes?"

Grainger hesitated to consider the ramifications. As CIA director, he not only answered to the president, but also to the director of National Intelligence and two congressional intelligence committees. And Congress had established strict rules about what the CIA could and could not do after the scandals revealed in the mid-1970s committee hearings held by Senator Frank Church.

Regardless of what President Austin called it, Grainger understood what he was being asked to create and if word leaked out, his career would be ruined. Even worse, depending on what the KTB team did, he could face prison time.

"Second thoughts, Director Grainger?" the president asked.

"Just contemplating a worst-case scenario. Your enemies always find out and use anything and everything negative they learn against you."

"That may be true about Congress and contractors," President Austin replied, "but I'm talking about the CIA, which is supposed to keep covert operations secret. By law it is a closemouthed group. I'm talking about you and me and three or four key people."

Grainger nodded but still was clearly pondering the dangers versus the rewards. "President Austin, the law is clear but so is history," he said. "Any operation this important WILL leak to the media sooner or later and Congress will start asking very tough questions."

"Director Grainger, I've asked you a simple question. Are you in or out?" Austin replied, ignoring the history lesson. "You want to remain director or hand in your resignation right now?"

"I would be honored to continue serving your administration," he declared. "But a part of my duties is to protect the president and, once again, I must remind you that all of us must follow laws, even you, sir, and I feel compelled to caution you that creating a team like what you are suggesting and keeping it secret from Congress could create a real legal quagmire for you as well as me."

"How thoughtful, Director Grainger," the president replied, not hiding the sarcasm in his voice. "I'm a lawyer just like you and I'm a damn good one. I also happen to be the president of the United States, and I'm going to be damn good at that job too. Now listen to me, Grainger. I will personally promise and guarantee you and the members of the KTB team that none of you will ever be convicted of any crime regardless of what you do in pursuit of the Falcon."

Grainger wasn't certain how the president could make such a blanket promise, but like President Austin, he also was furious that a terrorist had successfully killed a U.S. president in Washington, D.C. It showed weakness to the world and weakness always bolstered America's enemies. The United States needed to flex its muscles and he was being offered that opportunity.

"I want you either a hundred percent in or a hundred percent out," the president said, "and I'll not ask again. The good book warns us 'you are like lukewarm water, neither hot nor cold, I will spit you out of my mouth.'"

"I'm in. I'll form your KTB team."

The president walked from behind his desk to shake Grainger's hand, sealing the deal. As he did, he pulled Grainger closer. "There's one last request, Director Grainger, and her name is Major Brooke Grant. This son of a bitch Falcon has killed almost everyone precious to her. She has more reason than any of us to want him dead, and I think she can be useful. She's actually spoken on the phone with him. Besides, there's nothing like hatred and a need for revenge to motivate someone. I want Major Grant on our KTB team."

CHAPTER THIRTEEN

Frank's and Geraldine's House
Northern Virginia suburb

Major Brooke Grant opened her eyes in the bedroom where she had slept as a teenager, and in that moment, she wondered what her aunt Geraldine was fixing for breakfast downstairs. Then she remembered.

Mixing trazodone, alprazolam, and Johnnie Walker Black Label whisky could have been fatal according to the stern DO NOT DRINK ALCOHOL warnings on the medicine bottles. But Brooke had wanted to escape the pain, even if for only a few hours. The booze and pills worked. She had slept but it was temporary. There were no combination of pills and alcohol that could keep her from replaying the nightmare of her wedding day and the terrifying moments in the Heurich House Mansion basement when she felt the earth tremble, heard a momentarily deafening boom, and realized that the massive stone house above her and Jennifer was collapsing.

Her parents had been killed in a collapsing tower, and during the explosion at her wedding, she had thought she and Jennifer were going to die much the same way—buried in rubble.

When her parents died, Brooke had been traumatized, but with the love and support of her aunt and uncle, the teen had continued on.

Now all of her family support was gone. Her three brothers from Tulsa had come to her wedding. Her three cousins. All of her closest and dearest friends. The Falcon had stolen her past from her. Her family had been the memory keepers. Now who would know that she had refused to wear dresses when she was a little girl because she demanded to be treated like her brothers? Who would remember the time when her preacher father had caught her cooling off on a blistering Oklahoma afternoon by taking a dip in the church's baptismal tank under the stained glass window of Jesus praying? Who would recall how Aunt Geraldine was famous for her egg salad sandwiches that she had brought to family picnics or Uncle Frank's love of mint chocolate chip ice cream on peach cobbler? Those threads were part of her life's tapestry. The tricks Aunt Geraldine had taught her when braiding her hair into cornrows. The rivalry during the annual Army versus Navy game that pitted her uncle and cousins against her. These moments were important to her and now only she knew them.

There was more. Brooke had always strived to please her parents and later her aunt and uncle. She had worked to earn their approval and now there was no one for her to please. She had felt safe with them. She could always go home.

If the Falcon had stolen her past, he'd also stolen her future. She had fallen deeply in love with Walks Many Miles and had been eager to begin her life with him and Jennifer. On her wedding day, she had looked into their future and saw them having their own children, blending his Crow Indian culture with her African American history. There would be nights of passionate lovemaking, days of stealing knowing glances. In sickness and in health. In good times and bad. Till death do them part. They'd always laughed on Valentine's Day at the gushy Hallmark cards with their overwrought writings. But those gooey sentiments actually described how she had felt. He had been her knight in shining armor and now he was dead.

When the Falcon had issued his fatwa against her, he had boasted that he would murder everyone whom she loved before finally killing her. He had wanted revenge because she'd spoiled his plans to kill hundreds in Somalia outside a mosque. From that moment on, the Falcon had become her faceless tormentor.

Brooke slipped from the sheets in her childhood bed, grabbed a robe, and started downstairs. She had not gone to the Victorian house that she owned outside Berryville, Virginia. Instead, she had returned to the house where she had grown up as a teen. She was not ready to let go of her family. But there was another reason why she had come here.

The media.

Reporters wanted her reaction. They were clamoring for a much-coveted exclusive interview. What was there for her to say? She had turned on the television in her old bedroom and watched the mob of reporters and camera crews camped outside her Berryville home in Virginia. Vultures staking out her property, circling for a photo op. *How does it feel to have the president die on your wedding day? How does it feel to lose your fiancé and entire family in one blinding flash?* Everyone knew what had happened, so the only news was in asking her to expose her innermost feelings.

The Falcon had taken everything from her except Jennifer. Brooke would keep her feelings bottled up inside her, protecting them, because they were hers and hers alone.

As she descended the steps to the main floor, she paused on each one to examine the family photographs that her aunt had hung on the staircase wall. A part of her couldn't believe they were dead. She half expected to find her aunt and uncle having coffee in the kitchen.

Why had she survived? By the time Brooke reached the bottom step, her eyes were wet with tears.

She continued down the center hallway to the breakfast nook in the kitchen. Two bottles of prescribed pills and her uncle's scotch whisky were waiting on the table. She poured a healthy shot of Johnnie Walker into the same glass that she'd used before going to bed, but as she was raising it to her lips, she thought of Jennifer and lowered it to the table. She stared at the caramel-colored liquid for several minutes, lost in her thoughts, before going upstairs to shower and dress.

As she was returning downstairs to fix breakfast, someone knocked on the door. The twenty-four-hour security guards who had been stationed at the front gate to protect the chairman of the joint chiefs of staff had been recalled by the Pentagon. The rest of the world was moving on without her. Brooke fetched her Beretta M9 pistol from a table near the door and glanced through a side window at the man waiting on the stoop. She recognized him and invited him inside.

"I've come to comfort you, Miss Brooke," the Reverend Dr. Thaddeus Taylor explained. "We also need to discuss funeral arrangements and I thought we could pray together. I want you to know that God feels your pain."

Aunt Geraldine had been a devout Christian, and when Brooke had lived under her roof, Geraldine had insisted the two of them attend church every Sunday. It was more than the standard one-hour commitment held at most white churches. Depending on how moved the minister was, a Sunday session could easily last two hours or more.

Reverend Taylor was the co-pastor at Aunt Geraldine's church, but he had not been her aunt's favorite. That honor had fallen on the Reverend Dr. Charles Fowler—the preacher who Aunt Geraldine had asked to perform Brooke's marriage ceremony. He, too, had died during Saturday's bombing.

"I brought coffee," he announced as he followed her into the kitchen. He was carrying two cups from Starbucks in a container in his right hand and his well-worn Bible in his left. He noticed the open bottle of whisky, glass of Johnnie Walker, and pill bottles on the table. Without asking, he pushed them aside as Brooke took a seat opposite him.

"Let's pray," he said, opening his Bible.

"Let's wait on that," she answered. "There's something I need to give you." She excused herself and returned with an envelope with her aunt's handwriting on it.

"Aunt Geraldine wrote down exactly what she wanted done at her funeral. She did it when she and my uncle were drawing up their wills. You'll find her favorite Bible passages and the hymns listed just as she wanted them sung."

"That was very thoughtful of her—relieving you of this burden."

"When it comes to my uncle, I've already made arrangements for him and my cousins to have a joint funeral service presided over by the chief of chaplains of the Army with full military honors in Arlington National Cemetery. Given my uncle's position, it will be held at Fort Belvoir."

"I see," he replied. Nodding toward the bottle of whisky and pills, he said, "Brooke, I lost a good friend, my co-pastor, when that bomb exploded. It hurts, but you will not find peace by turning to drink and medication. Only God can help you through this and I think reading a few Scriptures and praying together will help show you the way."

"God?" Brooke replied in a mocking voice. "You think God will help me through this now? Tell me, Reverend Taylor, where was God when that bomber killed everyone—my future husband, my aunt and uncle, my complete family except for Jennifer, our president, and Reverend Fowler? Where was God when my parents were killed, along with twenty-five hundred other innocent people in those twin towers? If he didn't help them, what makes you think he is going to reach down and comfort me now?"

"Brooke, you're upset and you're going to be for some time. Are you familiar with the five stages of grief? Denial, anger, bargaining, depression, and finally acceptance."

Brooke leaned in close to the reverend, her intensity rising. "Denial? It's a bit hard to deny when photos of the bombing are being broadcast over and over again on television. But anger, yes. You're damn right I understand anger. I am angry at the man who did this to me and angry that someone in the CIA or FBI or Homeland Security didn't do their job and stop him from detonating that bomb on my wedding day and destroying my life. I'm angry the Falcon has become fixated on killing me and murdering everyone I love. And I'm angry that Jennifer has been so shocked by what happened that she has retreated into an imaginary world from which she may never return. Yes, Reverend Taylor, I'm angry, so angry, and while we're at it, I can tell you that I'm not too keen on praying right now because I have no intention of talking to a God who would let my aunt Geraldine, who was as kind and good and decent as a woman could be, die and let someone like the Falcon continue to slaughter innocent people."

"Brooke, I've known you since you first came to live with your auntie and uncle. Your anger will destroy you. Don't blame God for the evil acts of man."

"Reverend Taylor, if you have come here to tell me my aunt and uncle and the man I loved are in a better place now or that their deaths are part of some bigger plan or that God works in mysterious ways or that my aunt and uncle have been called home to God because they were his faithful servants, save your breath."

"Brooke, you aren't the first to lose someone. You aren't the first to express misplaced anger at God. I know how you feel and—"

"You know how I feel?" she repeated. The hostility in her voice surprised even her. "How dare you say that to me. Yes, you lost your friend Reverend Fowler. But have you lost your parents to terrorists? Have you lost your aunt and uncle to a Muslim fanatic? Has the person who you planned to spend the rest of your life with been blown to pieces by a suicide bomber? Has anyone ever issued a fatwa against you, demanding you be killed?"

"Your aunt would want you to seek comfort from God. She would not want you consumed by hate. And she certainly would object to you blaming God."

"Okay, you tell me. If God is all-powerful, then why did he let this happen? Why did he allow terrorists to crash two airplanes into the World Trade Center, killing my parents? Why did he allow a suicide bomber to kill himself and everyone at my wedding?"

"God is not responsible for any of this. There is evil in the world. Have you read the Book of Job?" he asked, flipping through his Bible.

Without waiting for Brooke to answer, he explained that the author of Job had addressed the universal questions that she now was asking: Why did bad things happen to good people? "It's an Old Testament book that comes from Judaism and there's even a version of it in the Quran. You see, Brooke, in times like this, everyone asks, Where was God?"

"So where was he?"

"In Job, Satan tells God that the only reason why Job worships him is because Job is rich and has a carefree life, with a loving wife, wonderful children, and good health. God tells Satan that he can do whatever he wants to Job to test his faith, except kill him."

"Is that what you think this is?" Brooke asked. "Do you believe God is testing my faith by killing everyone I love? What kind of a God would do such a thing?"

"Let me finish. Satan takes away Job's wealth, kills his children, and afflicts him with the most painful physical ailments. Three of his friends tell Job that God is punishing him for some sin he committed. They urge him to repent. His wife urges him to curse God. Even Job in his frustration demands to know why he is suffering when he is a believer and faithful servant, and people who are not believers and are truly evil are prospering. Job remains faithful, but at one point he shakes his fist at the heavens and demands that God explain himself. That's when God appears to Job in a whirlwind."

Reverend Taylor found the Scripture passage in the Book of Job, chapter 38, verse 4, that he had been hunting. "Listen to what God says: 'Where were you when I laid the foundations of the earth? Tell me, if you have understanding. Who determined its measurements? Surely you know.'"

"That's it?" Brooke replied, clearly unimpressed.

"Yes, Brooke. There is no single answer that explains why God allows bad things to happen. Only God knows why and he is our creator. So instead of being angry that your uncle, aunt, groom, and all the other guests died, you should be grateful that God created them and for the time that you were together with them on earth. Suffering is part of life and suffering is what allows us to build our character and develop a stronger and more meaningful love for God. Without suffering we could not appreciate him. You see, everything that happens is God's will and we have no right to question it. There is a better world that awaits us. A place where the lion and lamb will lie down together. You will receive your reward in heaven and God will deal with this Falcon accordingly."

"I know you mean well, Reverend Taylor," Brooke said, "but you can't have it both ways. You can't expect me to give God credit for everything good that happens in my life and then not blame him when something bad happens."

"But, Brooke, the only reason you have a life is because he gave it to you. It is his to take whenever he wishes because it was a gift. Your aunt understood this. She would tell you to believe all things happen for a reason. God knows. We just don't."

"The only reason I see is that a radical Islamic terrorist murdered my family and the only peace I will ever feel is when I track him down and kill him. That's justice."

"No," he replied, "that is hatred and revenge. You need to forgive him and let God deal with his actions on earth."

"Forgive him?" Brooke snapped. "You come to me two days after my family has been murdered and talk to me about forgiving the bastard responsible?"

"Brooke, the Bible warns us in the New Testament in Romans: 'Do not take revenge, my dear friends, but leave room for God's wrath, for it is written, "It is mine to avenge: I will repay," says the Lord.'"

Brooke rose from the table and jutted out her hand. "Thank you for coming by this morning to ask about my aunt Geraldine's funeral arrangements. But if you don't mind, I'd like to be alone right now."

"Brooke," he said in a soothing voice, "it's not easy being a Christian. It's going to take you time to find your footing but I will be praying for you and I know you are a good person and you will find it. Don't let hate and vengeance turn your heart away from the light. Don't let it destroy you, because it will."

"Right now, Reverend, hate and revenge are the only feelings that are keeping me from losing my mind. Love and forgiveness won't stop the Falcon from killing more innocent Americans and eventually me. And if God is as wise and all-knowing as you say he is, then he will understand what I must do to stop this monster."

"I will pray for you, Brooke," Reverend Taylor replied. "I will pray that you will not become like the terrorist who you plan to track down and kill."

Ten minutes after he was gone, there was another knock on the front door. Once again, Brooke glanced through a side window before answering it. Three black SUVs were parked in the driveway and a cadre of men and women in black business suits wearing flesh-colored earpieces had created a protective perimeter around the second vehicle. When Brooke opened the house's front door, the security officer, who had knocked, signaled his colleagues, and CIA director Payton Grainger emerged from the second SUV.

After Grainger entered the foyer and offered her the required sympathies that politeness dictated, he followed her into the living room and took a seat on a brown leather sofa while she slipped into a matching high-backed chair next to it.

"Major Grant," he said, "President Austin has asked me to form a special team. He specifically wants you on it."

"What sort of team?"

"The Falcon has obtained a nuclear bomb and it is imperative that we hunt him down and kill him. Our no-nonsense president is calling it the 'Kill That Bastard team.'"

Major Brooke Grant smiled.

PART TWO

—⚌—

NO ONE WALKS LONG ON A KNIFE'S EDGE

"Let not any one pacify his conscience by the delusion that he can do no harm if he takes no part, and forms no opinion. Bad men need nothing more to compass their ends, than that good men should look on and do nothing."

—John Stuart Mill, 1867 British philosopher and political theorist

CHAPTER FOURTEEN

Near the Khyber and Darra Adam Khel Passes
Northwest Frontier, Pakistan

Reporter Ebio Kattan felt no pity for Major Brooke Grant.

Why would she? The two women had first met in Somalia when the Al Arabic television correspondent was broadcasting stories about the rushed reopening of the U.S. embassy in Mogadishu. When that embassy had been overrun and burned by the Falcon's followers, Kattan had broadcast a flowery documentary that portrayed Brooke as a modern-day American superhero in a fight against the notorious Falcon. In Kattan's mind, she had created Major Brooke Grant in her media reports.

What had the American done for her in return?

Nothing. Brooke had returned from Somalia to the United States and had attempted to live an ordinary life. She'd shunned publicity and refused to grant Kattan exclusive interviews; most recently, Brooke had declined repeated email and telephone requests from Kattan about the bombing.

Major Brooke Grant had turned her back on the Al Arabic network's most watched, admired, and influential personality, and Ebio Kattan was bitter. If Brooke had cooperated, they could have both become international celebrities with all the fame and wealth that notoriety brings with it.

Now, Ebio Kattan would show her and the world just how important she was. She was about to accomplish what Brooke and her fellow Americans could not. If Brooke wouldn't talk to her, she'd found someone even better. The Falcon.

After the wedding bombing, Umoja Owiti had contacted Kattan. She'd known for months from her sources that Owiti knew how to reach the elusive jihadist and she had met with the African billionaire several times in secret but without luck. Then he'd called.

She'd immediately agreed to all of the Falcon's conditions, which explained why she was now riding with a black hood over her head inside the backseat of a Range Rover. It was the third vehicle that she had ridden in while hooded and she had been traveling for so many hours she'd lost track of time. When the hood was finally removed, she had no idea what time of night it was, only that the Range Rover had parked along a trail in the White Mountains, which separated Afghanistan and Pakistan.

"From here, we walk," one of the four armed men escorting her announced. For the next hour, they made their way along a narrow footpath in the moonlight up the rocky terrain through the snow until they reached a slit in the snow-covered mountainside. The two men in the lead turned sideways for about ten feet so they could squeeze through the narrow passageway; then they dropped down and crawled into a rabbit hole–like opening. Following them was difficult for Kattan because she was wearing an abaya, and the long cloak dress made it hard for her to drop onto her knees and crawl. Fortunately, once she slipped through the opening, she entered in a cave large enough to stand. From there, she was escorted through a narrow tunnel into a brightly lit room, which caused her to immediately squint until her pupils adjusted.

One of her escorts motioned for her to sit on a rug in the center of the carved out chamber, which was rectangular and about twelve feet across, seven feet tall, and fifteen feet deep. She suspected this cave was somewhere near the village of Darra Adam Khel, one of the region's most lawless outposts, known for being home to a notorious gun market. Nearly all the adults among the village's five thousand residents were engaged in either making or selling weapons.

Her four escorts remained standing, creating a perimeter around her. Ebio Kattan was not afraid. If the Falcon had wanted to kill her, he already would have. He hadn't needed to bring her to this remote cave hideout to end her life. She was more worried about the Americans tracking her and firing a missile into the mouth of this mountain hideout in an attempt to kill the Falcon, ending her life as collateral damage.

In her midthirties, Kattan had been hired by Al Arabic after winning the World Muslim Woman competition, an international pageant exclusively for Islamic women in which they were judged on their piety and knowledge of the Quran as well as their physical attractiveness. Much to her new bosses' surprise, Kattan had proven to be more aggressive, smarter, and more talented than her mostly male colleagues. Having graduated with honors from Georgetown University, she spoke English fluently as well as several other languages, and she'd shown herself to be a fierce and fearless competitor who didn't balk at reporting from war zones or resist potentially life-threatening assignments.

Her gut had told her that someday she would interview the Falcon. He was a narcissistic psychopath and that made him no different from any other self-obsessed religious crusader who was convinced that only he spoke the divine truth. Such an individual needed a stage. In preparation, Kattan had spent hours and hours watching YouTube videos and reading every scrap of information about him that she could find.

"May I have my camera now?" she asked, directing her question to no one specific guard.

One of the men handed her a black leather case that he'd been toting. Normally, Kattan worked with a camera operator and sound technician, but the Falcon had demanded that she come alone. She installed her Canon EOS C300 on a tripod and focused it on an area where a handmade rug was resting beneath the black flag of ISIS tacked to a wall. White lettering across the banner spelled out the *shahada*: THERE IS NO GOD BUT ALLAH. MOHAMMAD IS THE MESSENGER OF ALLAH. Underneath those words was a white circle, with black lettering that read: MOHAMMAD IS THE MESSENGER OF GOD.

"I'm ready," she announced.

"You must wait for him," a guard replied.

"How long?"

"He comes when he comes."

"I need water," she said. She was thirsty but she also wanted to make a demand, to demonstrate that her escorts did not intimidate her.

One of the men handed her a plastic bottle of water.

Kattan had done enough interviews to understand that her subjects often made her wait as part of pre-interview posturing. But in this case, she assumed the Falcon was being careful. If an American drone had followed her to this cave, its operators might presume the world's most wanted terrorist already was inside. Waiting could make it appear her interview was under way, in which case, they might fire a missile. Better that she die than him rushing into a trap to meet her.

For Kattan time seemed to slow. She began to feel claustrophobic waiting in the underground room. Sitting in silence. A minute seemed to take ten minutes to pass. After an hour, she announced: "I need to stretch my legs." She stood up suddenly, which surprised her guards.

"You may not leave," one said.

"What if I wish to use the toilet?"

The question flummoxed him.

"We can bring you a plastic container. Perhaps you should not drink so much water."

Cute, she thought.

Another insufferable hour passed before she heard muffled sounds coming from behind her. Several bodyguards entered the room followed by a man dressed completely in black with everything except his eyes concealed. He strutted directly to the carpet under the flag and dropped to the floor across from her camera.

"With the blessings of Allah, praise his holy name, we may now begin," he declared.

Kattan switched on her camera, checked the focus, and started her tape recorder.

"Are you responsible for the truck bombing in Washington that killed the U.S. president, Sally Allworth?" she asked in Arabic.

"We will speak in English because I want the West to understand my words. Yes, I was responsible but no, I was not responsible."

"Forgive me, but I don't understand that answer."

"The Americans brought this on themselves by waging war upon Islam. They desecrate his prophet, Mohammad, blessed be his name. I simply delivered Allah's justice to them."

From his bilingual speech, she assumed he had been educated abroad, but where? No one knew his background, his age, or even his name, although there had been many theories and much speculation. One of the conditions he had insisted on prior to their interview was that she could not ask him a single question about his personal life or past.

Feeling exhausted by the trip and long wait, Kattan got right to the point.

"Were you trying to kill the president of the United States, Sally Allworth, or the bride, Major Brooke Grant? Isn't it true you have issued a fatwa against Major Grant?"

"I did not invite you here to discuss this American pest. I have a message for the American people. What happened at the wedding was a prologue."

"Are you saying there will be more attacks in the United States?"

"'Kālo'smi lokakṣayakṛtpravṛddho lokānsamāhartumiha pravṛttaḥ.'"

It took Kattan a moment to understand. "If I am not mistaken, you have just quoted *The Bhagavad Gita*—the famous statement that the American scientist J. Robert Oppenheimer repeated after helping invent an atomic bomb."

"Your education at Georgetown University is proving useful to you," he replied—a subtle reminder that he, too, had studied her past before their interview.

"Yes," she said, "it means 'I am become Death, the destroyer of worlds.' Are you implying that you are the 'destroyer of worlds'?"

"In time, you and the world will have your answer. What is your next question?"

She was irritated that he was not being clearer in his answers. She hadn't come all this way and risked her life to listen to riddles. She needed something dramatic to make her interview newsworthy. Kattan decided to provoke him, but only a little.

"As you know, many Muslim leaders condemn you. They believe all religions should exist in harmony. What do you say to them?"

"I spit on them. No one can balance on a knife's blade. You either fight to defend Islam and Mohammad against Western evil or you are our enemy. Every Muslim must make that choice."

This is more like it, she thought. "What about Muslim women, children, and the elderly who cannot fight? Are they your sworn enemies?"

"The elderly cannot take up arms, but they are expected to teach the truth to those who are younger. All others must join our war. If a Muslim lives in harmony with a nonbeliever, he is an offense to the Prophet and deserves the same fate as infidels."

Knowing most of her viewers were peace-loving Muslims, she pushed a bit harder: "You are condemning anyone who doesn't agree with you?"

"I am condemning anyone who does not follow the teachings of the almighty Allah. There is only one God and he is Allah. All other religions are a blasphemy. There is only Sharia law—not laws or governments based on the whims of men. Men have no authority over Allah. It is Allah who has authority over all men. This is the truth."

Before she could ask her next question, the Falcon said, "The West, especially the United States, has superior weapons, but they will lose this battle just as the French, the British, the Russians, and the Jews who have attempted to control and invade our lands. The Americans grew tired of dying in Vietnam. This is their way. They enter a war with their bombs and they believe their superior weapons will give them victory. But this is not their land. Allah has given his land to us and he expects us to die for this land. A foreigner eventually seeks to negotiate. There will be no such negotiations. There will be no end to the war because Allah has ordered me to reclaim what is his. They will try to flee but I will follow and destroy them."

"You are against a negotiated peace in the Middle East even if the Americans agreed to leave?"

"If you catch a dog entering your house to steal your food and chase it out, it will run away but will soon become hungry and return. The only way to stop the dog is to kill it. The Americans want our oil. They bring with them fleas—Catholics, Christians, Zionists—who teach blasphemy. You cannot live with fleas any more than you can live with a dog that will take what is yours. Negotiation acknowledges their false beliefs and that is an insult to Islam."

"Not every group feels as strongly as you about fighting an endless war. I've been told Al-Qaeda in the Arabian Peninsula has rejected you as its leader and in Somalia, Al-Shabaab is rebelling against your leadership."

"I did not invite you here to spread Western lies and propaganda."

"Then you are denying these rumors of dissatisfaction?"

In an agitated voice, the Falcon said, "What does the West call me? The Falcon. I will explain this in ornithological terms. Do you understand murmuration?"

"No, it's not a familiar word."

"Despite your American education." He smirked. "Yet you have witnessed murmuration each year when European starlings form dark clouds across our skies as they migrate from Russia and Eastern Europe, flying together in unison. They dart across our skies as if they are one, physically connected, switching directions in a glance. There is no individual leader in murmuration; each fish or bird watches the one next to him as they join together to avoid predators."

"I'm not quite certain I understand your point."

"Allah is our leader, but each true believer is like one of those starlings who flock together. The West hopes to split us apart so it can destroy us one by one. But we all follow Allah. We are part of his flock. There is no Al-Shabaab, Boko Haram, Al-Qaeda of the Arabian Peninsula, ISIS. There is and can be only one. A single fist."

"There are reports in the West that you have lost territory and with that, you have lost millions in oil revenues. The West accuses you of raising funds by looting and selling antiques and artifacts, taxing and extortion, drug dealing, even sexual slavery."

The Falcon leapt to his feet. "The power Allah has awarded me is far-reaching, Ebio Kattan. Do not tempt me to use it. I can reach into your bedroom when you sleep and tighten my hands around your throat."

She had pushed him as far as she could, and it had worked. "I did not mean to offend," she said, slowly standing to be eye to eye with him. "Journalists ask questions, including difficult ones."

"And journalists bleed and die."

Kattan removed the camera from its tripod and focused in on his masked face. "May I ask one more question? Why did you finally agree to speak on camera to me?"

"Because I have a message to the United States. You Americans soon will learn what it is like to be afraid, to feel suspicion when you encounter a stranger walking toward you on the street. To be fearful when you enter a park, a café, an airport, a sports playing field, a church, a museum. For decades you have believed you are invincible, as if nothing can touch you, but I will. I am bringing death to your shores. Your mothers and fathers, brothers and sisters, young men, young women, and babies will be slaughtered before your eyes and your land will be saturated with your blood."

Kattan beamed. She'd done it.

CHAPTER FIFTEEN

Nondescript building
Reston, Virginia

Major Brooke Grant noticed a stranger enter the briefing. From his dress, he was clearly a Saudi. He was wearing a long, loose-fitting white shirt, known as a *thawb* with slits on its sides that extended to his ankles. His head was covered with a piece of red and white checkered silk cloth held in place by an igal, a black cord worn doubled across the forehead.

What was he doing here?

This was a classified briefing. Most attendees had top secret clearances or higher and yet a foreigner was listening in. She noticed he was scanning the room and when their eyes met, he nodded politely as if they were acquaintances. Brooke averted her glance and when she looked back, he was gone.

She returned her attention to the briefing.

"From identifying stamps on various parts of the rented truck, we've learned it came from an Easy-Haul facility in Newark and was painted to mimic a Coswell's Catering delivery vehicle," the briefer explained. "The names listed on the rental papers were fake and there were no security cameras inside the facility but there was an ATM across the street and it captured this view."

The blurry image of a man appeared on the briefing room monitor. His face was largely a collection of unrecognizable black and white dots.

"We were able to obtain DNA from inside the truck cab but it didn't match anyone in our databases."

The briefing officer clicked his handheld remote, causing a photo of a smiling young man to appear. "Despite these obstacles, we have confirmed the identity of the driver. His name is Salman Basra, a twenty-one-year-old Arab American from Jersey City. This photo was obtained from the employee badge issued to him when he was hired to work as a fast-food server inside the Walt Whitman Service Area on the New Jersey Turnpike—"

Brooke interrupted him. "How exactly were you able to identify Basra?"

Everyone turned and looked at her. Like the stranger, whom she had noticed, Brooke had entered the briefing after it had already started and had chosen a seat at the rear of the room to avoid being approached by workers offering condolences or whispering about her returning to work on this Wednesday, only four days after the Saturday explosion.

"Please hold your questions," the briefer replied. Continuing, he said, "By using facial and body recognition software, we have been able to determine that Salman Basra is not the same individual whose image was captured by the ATM outside the truck rental agency. Clearly, we are dealing with two individuals."

Next, a photo of a parked car appeared on the screen. "We were able to confirm that Basra was the suicide bomber and that he had an accomplice when we found this Honda Civic in the long-term lot at the Philadelphia International Airport. It is registered to Basra's parents."

Interesting, Brooke thought. Someone had identified Basra as the suicide bomber before his parents' car had been discovered.

"Security cameras captured images of a man driving the car into the parking lot and later when he walked through the airport terminal. When we compared the ATM footage captured outside the truck rental agency to the images from the airport's security tapes, we were able to confirm that they are the same man—Basra's accomplice, the second terrorist. Based on this evidence, we concluded that his accomplice delivered the rental truck to Basra at the Walt Whitman rest stop where he was at work that Saturday morning and then drove Basra's Honda to the airport."

The monitor momentarily became blue, waiting for the next image.

Several popped on the screen in rapid progression, showing a thin figure at different stages as he walked through the terminal. "At this point, we did not have a clear photo of the second terrorist's face because he was wearing a New York Giants cap, large sunglasses, a heavy beard, and turned up collar, but we were able to track his movements to a specific boarding gate. With assistance from the airline, we determined he was traveling under a French passport and the name Saleem Antar. We tracked him to London and then on to Paris, where he purchased a ticket to Morocco. That's where we lost him."

A new image appeared showing a passport photo. "His name is not Saleem Antar. It is Hakim Farouk. He is known in radical Islamic circles as 'the Destroyer' because he is an expert bomb maker. This photo is several years old."

Brooke studied the image. It showed a bearded man wearing bottle cap glasses and a turban that made it appear as if he were a Sikh, not a Muslim. It was obvious to her that the large glasses and headwear were an attempt to conceal his looks.

When the briefer finished five minutes later, Brooke raised her hand.

"I asked earlier how you were able to identify Salman Basra, the man who committed suicide by detonating the truck bomb?"

"A cooperative foreign intelligence agency provided us with Basra's name. Now if there are no more questions."

Without raising her hand, Brooke called out, "Who confirmed that Basra's accomplice was Hakim Farouk, this so-called Destroyer?"

"Again that confirmation came from a cooperative intelligence service," he said.

No one else had any questions, so Brooke slipped out of the room quickly and made her way down a gray-walled corridor to a solid steel door with a red stop sign decal attached to it at eye level:

RESTRICTED ACCESS

A camera in the ceiling videotaped everyone who entered or left the room. None of the analysts at the early morning briefing were aware of what was happening behind the steel door. It was not uncommon for intelligence operatives to work independently, strictly on a need-to-know basis, and to be heavily compartmentalized within the same leased building. Being too curious about another employee's assignment could make others wonder about your motives, especially because of spying scandals at both the CIA and FBI in earlier years. Given that Brooke had just survived an explosion that had killed the president, she was certain her appearance at the briefing might have surprised some, but she was equally certain those present had no idea the president had created a KTB team and that she was on it.

She punched the correct code into the electronic lock and then pressed her right thumb onto a verification screen. As soon as the dead bolt slid back, she tugged open the heavy door and stepped into a compact office area that held five glass-enclosed cubicles, a conference room, and a break room exclusively for use by President Austin's so-called Kill That Bastard team.

The offices were empty, which didn't surprise her. As far as Brooke knew, she was the only KTB team member. She was about to enter her office when she heard the bubbling sound of an old-fashioned coffee percolator coming from the closet-sized break room. Clearly, someone was there. She went to investigate and almost collided with the Saudi, who she'd seen earlier, as he was exiting from the break room.

"Good morning, Major Grant," he said, offering her a Styrofoam cup with steam rising from it. "I've taken the liberty of brewing coffee. I was unable to learn from your dossier if you take sugar or like it black."

She didn't reach for it. "Who are you? Why are you in a restricted area? And why were you reading my dossier?"

"Oh, I apologize," he said, still holding the coffee for her. "My name is Khalid and I'm from the GID. Your CIA director, Payton Grainger, has authorized me to join your team."

Brooke was used to intelligence officers using only one name, generally an alias, so she didn't bother asking Khalid for a last name, but she wasn't going to take his word that he was from the Saudi's General Intelligence Directorate without verifying it.

"Follow me, please," she said, directing him into the nearby conference room. As she sat down, she sized him up. In his early forties, she guessed, and a big man, at least 240 pounds but tall enough that he carried it well and didn't appear pudgy. His face reminded her of the famed actor Omar Sharif, whom she'd seen in a college film studies class that included the classics: *Lawrence of Arabia* and *Doctor Zhivago*. She used a secure phone to dial a phone in Director Grainger's office.

"Okay, you're legit," she said moments later after hanging up.

He offered her the same coffee that he'd been carrying and she accepted it, but before taking a sip, she said, "Can I assume it was Saudi intelligence that identified Salman Basra and confirmed the true identity of Hakim Farouk, this bomb maker called 'the Destroyer'?"

"Only one name came from us," he answered. "Salman Basra." Glancing around, he said, "May we go into your office or would you prefer to use mine? Although it was assigned to me only this morning and only contains an empty file cabinet, a computer with restricted access, a rather uncomfortable chair, and a metal desk. I must tell you that in my country, our offices are a bit more plush."

"It's called 'buying from the lowest bidder,'" she replied, following him inside his cubicle.

"Major Grant, before we begin, may I ask you who these people in the briefing were this morning?"

"They're from the agency or other intelligence groups investigating the bombing and international terrorism. We'll receive copies of all their reports. It's our job to analyze every scrap and then use our own skills to locate the Falcon."

"Don't you mean kill that bastard?" he replied. "I believe that is the title of our group—KTB. By the way, how many more of us will there be?"

She shrugged. "All I know about is me and you. Now, tell me how the GID identified Basra so quickly."

"First let me express my condolences for your multiple losses. I'm certain this is a very difficult time for you."

"I appreciate that, but I'd rather have you answer my question."

"You've only tasted the coffee. Would you like a fresh cup?"

"No, I'd like you to answer my question about Basra."

"Did you know," he said, "it was an Ethiopian goat herder who made the first cup of coffee? My people have been making and drinking it much longer than you Americans."

"Khalid, I really don't care about who invented coffee," she said firmly. "What I care about is how you were able to identify Basra when we didn't have a clue who he was?"

"Yes, that's understandable, but first a question for you. Today is your president's funeral. Sally Allworth. Yet, you are not there."

"I don't see how any of this is your business, but if you must know, I didn't want to deal with the media. I'm not terribly fond of them feeding on my grief."

"Nor are reporters a favorite of mine, but indulge me with one more question, please. It has been only four days since the bombing. Why are you here and not home grieving?"

"How I choose to vent my grief is my business," she replied in a stern voice. She was losing her patience with his personal questions.

"A fair point, but I want to be certain your mind is clear and focused, since we are now partners."

"Then test me by answering my question. How was the GID able to identify Basra so quickly when our people didn't have a clue who he was until you told them? Was he someone on your radar who slipped through the cracks?"

"No. As far as I know, he was not on anyone's watch lists. We had never heard of him until his mother called us."

"His mother?"

"Yes. Nadia Basra contacted us in Riyadh, or I should say she contacted some very influential people in Riyadh who asked us to look into this matter."

"What am I missing here?" Brooke asked. "Basra's mother calls someone in Riyadh and the GID immediately sends you to Washington?"

"Nadia Basra is married to a Pakistani but she actually is a Saudi and not just any Saudi. She is a member of the House of Saud."

"She's royalty? If she's royalty, why is she living in New Jersey and not in some Manhattan penthouse?"

"Ah, the answer is complicated. You see, all Saudi men and women must obtain permission from the government if they wish to marry a non-Saudi."

"You're joking? Your government has to approve every marriage if a Saudi wants to marry someone from a different country?"

Brooke glanced at Khalid's fingers and noticed he was not wearing a wedding band. But she also knew some Muslims did not wear them because they considered it forbidden.

"Our government takes marriages between Saudis and non-Saudis very seriously, especially when the bride is part of the royal bloodline. Having someone of her standing marry an outsider is virtually unheard of."

"Montagues and Capulets."

"Exactly, Romeo and Juliet, and like that Shakespearean tragedy when Nadia asked for permission to marry a non-Saudi, it was quite scandalous."

"Let me guess. The government gave her permission because of her connections."

"No, exactly the opposite. It denied her request, so she abandoned her native land to marry. Even worse, she married a Pakistani."

"Why's that worse than marrying any other non-Saudi?" Brooke asked.

"Let's just say Pakistanis are not on the same level as us Saudis."

"Meaning you Saudis think you are better."

Her judgmental tone irritated him. "Major, have you ever been to Pakistan and witnessed for yourself how they live? They are only one step up above their Indian neighbors."

"I imagine Pakistanis believe they are superior to Saudis and the residents of India believe they are superior to both Pakistanis and Saudis."

"You Americans believe you are superior to us all."

"In case you haven't noticed," she replied, "I'm black. My descendants were slaves and we have been fighting prejudice for as long as your people have been making coffee."

"Touché," he said, raising his cup. He seemed to enjoy their verbal sparring. "Nadia contacted us because she suspected her son was involved the moment she heard about the bombing. She wants someone to punish the Imam who radicalized her son, and his mosque is not far from here."

"What made her so certain it was her son?"

"I was not told. The royal family simply told me to come here and help you."

"Okay, who is this Imam and where is his mosque? Virginia, Maryland, or D.C.?"

"Maryland. His name is Mohammad Al-Kader. Perhaps you are familiar with him."

"Familiar? Very familiar. He's the same Imam who radicalized a Somali American couple named Cumar and Fawzia Samatar. They attacked President Sally Allworth when she was attending a funeral at the National Cathedral."

"I remember. The woman lit herself on fire and tried to throw herself onto your president. Meanwhile, the man blew himself up with a suicide vest while leaping against the presidential limousine. Can I assume that you have questioned this Imam?"

"No, you may not assume that. I've always wanted to interrogate Al-Kader but he's a spiritual leader. He has lots of lawyers and, as shocking as it sounds, he is an American citizen protected by our constitution. But I've always suspected he was linked to the Falcon in some way."

"I believe this is an issue we should discuss with Director Grainger."

"I agree," she replied. "Now tell me about Hakim Farouk. You just said the GID wasn't responsible for fingering him. Who did?"

"The Mossad. It has been tracking him for a long time and it positively identified him based on the pictures taken at the airport and his passport photo."

"Why would you know what the Mossad is doing?"

"Because they told us."

In a surprised voice, Brooke replied, "Since when did Saudi intelligence and the Mossad begin sharing information?"

"Major Grant, the Saudis and the Israelis and most other Arab nations have one common enemy. None of us want the Iranians to grow any stronger than they are. They are the biggest sponsors of terrorism in our region. Surely you know this."

"No, I wasn't aware. I'm not an expert on Middle Eastern politics. I got dragged into all of this when my parents were murdered and years later when the Falcon decided to make killing me a priority. Now tell me what the Israelis know about this Destroyer."

"Your wedding party was not Hakim Farouk's first victims. The Mossad has linked him to at least seven other major bomb explosions across Europe and in the Middle East. He is a psychopath."

"Aren't they all?"

"No, jihadists come in different flavors. This man is in a special category. He enjoys killing. He derives personal pleasure from it."

"Did the Mossad tell you that too?"

"I know because he kills people when he doesn't have to. Innocent people, especially Muslims. In every city, before one of his bombs explodes, there is a death or maybe two that ultimately gets tied to him; there is usually a murder that involves a slit throat or stabbing. Farouk always uses a knife. It makes it intimate. He likes to watch people die when they are a breath away from him."

"What makes a man that way?"

"Ah, shall we have a psychological conversation? Nurture or nature? I'm afraid it is an old argument. Farouk often tells people he is from Yemen and his wife and daughter were murdered by an American missile. He even has names for them—Ayeesha and Leyia. But no one has ever verified any of that. Our sources believe he was an illegitimate baby discarded at an orphanage in Oman. Such children are treated cruelly, frequently beaten and starved. Perhaps his wife and daughter are a fantasy he developed because of his loveless childhood. An imaginary family, but they also could be real. Who knows and does it matter? He is a religious fanatic who enjoys killing. There's no reason to learn anything else."

He finished his coffee and said, "If I can make an assumption. Salman Basra was radicalized—that is why he detonated the bomb that killed your family, friends, and the president. But someone like Hakim Farouk is a true serial murderer who hides behind piety."

CHAPTER SIXTEEN

Port of Tanjung Priok
Jakarta, Indonesia

Hakim "the Destroyer" Farouk inspected the day laborers loitering along the street on this hot Wednesday and chose a strong-looking twentysomething worker who said his name was Kevin, one of the most common first names in Indonesia.

They had ridden together in Kevin's pieced-together Suzuki Carry Truck to the docks, where the cargo ship *Sea Voyager* had dropped anchor.

The ship's captain greeted Farouk personally. He had no idea what was inside the large wooden crate marked SEA TRIDENT SHIPPING that he'd brought from North Korea. But he'd been warned that the box contained something extremely important to the ship line's owner, an African billionaire named Umoja Owiti, so the captain had made certain it had been unmolested during transit.

The ship's deck crane raised the wooden carton from the cargo hold and deposited it on the dock, where a forklift transferred it onto Kevin's flatbed. Farouk and Kevin drove west out of Jakarta after covering the container with a heavy green tarp.

They'd gone only a few miles when Kevin announced that he needed gasoline and asked Farouk for enough rupiahs to fill his tank. Farouk handed him cash and wandered into a nearby store, where he bought bottled water, a container of *nasi goreng* (fried rice), *uli petataws* (sweet potato fritters), *sambal kecap* (chili and soy sauce), and finally a kakoa chili chocolate bar, a gourmet Indonesian candy made of dark chocolate and organic red chili mixed together.

As Farouk was paying the owner, he happened to glance through the store's smudged windows and noticed that Kevin was talking on his cell phone while filling the truck's tank.

When they restarted their trip, Farouk offered Kevin a bottled water and piece of kakoa chocolate, both of which he eagerly accepted.

"Thank you, boss!" he exclaimed enthusiastically. "I work hard for you!"

They'd gone only a mile from the gas station when Farouk said, "Pull to the side of the highway and please turn off the engine."

"Much too dangerous, boss!" Kevin said. "Look. Too many cars on road. We get hit."

Reaching down, Farouk removed a large handgun from a black gym bag at his feet.

Kevin's carefree demeanor instantly turned to fear.

"Recognize this?" Farouk asked casually as he aimed the semi-automatic pistol at Kevin's chest. "It's a Pindad PS-01 assault pistol—a handgun that your government stopped making years ago because it was so heavy and bulky, but it is still being sold on the black market in Jakarta."

Drivers in Indonesia travel on the left side of the road, and Farouk again told Kevin to pull onto the shoulder along the busy thoroughfare.

"Okay, okay, boss, but what's this?" he stammered. "You no need point gun at me."

"Let me tell you a story," Farouk said, keeping the pistol aimed at the center of Kevin's badly soiled wife-beater T-shirt. "I had a driver take me to Bandung yesterday and we were stopped four times by policemen on this very road. They all made some flimsy excuse that required me to pay an on-the-spot fine."

"Bribes," Kevin said. "The cops, they do that. But why gun? Why stop?"

"Yes, I had to pay each one seventy thousand rupiahs—about five U.S. dollars."

Kevin's eyes remained fixed on the barrel aimed at him.

"Bribing police," Farouk continued in an eerily calm voice, "is a mere inconvenience, a cost of business. But my driver yesterday also mentioned the real problem was bandits attacking trucks, especially on the stretch of highway that climbs the mountains into Bandung."

Tilting the huge pistol slightly upward so it was now pointed directly at Kevin's face, Farouk said, "I want you to know that I will shoot you first if anyone tries to hijack my cargo."

"Boss," Kevin sputtered. "I no bandit."

"The cell phone call you made when you were pumping gas."

"A woman. She nobody."

With his free hand, Farouk removed Kevin's cell phone from a holder attached to the truck's dash. "You might want to call this woman back and explain to her that I will kill you and anyone else who tries to steal my cargo."

Farouk hit redial on the cell phone's touch screen and handed it to Kevin.

When a man's voice answered, Kevin spoke rapidly in Indonesian before hanging up.

"Should we expect bandits?" Farouk asked rhetorically.

"No bandits. I promise, boss man. No bandits today for us."

"Good," Farouk said as he tucked his handgun between the passenger door and the truck's seat so it was out of sight but within easy reach. "Just remember, you die first."

As they pulled back onto Highway One heading west, Farouk said, "Tell me who you are."

"I'm nobody."

"Wife, children?"

"Never. No."

He offered Kevin another piece of chocolate, which left a spicy, hot taste after the initial sweetness, and suggested that Kevin relax. Having made this same drive the day before, Farouk knew they would be traveling together for at least three hours.

"Girlfriend?" Farouk asked.

"No," Kevin said, exposing a near empty mouth of missing teeth. "Kevin knows many girls. Much fun. You want meet? I get. Good prices."

"How much do you pay a woman for sex in Jakarta?"

"Six hundred thousand rupiahs—fifty dollar U.S. Good woman. Young. Virgin. Or maybe you want boy."

A rare flash of anger swept across Farouk's face. "Sleeping with prostitutes is haram and I am not a pedophile or homosexual."

"Sorry, boss man. Lots of foreigners come for sex. Lots want boys. What was that word you said?"

"*Haram*? It means prohibited. I'm a Muslim."

"My mother Catholic, but too much bother for me. She always praying, lighting candles. But God do nothing for Kevin."

Farouk broke the last piece of chocolate in half and shared it with Kevin.

"Why you come here, boss?" Kevin asked. "Something important in Bandung."

"How many rupiahs do you earn in a year?" Farouk asked.

Taking his eyes off the road momentarily to glance at his passenger, Kevin replied, "Twelve thousand U.S."

Farouk suspected he was lying but didn't care. "And how much comes from tipping off your friends about trucks they can hijack?"

Kevin shook his head. "You got me wrong, boss. Mistake. I work hard."

"The Holy Quran says: 'As to the thief, male or female, cut off his or her hands: a punishment by way of example, from Allah, for their crime.'"

"You hire me to drive to Bandung," Kevin said. "You ask about prostitutes. You call me a bandit. You ask me about money. Then you quote the Quran. Cut off hands. Why you do this?"

Farouk reached into his satchel and opened another bottle of water, which he handed to Kevin. "Forgive me for being rude. I want you to forget what we agreed on earlier. I will give you a thousand dollars U.S. to get me to Bandung and then forget me and the box we are carrying. Do you accept?"

"How about two thousand. For that I forget everything—for two thousand." Kevin spotted a police officer ahead of them waving over vehicles. "What you say, two thousand?"

Farouk replied, "Yes, two thousand."

The policeman motioned for them to stop and walked around the truck. The green tarp was not correctly lashed over the cargo, he announced.

"You pay fine—seventy thousand rupiahs—now," he said in broken English. Farouk handed him the money and the officer let them continue.

As they neared the town of Karawang, another policeman stopped them and demanded 70,000 rupiahs for too loud of a muffler, and it happened a third time when the highway divided and they turned onto a road that would take them first to Purwakarta and then into the volcanic mountains that surrounded the mountain hideaway of Bandung.

None of the police officers showed any interest in what the rectangular container under the tarp contained. Instead they picked some violation related to the flatbed truck, which admittedly, gave them plenty of legitimate choices.

However, when they were five miles outside of Bandung, they were stopped again and this officer peeked under the tarp.

"What's in big box?" he demanded.

"Parts for machines that make ice cream," Farouk replied, having read enough about Indonesians to know they were huge consumers of ice cream products.

"You open."

Farouk clearly couldn't open the container because it contained a nuclear bomb. Yet he couldn't shoot the officer because that would raise undo attention. The best alternative was to offer him a higher bribe but he needed to be smart about it. If he offered too much that could make the dishonest cop even more curious. It was not uncommon for policemen to help themselves to goods being transported. He needed a reason that would justify offering more rupiahs without calling attention to the cargo.

"We're running late," Farouk said. "My boss is losing thousands of rupiahs each minute we aren't selling ice cream and we can't sell ice cream if our machines are broken." Farouk reached into his shirt pocket and removed the equivalent of $20, which he handed to the policeman. The cop grabbed it like a wolf locking its teeth onto a newborn bunny and said, "You open box now."

"I can't. My boss will think someone stole something from it."

The policeman drew a Taurus M82 revolver from his holster and waved it at Farouk. Letting out an exasperated sigh but showing no fear, Farouk calmly took a wad of 1 million rupiahs, about $75, from his pocket. "Like I said, we need to get going."

The policeman fanned the bills and broke into a smile. Returning his pistol to his holster, he said, "Next time bring beer. We can drink together." He let them through.

"You cool customer, boss," Kevin said.

As they entered Bandung, Indonesia's third largest city, Farouk used a GPS to direct Kevin to a small warehouse that he'd rented the day before. It was a 3,500-square-foot unit that came with a restroom, a small kitchen area, a single office, and a forklift that Farouk had paid extra to have on hand. His was one of five identical warehouse units joined together in a row protected by a ten-foot-tall security fence and two security guards stationed at its gated entrance.

Farouk used a handheld opener to raise his warehouse's larger door, which was big enough for Kevin's truck to drive through. He closed the door after the truck was parked safely inside.

"Boss, you going to kill me now?" Kevin asked.

Farouk feigned shock. "No, I'm going to pay you a thousand U.S. dollars after you help me unload and then you can return to Jakarta." As a sign of good faith, he inserted the pistol back into the gym bag, which he zipped closed. "It was so old it probably would have exploded if I pulled the trigger," he chuckled.

Farouk walked from the truck to the warehouse office, where he dropped the gym bag on the floor. He closed the office door and locked it. "Here. You can hold on to the key. No gun. You help me unload. Eat the food I bought for you and then you go." Reaching into his pocket, he removed a big wad of rupiahs that he handed Kevin.

"With thirteen million rupiahs," Farouk added, "you can buy many girlfriends."

"And whisky!"

"Can you operate a forklift?" Farouk asked.

Kevin climbed onto the forklift and started its engine. Within minutes, he had expertly inserted its two front blades into the openings in the pallet under the cargo box and lifted the container from his truck.

"Where you want?"

Farouk directed him toward a large square of plastic spread over the concrete floor. "Here," he said, pointing at its center.

Kevin drove the forklift to the spot and began lowering its cargo.

"Stop!" Farouk yelled. He bent down and glanced under the cargo box that was now teetering about four feet above the plastic. "I think you punctured something with the forklift."

Kevin hurried down from the driver's seat, joining Farouk on the plastic wrap. He glanced under the pallet.

"No, boss, everything okay."

Before Kevin could utter another word, Farouk stabbed him in the back. The downward angle of the six-inch blade sliced through Kevin's aorta and pulmonary artery as its tip pierced his left atrium. Kevin's body collapsed onto the plastic. There was no blood gushing from his wound. A signal his heart was no longer pumping.

Farouk wiped his blade against Kevin's shirt and removed everything from the worker's pockets, including his identification card, driver's license, and the wad of rupiahs that he'd given him moments before.

Getting behind the forklift's wheel, Farouk turned the vehicle around and drove off the plastic to a nearby corner where he lowered the pallet onto the concrete floor. Using a crow bar, he opened the wooden Sea Trident Shipping container and lifted several boxes of supplies from it. Next, he wrapped a piece of heavy chain around the nuclear bomb. He took the loose ends of the chain and attached them to the twin blades of the forklift. By raising the blades, he was able to remove the heavy bomb from the container, drive it to a better location, and lower it to the floor.

Dismounting from the forklift, he returned to Kevin's corpse, which he rolled into the plastic that was spread across the floor.

Returning to the forklift, he drove to the corpse and attached the chain to the plastic-wrapped human burrito that he had created. As he had done with the bomb, he used the vehicle's blades to lift Kevin from the concrete. Within five minutes, Farouk had deposited the corpse into the wooden cargo container, nailed its wooden top into place, and used the forklift to place the box into a corner of the warehouse.

He checked the time. He had missed the fourth of Islam's five mandatory prayers while driving to the warehouse. Now it was time for the fifth and final prayer of the day. He retrieved his prayer rug from the office and hurried into one of the bathrooms to do the required washing before praying. When finished, he stood in the warehouse a few feet from the nuclear bomb that he had brought there. Standing above his prayer rug facing the holy city of Mecca. Raising his hands upward at the elbow in adulation, he then crossed them in font of his chest and chanted:

"Allah is the greatest.
"In the name of Allah, most gracious, most merciful
"All praise is due to Allah, Lord of all that exists
"The most gracious, the most merciful
"Master of the day of judgment
"You alone we worship, and you alone we ask for help
"Guide us to the straight way
"The way of those on whom you have bestowed your grace
"Not the way of those who earned your anger, nor of those who went astray
"Oh Allah accept."

His words were the opening lines of a *Rakat*, the first of two said aloud, the final two in silence. At one point while praying, he would kneel, touch his forehead to the floor, and say, "My Lord forgive me."

After he was finished, he removed the license plates from Kevin's truck and fetched several tins of paint from supplies that he had brought to the storehouse the previous day. He mixed the colors to match the badly mangled plates and carefully changed a 3 into an 8. Satisfied, he used a spray gun that he'd purchased the day before to repaint Kevin's truck from white to a dull red.

Farouk wanted to be relaxed when he began the next step in his plan. Only a fool hurried when building a detonator, so before he rested on a cot in the office, he took several moments to examine the nuclear bomb that had been entrusted to him. He needed to ensure that no one had tampered with it since he'd last inspected it in North Korea. He gently caressed its metal shell like a lover. The killing power under his fingertips excited him. He closed his eyes and imagined the bomb exploding, creating a giant mushroom cloud, and obliterating everything around it. He could see the burning bodies, the crumbling buildings, the thousands of deaths. Such destructive power.

Yes, Allah, I am the Destroyer.

CHAPTER SEVENTEEN

Geraldine and General Grant's house
Northern Virginia

Shortly after speaking with her new KTB Saudi team partner, Brooke Grant exited the secure Reston office building. The parking lot was empty. Everyone else who'd attended the early morning Wednesday briefing had already departed to watch President Sally Allworth's eleven o'clock funeral service being broadcast on television. Brooke had no interest in seeing it. She had told Khalid that the media had kept her from attending in person. There was more to it than that.

She felt responsible—just as she felt responsible for all of the deaths at her wedding. It was easier to remain secluded and pour over intelligence cables and background information in pursuit of Hakim Farouk, the missing nuclear bomb, and the Falcon than to face the public or her own conscience.

For some time, she'd suspected African billionaire Umoja Owiti was secretly supporting the Falcon. She was not the only one who believed this. The agency had him in its sights. Again, it was the Mossad who had the best intel in the region and it had sources who claimed the Falcon had once visited Owiti at his El Wak compound. Not long after that reported meeting, three supertankers carrying oil owned by one of Owiti's companies had vanished in the vast Pacific Ocean. Trading oil to the North Koreans would have been an astute way for Owiti to avoid leaving his fingerprints behind when purchasing a nuclear bomb.

Brooke was still hiding out at her aunt and uncle's home, and after parking her car in its garage to hide it, she went into the dining room to work. She couldn't bring herself to use Uncle Frank's office. In her mind, it was still his private space even though he was gone.

She was so engrossed in her research that she jumped in her chair when someone rapped on the door. Grabbing her Beretta, she peeked outside. Congressman Rudy Adeogo was raising his hand to knock again.

"I came to tell you how sorry I am for your losses," he said as soon as she let him inside the foyer.

"How's Jennifer?" he asked, clearly concerned.

"She's getting treatment for post-traumatic stress. She's in a safe place. It is going to take time." Brooke didn't want to go into detail. It was too painful to recite.

"I'll tell Cassy that Jennifer is doing fine. She's worried about her best friend. Hopefully we can get them together soon."

Leading him into the living room, she asked, "Why aren't you at President Allworth's funeral?"

Casting his eyes downward, he replied, "It shows a lack of courage on my part. Better than anyone else, you are aware that my youngest brother, George, was radicalized and a terrorist."

"I knew him as Abdul Hafeez," she said. Brooke understood why the congressman was avoiding the funeral. It was nothing he had done personally, but the media would ask him about his brother's radical-ization and if Abdul Hafeez had any possible connection with the suicide bomber.

"I've actually have come to ask for forgiveness," Adeogo said, sur-prising her.

"My forgiveness for what? You certainly didn't have anything to do with the bombing."

"It's not about the bombing. It's about resentment that I am ashamed to admit."

"Against me?"

"No, the man you were to marry—Walks Many Miles."

From the puzzled look on her face, Adeogo could tell she was con-fused.

"He was responsible for my youngest brother's death in Mogadishu."

"Walks Many Miles killed your brother because Abdul Hafeez was about to detonate a suicide vest and car bomb outside a mosque, possibly murdering hundreds of innocent people."

"Yes, yes, I understand. If Miles had not shot him, George would have done exactly what you say. I am so ashamed because he was my brother. Yet, he was my brother and my parents and brothers and sisters and I have never had a chance to have a funeral for him. Nor have we ever talked about him because it is so painful. We have no idea how he became radicalized. We have always been a close family and it is as if we have washed him from our memory banks, or tried to. The truth is that I felt a certain animus against your Walks Many Miles even though I understood he needed to kill George. I have come now to ask if you will forgive me for those inappropriate feelings. The bombing at your wedding has reminded me of just how evil my brother had become because of the Falcon and his false teachings. Once again, I feel great shame."

"Miles and I talked about you and your brother, and this is going to surprise you, but both of us thought you showed tremendous courage when you revealed at a press conference that Abdul Hafeez was actually George Adeogo. We thought it was incredibly brave for you to do as a congressman."

Adeogo remained quiet for several awkward moments.

"Would you like to know why I acknowledged my younger brother was an extremist?" he asked. "It wasn't courage; it was because I was forced to. I was being blackmailed."

"Blackmailed? Who was blackmailing you?"

"Mary Margaret Delaney, the Washington lobbyist. Somehow that witch discovered our family secret. She learned Abdul Hafeez was my youngest brother and she threatened to expose it. She said I would never get reelected if people knew."

"She was trying to get money out of you?"

"No and yes. What she wanted was to control me. She said her clients would pay her large sums of cash if they knew she had a member of Congress under her thumb. But it was more than that. It was personal between us. She hated me."

"So rather than become her puppet, you announced that Abdul Hafeez was your brother at a press conference. You took away her power."

"And, most likely, I will pay a price. My first term in the House may easily be my last. There are already rumors circulating in my Somali American district about a young community organizer who is thinking about challenging me. What has always troubled me is how Delaney discovered my brother was a terrorist."

"I'd assume she went to Minneapolis and dug into your family history, talked to people who knew him when he was a child."

"And that's what I assumed too until she came to my house and showed me documents that were from an old juvenile court record. They showed that my brother had legally changed his name from George Adeogo to Abdul Hafeez. A local family court judge had sealed those documents but someone had obtained copies illegally and provided them to her. I am convinced she was working as a straw man. I've given it much thought and I believe it was Omar Nader, the Washington head of the OIN."

Again, Brooke looked perplexed. "Omar Nader is a fellow Muslim. He should have been supporting you politically, if only for religious reasons. Why would he want to harm your career? It doesn't make sense to me."

"I have disagreed publicly with him and the OIN. I've said Arab nations need to do more to clean their own houses. I've criticized them for saying they oppose terrorism while quietly supporting terrorists. What really has angered Nader is how I have humiliated his home country. I've spoken openly about repression in Saudi Arabia and its strict adherence to Sharia law. It's an undemocratic regime that actually is little different from what the Falcon and his followers are hoping to duplicate throughout the Middle East. Omar Nader is shrewd enough to know that he can't threaten me openly. You can't have an organization like the OIN attacking the only Muslim member of the U.S. Congress. This is why he recruited her. Nader must have obtained the juvenile court information somehow and provided it to her."

Brooke left her seat and returned to the foyer where Aunt Geraldine had put aside the large manila envelope that had been hand-delivered to Brooke on her wedding day.

Returning, she explained, "A very determined Park Police officer named Cindy Gural brought me this. She's the officer who found Delaney's body in her car parked along the G. W. Parkway."

Brooke paused to control her emotions. "After dropping off this packet at my house, she went to my wedding. She'd been a former D.C. police officer and wanted to earn some extra money helping provide security. She was killed with everyone else."

Brooke removed a set of 8-by-10-inch photos from the envelope. "This is all coming back to me now," she explained as she glanced at the first picture. "On the night Mary Margaret Delaney was found dead, she had been out celebrating with a girlfriend at a popular bar called the After Hours Club in D.C. Her girlfriend said Delaney was bragging about some big client she'd nabbed. She was buying expensive champagne because this client was going to pay her big bucks. The two of them were having a great time, flirting with men and drinking until Delaney got a phone call and literally ran out of the club to go meet some man. Her girlfriend thought it was her new big-time client."

Brooke handed the first photo to Adeogo, explaining, "This photo was taken by the club's outside security camera. It shows her leaving, getting into her car, and driving away. It has a time and date stamp on it."

Brooke removed a second photo. "Now this one was taken by a stoplight camera at a D.C. intersection. It photographs drivers who speed through a red light."

Delaney was clearly visible behind the wheel of her BMW failing to make it across the intersection before the light turned red. The shot had a time and date stamp.

"I've been caught by these cameras near my house," Adeogo volunteered as he inspected the photo.

"Anyone who actually stops for a yellow light in downtown D.C. is going to get rear ended," Brooke joked. She looked at the third photo from the envelope and gasped.

"What?" he said, eager to see.

"It's another traffic photo but until this moment, I didn't recognize the driver. Quick, what's the time stamp on the photo of Delaney running the red light?"

Adeogo read it to her.

"This photo was taken exactly three seconds later at the same intersection. This car must have been directly behind Delaney's BMW, chasing her."

She handed Adeogo the photograph.

"The passenger in this car is Omar Nader!" he exclaimed. "But who is the driver?"

"I met him today. He said his name is Khalid. He's GID."

Adeogo gave her a blank look.

"Saudi General Intelligence Directorate."

"Such a man would know how to obtain information that most cannot get. Privileged information possibly through some backdoor intelligence channel about my younger brother being Abdul Hafeez, a terrorist. He must have been Nader's source."

Brooke pulled several typed reports from the large envelope. One was a facsimile of the official Park Police log that showed when Officer Cindy Gural had reported finding Delaney's body. The next several pages were copies of her official on-the-scene report, in which she noted that Delaney had been shot in an upward angle through the roof of her mouth. The .22-caliber round apparently had been fired from a "double derringer" found on Delaney's lap. Made in Italy, the tiny two-barrel pistol was more than fifty years old, making it impossible to trace. A second .22 "short" bullet was found loaded in the second barrel's chamber.

Officer Gural noted that one of Delaney's earrings had been ripped from her earlobe and one of her fake fingernails had been ripped off, which caused Gural to speculate there had been a struggle inside the car because both the missing earring and fingernail tip had been found on the floor.

Her superiors and the Virginia medical examiner had disregarded Gural's theory of a violent struggle and had ruled Delaney's death a suicide.

"Wouldn't a GID officer like this Khalid know how to stage a death, even bringing along a pistol that would be impossible to trace?" Adeogo asked.

"These photos prove Omar Nader and Khalid were directly behind her, but that doesn't link either to her death."

"Every detective show I've watched on television talks about opportunity and motive. I believe the photos show opportunity and I have just given you a plausible motive. After I announced Abdul Hafeez was my brother, Omar Nader must have panicked."

"I'm not following your logic."

"Let's assume Omar Nader was Delaney's big client and he was the one who got the information about my brother—information that enabled her to blackmail me. He would not want to risk having Delaney go public and reveal his role in any of this. It would have been too scandalous for him and the OIN. Who knows? Delaney may have attempted to blackmail him. What I do know is that Omar Nader would not hesitate to solve an embarrassing problem, such as this one, by summoning a Saudi intelligence agent to kill Delaney. It's how his mind works."

Brooke began putting the photos and reports back into the envelope but stopped to take a second look at the photo of Khalid behind the wheel. There was no doubt it was him.

"What are you going to do with these?" Adeogo asked.

"Cindy Gural is dead and I have no jurisdiction, so I'm going to turn them over to the director of the CIA. If Saudi intelligence murdered someone on U.S. soil, he'll know how to proceed."

Minutes later, Adeogo left the house and the reality of what Brooke had discovered settled in. It appeared that Khalid was a GID assassin. A part of her had considered the title—Kill That Bastard—mostly bluster, an angry response to a mass murder. But she now believed it was not hyperbole.

Her cell phone rang. The number on its screen showed it was Director Payton Grainger's private cell.

"Are you watching television?" he asked.

"No, I haven't had it on all morning."

"Turn it on now!"

CHAPTER EIGHTEEN

Dubai Media City
United Arab Emirates

It's unbelievable!" Al Arabic's news director gushed as he hurried into the network's master control studio housed inside one of the fourteen skyscrapers that made up the Middle East's largest media broadcasting hub.

"We're only five minutes into your exclusive interview with the Falcon and we've already gotten close to fifty-five million viewers," he told Ebio Kattan, who was overseeing the broadcast. "Fifty-five million! Including large numbers in the United States, Germany, France, and England."

No journalist had ever interviewed the Falcon face-to-face and broadcasting it the same Wednesday as President Allworth's funeral was proving to be a ratings bonanza. Her exclusive hit the airwaves at 10:00 p.m. UAE time, which was eight hours ahead of Washington, D.C. It was reaching U.S. viewers almost immediately after President Sally Allworth's morning service and graveside ceremony.

"Our numbers are still going out of sight. Word is spreading on social media. We've already got more Americans watching us than they did the winter Olympics."

An aide slipped inside and informed Kattan that the lobby security guard was trying to reach her.

"I'm busy," Kattan snapped as she focused on the screens before her, reveling in her international scoop.

"Ms. Kattan, the guard says a courier has brought you a package from the Falcon."

Kattan bolted from the room down to the lobby, where she retrieved the package. It contained a flash drive. Nothing else. Hurrying upstairs, she inserted it into a computer with her news director watching over her shoulder.

The Falcon's masked face appeared on the computer screen in a video recording that was poorly lit, slightly blurry, and of amateurish quality.

"American infidels and Zionist devils. Allah, bless his holy name, has called on me to bring justice upon you. Believing only you could possess nuclear bombs reveals your arrogance and ignorance. I am coming to America to destroy three of your cities."

He paused, for unneeded dramatic effect, before adding, "Hiroshima, one hundred and forty-six thousand killed. Nagasaki, eighty thousand murdered. How many Americans will die at the hand of Allah? Prepare yourselves for my nuclear sword."

The screen went black.

"We must go live right after my taped interview ends!" Kattan gleefully exclaimed. "If you think the ratings are high now, just wait!"

"Kattan, he's talking about murdering possibly millions of Americans. We can't be happy about this."

"Which is why it's our duty to broadcast this as a warning."

"But what if it isn't true?" the news director asked. "Where would he get three nuclear bombs? This will cause complete panic in the United States. Think of our responsibility here. Shouldn't we turn this over to proper officials? Shouldn't we warn the U.S. government before possibly causing mass hysteria?"

"If a nuclear bomb goes off tonight in Washington, Boston, or New York and the world learns we had this warning and didn't broadcast it, we would be called coconspirators. Our job is not to worry about what might happen. Our job is to tell the public and let it decide how it wants to react."

"Kattan, I think we should clear this threat with the authorities."

"And what? Have them confiscate it and refuse to let us broadcast it."

"But you and I and the network could get into serious trouble."

Clutching the flash drive in her hand, she angrily proclaimed, "He sent this to me and if you don't have the balls to put it on the air, then I will sell it to another network that does and watch their ratings sky-rocket."

The director gave in. "We'll put you on the air at the very end of your broadcast with the Falcon and while you're playing it, I'll notify the proper authorities."

"Don't you dare do it until I'm showing it live," she warned.

Rushing to her dressing room, Kattan opened her closet. On tele-vision and in public when she was in most Arab countries, she always dressed conservatively. But Dubai was more tolerant of stylish Western garb and she had not planned to appear on camera tonight. She slipped out of her Italian Punto Milano straight leg pants, Armani floral silk satin blouse, and Jimmy Choo heels and took a one-piece, dull gray abaya—a loose-fitting cloak that ran from her shoulders to the floor—from her closet rack. Regardless of where she was, Kattan always wore a hijab that covered her head and neck. Even in such a modest garment, her oval face, dark eyes, and full lips made women envious and often caused men to act like fools, hoping to impress her but knowing she was unattainable. Kattan understood this and used her striking features to her full advantage.

Back in the Al Arabic studio, she anxiously waited, standing next to a large flat-screen monitor for her taped programming to end. As soon as it did, the camera focused on her.

"We have an extremely important news story to tell you!" she breathlessly revealed. "A story that has shocked even us. A courier arrived only moments ago with a package addressed to me from the Falcon."

As if viewers needed a reminder, a photo of the Falcon's masked face appeared on the monitor next to her.

"The Falcon sent me a flash drive message and it is such an im-portant announcement that we have no choice but to broadcast now, completely unedited despite its rather poor technical quality."

On the monitor beside her, the Falcon appeared sitting cross-legged underneath a jihadist flag with an AK-47 resting across his lap. After broadcasting his unedited video, the studio cameras focused on Kattan, who looked down at a notepad and quoted this snippet:

"American infidels and Zionist devils. Allah, bless his holy name, has called on me to bring justice upon you. Believing only you could possess nuclear bombs reveals your arrogance and ignorance. I am coming to America to destroy three of your cities."

Raising her eyes and looking directly into the camera, she said, "We don't know if the Falcon actually is in possession of any nuclear bombs, but his reference to two Japanese cities the United States destroyed with atomic bombs at the end of World War Two suggests that he does. Five days ago a suicide bomber detonated a truck bomb in Washington, D.C., that killed the U.S. president and some three hundred others."

She took a step away from the monitor, placed her notepad on a table, and clasped her hands at her waist—the image of a modest, trustworthy, and concerned Arab woman. "Speaking as the only reporter who has ever met with the Falcon and spoken directly to him, I feel strongly these new threats are genuine. America, please do not take these threats lightly. You need to prepare yourselves for his 'nuclear sword.'"

Kattan cast her eyes downward as the camera pulled away, saying in a quiet voice, "This has been an Al Arabic news exclusive. Keep your television tuned to our network to get the latest headlines."

Within moments, she was back in her dressing room changing into her Western clothes. When she emerged, her news director was pacing in the hallway.

"The State Security Service is on its way. They want all of your footage of the Falcon and the flash drive."

"Tell them no," Kattan replied. "Tell them journalists don't help governments. If the Falcon believes we are helping them and U.S. intelligence agencies, all reporters will be in danger."

A look of disbelief swept across his face. "Have you forgotten where we are? This is not the United States. I am not going to prison for life or even worse. Give me the flash drive now!"

"Fine, it's still in the control room. Go get it yourself, but I don't want to be questioned about my interview or about how I was able to find the Falcon. I'm leaving."

"Where will you go? There's no place for you to hide."

"Just tell them I left and am not available."

Kattan should have been afraid of UAE intelligence, but her thirst for a worldwide scoop overrode any trepidation that she might have felt. Besides, she was now even more famous than ever before. Who would dare touch her?

She was schoolgirl giddy by the time the elevator reached Al Arabic's secure underground parking garage, where her Mercedes-Benz SL-Class white convertible was parked in her reserved space. She used her key fob to both unlock her car and start its engine as she emerged from the lift.

She had walked about ten feet from the elevator when she heard someone running up behind her. Turning to look, she was hit with a 50,000-volt jolt, causing her to collapse. Four hooded figures surrounded her as she felt another jolt from the handheld device. A strip of wide tape was slapped against her lips, a hood was slipped over her head, her hands were handcuffed in front of her, and a long plastic strip was wrapped around her ankles and pulled taut. Now immobile, she was lifted into a waiting van.

The engine of Kattan's unoccupied Mercedes-Benz was still running when her news director exited the elevator on his way home and noticed she was not in her parked car.

He glanced around the parking garage. "Ebio!" he hollered.

There was no answer.

CHAPTER NINETEEN

Oval Office
The White House
Washington, D.C.

Three cities!" President Austin exclaimed before releasing a round of profanities that was even more intimidating because his deep religious convictions generally kept him from resorting to such vile language.

"Director Grainger," he snapped, "please explain to me why someone who you are supposed to be hunting down and killing is granting television interviews and sending flash drive threats to reporters? And after you explain that, please tell me if he has one, two, or three nuclear bombs!"

CIA Director Payton Grainger started to reply, but President Austin wasn't finished. Springing to his feet from behind his desk, he began pacing. "I have to go on national television tonight to assure the American public that this donkey-ass masked murderer is just trying to terrify everyone and they can go to bed tonight feeling safe and secure. Given that we just buried President Allworth this morning, that's going to be a tough sell."

Again, Grainger began to answer, but he could tell the president still had more to say. Turning his back on Grainger, President Austin walked to the windows behind his desk and said in a sarcastic tone, "When I get angry, the First Lady says I need to take a deep breath and smell the roses. Based on her thinking, I guess I should just discuss the rainy April weather tonight that is causing the West Wing flowers to bloom." Spinning around, he glared at Grainger. "Damn it, if an Arab television correspondent can find this terrorist, why can't you?"

"We have a team in Dubai as we speak analyzing those news clips," Grainger replied.

"What good is that? The entire world has already seen them."

"Most smartphones and digital cameras are embedded with GPS coordinates that identify where images were taken."

"The Falcon must know that. He and his followers are not a bunch of rubes when it comes to technology."

"I agree, sir, but we can't assume they turned off that feature on whatever smartphone or other device they used to film him threatening us."

"Which means," the president said, "the longitude and latitude could be on the digital images on that flash drive."

"Yes, sir, it may be a long shot, but it also might be a mistake that could reveal where the Falcon is currently hiding—if we can get there fast enough."

"How long do we have?"

"The Falcon likes to move around but the weather in Afghanistan has been colder than normal, especially in the White Mountains, which are favorite hiding spots for jihadists. Plus there are storms under way right now, which might discourage travel. We don't have time to fly the KTB team to Afghanistan. That would take seventeen hours. But I have a unit standing by in-country. If we get a GPS reading, consider them there."

A hopeful look appeared on the president's face. "Sometimes you just got to hand these things over to God and say, 'God, fix this' and by golly, God always does for America."

He returned to his desk and sat down. "Let's talk alternative. If there's no GPS trail or if the Falcon already has fled, what's your plan?"

"The KTB team has identified the Imam who radicalized Saturday's suicide bomber. Clearly, he has ties to the Falcon."

"You interrogated him yet?"

"His name is Mohammad Al-Kader and he operates out of a Maryland mosque just across the D.C. line, but to answer your question, no, sir, we haven't touched him."

"Why the heck not?" the president snapped.

"It's complicated, sir. In the 1980s, Al-Kader was recruited by our government to fight the Russians in Afghanistan. At one point, Al-Kader became friends with Osama bin Laden. When the Russians fled, Al-Kader got himself into trouble with the factions jockeying for power and a decision was made by my predecessor to bring Al-Kader here to the United States and grant him U.S. citizenship."

"The Imam who radicalized a suicide truck bomber is an American citizen and a buddy of the Falcon. Is that what you're telling me?"

"He didn't appear to be a threat when his citizenship application was green-lighted by our agency. But yes, sir, he's protected by the same constitutional rights as you and me. Plus, I'm certain he has a list of Washington's best civil rights lawyers on his speed dial."

"I don't care about his lawyers or his civil rights. If your technicians can't use that flash drive to flush out the Falcon, I want you to snatch up this Imam."

Grainger shifted uncomfortably in his chair across from the president. "As you know, Mr. President, the CIA is barred from conducting any operations inside the United States. We don't have the authority to arrest someone. That's the FBI's job."

"I don't need a civics lesson and I don't need you to tell me what you can't do—start telling me what you are doing. If the Falcon is about to destroy three cities, then you need to detain and interrogate that Imam. Let the KTB team have a crack at him. Tell them to take off the gloves somewhere his lawyers can't find him."

"Mr. President, Senator Frank Church's hearings about abuses by my agency and restrictions by President Barack Obama's administration put limits on what we can do," Grainger said, sounding very much like the lawyer he was.

"Trust me, I know all about how the Church Committee put an end to your agency plotting to assassinate foreign leaders. I remember watching those hearings and the list of bad guys who'd been targeted."

He recited the names: Patrice Lumumba of the Democratic Republic of the Congo, Rafael Trujillo of the Dominican Republic, the Diem brothers in Vietnam, and Fidel Castro.

"Everyone my age remembers how you provided poison to the Mafia to slip into Castro's food. And yes, I am fully aware of President Obama's ban of waterboarding. To me, it's a bunch of hair-splitting. You tell me, Mr. Director, what's the difference between an assassin's bullet and killing someone with a missile fired by a drone?"

"Sir, we use drones to eliminate enemy combatants, not leaders of governments we don't like. And we certainly can't detain an American citizen and interrogate him without probable cause and reading him his Miranda rights. In fact, the CIA can't touch anyone on U.S. soil."

"You still don't get it, do you, Director Grainger?" President Austin asked, clearly irked. "I want to hear solutions, not problems. I want a director who is willing to step out of the box when it's necessary for the greater national good. I want you to pick up that Imam and start interrogating him in a jail his lawyers can't find. You let me deal with the attorney general and the Justice Department."

"But, Mr. President, neither of us can ignore the Constitution. Al-Kader is an American citizen. I would be breaking not one but a number of laws."

Opening a desk drawer, President Austin withdrew a blank sheet of White House stationery and with a pen, began writing. When he finished, he slid the sheet across his desk for Grainger to read.

"You want to talk about Constitutional rights," President Austin said. "Let's discuss Article Two, Section Two, and I quote, 'The president shall have power to grant reprieves and pardons for offenses against the United States, except in cases of impeachment.' Now I've just given you a sheet that is a blanket pardon—that's right—a blank check for you to go do whatever is necessary without being held legally accountable when it comes to finding and killing the Falcon. I'll take the heat if they come after me on impeachment charges. But you will be immediately pardoned."

Grainger had never conceived of such a document.

"Mr. President, as a lawyer—"

President Austin cut him off. "Director Grainger, you need to start thinking like the head of a spy agency and less like a lawyer. I just explained my constitutional powers. If you need a wiretap, install one without going before the FISA court for permission. If you need to burglarize a mosque, grab and interrogate the relatives or family members of a suspected terrorist, or get rough with this Imam, just do it. And if someone bellyaches and you get indicted, you can take out that little sheet of paper with my signature, date it, and bingo, you have a presidential pardon for any and all criminal acts that you committed."

Grainger reread the paper in his hands. Part of him was saying this was insanity. The image of him being questioned by a hostile congressional oversight committee flashed through his mind. It was followed by him being indicted by a grand jury, tried in a courtroom, and led to a prison cell. And then another image flashed in his mind: 1974. President Gerald Ford being sworn into office and immediately pardoning his predecessor for his involvement in the Watergate scandal. Richard M. Nixon walked away in shame, but free.

Grainger took a deep breath and said, "Sir, it's not only my people who I am considering. It's you. Your political opponents will destroy you."

"For the good of our nation, I'm willing to risk that. Are you? We now have a clear warning that our enemies are going to try to destroy three American cities. That could mean more than a million American lives could be lost. Have you considered that your actions may save those millions of Americans?" he asked. "Director Grainger, if you are not up to the task, I will accept your immediate resignation and I will find someone who is."

Grainger paused. "Sir, I will do what you have asked me, but there is a caveat. You specifically told me to include Major Brooke Grant on our KTB team, which I have done, but I'd like to keep her out of the loop when it comes to some of what we might end up doing."

"You don't trust her?"

"I'm not certain she'd agree with the tactics that might be required and she is well known by the media and the public. I'll utilize her expertise in identifying our target, but it would be better if she were not directly involved in some circumstances that might later raise potentially embarrassing questions."

"I understand. Tell her what you want. Now, let's move on. Did the Falcon get one nuclear bomb from the North Koreans or, God forbid, three of them?"

"We have a high degree of certainty that he obtained one nuclear bomb from North Korea. Not three. What we don't know is what other materials he may have gotten from them or if he knows of some way to convert that singular nuclear bomb into three nuclear weapons."

"Is that even possible? Splitting a nuclear bomb into three baby nuclear bombs?"

"Our top scientists say it would be extremely unlikely and counterproductive. But if the North Koreans sold him a nuclear bomb, they might also have provided him with other materials that he could use to make dirty bombs. I've prepared a briefing paper for you."

He reached to the side of his chair and removed a report from his briefcase that he placed on the president's desk. "A dirty bomb is not a nuclear bomb. It is not as powerful and destructive because it does not create a deadly radiation cloud that can spread for tens to thousands of miles. It's made by combining an explosive with radioactive materials. The actual killing power comes from the explosives and most dirty bombs would release only enough radiation to cover a few city blocks. But the real damage would come from causing widespread panic, fear, and major contamination around the blast site that would be expensive and could require years to remove, potentially making an area uninhabitable."

"We talking about a briefcase bomb or larger?"

"The blast would depend on how many explosives are packed around the radioactive materials. But let's use Saturday's truck bombing as an example. If that Coswell's Catering truck had contained radioactive matter as well as explosives, in addition to the immediate carnage, it would have made the Heurich House Mansion area and Dupont Circle neighborhood unsafe for a generation, much like Chernobyl."

"We need to avoid panic," President Austin said, "which is exactly what the Falcon wants to exploit. When I go on television tonight, I will assure the public that our borders are secure and our cities are safe. There's no need for me to mention we know North Korea already has sold him one. That will cause more alarm. I'm not going to lie, but I'm also not going to reveal everything we suspect."

There was a rap on the Oval Office door and the president's executive secretary announced that his newly hired White House chief of staff urgently needed to see him. When the president invited him in, he went directly to one of the televisions that Austin had installed and turned the channel to CNN.

Its chief Washington correspondent appeared standing outside the White House grounds speaking with former White House chief of staff Mallory Harper.

"Is the Falcon trying to scare us or has he obtained one or more nuclear bombs?" the reporter asked Harper.

Looking directly into the camera, she replied, "I know for a fact the Falcon has obtained at least one nuclear bomb. Our intelligence sources confirmed that information on the same day President Sally Allworth was murdered."

"This is information that you were privy to before you left the White House and President Austin replaced you with his own chief of staff. Is that correct?"

"That's correct. I was in the Oval Office when President Sally Allworth was briefed about the nuclear bomb. This briefing happened before she left for Major Brooke Grant's wedding, before she was murdered."

"Just to be one hundred percent clear. You are telling us that the Falcon has in his possession right now at least one nuclear bomb?"

"That's correct. He does and President Austin knows it."

The president's new chief of staff switched off the television and asked, "Mr. President, how do you wish to respond to her statement? It is spreading across social media like a wildfire."

President Austin's mind flashed back to the day when he fired Mallory Harper and her parting Lyndon Johnson quote about being on the outside of the tent pissing in. She was getting her revenge, or so she thought.

"Get the attorney general on the line," the president ordered. "Mallory Harper has just violated security laws by talking about a gigantic secret that I have not declassified. I want her arrested.

"And get me my speech writer," he added. "Now!"

CHAPTER TWENTY

Oval Office
The White House

L ate Wednesday night, President Wyatt Bowie Austin appeared on television, looking directly into the television lens focused on him. His rugged outdoor looks and square jaw gave him the appearance of an All-American hero full of confidence and strength. He had rejected the idea of holding a news conference because he didn't want reporters rudely shouting questions at him. He was at his best when he spoke directly to the American people and he was doing it sitting behind his desk, inviting himself into each home's living room.

"My fellow Americans," he began in a serious voice. "Earlier this morning, we buried a president and within hours after paying her our deepest respects and offering our most profound gratitude for her leadership and public service to our great nation, a masked coward appeared on the Al Arabic network, taunting us, claiming responsibility for her murder and bragging about the slaughter of some three hundred other proud Americans during last Saturday's bombing here in Washington.

"If his insolence was not enough, this miscreant announced that he would destroy three of our cities sometime in the near future. I come before you tonight to say that we Americans do not fear those who hide behind masks, afraid to show the civilized world their faces as they perpetuate evil. It is they who need to fear us."

President Austin understood that television was about emotion and appearance more than it was about the words he actually spoke. As a young politician, he'd practiced before a full-length mirror, learning how to lift an eyebrow, quiver a lip, crack a smile—all subtle signals aimed at winning trust and exuding confidence, and he had become damn good at it.

"Like so many of you, I am grieving and still hurting but I have come to tell you tonight that my grief and hurt will not cripple me nor weaken my resolve—our resolve. Adversity and threats do not intimidate us. They do not panic us. They do not alarm us. They make us more resilient, more unified and stronger in our determination to bring justice to those responsible.

"Threats and boasts are easily made. Any fool can clamor and puff out his chest. Do not be deceived by cheap words uttered by some primitive in his underground hole. The United States of America is the most powerful nation in the world, with a military unmatched by any other, an intelligence service unmatched by any other, and a citizenry unmatched by any other.

"Undoubtedly, you have heard speculation that this liar and butcher of children has obtained a nuclear bomb. We are in the midst of investigating his claim to determine if it is his delusional bluster. If he has somehow gained possession of such a weapon, it was provided to him by an irresponsible and reckless rogue nation. If he dares attempt to use it against us or our allies, those responsible for his treachery will be held accountable just as he will be held accountable and we will extract a heavy price for their misdeeds. There will be no safe place for them to hide on this planet, no hole deep enough for them to burrow into, no friendly face to ever greet them."

Narrowing his eyes and staring even more intensely into the camera, he said in a forceful voice, "Let me be clear. Any nation, any government, and any individual who is supporting this enemy of all civilized nations give heed to my words. Any attack on the American people or our allies will be considered an act of war and those who give shelter and comfort to this renegade terrorist will be judged by us to be equally guilty. We will not—will not—ignore or forgive their collusion and depravity. They will be punished harshly by us and our allies.

"My fellow Americans, my administration is committed to protecting our nation and our liberties. Over the next several days, my cabinet and I will discuss how best to address these threats. Meanwhile, I will be taking specific steps to safeguard our borders, increase security in our cities, and hunt down and kill this masked murderer who deserves neither respect nor mercy. I pledge to you tonight as your president that we will find him and he will rue the day of his birth.

"Let me close by asking you tonight to shut your eyes and observe a moment of silence with me now in honor of our fallen president and the other Americans who were slaughtered. If you are near someone extend your hand and take their hand into yours because in this cause we are not strangers but proud Americans, bound to each other, brother to brother, sister to sister, friend to friend, parent to child."

The president lowered his eyes and counted out sixty seconds in his mind before again speaking.

"Now I want you to pray with me, regardless of your faith and religious beliefs. Pray with me for strength, pray with me for unity, pray with me for peace, and let us all ask God Almighty to give us an iron fist to smite our enemies and those who would do us harm."

Again, he closed his eyes but only for a few moments before he declared, "God bless you, my fellow Americans, and God bless the United States of America."

CHAPTER TWENTY-ONE

Several miles south of Deh Bala
The White Mountains, Afghanistan border

We're approaching the drop point," the Blackhawk pilot announced through his headset to Peter Wolf as the helicopter they were riding in crossed a snowcapped ridge in the predawn Friday darkness.

The CIA's Special Activities Division team under Wolf's direction consisted of highly trained combat veterans who frequently teased their leader because of his name's similarity to the Russian children's story *Peter and the Wolf*. But if anyone outside their tightly knit group dared say a critical word about him, they would have paid a heavy price. Wolf's men respected and trusted "the Wolf" with their lives. As the often-quoted poet Lord Alfred Tennyson wrote, they were prepared to follow him "into the jaws of death, into the mouth of hell."

It had been less than thirty hours since the Falcon had declared his televised nuclear threat, and the "echelons above reality"—soldier talk for "higher headquarters where no one has an idea about what is really happening"—had made a decision to send them into harm's way in the morning blackness somewhere near the Durand Line that separates Afghanistan and Pakistan. That hurriedness worried the Wolf. Hasty decisions increased the chances of failure and with failure all too often came death.

CIA director Grainger's prediction to President Austin that longitudinal and latitudinal coordinates might have been embedded in the flash drive recording made by the Falcon had proven true. Intelligence gleamed from that drive had been directed to the National

Geospatial-Intelligence Agency, which had pinpointed the coordinates to what appeared from the sky to be the entrance into one of the peaks that made up this snow-covered range. A drone had been dispatched but it had been forced to fly low and that further troubled the Wolf because it increased the chances of its propeller being heard by those on the ground, alerting them. He'd studied the footage that the drone had captured: two figures first spotted walking among a large group of jagged boulders before they'd virtually disappeared into the mountain's belly.

"Why aren't we just pounding the hell of that cave, if there is one?" asked Shorty—so nicknamed because he stood six feet, four inches tall.

"Two reasons," replied the senator, who hailed from Washington, D.C. "Number one: the closest village is Deh Bala."

"Just a tiny crap hole in this giant crap hole of a country," Shorty replied.

"In 2008," said the senator, who considered himself an amateur military historian, "we accidentally bombed a wedding party just outside the town. Killed forty-seven, including kids and, oh yeah, blew away the bride and groom too."

"Hey, there's a war going on," Shorty replied unsympathetically. "You shouldn't be getting married in the middle of a war."

"You shouldn't be getting married ever," the senator retorted, laughing.

"What's the second reason besides not wanting to blow a couple of goat herders to hell?"

"Most likely Tora Bora," the senator replied.

"Torro burrito?" Shorty repeated, smirking. "I think I ate one of those once and was in the shitter for a week."

Even the Wolf smirked.

"When we first invaded this hellhole years ago, none other than Donald Rumsfeld himself said Tora Bora was the hideout of Al-Qaeda bogeyman Osama bin Laden. The story got bigger with each telling. Soon there were thousands of Johnny Jihads hiding underground in an impregnable cave fortress with its own hospital, hotel, and roads large enough to drive tanks into and even a hydroelectric power plant and indoor plumbing. We bombed the hell out of it for seventy-two straight hours, good old American 'shock and awe' that cost millions and there was nothing there."

"Indoor plumbing?" Shorty laughed. "Imagine Johnny Jihad with a functioning toilet? Everyone should have known that story was bullshit." Those sitting around him chuckled.

"If there's nothing to this cave, no one wants to explain to Congress why they blew up an empty hole with expensive taxpayer bombs."

"That's why they're sending us," Shorty replied. "As my grandfather said in Korea and my pappy said in Vietnam, *bo-HEE-ka*"—using an Army term for "we're about to get screwed as usual."

"Christians in action," the senator replied, citing the CIA's slang name.

The Wolf understood his men's idioms, as well as their pet names, were important to team camaraderie in the insular and deadly world they operated in, so he answered with perhaps the best known phrase among troops fighting in Afghanistan.

"Time to embrace the suck."

They dropped in four miles from where the suspected cave entrance was located at exactly four hundred hours local military time and moved slowly across the frigid mountainside in radio silence wearing night-vision gear that turned the blackness into an eerie slime green of shadows. The Wolf stopped about three hundred yards from the boulders where the cave's entrance was supposed to be located.

Hoping to see some sort of light being emitted from a hidden campfire or some other thermal imagery, he scanned the rocks with night-vision binoculars. There were no telltale signs of anything except snow-encrusted stones. The team's sniper and his spotter settled in as the other nine cautiously continued forward. When they were within fifty feet, the Wolf finally spotted a yellow flicker that had found its way up and out a narrow crack. It was the size of a flame from a cigarette lighter.

The senator and Shorty moved forward and were the first to reach a narrow crevice that cut through the rocks. When they shimmed between the jagged stones, they came to a round opening about the size of a standard car tire. There was light emitting from it and the muffled sound of men talking from beneath the surface. Worried about possibly killing innocent civilians and having their names plastered on the front page of the *New York Times*, they tossed two flash bangs into the opening. The explosive devices produced a blinding flash of light and an intensive bang to disorient potential combatants without permanently harming them. As soon as the devices exploded, the two Americans scrambled through the hole into a larger chamber, and that is when all hell broke loose.

They'd entered a trap created specifically for them. Two jihadists ran toward them from side tunnels wearing suicide vests, killing themselves and both Americans but not before hitting a master detonator wired to more than thirty IEDs positioned outside the cave entrance.

The Falcon's fighters had buried the unexploded ordinance left behind by the Soviets in seven concentric circles with a ten-foot annulus between them. Their location created a kill zone in all directions that was large enough to hit every SAD team member except for the sniper and his spotter, who were helpless to do anything but observe the carnage. The daisy chain series of explosions came so rapidly that the moment the soldiers comprehended what was happening, they were being struck. The blasts blew fragments of rock and steel projectiles packed around the old shells and bombs in every direction, shattering bones, puncturing organs, and ripping away limbs of the Wolf and his teammates. The few who survived would die before rescue helicopters could reach them. It was a massacre.

In that instance, the unbiased nature of war showed its ugly face. No matter the American's childhoods, their religious beliefs, their schooling, their military training, their individual wants, desires, fears, loves, and hopes—everything that mattered about them and made them special ended in a few fleeting moments that cared nothing about freedom or heroism. At a minimum, they would receive burial and a tombstone in Arlington Cemetery and perhaps a posthumous written citation awarded in secret to their families for having been killed pursuing a jihadist phantom on a craggy mountainside at a place identified only by longitudinal and latitudinal coordinates carrying out a covert mission that would never be made public.

More than six thousand miles away, CIA director Grainger informed President Austin personally at the White House about the debacle. Frustrated and embittered, President Austin ordered Grainger to green-light the backup plan they'd discussed earlier in their quest to locate the Falcon.

The parking lot that encircled the Great Mosque of Allah located just outside the D.C. line in Maryland was nearly full as the faithful gathered before dusk for the Friday evening Maghrib prayer.

Two unmarked cars and a paddy wagon raced forward, coming to a screeching halt directly in front of the worship center's double-door entrance. A dozen men wearing masks, dressed in all black, with bullet-resistant vests stenciled with the single word POLICE in bright yellow letters, burst from inside the vehicles.

Their unexpected arrival shocked and frightened the mosque's members. With more than three thousand adherents, the mosque had operated quietly for decades, living in peace with its non-Muslim neighbors. It was especially well known for raising money and collecting food, clothing, and other items for the homeless, who had been growing in numbers despite the affluence of the surrounding suburban neighborhoods.

The officers swept in tandem into the three-story rectangular mosque, which had two wings attached to its main building. A stunning blue, white, and gold minaret with a half-moon atop its tower clearly identified it as a Muslim place of worship.

The appearance of armed, hooded men entering the building's main hallway lined with children's classrooms seemed unimaginable to the devotees in the massive prayer chamber who were now witnessing the intrusion. The men marched directly to Imam Mohammad Al-Kader's study and pushed open its door.

As a former Afghan freedom fighter, Al-Kader was not easily intimidated, but the boldness of these masked intruders surprised even him. Without uttering any explanation, two of them stepped forward, jerked him to his feet from behind his desk, twisted his arms behind him, and secured his wrists with plastic strips.

By this point, word of what was happening had spread throughout the entire mosque and the hallway outside the office was crowded by confused members. Someone yelled, "They're arresting the Imam!" Another hollered, "The media is here!"

Acting on an anonymous tip, television correspondents and news reporters had arrived moments ago. The media bullied their way into the hallway, adding to the chaos.

Like football players protecting a quarterback, the officers formed a two-man-deep shield around Al-Kader and began pushing their way through the hallway mob toward the front exit.

"Where are you taking him?" someone demanded.

"Stop them! They have no right!"

"Identify yourselves! Are you really police?"

"I'm an attorney," yelled one. "Where is your warrant?"

Egged on by the television cameras, several young worshippers decided to stand their ground in the hallway, refusing to budge, blocking the intruders about midway between Al-Kader's office and the mosque's front doors.

The three officers at the front pressed their clear, polymer alloy riot shields against the protesters blocking their path, causing a pushing tug-of-war. When it became clear the crowd was too big to shove through, the masked men drew police batons.

It was Mohammad Al-Kader who yelled out to those blocking the hallway.

"My brothers! Let us not pollute this sacred ground. We are a people of peace, of justice, not tyranny."

By this point, dozens and dozens of cell phones were filming the standoff—a fact well noticed by Al-Kader.

"Our mosque is open to all who seek wisdom, even those who desecrate it. Let these hooded invaders pass because it is their hope we will fight them. Show the world they are the aggressors, the violence seekers, and we are the peacemakers."

With that, the worshippers reluctantly stepped aside, as one reporter later noted during his news report, "parting like Moses crossing the Red Sea."

Moving quickly amid verbal jeers and spitting, the harried squad hurried Al-Kader into the paddy wagon and raced away, leaving reporters behind to interview the still-startled mosque members.

Calls by reporters and attorneys representing Al-Kader revealed the masked team had not been sent by any local or state law enforcement agencies. The FBI, Justice Department, and Homeland Security all refused to comment. No one appeared to know where Al-Kader had been taken or what charges had been filed against him. Camera phones captured the license tags of the two unmarked cars and paddy wagon exiting the mosque parking lot, but when the news media checked, they discovered there was no record of them ever being issued to any local, state, or federal agencies. This immediately led to speculation that the CIA was somehow involved, but reporters reminded viewers that the agency was prohibited by law from operating inside the United States.

Because the high-profile D.C. legal firms retained by Al-Kader had no idea who had taken him or where he was being held, they prepared writs of habeas corpus to be filed in shotgun style in Maryland, Virginia, and the district's courts. But it was Friday night and that meant nothing could be done legally in a courtroom until after the weekend.

Concerned followers of Al-Kader, as well as reporters, staked out Dulles International Airport and Ronald Reagan Washington National Airport. Others scurried to the perimeter gates of Joint Base Andrews, the military airfield closest to the district, thinking Al-Kader might be en route to a foreign interrogation site.

Al-Kader had vanished.

President Austin watched the late-night news coverage from the Oval Office. He had ordered his staff to anonymously tip off the media about the abduction because he wanted the entire country to see the Imam being taken from inside a mosque. He had wanted to send a clear message to the world. The United States, and more importantly, his administration, was taking steps to punish those believed to be involved with aiding and abetting international terrorism.

Given the investigative skills of the media, the president correctly assumed that by Saturday morning, every major news outlet in the country would have identified Mohammad Al-Kader as the Imam who had radicalized the Saturday truck bomber responsible for the murder of President Sally Allworth and the wedding guests.

There would be no sympathy for the Imam, even after the public discovered he was a U.S. citizen.

CHAPTER TWENTY-TWO

CIA Headquarters
Langley, Virginia

Major Brooke Grant struggled to control the fury inside her as she waited Saturday morning outside Director Grainger's office. When she was finally shown in, she found him calmly sipping tea with Khalid in two overstuffed chairs next to a sofa in his spacious office. That angered her even more.

"Major Grant, come join us," Grainger said.

"Sir," she replied, still standing and in a voice edged with indignation said, "I was not informed about a CIA team being dispatched to the White Mountains yesterday, nor was I told about Al-Kader's arrest and I've just read a for-your-eyes-only report written to you by Khalid that describes him questioning the Imam late last night."

"Let me fix you some tea. I promise it is as good as the coffee I brew," Khalid volunteered, rising from his seat and walking toward a number of beverages on a counter in the director's suite.

"With all due respect, I don't want any damn tea. I want answers. How can I do my job if I am being excluded? Why did you have Khalid interrogate the Imam and not me?"

"Major Grant," Director Grainger said in a stern voice, "let me remind you I am in charge, not you, and I will be the one who calls the shots. Secondly, reports about the failed attack and Khalid's interrogation were given to you—so you were not excluded. And finally, I shouldn't have to remind you that you were preoccupied Thursday and Friday, were you not?"

Brooke could feel herself blushing. Grainger was referring to the funeral services for her aunt Geraldine on Thursday and for her uncle and cousins at Arlington Cemetery on Friday. Walks Many Miles's body had never been recovered and his Crow family had bitterly opposed any memorial service being held in Washington, D.C. Nor had they invited Brooke to the Montana reservation for a burial ceremony—a snub that had further depressed her.

"Director Grainger, I appreciate your concern," she answered, "and yes, I was unavailable for personal reasons. But I should have been informed and been allowed to participate in the interrogation of Imam Al-Kader. He is a U.S. citizen but, according to Khalid's report, the Imam was interrogated at an unknown location without witnesses." She pointed at Khalid. "A GID foreign intelligence officer left alone with Al-Kader without any lawyers being present."

"I really didn't interrogate him," Khalid said in an unconcerned voice. "I merely asked him a few questions as one Arab to another. Why would two men speaking require the attendance of a lawyer?"

"That's bull and all three of us know it. We can't use anything in court unless he was advised of his Miranda rights and I doubt you even know what those are."

Brooke was spitting mad and she had no intention of trying to conceal it.

"If you read my report," an unshaken Khalid said, "you will see the Imam didn't tell me anything of importance. We spoke only briefly."

Brooke didn't believe him. She suspected the report was a sham, written to cover up what really happened.

"Major Grant," Director Grainger said, "it was my decision to allow Khalid to speak alone with Al-Kader. The president, the attorney general, the Justice Department, and the FBI are all aware. His rights as an American citizen were protected."

That was a lie, but Grainger hid it well.

In an unsympathetic voice, Grainger continued. "Major Grant, if you don't agree with my decisions, I'd suggest you resign."

"Yes, sir," Brooke said, still smoldering.

"Yes, sir, you are resigning?" he asked. "Or yes, sir, you understand?"

"I am not resigning, Director Grainger."

"How about that tea, then?" Khalid offered in a patronizing voice.

"If I might, sir, may I speak to your privately?" Brooke said, glaring at Khalid.

"Major Grant, you just complained because you were not privy to my decision making," Grainger dryly noted, "and now you want me to excuse the only other member of your team so we can speak privately."

"Sir, this is not about the KTB team, the Falcon, or Hakim Farouk."

Khalid said, "I will be happy to give you privacy. Besides, our conversation is done, is it not, Mr. Director?"

"I'll get you an escort," Grainger said, touching a button on his phone that summoned his executive assistant.

It was CIA protocol that all non-CIA personnel be escorted whenever they were inside the Langley headquarters. Khalid had been granted restricted access at the satellite Reston facility but nowhere else.

After Khalid exited, Brooke opened her leather satchel that served as a combination purse and briefcase.

"I believe you need to see this," she said, handing Grainger the manila envelope that contained Park Police officer Cindy Gural's reports and the photographs taken on the night Mary Margaret Delaney's body was found.

Grainger shuffled through them quickly, clearly unsure why Brooke was troubling him, until he saw the traffic stoplight photo of Khalid driving the OIN's Omar Nader.

"What's this about?" he asked suspiciously.

Brooke quickly told him about her conversation with Representative Rudy Adeogo at her house and his suspicions that Khalid and Omar Nader might have murdered Delaney and staged her death to make it appear like a suicide.

"This Saudi is a possible murderer and you are trusting him to be part of our hunt," she bristled.

"First, you have no real evidence, and second," the director said,

"Khalid has diplomatic immunity. Officially, he is a cultural attaché on a temporary assignment at the Saudi embassy and is on loan to us."

"So he may be untouchable. What about Omar Nader?"

"Major Grant, you are talking about an extremely important figure in Washington with influential friends. As I'm certain you know, the OIN is a worldwide Arab organization and although Nader has no diplomatic immunity, it's going to take a lot more than a photograph of him riding as a passenger in a car through a red light for a prosecutor to charge him with murder."

"I felt it was important for you to know, sir, especially about Khalid's possible involvement. This isn't something that should simply fall between the cracks."

Grainger slipped the photos and police reports back into the envelope. "You obviously care about this case, Major Grant. You've made that perfectly clear. What I don't understand is why?"

"Why?" she repeated. His question surprised her. If Mary Margaret Delaney was murdered, that should have been reason enough, especially if the lobbyist was killed by Khalid, a GID operative terminating an American on U.S. soil.

"In addition to the obvious," she replied, "I made a promise to both Representative Adeogo and Officer Gural that I would look into this." She paused before adding, "Officer Gural was helping provide security at my wedding. She's dead."

"Oh, I see," Grainger said. "Okay, I agree. This matter deserves further investigation and you were right to bring this to me. I will look into it. Now if there is nothing else, I'd suggest you get back to work before the Falcon attacks three of our cities. And while you are at it— stop questioning me about my actions."

CHAPTER TWENTY-THREE

Rented Warehouse
Bandung, Indonesia

Hakim Farouk jerked back his hand.

In his exhaustion, he'd nearly made a wiring mistake that could have sparked an explosion, killing him.

He immediately began thanking Allah for sparing his life. A walk outside in the mountain air might help refresh him, even though it was hot with temperatures in the mid-80s on this Saturday. That was cooler than inside his rented, windowless warehouse. With no air-conditioning and only a portable fan that he'd bought to circulate the stale air, Farouk found himself drenched with sweat.

Soon, he thought. *Soon I will be finished.*

Farouk had gone outside only twice since he'd arrived. There was no need to call attention to himself. He had learned about the Falcon's televised interview and newest threat through social media. He'd watched video of Al-Kader's arrest live-streamed by members of the mosque on their smartphones. According to local Indonesian news reports on his computer, demonstrators were assembling outside the U.S. embassy in Jakarta nightly to protest the arrest of an Islamic holy man from inside a sacred mosque.

Initially, Farouk had wondered why the Falcon had warned the United States, but that was before Farouk had seen news reports from America. Despite the president's call for calm, that nation was consumed by fear. Military troops were patrolling Manhattan subway stations, the U.S. Capitol had been closed to tourists, and no vehicles were allowed within a four-block perimeter near it or the White House. Travelers were told to report to airports three hours before departure because of increased TSA security, random checkpoints had been erected on major highways, and the U.S. Coast Guard was boarding twice as many ships as usual as they neared ports. The entire country was readying for a nuclear attack. Grocery stores couldn't keep their shelves stocked. Sales of assault rifles and ammunition skyrocketed. There was widespread talk on radio and television shows about possible riots if there was a nuclear blast. Yellow and black FALLOUT SHELTER signs that hadn't been seen since the 1960s reappeared in government buildings and schools.

The Falcon was achieving his goal. Farouk should have anticipated the Americans' reaction. After the 9/11 attacks, nearly every U.S. mayor had thought his city could become a target. The San Francisco–Oakland Bay Bridge, the Hoover Dam, the Las Vegas casino strip—all had been mentioned. South Dakota's governor had dispatched fully armed National Guard troops to the tiny Rapid City regional airport to prevent jihadists from blowing up the presidents' faces carved into Mount Rushmore. The threat of a nuclear bomb—or three—being detonated in a major city would have alarmed every nation, but especially the insufferable United States.

While he took pleasure in the terror that now engulfed the Great Satan, Farouk was not pleased by the arrest of the Imam Al-Kader. They'd never met, but Farouk knew the Imam was one of the Falcon's most trusted advisors. No matter how faithful the Imam might be, every human had a breaking point and that made him a threat.

Concerned, Farouk had stayed at his workbench without taking breaks and barely sleeping. This morning's possible mishap had jarred him. He did not fear death. He feared failure.

His short walk outside the warehouse turned into a much longer one and Farouk eventually found his way to a *kedai* (coffee shop) on Gegerkalong Girang Street. He entered through the open door and took a seat close to the shop's front window. He ordered coffee and as he sipped it, a boy, perhaps eight or nine years old, darted through the entrance to where he was sitting and stretched out his hand while his eyes nervously glanced around.

Amused, Farouk gave him 1,000 rupiahs and the youth bolted outside before the shop owner noticed him. In less than a minute, another beggar appeared. Farouk handed him 1,000 rupiahs but this time the owner spotted the boy fleeing. Farouk watched him draw an arm-long wooden club from under his store counter.

From his seat, Farouk could see the first two boys talking to a third. It was now this boy's turn but as he neared the door, he hesitated. Farouk pulled a 1,000-rupiah note from his pocket and waved it over his coffee cup as bait, luring the skinny child closer.

The boy made a run for it.

The waiting shop owner smacked the boy across his back hard, causing him to scream in pain and fall forward onto the floor at Farouk's feet.

The youth looked up at Farouk, who was still holding the 1,000-rupiah note, and then at the approaching shop owner, who had raised his club again. Farouk paused; keeping the hopeful boy stalled at his feet, he dropped the bill when he was certain the shop owner was close enough to strike the child again. This time his club hit the boy's buttocks, causing him to yelp. He began crawling toward the door, eager to escape another blow. The shop owner lifted his stick a third time but before he could hit the beggar, Farouk shot from his seat and grabbed the man's arm.

Startled, the club owner stared into Farouk's eyes. He had not seen anyone with such dead eyes, empty pools, like those of a killer shark searching for prey.

The shop owner relaxed his grip, letting the club drop onto the floor as the street urchin escaped. Turning, Farouk tossed some cash on the table and followed the boy outside.

Four beggars, all children, including a girl, rushed toward him. Others walking on the street noticed the commotion and a Bandung police officer wearing a bright blue beret began walking in his direction to shoo away the pests.

Farouk grabbed a handful of rupiah notes from his pocket and flung them into the street between him and the policeman, creating mayhem and distracting the officer long enough for him to turn onto a side street and begin running.

As he did, he cursed himself for being foolish. The shop owner might complain. *Why had he risked a violent confrontation?* he wondered, but only for a second. He knew why. Stopping the shop owner had nothing to do with protecting the child. He'd intervened because he could and the threat of an altercation with the beefy shop owner had excited him. Despite the foolishness of his actions, he was disappointed. He had hoped for a fight, the spilling of blood and the feeling of a returned punch, the cracking of teeth.

By the time he reached the warehouse, he was ready to return to his handiwork.

CHAPTER TWENTY-FOUR

An empty room
Somewhere outside Dubai, UAE

Remove your clothes."

"I certainly will not," Ebio Kattan answered. She had been given an injection when she'd been abducted and tossed into a van and had no idea what day it was or whether it was daytime or nighttime outside. "Who are you?" she demanded.

The woman ordering Kattan to strip was wearing a tight tan undershirt and camouflage military pants with high laced military boots. There were no insignias that would reveal her branch of service or nationality, no dog tags dangling from her neck, but she appeared to be either Eastern European or Middle Eastern because of her brown complexion and thick black hair. She was in her early thirties and not particularly attractive, given what appeared to be a nose broken more than once and a nasty scar on her neck. What Kattan noticed the most was the woman's physique. Using her own height and weight to help her judge, Kattan guessed the woman stood about five foot seven and weighed only around 130 pounds. She assumed from the thickness of her biceps that she regularly lifted weights.

There was something else that Kattan spotted. Having spent time in several war zones as a reporter, the Al Arabic correspondent prided herself on being able to separate pretenders from combatants. The woman before her was no pretender.

The woman stepped closer, looked directly into Kattan's eyes, smiled, and sucker punched her in the abdomen.

Kattan gasped for air as the woman took one step back and said, "If you don't disrobe, I will do the job for you, or maybe you would like for me to call in two men from the hallway to strip you."

Slowly regaining her breath, Kattan said, "You can't do this to me. I'm with Al Arabic. I'm known by the world."

The woman stepped forward again and with her right hand slapped Kattan hard against her cheek and then punched her again in the abdomen. The blow caused Kattan to fall onto her knees on the dirty concrete floor.

"What makes you think you will leave this room alive?" the woman asked.

Kattan was stunned. She had mistakenly believed that her notoriety and being a news reporter had protected her from violence and certainly from being murdered.

"What do you want?" Kattan stammered without attempting to stand.

"I already told you. Strip. Everything."

Kattan began removing her Armani floral silk satin blouse and by the time she was nude, she felt totally humiliated. Without saying a word, the woman collected Kattan's clothing and exited the room, leaving Kattan naked, trying to cover herself with her hands.

Only a few seconds passed before the sound of a massive explosion jolted Kattan upright to her feet. As she looked wildly around the room, ears ringing, for the source of the sound, it was replaced by the ear-piercing whine of a shrill whistle. Forsaking modesty, Kattan covered both ears just as screeching noises—the sound of a thousand fingernails being scrapped against a blackboard—were added to the clamor. Animal yelps and squeals, machine-gun fire, children crying, women screaming, a man singing loudly, *Star Wars* lightsaber pings— every sound an affront to her senses.

The room became dark before being flooded with flashing strobe lights, some like lasers, blindingly bright, as if she were in a nightclub only without music, only screeching noise so loud she thought her eardrums would burst.

Kattan squeezed her eyes shut, but even closed she could sense the intense lights tormenting her.

How long would this pandemonium last?

Kattan lost track of time because the sensory bombardment was so intense it completely disoriented her. When it finally stopped, Kattan found herself curled in a fetal position on the cold floor. Breathing rapidly, she felt heat blowing in from ceiling vents as she righted herself into a sitting position. Within seconds, the chamber was a sauna and Kattan was perspiring. There was no escape from the smothering temperatures.

The heat stopped as abruptly as it began. Fans sucked it from the horror chamber.

The woman reentered the room. "What airport did you fly into when you met the Falcon?" she asked.

So this is why she had been abducted and now was being tortured, Kattan thought.

The woman was holding Kattan's silk underwear. "Tell me the name of the airport and I will return these to you."

"Reporters protect their sources," Kattan declared.

"You're not a reporter," the woman calmly replied. "You're a fosterer of terrorism. The Falcon used you as a tool, a vehicle, and that makes you his accomplice, no different from you driving a robber to a bank. Now what airport did you fly into?"

"Go to hell!" Kattan spat.

The woman turned, exited, and within seconds, the frantic noises and strobe lights started again. Kattan immediately dropped to the floor, sliding backward into a corner with her back against the wall and her knees pressed against her breasts. She covered her ears, pressed her closed eyes against her uplifted knees, and tried to focus on something pleasant—a vacation with a friend to Italy. *Mind over reality*, she thought. *I can get through this.*

Cold air this time. Blowing through the vents, turning the room into an icebox. The door opened and Kattan lifted her eyes and, to her horror, saw two men approaching. Naked and vulnerable, she felt panicked. But they did not touch her. Instead, they doused her with icy water from buckets they were carrying.

She clenched her teeth. Shivered. And felt hatred rising up inside her.

More noise, more blinding lights. The door opened again. Two men, this time dragging a fire hose. The pressure stung like a hundred biting bees as she turned her back to them and pressed herself into the corner wall.

"Islamabad!" she screamed, hoping not to drown from the water splashing across her face. "Islamabad!"

The hosing stopped. The men exited. The noise stopped. Followed by the blinding, flashing lights. Kattan felt the hot air return. It dried her skin and stopped her shivering. Welcomed at first, the heat now great more intense, causing the water on the floor to steam, making it difficult for her to breathe. Hotter. Hotter. Well over a hundred degrees now in the brightly lighted room. Once again, she crouched to avoid the hotter air rising upward. Her nostrils were burning. Each breath thrusting heat into her lungs.

Darkness. The frenzied noises returned. The strobe lights.

How many times would she be forced to endure this sensory cycle?

If you plan to kill me, do it!

"I told you what you wanted!" she screamed inside the empty room. "Stop! Please stop!"

The room became silent. The strobe lights stopped. The hot air stopped.

"You lied," a voice from the ceiling announced. "You flew into Kabul."

The woman entered the chamber again, this time holding an 8-by-10-inch, black-and-white photograph, which she held up in front of Kattan's face.

"Here you are arriving at Hamid Karzai International Airport."

"Why did you ask if you already knew?"

Leaning down to where Kattan was still crouched on the floor, the woman said in a sympathetic voice, "Do you think I enjoy doing this to you?" She reached over and gently touched Kattan's hair, causing her to pull back her head. "I have watched you on television for years," the woman said softly. "I greatly admire the work you do. But you cannot be independent here. You are a smart woman, so you must know neutrality helps the oppressor, never the victim."

Kattan had heard that phrase "Neutrality helps the oppressor, never the victim." *Who? When? Focus*, she told herself. *Think beyond the moment.*

It came to her. The exact quote was "We must take sides. Neutrality helps the oppressor, never the victim. Silence encourages the tormentor, never the tormented." It was from the Jewish writer Elie Wiesel.

"You're Mossad," Kattan whispered.

"Who I am doesn't matter. Your fate is not in my hands. This is your choice and only you can end it." The woman produced Kattan's bra and panties again. "Don't you want these? Don't you want to go back to your apartment and to continue being famous? Or do you want to die here naked and alone?"

Kattan's entire body began trembling. It was not the temperature in the room.

"Please, take them. I am giving these to you," the woman explained, holding out Kattan's underwear. "Put them on. Be decent."

Kattan hesitated for a second, thinking it was a trick, and then snatched both items and slipped into them.

"You are an intelligent woman, Ebio Kattan. Why are you suffering to protect an extremist, a violent jihadist who would murder you in a second? How many will die because of your silence? You are a Muslim. Does this zealot represent your Muslim father and mother? Can you live with the blood of innocents on your hands?"

"I just report the news. I don't make it."

"Nonsense. You decide what is news and that decision is helping him, assisting his campaign."

"Even if I wanted, I couldn't help. Yes, I arrived in Kabul, but it took me hours of traveling to reach him and I was wearing a hood. When it was removed, I was already at the foot of a cave. I don't know where that cave is."

"How did you make contact with the Falcon?" the woman asked. "Tell me, and I promise, you will be given your clothing and released outside your apartment."

"I don't believe you."

The woman shrugged. "You are not our enemy unless you continue to protect this mass murderer." She glanced around the room. "I have seen strong, big men brought here and those that leave are always broken and sobbing. This interrogation will not end until you help us or you lose your mind. I have seen men dragged away with drool flowing from their lips. Do you want to lose your mind for this killer?"

"Umoja Owiti," Kattan said quietly. "He was my conduit to the Falcon."

The woman exited and Kattan crawled back to her corner, afraid of what might happen next. Would it be more sounds, more lights, more water hoses or even worse—her execution? Her mind told her, *They will never let me leave*. She was an Al Arabic correspondent. Before they began torturing her, she thought of it as a shield. Now she feared they wouldn't want to release her because she would tell the world what they had done to her.

She heard the door opening and turned away, expecting the worst. Instead it was the woman carrying the rest of Kattan's clothing.

"I have a few more questions to ask you in a more comfortable surrounding. If you cooperate, you will be returned to your apartment and no one will ever know this happened unless you tell them. If you refuse to cooperate, you will be brought back here. Do you want that?"

Looking at her clothing, Kattan realized it was fruitless to resist. She wanted to live. She wanted to go home. She reached out and quickly dressed.

CHAPTER TWENTY-FIVE

Longworth House Office Building
Washington, D.C.

"We've come to demand your help!" Omar Nader declared as he strutted into Representative Rudy Adeogo's congressional office on this Monday morning, followed by representatives from the National Muslim Lawyers Association, the American Civil Liberties Union, and the United Nations International Court of Justice.

Nader quickly introduced the delegation that he'd assembled. One by one, each shook hands with Adeogo before sitting.

"You must do something about the abduction of the Imam Mohammad Al-Kader on Friday night," Nader began. "We can't have our people being grabbed inside mosques. It's outrageous!"

"I share your concerns but it is a bit premature for me to share your anger," Adeogo said calmly. "This weekend Al-Kader was identified as the Imam who radicalized the suicide truck bomber. If true, he was an accomplice in the assassination of a U.S. president."

"Where is he being held?" Nader demanded.

"Holding him in a secret location over the weekend until the courts open could be for his own safety, especially given the current political climate and heated rhetoric."

"I couldn't disagree with you more," Nader declared.

Adeogo searched Nader's face for some hint of the mutual hatred they shared but the OIN executive director was much too slick to reveal his innermost feelings in front of the representatives whom he'd brought with him.

Omar Nader was a talented Islamic lobbyist. Educated at the best private schools in England, he'd later graduated at the top of his class in International Affairs at Harvard. He was well liked by the Saudi royal family, so much so that he'd served as the Saudi's United Nations ambassador before being asked by the king to accept the OIN's leadership post in Washington. He was recognized worldwide as an important leader in the Arab world, something he never failed to remind those around him.

"You are a congressman," Nader said, "and a Muslim. It is imperative that you protest Mohammad Al-Kader's arrest inside a mosque." With a glint in his eyes, he tweaked Adeogo. "The United States, and you in particular, have criticized other nations, including my own, for allegedly violating human rights. Does not your Sixth Amendment guarantee the accused a speedy and public trial by an impartial jury?"

The ACLU lawyer joined their conversation. "I've brought the exact wording of the U.S. Constitution's confrontation clause with me." Slipping a folded sheet from inside his jacket pocket, he read, "'In all criminal prosecutions, the accused shall enjoy the right to—'"

"Gentlemen," Adeogo said. "I'm familiar with the Constitution."

"Then you are aware that in addition to a speedy and public trial," the lawyer continued, "it guarantees every citizen the right 'to be confronted with the witnesses against him.'"

"Let's not forget the presumption of innocence until proven guilty," Nader added. "Congressman, do you have any idea who arrested him, or if he even was arrested? Any idea what charges are being levied against him and, if so, in what jurisdiction?"

"I placed a call early this morning both to the White House and Justice Department but neither has yet been returned it."

"As the only Muslim member of Congress, it is imperative for you to take the lead on this," Nader said. "Muslims are afraid, not only here in the United States but overseas. America is supposed to be the model of religious freedom and yet here are these jackboot storm troopers abducting a holy man out of a mosque!"

"None of us want a repeat of what happened to Japanese Americans during the war," the ACLU lawyer chimed in.

"Gentlemen, please," Adeogo said. "Comparing Mohammad Al-Kader's disappearance to the creation of large-scale internment camps is quite a leap. Let me also remind you that a majority of Americans later were ashamed. In 1988, President Ronald Reagan signed an act that compensated more than a hundred thousand Americans of Japanese descent and issued a formal apology."

"Far-fetched?" Nader sneered. "Have you read what happened in Arkansas over the weekend?"

Adeogo knew the story. While stopped at a red light in a busy intersection, a man had been fatally shot by two men in a pickup truck. "This is what you get for what you've done to us!" one of the attackers yelled before the truck sped away. The victim was not a Muslim. He was a Sikh wearing a turban.

"If Al-Kader is not brought into a court by this afternoon," Nader continued, "we'd like you to make a speech on the House floor demanding that President Austin's administration give a full accounting to the American people and the world about what has happened to the Imam."

While Adeogo was considering that request, Nader continued speaking. "My colleagues and I are planning a news conference this afternoon in front of the Justice Department to protest and we need you to join us."

"I'd like to speak to the president or attorney general first before making any commitments," Adeogo replied.

"Why?" Nader demanded. "You need to honor your obligations as a devout Muslim."

"Before I defend Mohammad Al-Kader, I want to know what he has been accused of plotting," Adeogo said.

"It shouldn't matter," the ACLU attorney complained.

"Not to you, but it does to me."

As if on cue, Adeogo's staff director interrupted them. "I apologize, sir, but the attorney general is on the line."

"If you gentlemen will excuse me, I'd like to take this call in private. You may wait in my outer office."

As soon as they exited, Adeogo picked up his phone. The attorney general was brief: Mohammad Al-Kader was being charged in the U.S. District Court for the District of Maryland in Baltimore with seditious conspiracy. He would be brought into the court at four o'clock for his arraignment.

Before Adeogo invited the others to return to his office, he typed *seditious conspiracy* into his computer:

> **Seditious conspiracy** *(18 U.S.C. 2384) is a crime under United States law, stated as follows:*
>
> *If two or more persons in any state or territory, or in any place subject to the jurisdiction of the United States, conspire to overthrow, put down, or to destroy by force the government of the United States, or to levy war against them, or to oppose by force the authority thereof, or by force to prevent, hinder, or delay the execution of any law of the United States, or by force to seize, take, or possess any property of the United States contrary to the authority thereof, they shall each be fined or imprisoned not more than 20 years, or both.*

CHAPTER TWENTY-SIX

President Austin was in front of a television camera once again Monday afternoon, speaking directly to the public. He was intentionally avoiding the White House press corps, cutting them out as middlemen, so that he could make his points directly without being challenged or interrupted.

Major news outlets had criticized him over the weekend for having former White House chief of staff Mallory Harper arrested on charges of leaking classified information and many of those same networks were pressuring him for more information about the disappearance of the Imam Mohammad Al-Kader.

Editorial writers and talking heads on Sunday news shows accused the president of having Harper jailed for personal reasons, not because she had revealed the Falcon had obtained a nuclear bomb. In some circles, she was being hailed as a hero for warning the public. *Why had the president not confirmed immediately after the Falcon's threat that the radical Islamic terrorist did, in fact, have a nuclear weapon?*

In addition to those complaints, civil rights activists and Muslim groups were demanding to know the whereabouts of the Imam, who'd not been seen since he'd been forced from his Maryland mosque.

President Austin was about to explain both his actions and he felt confident a majority of Americans would fully support him.

"Last Wednesday night our nation was threatened by a radical Islamic terrorist, a masked coward, and a despicable cur. I promised immediate action and, my fellow Americans, I have kept my word.

"My first action was to have my predecessor's White House chief of staff arrested after she revealed classified information. While this was highly unusual, during this critical time our government cannot afford to have anyone—regardless of their prominence—revealing our secrets to our enemies. Exercising extremely poor judgment, Ms. Harper aided our enemies by sparking fear and spreading a rumor as a known fact. As I said last Wednesday and will repeat now, we are still investigating whether or not our adversary actually has obtained nuclear weapons. No one, no matter how important they have been in our government, can simply decide to leak classified information. Her arrest should send that warning to those who take it upon themselves to disclose our secrets.

"Two days later, on a Friday night, a Muslim cleric named Mohammad Al-Kader was arrested inside a Maryland mosque where he had been spewing hatred and openly calling for the destruction of the U.S. government. He was not born here, but he is an American citizen and under our laws, he deserves a fair trial, so I will not explain to you the evidence that led to his arrest.

"But, my fellow Americans, I will address critics who have protested because this alleged spiritual leader was apprehended inside a place of worship.

"I grew up in the proud state of Texas and as a young man hunting jackrabbits with my twenty-two rifle, I quickly realized that if you wanted to hunt rabbits, you didn't search for them in the trees."

He paused long enough to let viewers grasp his allegory.

"Claiming to be a religious leader and hiding inside a mosque does not take anyone out of the reach of law enforcement officers. His arrest was not an insult to Islam. The law does not end at any church's front door. If it did, our churches would be filled with criminals taunting us."

Growing sterner as he spoke, he reminded viewers of several incidents where preachers and other religious cult leaders had been arrested: James Baker, a popular televangelist; Yahweh Ben Yahweh, founder of the Nation of Yahweh, who was convicted of conspiracy in fourteen murders; David Koresh of the Branch Davidians; and

Charles Manson, who served as the spiritual guide of "his own family of misfits."

"Anyone with access to the Internet can buy a certificate that confers on them a minister's license," President Austin said. "Does this make them immune from prosecution? Just the other day, I was told by the Justice Department that a bunch of federal convicts created their own church behind bars called the Church of the New Song—or CONS—and filed a legal suit demanding religious protections. I was told prison officials were fully expecting to be asked for Jack Daniel's and steaks to be used as holy sacraments!"

Nodding his head in disgust, he continued. "Our history is filled with egomaniacs who claimed divine guidance and justified murders. The Reverend James Jones, a Communist and ordained minister in the Disciples of Christ Church, was responsible for the mass suicide of nearly a thousand of his followers who drank poisoned Kool-Aid in Guyana. More recently, there was the Heaven's Gate suicides where thirty-nine members of a religious millenarian group participated in a mass suicide because they believed their deaths would lead to them being taken on an extraterrestrial spacecraft following a comet called Hale-Bopp.

"We are tolerant of different religious beliefs. Religious freedom is why our forefathers came to our great nation. Religious freedom does not, however, protect a citizen who is promoting sedition and the overthrowing of our government. It does not give anyone the right to promote the killing of another person simply because they don't believe in the same God.

"Any so-called spiritual leader who calls themselves a holy man but preaches hate and intolerance and calls for the ripping up of our Constitution is no different from those criminals who demand steaks and whisky under the guise of exercising their religious rights.

"Tonight, I am rescinding my predecessors' presidential orders that prohibited federal investigative agencies from infiltrating radical religious organizations that are known to promote terrorism and anti-American sentiment.

"If you're praying and worshipping your maker, whether you want to call him God, Jehovah, Allah, or some other name, we embrace you. But if you're encouraging a suicide bomber to blow up a wedding and kill a sitting U.S. president, then we're going to infiltrate your followers, catch you, and punish you no matter how tightly you wrap yourselves in religious garments.

"Because of the Falcon's threats and turmoil in the Middle East, we are specifically going after radical Islamic terrorists. My predecessor refused to utter those words in the mistaken belief that it was unfair to believers of Islam. She thought it unjustly linked the Muslim faith with brutality, cruelty, and murder. Her desire to appear nonjudgmental ignored the obvious. Radical Islamic terrorists are exactly what they are: radical Islamists terrorists. To deny they are religious fanatics is nonsensical. I have Muslim friends and have no malice or prejudice against those Americans who believe Islam is a religion of peace and tolerance. Our campaign is not aimed at them. It is aimed at identifying and eliminating the fanatics who are threatening us.

"If these fanatics were Christians, and repeatedly cited Bible verses as inspiration for their attacks, we would identify them as radical Christian terrorists. Those making threats against us claim Allah has instructed them to murder anyone who disagrees with their interpretation of the Holy Quran and that includes other peace-loving Muslims. They have pledged to kill all infidels, who they identify as everyone who dares disagree with them—including fellow Muslims who do not subscribe to their extremist interpretations.

"Those of us who are not Muslim and are unfamiliar with the Quran will never be able to expose their false teachings as corruptors of Islam. This is why I am calling on all faithful Muslims to join us in condemning these heretics. It is you who must challenge their lies and reveal them as the barbaric criminals they are. It is the faithful among you who must drive them from your mosques and teach your children that Islam is a religion of peace, not violence, a religion of love and tolerance, not hate and prejudice.

"Rather than denying that these radical Islamic terrorists have any connection with Islam, you must acknowledge that they do and show the world how they are abusing your faith and defaming the teachings of the Prophet Mohammad by their actions.

"In addition to freeing our law enforcement agencies to do their jobs, I am instructing the Immigration and Naturalization Service to significantly tighten its procedures when it comes to background investigations. I want us to know exactly who we are allowing to enter our country and why they are coming here. In addition, I am restricting the number of visas and barring entry to our nation from six countries that are openly hostile to the United States.

"Make no mistake about this, my fellow Americans. We are at war with evil. You would not welcome a burglar, a rapist, or a murderer into your home and as long as I am your president, our nation will not open its doors to those intent to destroy us. God bless you and God bless America."

Within minutes after President Austin's speech, Omar Nader began making the rounds from one television network show to the next, expressing his outrage at the president's speech and actions.

"President Wyatt Austin is a bigot who is clearly promoting Islamophobia," he declared. "He is insulting all Muslims, turning us into enemies of the American people because of our Islamic faith. As the chief spokesman for the OIN, I will be calling on members of the U.S. Congress, America's top business leaders, and all religious leaders in the nation and around the world to join me in demanding an end to this despicable profiling, promotion of racism, and religious intolerance! We will be protesting, organizing demonstrations, and fighting for our rights in court."

President Austin listened carefully to Omar Nader. The Texas-born president came from a long line of rough-and-tumble lawmen who had never run from a fight and who had seen themselves as being called on by God Almighty to defend those unable to protect themselves. For Austin, it had started in the third grade when he'd gone heel-to-toe with a sixth-grade bully picking on a kid with intellectual disabilities. Austin had taken more punches than he'd thrown but he'd physically outlasted the bully, taking his blows until sheer exhaustion had given the dogged Austin his first taste of triumph as a champion for an underdog. Those punches had taught him a lesson. You can survive a beating by a bully. But you can never regain your manhood if you shrink away. That had been drilled into him by his father and grandfather, just as it had been passed down to them from their fathers.

Omar Nader had made a poor choice in publicly challenging President Austin. And the president would make certain that the Saudi lobbyist would pay dearly for his words.

CHAPTER TWENTY-SEVEN

Owiti's private compound
Near the Somalia/Kenya border

After watching President Austin on television via his own satellite connection, Umoja Owiti used his ever-present iPad to summon Ammon Mostafa.

A former member of Egypt's elite special forces—known only as Task Force 999—Mostafa oversaw a force of sixty security guards at the El Wak compound. He found Owiti in the house's domed main room admiring his oversized statute of a Maasi warrior.

"You're an Egyptian," the billionaire noted, "so you may not know my father's Maasi history. In my father's generation, all Maasi males had to kill a lion as a rite of passage. It was how a Maasi man earned his name. Did you know this?"

"No, sir, I've only heard stories about how fierce Maasi have fought and killed."

"Yes, and unlike many such legends, those stories are true. Like all Maasi children, my father was given two names when he was an infant. One was his father's name; the second honored a family friend. When my father was circumcised at age seventeen, he was called Moran, which is what every teenage man was called. He would be called that until he killed a lion and only then would he be allowed to take his own name as a warrior, a name that represented the characteristics of both the warrior and the lion."

Mostafa listened without interrupting, a carryover from his military training. He also knew that Owiti liked to hear himself talk, especially about himself.

"My mother was Somali and my father did not honor me with either his father's name or a Maasi name because of my impure blood. But when I became wealthy, I defied him and killed a lion."

Owiti pointed to a nearly two-foot-long cord made of hair draped around the statue's neck. "That is the tail of the lion I killed. I had a Maasi elder come here to stretch and soften it the traditional way before giving it to a woman to bead. It is considered the most important part of the lion and it must be kept in the warrior's *manyatta*— his camp—which is why I keep it here. It protects me."

Owiti turned his eyes away from his prized statue for the first time, looking at Mostafa. "Today," he said, "I will need more than mystical powers to protect me."

"When do you expect trouble?"

"We can take no chances. You need to assign more guards to each shift. I do not want any of them going into town to get drunk and sleep with whores. They are to remain here in their underground quarters, ready to fight."

"Who will we be fighting?" Mostafa asked.

"The Americans or their surrogates."

"Killing American soldiers always causes problems. Americans are overly loyal. They will send fifty to rescue a single soldier. Would you be safer in one of your other homes, maybe in China. The Chinese have no love for the Americans."

"The Chinese can't be trusted. They always look for a way to benefit and they will turn me over to the Americans for profit. No, here in Africa is where I will stay. The Americans cannot extradite me. I can buy politicians for mere pennies or kill those who would betray me."

"When do you expect the Americans to come?"

"Soon," Owiti said. "Very soon."

PART THREE

—◊—

ON A BOMBER'S TRAIL

"There is no hunting like the hunting of man, and those who have hunted armed men long enough and liked it, never care for anything else thereafter."

—Ernest Hemingway, American author

CHAPTER TWENTY-EIGHT

Brooke Grant's Victorian House
Berryville, Virginia

Finally, Brooke had returned to her own house. After waiting for ten days after what the media was now calling "the wedding bombing," the reporters camped near her driveway an hour outside of Washington, D.C., had given up. She was in her bedroom but not asleep. Because of a recurring nightmare, she was afraid to close her eyes. Her cell phone rang at 3:35 a.m.

"Get to Dulles," CIA director Grainger said. "You and Khalid are going to Africa to confront Umoja Owiti."

"With what evidence? All we have is an unverified Mossad report that he met with the Falcon and speculation he exchanged three supertankers for a nuclear bomb."

"Use your unquestionable charm."

Brooke found Khalid waiting on the tarmac next to a private jet.

"We the only ones going?" she asked.

"No, I think we should take the pilots too."

So this is what she signed up for? Smart-ass remarks from both Grainger and Khalid?

"You best enjoy the luxury this jet has to offer," he said, "because we'll not be riding in such comfort after we reach Africa."

Brooke didn't like that Khalid knew more about this mission than she did. She didn't like that he had interrogated the Imam Mohammad Al-Kader alone without her participation. She didn't like that Director Grainger appeared to trust Khalid more than her even after she'd turned over photos and police reports implicating him in the death of Mary Margaret Delaney.

"Your CIA director has an odd sense of humor," Khalid said when they were airborne.

"Why's that?"

"His choice of this jet."

Brooke glanced at the opulent interior of the aircraft. It was divided into three chambers, two of which had twin beds while the one, in which they were seated, had plush captain's chairs, a table, and a galley.

"What's funny about Grainger's selecting this jet?" she asked.

"Its manufacturer is Dassault and this model is called the Falcon." Khalid laughed at his own joke.

Despite her mistrust of the Saudi, they were partners and Brooke needed to cooperate with him if she wanted to track down Hakim Farouk and the Falcon.

"I think this is the first time we have been together when you haven't been trying to serve me tea or coffee," Brooke said.

"Would you like me to act as your stewardess on this flight?"

"We call them flight attendants."

"Ah, yes, always with the American political correctness. In my country, we call them stewardesses and we much prefer attractive women to attend to passengers, not men. But let me see what I can find in the galley since I've flown on a Dassault before."

She ignored his sexism and replied, "That's kind of you."

Moments later, he offered her milk, coffee, and breakfast pastries. She accepted the milk and watched him eat a pastry.

"Do you come to the United States often?" she asked.

"Whenever my king sends me. You should try one of these pastries. They taste better than they look."

"Does your king send you to the United States very often?"

"Major Grant, it appears you are determined to get an answer. Is this an interrogation?"

"I believe interrogations are your specialty," she replied.

He grinned. "Still upset that you were not included in my conversation with the Imam Mohammad Al-Kader, aren't you?"

She shrugged. "It's a long flight to Africa. I thought it would be nice to get better acquainted. I've never met anyone from the GID."

"From our earlier conversations, I've detected a certain hostility," he replied. "What can I tell you about myself? I have spent most of my time in New York when I have traveled to the United States. If you understand intelligence gathering, this should not surprise you."

"I didn't know Manhattan was better than Washington for spying."

He gave her a curious glance. "You really aren't a trained intelligence officer, are you?"

"You read my dossier. I'm a Marine who worked as a military attaché before the Falcon decided he'd focus on making my life a living hell. So, no, I've never been a spy."

"Nor have I."

"You're not a spy? Then what are you?"

"One could argue it's semantics. A spy is someone like your famous American general Benedict Arnold—who was recruited to provide information to an enemy. The person who convinced him to become a spy was his handler, an intelligence officer."

"Tell me why Manhattan is better than Washington for recruiting spies."

"It's home to the United Nations. In Washington, people notice if two members of the diplomatic corps meet for a lunch. In New York, it is expected for a diplomat such as me to socialize." He grinned again at his own humor, having referred to himself as a member of the diplomatic corps.

"When I was stationed in London, I thought it was fairly easy to pick out who was, say, a Russian diplomat and who wasn't."

"Ah, please tell me. You can teach me something."

"Real Russian diplomats were always too busy doing their jobs to attend parties and ceremonies but the spies—excuse me, the 'intelligence officers'—were always trolling on the dip circuit, drinking too much, talking too loudly, trying to be overly friendly."

"Maybe these men were simply flirting with you. In the GID, we have found women intelligence officers are not very effective, except as secretaries or in seducing potential spies."

"Tell me, Khalid, since you are being so frank about your trade craft, what's the best way to turn someone into a traitor?"

"Traitor? One nation's traitor is another country's hero, is he not? Benedict Arnold is a traitor to you and a hero to the English. But I will answer your question. When recruiting Americans, there has never been any mystery. Money. The only exceptions are the Jews, who feel a loyalty to spy for Israel."

"And in other countries?"

"It depends. For some, it's political or in the Middle East, it can be for religious reasons. Others can be turned because they are homosexuals who are easy to blackmail. Being gay can be a death sentence in an Arab country. Then there's always sex."

"Yes, you said earlier women were only useful as secretaries and to seduce men. Does the GID have men who are used to seduce other men?"

She could tell from the tightening of his jaw and piercing look that she had offended him.

"The best way to turn someone," he said, "is the most insidious."

"And what way is that?"

"You become their best friend and convince them their loyalty to you is a more important than their loyalty to their own country."

"Can I assume you were good at becoming someone's best friend? Was one of your tricks offering them milk, coffee, and pastries?"

Again she saw a tightening of his jaw and his penetrating look. He clearly did not like her mocking him.

"My real talents are in other areas. Not recruitment."

"And what areas are those?"

"Major Grant, playing dumb doesn't suit you and insults me. I am a fixer, or what some call a ghost."

"An assassin," she replied.

"What is it that you want of me, Major Grant? From the tone of your voice and rudeness of your questions, it is clear you do not care for me as a partner and yet, here you are on a private jet flying with me to Africa to do what? Will you not kill Hakim Farouk? Will you not kill the Falcon? Are you not an assassin?"

"I am a soldier searching for an enemy combatant."

"Ah, so you will have us playing with semantics once again. Tell me, Major Grant, are most American soldiers driven by patriotism or do they kill because of a personal grudge and hatred? Are you not seeking vengeance and does that not blur the line between a soldier and an assassin?"

Brooke turned her head away from him. She was tired of their verbal sparring. For several moments, she stared out the window, alone with her thoughts. When she spoke again, she said, "Surely you didn't spend all of your time in New York. You seem to know Washington well."

"Not really. This assignment is my first visit. When we have completed our assignment, I may ask you to show me your beautiful capital."

She yawned and quickly covered her mouth. "I've not been sleeping too well. Do you have a preference of cabins?"

"You decide. I will be working during our flight."

Brooke settled into the cabin closest to the jet's tail and removed her Beretta from her satchel. She slipped it under the light running jacket that she had been wearing. It was in easy reach. Khalid had lied about never before being in Washington. He'd been there the night Mary Margaret Delaney had died and he'd admitted to being a fixer. She had no interest in playing tour guide after their forced partnership ended.

CHAPTER TWENTY-NINE

Rented Warehouse
Bandung, Indonesia

The pungent smell of death filled every pore of the room.

How had flies found a way to lay their eggs on a decomposing corpse wrapped in plastic and nailed inside a discarded shipping box?

Farouk had no idea. He was wearing a paper mask that covered his nose and mouth but it couldn't block out the putrid odor. He was happy he had less than an hour of work to complete.

As he worked, he complimented himself. He had outsmarted everyone. Because of the Falcon's televised threat to destroy three cities with a "nuclear sword," the Americans had been deceived into believing Farouk either had obtained three nuclear bombs or was somehow dismantling a single bomb and creating three dirty bombs.

Fools.

Taking apart a nuclear bomb would have been counterproductive. Why reduce its killing power? And while making a dirty bomb was a popular plot for moviemakers and novelists, actually constructing one would be extremely difficult, or so the world thought.

Farouk had been studying the problem of making a dirty bomb for some time. In 2004, authorities had arrested a British national who was sentenced to life in prison for, among other things, writing a document called "Final Presentation" that was a how-to kit for constructing a dirty bomb. That paper proved it was possible, although highly unlikely.

The difficulty was obtaining enough radioactive materials to cause massive damage without exposing yourself and dying while making the dirty bomb.

The first reported "dirty bomb" attack came in November 1995 when men claiming to be Chechen rebels boasted to a Russian television station that they had buried radiological materials in Moscow's Izmaylovsky Park. Authorities found a container of radioactive material, but there had been no explosives attached to it that could have blown contaminants into the air. Either the alleged Chechen rebels had no idea how to best use the radioactive matter or, more likely, the Russian government had planted it to whip up political support for its war in Chechnya.

Hakim Farouk had read dozens of stories about attempts by various terrorist groups to obtain stolen radioactive materials, mostly in former Eastern European countries. One involved the arrest of a British national and six others who attempted to buy a "radioisotope bomb" from the Russian mafia in Belgium for Al-Qaeda.

Although there were occasional news stories about radiological materials gone missing, most nations closely monitored uranium, plutonium, and spent nuclear fuel. According to one prestigious scientific journal, as little as four pounds of radioactive material without shielding around it would broadcast such a strong signal that every developed nation's military would immediately track down and contain the source.

This was another hurdle to making a dirty bomb: secretly obtaining enough radioactive materials to make the bomb worth building.

There was still a third complication. Explosives. How did someone obtain enough explosives to spread the radioactive contaminants?

Given the drawbacks, most of the world's scientists tended to dismiss the threat of a dirty bomb actually being made.

Hakim Farouk laughed at them. They had underestimated the Destroyer. It had taken him months of coordinated planning with the African billionaire Umoja Owiti to set into motion his intricate plan.

Some 2,500 feet above sea level in the city of Bundung, resting in a river basin nestled between volcanic mountains, Farouk had taken the final critical step in creating three powerful dirty bombs.

And he had done it without tampering with the North Korean nuclear bomb entrusted to his care by the Falcon. He was not handling any easily detectable radioactive materials. There were no toxic lead containers of enriched uranium smuggled with him into the warehouse where he now worked. Nor did he have tons of explosives with him.

The solution to building a dirty bomb had come to him one night after many, many nights of restless sleep thinking about how to create one. When he had solved the puzzle, he had laughed at how simple the solution was.

To make a dirty bomb, he needed explosives, radioactive matter, and a detonator. The solution: have Owiti's Sea Trident Shipping Company load some form of radioactive matter and explosives on one of his ships and send it to Jakarta. All Farouk had to do was provide a detonator.

Simple.

His sophisticated detonators would cause an explosion that would set off a chain reaction with other explosives bursting the lead containers shielding the radioactive matters and disperse them into the air.

Incredibly simple.

The pièce de résistance was the choice of radioactive material that the ships would be transporting. Through his many different companies across the globe, Owiti had been amassing a sparkling blue powder known as cesium-137, a highly radioactive substance that had a number of practical uses. Small amounts could be utilized to calibrate radiation-detection equipment. Medically, it was used in cancer radiation therapy and industrially in flow meters.

However, in large amounts it was extremely toxic, and Owiti had collected large amounts.

In Goiânia, Brazil, a scrap-yard worker had found a lead canister scavenged from an abandoned cancer treatment center that contained a small amount of cesium. Not knowing what it was, he sold the salt-like crystals to his friends, exposing more than two hundred people to radiation poisoning, including a six-year-old girl who rubbed it over her body and hair so that she glowed. That incident was sec-

ond only to the Chernobyl nuclear power plant calamity. The release
of cesium-137 into the air at Chernobyl had resulted in more than
4,000 incidents of cancer and prompted some 150,000 elective abor-
tions performed on women who suspected their unborn children had
been contaminated. Only fifty-six pounds of the stuff had been dis-
persed and sixteen years later tests showed that a 2,500-mile area near
the plant still contained too much cesium-137 to be inhabited.

Owiti had arranged for three ships to arrive in the Jakarta port, each
carrying explosives and cesium-137. All Farouk had to do was add the
detonators that he had been constructing in his warehouse hideout.

Voila!

And what of the North Korean nuclear bomb? Ah, Farouk had
other plans for it.

By late evening, Farouk had finished nailing shut the final wooden
crate that he'd constructed to conceal the last of the three detonators
that he had built along with a fourth cargo container, in which he had
hidden the North Korean nuclear bomb. Each was carefully marked
SEA TRIDENT SHIPPING. He used the forklift to load the four boxes
onto the back of his stolen Toyota truck and opened the warehouse
door.

Removing his paper mask, he sucked in the warm night air, clearing his lungs of the stench from inside the warehouse.

It was a good night.

CHAPTER THIRTY

Longworth House Office Building
Washington, D.C.

Were you recognized?" Congressman Rudy Adeogo asked.
"I don't think so," his press aide, Fatima Olol, responded. "The reporters who cover Congress and know I'm your press secretary are different from the ones who cover terrorism and criminal trials."

The two of them were in Adeogo's office, which was decorated much like the offices of every other member of Congress, with awards and photos of the elected politician being sworn in, shaking hands with the party's ranking leaders, and smiling at photo ops with various Washington dignitaries. Everyone, of course, was required to have at least one family photo on his or her desk. Adeogo's framed picture showed him with Dheeh and Cassy, all smiles, the perfect image of a happy family.

The congressman had dispatched Olol to the U.S. courthouse in Baltimore to take detailed notes at the Imam Mohammad Al-Kader's first public court appearance, which had been delayed several days after his Friday night arrest thanks to intentional Justice Department foot-dragging.

"Tell me exactly what you saw," Adeogo said.

"Al-Kader was wearing an orange jumpsuit when they brought him into court in handcuffs and leg chains. The judge read the charges against him and then asked Al-Kader how he wanted to plead. Two court-appointed lawyers were standing next to him, but before either of them could answer, Al-Kader said he intended to represent himself...well, he sorta said that."

"How does one sorta say something?"

"Al-Kader told the judge the court didn't have authority over him because he only recognized Sharia law. He called the trial 'an attack on the words of God' and said the United States was 'an enemy of Islam' that was intent on giving him 'a slow death' in retaliation for the bombing that killed President Allworth. The judge kept pounding his gavel telling him to be quiet, but the Imam just kept talking until he'd said everything he wanted to say and then he refused to say another word or answer any questions."

"Did the judge agree to let him defend himself?"

"He took that under advisement but cautioned the Imam against trying to represent himself. The judge asked prosecutors to explain what evidence they had in general terms and it got really interesting because they said the government had tape recordings of Al-Kader preaching in his Maryland mosque."

"Recordings from inside the mosque?" Adeogo repeated, clearly surprised.

Olol nodded as she flipped through her notes. "They said Al-Kader could be heard on the tapes saying every Muslim had a duty to wage jihad to install Sharia law based on the strictest Islamic laws. They had tapped his phone calls but the really good stuff came from a paid informant who infiltrated the mosque and secretly wore a wire just like on those crime dramas on television. This was someone Al-Kader had trusted and he got lots of incriminating conversations."

Again, she read from her notes. "Al-Kader can be heard complaining on the tape recordings about the corrosive effect on Islam because of the materialistic and hypersexualized West and discussing how Muslims need to return to fourteenth-century Quranic interpretations that he said obligated faithful Muslim to *kill* rulers who did not follow Islamic law. That kill rulers statement sounded really damning."

"How did Al-Kader react when he learned someone inside the mosque had betrayed him?"

"He just stared straight ahead with his face sorta frozen like he wasn't even listening."

Flipping to another page in her handwritten notes, Olol continued.

"The confidential informant recorded what they called a 'counseling' session between the Imam and Salman Basra—the suicide truck bomber. That was a really huge bombshell in court!"

Olol winced, having realized she'd mentioned the truck bomber and the word *bombshell* in the same breath. "That probably wasn't the best choice of words. Anyway, the prosecutors hinted the government had more than enough evidence to convict Al-Kader of being a coconspirator to the wedding truck bombing."

Referring to her notes again, she said, "The attorneys explained that seditious conspiracy laws were written during the Civil War to punish Confederates who still wanted to overthrow our government." The law didn't require linking a defendant to any specific act of violence, she explained, although the government had claimed it could link Al-Kader to the bomber. The law merely said that conspiring to overthrow the U.S. government could be enough for a conviction.

"Al-Kader didn't appear to be the slightest bit worried," she said.

Adeogo had heard enough. "You did a great job, Olol. Thank you."

"Congressman, I've already gotten a ton of media requests asking you to come on news shows because you're the only Muslim here. *Fox and Friends* has really been asking about you."

Olol seemed apprehensive, momentarily averting her eyes from his before she added, "The federal prosecutors in Baltimore mentioned your brother. They said Al-Kader had taught at a mosque in Minneapolis and your brother was one of several Somali Americans who got radicalized there."

"That's why everyone wants me to be a guest on their programs," he replied.

"I hope this wasn't out of line, but I asked one of the prosecutors if he could tell me more about Al-Kader's relationship with your younger brother. He told me the Imam had been a father figure to him but wouldn't say anything else."

"You did a fine job, Fatima."

"Sir," Olol said, "if this case goes to trial, all that horrible stuff about your brother and what he did in Somalia will be brought up and we'll be getting lots of negative press again. It's really going to hurt your reelection chances."

"It will come up," Adeogo replied in a weary voice, "regardless of what we do. The White House and Justice Department are not going to allow the Imam to cut a plea deal to avoid a trial. President Austin wants to show that his administration is cracking down on terrorism."

Olol reached over and touched the top of her boss's hand. "There's a good chance the stuff about your wife and you having marital problems will come out, too, then. I've already had a Minneapolis reporter snooping around. You need to talk to Dheeh and see if she'd stick with you. If a reporter learns you were having an affair with a Washington lobbyist who later ended up committing suicide, the tabloids will be all over it."

Slipping his hand out from under hers, he said, "I want you to contact the U.S. attorney prosecuting Al-Kader and the attorneys defending him and tell them that I want to meet privately with the Imam."

"Oh, sir! That's really not a wise decision. Even if they promise you, they'll tell someone and the media will jump all over your visit."

"You don't have to tell me the obvious," he said, rebuking her.

Olol looked hurt. "If I may then, sir, may I ask you why you want to meet him knowing it could possibly destroy your political career and lead to more reporters looking into your personal life?"

Adeogo thought for a moment about her question. "I owe you that, as my press secretary and friend. I need to understand how my brother was radicalized. All of us have read the newspaper accounts. We've heard the experts. But this was my brother and I want to hear it myself from this Imam. How did he turn my little brother into a cold-blooded killer? You saw what he did in the YouTube videos. How he chopped off a man's hands. I can't move forward without knowing."

CHAPTER THIRTY-ONE

En route to Owiti compound
Northern Africa

Brooke and Khalid landed at Addis Ababa Bole International Airport in Ethiopia, where they taxied directly into a private hangar so neither of them would be required to clear customs and explain why they were armed. They were fortunate that the jet, like Owiti's private plane, had enlarged fuel tanks.

Eager to stretch her legs, Major Brooke Grant followed Khalid down the aircraft's steps to the concrete and jogged in place for several minutes before doing knee bends. Khalid watched with amusement while chatting with one of the pilots who'd flown them there in shifts.

Ten minutes after they'd landed, Brooke watched a twin-propeller, badly weathered aircraft slowly making its way toward them from where it had been parked.

"Is that rust bucket our next ride?" she asked.

"I warned you it wouldn't be luxurious," Khalid answered.

"It's a Chinese-made Harbin Y-12," the pilot, who'd been speaking with Khalid, explained. "Probably one of the first generation made, which makes it, say, vintage 1984 or '85."

"We're flying it to Owiti's compound?" Brooke asked again in disbelief.

"You could have continued in our jet if Owiti had given us permission to land on his private airstrip," the talkative pilot explained. "Sorry, this is the end of the road for us."

"If we can't land at Owiti's airfield, where are we landing?" Brooke asked.

"El Wak doesn't really have a legitimate airfield. It's too small a town but there's a patch of hard dirt nearby, which is why we will be traveling there with a new crew in this fine specimen of a flying machine," Khalid quipped. "It *should* be able to land safely."

"'Should' is hardly reassuring."

"Major Grant," Khalid replied in a mocking tone, "this is considered one of the better airplanes for hire in Africa. Eleven Kenya diplomats and dignitaries flew onboard one of these on a special mission into Marsabit in 2013 for a big conference." He paused and then added, "It crashed and burned, killing everyone aboard while trying to land on that town's dirt airstrip. A year later, another crashed trying to land at El Wak."

Clearly, Khalid found his fatalistic sense of humor funny. Brooke didn't.

The Chinese aircraft came to a halt outside the hangar but the pilots kept its propellers running as Brooke and Khalid ducked around its wing to an open door near the tail, where a three-step ladder had been flipped outside for them to climb. A woman wearing a short-sleeve, light-blue, button-down shirt; black skirt; and sensible black shoes was standing in the aircraft's doorway.

"Hand me your bags," she said, extending a hand.

"I've packed light," Brooke replied, hoisting up a gray gym bag, which along with her satchel, was her only luggage. The woman grabbed the gym bag and tossed it behind her. Next, she helped Khalid aboard.

"The flight to El Wak could be pretty bumpy, so if you get airsick I'd suggest you take something now. I have pills," the woman offered.

Brooke and Khalid both shook their heads, indicating no as they buckled themselves into two seats divided by an aisle immediately behind the plane's two pilots. Unlike American airplanes built after 9/11, there was no wall or door separating the pilots from the passengers.

"I'll have bottled water, sandwiches, and fruit available after we take off," the attendant said.

The pilots turned the plane around and maneuvered it onto a narrow runway. As soon as they powered up the propellers, the entire fuselage began to shake and the racket from the engines became so loud those inside couldn't hear each other speak. The Y-12 started slowly but gained enough speed that it managed to lift off by the end of the runway. Once airborne, the engine noise lessened as the aircraft reached its cruising altitude of 23,000 feet. As warned, the flight was not smooth.

To take her mind off the bumpy ride, Brooke glanced out the window at the shadow of their aircraft as it raced across the barren African desert. As she had done every day since his death, she thought about Walks Many Miles. Her memory today was even more painful because Africa is where they had met and she had first fallen in love with him. She looked upward into the cloudless sky. Modern-day science had shown that space was a vast expanse of stars and planets. Yet Brooke's upbringing had drilled into her the concept of heaven, somewhere above her. *Is Walks Many Miles watching me now?* she wondered. *Is there really a heaven or hell, or are both make-believe to appease the masses who can't fathom that with death comes utter nothingness, no different from when they first were born?*

Brooke still was bitter toward God. *Why had he allowed that explosion?* The answer continued to elude her and yet, despite her doubts, she found herself shutting her eyes and offering an unspoken prayer. *If you are there, my darling, know I love you. Tell my parents and Aunt Geraldine and Uncle Frank that I miss them terribly.* When she opened her eyes, they were damp with tears.

They'd been airborne about a half hour when the air smoothed and the flight attendant appeared with water, fruit, and two sealed manila envelopes.

"I was asked to give each of you one of these," she said, before retreating behind a curtain at the rear of the aircraft.

Brooke shot Khalid a puzzled glance and when he didn't respond likewise, she suspected he'd been told about the contents of these envelopes beforehand.

Opening her envelope, Brooke found a flash drive and a twenty-five-page summary of what appeared to be several hours of an interrogation. Each line in the summary was annotated with a digital frame number, making it easy for the reader to locate the exact quote on the flash drive. She popped the drive into her laptop and video instantly appeared that showed Al Arabic correspondent Ebio Kattan seated at a steel table in a dark room. The camera was pointed directly at her face, so her questioner remained off camera but Brooke could tell from the interrogator's voice that she was a woman.

Question: How did you make contact with the Falcon?
Kattan: Through the African billionaire Umoja Owiti. I'd heard gossip in Dubai among prominent Muslim multimillionaires that Owiti was one of the Falcon's financial backers.
Question: You met with Owiti personally?
Kattan: Yes, several times but it didn't seem to be going anywhere until he called me after the Washington bomb exploded. That's when he told me the Falcon had agreed to meet with me.
Question: Did he ever try to hide his relationship with the Falcon?
Kattan: No, he didn't. From the beginning of our meetings he was quite open about it because he was trying to impress me. I could tell he wanted to have sex with me. That's why he wanted to meet me personally.
Question: Did you have sex with him?
Kattan: Yes, I did. More than once. I wasn't going to miss the opportunity for an exclusive. It was while we were in bed after we had sex that he bragged about his relationship with the Falcon. He said they were going to make hundreds of millions of dollars soon and he could tell me which stocks to invest in if I wanted to become fabulously wealthy.
Question: How did you respond to that?
Kattan: I laughed and asked if he could see into the future. How could he know which stocks would go up and which would go down? That's when he asked me if I knew what happened to world markets after the 9/11 attacks?
Question: And at that point did it become clear to you that the Falcon was planning a terrorist attack against the United States and Owiti knew about it?

Kattan: Not really. In retrospect, it seems obvious but men say many things when they're in bed that aren't always true, but it certainly concerned me.

Question: But not enough to contact authorities and report it?

Kattan: I'm not a policeman. Besides, I had promised him confidentiality. I swore I would never reveal his name in return for his help securing an interview.

Question: Did Owiti ever tell you about the Washington bombing or which three cities the Falcon now has targeted?

Kattan: No, absolutely not. I didn't know anything about the truck bombing and the first I heard about the three cities was when the Falcon sent me that flash drive. You've got to believe me. I didn't know.

Question: Owiti told you he was going to make millions because of a terrorist attack and you never asked when or where it would happen?

Kattan: No. Owiti told me that he had helped buy a "special package" for the Falcon from friends in North Korea and it was being delivered to a man known as "the Destroyer." In hindsight, I should have known. But I certainty didn't know it was a nuclear bomb until I got the flash drive. I swear it.

Question: You are making yourself sound very naïve.

Kattan: I wasn't interviewing him in bed. It was more like pillow talk and I didn't want to say anything that might hurt my chances for an interview. I just listened and kept my mouth shut.

Question: Did he tell you where this "special package" was being delivered to the Destroyer?

Kattan: Obviously Owiti knew where it was being delivered because he was responsible for buying it from the North Koreans, but again, I didn't ask any more questions because I didn't want to say something that might ruin my chances of getting my interview with the Falcon.

Question: And after all that, you still didn't think you needed to tell the authorities.

Kattan: I really wanted that interview and I thought maybe Owiti was testing me to see if I could be trusted.

The transcript and video of Ebio Kattan was why Director Grainger had decided to send Khalid and Brooke to confront Owiti. It was the smoking gun that linked the African billionaire to the terrorist.

One of their pilots removed his headset, looked over his shoulder, and hollered to his two passengers.

"Mr. Owiti has changed his mind. We have permission to land on his private airstrip."

Brooke tucked the flash drive and her computer into a zippered compartment of her shoulder satchel. She also checked the safety on her Beretta, which was in her bag.

"I wouldn't suggest taking that with you," Khalid said, having noticed the semi-automatic. "Your pistol will do us little good against his security guards and bringing it in will suggest we are ungrateful houseguests."

Leaning close to him so he could hear her, Brooke asked, "What do you plan to do if things turn ugly? Offer him coffee or tea?"

Owiti's private runway appeared like a black stripe painted across the barren brown desert. It was near dusk and the lights along the asphalt suddenly switched on, creating an even more surreal image—a mile of blacktop in the middle of nowhere. Brooke noticed two aircraft hangars and an entourage of five Land Rovers parked at the end of the strip. As their ancient airplane smoothly landed, she counted at least six armed security guards in uniforms standing next to the vehicles. All but one had an AK-47 slung over his shoulder. She decided Khalid had been right about hiding her Beretta. They were clearly unmatched.

Leaning forward, she called into the cockpit. "Are you staying with us while we are here?"

One of the pilots removed his headset. "What?"

"Are you staying with us or are you leaving and coming back for us later?"

"We were hired to stay here until you are ready to fly back."

Brooke removed her pistol and hid it in an airplane blanket that she found in the overhead luggage container above her seat. She had no clue where Khalid had hid his weapon.

Khalid let her exit the aircraft first and as she did, Brooke saw a broad-shouldered man wearing tan slacks and a brown shirt with a bright gold insignia on his breast pocket emblazoned with the initials UO. While his men wore black berets, his was bright blue, signifying his higher rank. It was perfectly positioned on his shaved head and underneath it was a pair of black mirror sunglasses and a menacing scowl.

"Major Grant, I am Ammon Mostafa, head of security here," he announced without extending a welcoming hand. "Before we return to his house, I must search your bags and those of your crew."

Khalid dutifully lined up next to Brooke and tossed his duffel bag onto the asphalt next to her shoulder satchel and gym bag. Two of Mostafa's men escorted the airplane's two pilots and the flight attendant from the aircraft and they, too, dropped their overnight bags on the runway for inspection. As his men examined the contents of each bag, Mostafa frisked Khalid and the pilots and then approached Brooke and the flight attendant. Raising his hand above his head, he snapped his fingers and a woman emerged from one of the Land Rovers with only her eyes visible under her burqa. She hurried forward and began feeling under Brooke's outstretched arms, mimicking what she had observed Mostafa do. Finding nothing, she moved to the flight attendant before hurrying back into the vehicle.

Satisfied, Mostafa said, "Mr. Owiti has prepared rooms for everyone, including the crew, where you can refresh yourselves. There is a sand storm coming, so you should be prepared to spend the night. I will leave two of my men here to guard your aircraft."

CHAPTER THIRTY-TWO

The Phoenix Tower
Dubia, UAE

After being abducted, held hostage, tortured and interrogated for more than a week, Ebio Kattan was released during the predawn hours near the rear entrance of the forty-two-story apartment building called the Phoenix Tower where she leased a flat. The Burj Khalifa, the tallest building in the world, overshadowed it, but only the wealthiest could afford to live there. The building's less expensive lease rate was not the only reason why Kattan had moved into a one-bedroom apartment. Most of the time, she was away from Dubai traveling on assignments and when she was home, she wanted to keep a low profile. Had she lived among the city's elite, she would have been constantly asked for favors or pressured to invite them as guests on the network. What better place to hide than in what passed as a mid-income building in a city of super wealth where residents who actually worked at daily jobs were her neighbors?

Because the building was older, there were no security cameras in its lobby and Kattan waited until she saw the night doorman leave his post to slip inside with her niqab hiding all but her eyes.

When she reached her one-bedroom home on the twenty-second floor, she discovered the Dubai police had stretched "Do Not Cross" tape across her door after having checked her apartment in their ongoing search for her. She unlocked her door, happily noting that it still required a key and not an electronic lock found at most hotels that recorded and alerted security whenever someone entered or exited. Ducking under the tape, she slipped inside and moved quickly to lower all of the window shades before going directly into the bathroom, where she switched on a light after closing its door.

Her reflection looked nothing like the perfect face that appeared regularly on the news. Her hair was dirty and tangled, both of her eyes were puffy, and the left side of her face was swollen.

Kattan stripped naked and reached into her shower to turn on the water, but when her hand touched the stainless steel knob, she froze. In that instant, her mind flashed back to when she'd been dosed with freezing water after she'd been abducted. She pulled her trembling hand back without switching on the water and instead retreated naked from the bathroom into the darkness of her bedroom. Slipping under the bedcovers, she tried to regain her composure but she couldn't escape her fear.

Kattan was certain it was the Mossad who had kidnapped and interrogated her. They had abducted her inside the very building where she worked, in what was supposedly a secure parking garage. The woman who had brutalized her had warned that they could easily abduct her again whenever they wished. She'd never be able to elude them.

At the same time, Kattan realized she had been videotaped identifying Umoja Owiti as the financer behind the Falcon. She'd told them about a "special package" from North Korea—a package that she now understood was a nuclear bomb that the Falcon was threatening to use against the United States.

In her quest to gain her exclusive interview, she had been drawn deep into a catch-22 from which she could not escape. She'd betrayed a billionaire and the Falcon. She also had to fear the Mossad. There was no way out.

Or was there?

Lying in the darkness, Ebio Kattan began going over possible solutions. Clearly her disappearance for several days had become an international story. Her reappearance would be equally newsworthy. *Why reappear now?* she asked herself. She needed time to think, and waiting two or three more days would only create more mystery about her disappearance. It would guarantee her a bigger audience and that, she decided, was her only safeguard. She needed notoriety to prevent

Owiti, the Falcon, and the Mossad from moving against her. That was all she had, other than simply going off the grid.

She quickly decided that vanishing was not something she wanted to do. She had worked too hard to become Al Arabic's most influential correspondent.

Lying there, she decided that she needed a story even more fantastic than the factual one. She would tell the truth about being abducted, but she would exaggerate the torture. Taking a pen and paper from her nightstand, she turned on the light. She would script her kidnapping just as she had scripted stories for her nightly newscasts.

As she wrote, she considered different ways to augment her tale. She had been raped. No, that was too much. She had been threatened with rape. That would outrage her modest Muslim viewers.

The more she plotted, the more optimistic she began to feel. She was convincing herself that what she was doing would work.

The fact that it was the Mossad that tormented her would further anger her largely Muslim audience and feed hatred for Israel. The Mossad might deny it, but who would believe it? She would play directly into her viewers' prejudices.

The problem would be Umoja Owiti. He was rich enough to be as dangerous as the Mossad. Although she had not known where the Falcon was located, that terrorist also might want to harm her for talking. No. He needed her. She was his mouthpiece. Surely Owiti and the Falcon would understand that she had been broken after being subjected to torture. That was it! She had said whatever her tormentors had wanted to hear. She had been fed information and had simply repeated it during the videotaped interview to stop the torture. Yes, this was her way out. To sweeten her story, she would claim the CIA had been in the room with the Mossad. It would add to the frenzy, the anger. Her Muslim viewers would stand behind her. They admired her—no, they loved her.

What happened to her was a travesty, an outrage, a violation that no Muslim woman should ever have to endure. The fact that she was an internationally known correspondent, a news reporter, showed how the Israelis and the Americans had no respect for the human rights

of all Muslims. She was a victim! Collateral damage like those innocents murdered when Western forces mistakenly fired missiles into
schools and hospitals. The more she considered it, the more plausible
it seemed to become. By attacking the Mossad and the United States,
she would please the Falcon.

She began scribbling specific lines that she would say and reviewing
her claims over and over again to ensure that she would not slip up
and make a statement that could be easily checked and proven false.

She worked on her script for an hour before exhaustion overtook
her. Kattan climbed into bed. She would not bathe or fix her hair to
make her story more believable. For how long? Another day or two or
three?

This could be decided tomorrow after she had gotten sleep, but she
had to be careful. If she were discovered hiding in her apartment, she
could be accused of staging everything. She had to be smart.

By the time that she drifted off, she had foolishly convinced herself
that what she intended to do would actually enhance her career.

It was a delusion, and as with all delusions, the person who deluded
herself lacked the insight to see what lay ahead.

CHAPTER THIRTY-THREE

Owiti's private compound
Near the Somalia/Kenya border

Security Chief Ammon Mostafa led the Land Rover caravan from his employer's private airfield to the walled compound of Umoja Owiti's estate without speaking to either Brooke or Khalid.

Two uniformed sentries were standing watch outside a heavy, motorized, ornate gate, and when they saw Mostafa approaching, they notified their supervisor and the gate swung open, allowing the vehicles to continue along the lush palm trees and tropical plants in a desert where water was always scarce and impoverished Somalis and Kenyans outside Owiti's personal paradise were dying from a drought and severe dehydration. The rest of the vehicles split away from the lead Land Rover, taking the two pilots and flight attendant into an underground parking facility and living quarters for servants, where they were to be fed and locked into their rooms until it was time for Brooke and Khalid to depart.

Owiti's chief butler, a thin, sixtysomething white man with an English accent and dressed in a white tunic, greeted them under the portico of the Moroccan-style main house with its huge golden dome center grand main room. Brooke, Khalid, and Mostafa followed the butler up four polished marble steps to the mansion's front entrance, where two armed guards dressed in blue uniforms—indicating that they were assigned to the main house—were on guard duty. The house's open foyer was three stories tall and had walls covered with gold leaf with shimmering black-and-white floor tiles.

As he always did, the butler recommended that everyone remove their shoes and as soon as they had, two women appeared and washed their feet from a nearby basin. The butler offered them a choice, either comfortable silk slippers or to remain barefoot, proudly telling them about the seventy-five slightly raised diamonds in each floor tile that Owiti believed helped increase blood flow.

Having never walked across a floor of raised diamonds, Brooke chose to cross barefooted, silently wishing she'd had the luxury of a pedicure before embarking on this trip. Khalid chose the slippers and seemed unimpressed as they strolled farther into the house. The chief butler escorted them along a series of hallways to where another pair of uniformed guards stood watch outside two twelve-foot-tall, ornately carved walnut doors.

The guards opened them for the two guests, who entered the great domed main room of the mansion. The chief butler excused himself, leaving Khalid and Brooke to take in the ostentatious décor. Khalid seemed accustomed to such lavishness. Without commenting, he sat on one of the half dozen settees, all covered with animal skins— giraffe, zebra, and leopard—placed in a semicircle facing a larger settee upholstered with the hide of a white rhino, which he correctly assumed belonged to the lord of the manor.

As she sat on a zebra-skin-covered settee, Brooke noticed several cameras strategically positioned and assumed their host had been watching them from the time they had arrived at his compound.

Owiti entered the room moments later, causing both to rise from their seats to greet him. He was dressed in black pants and a dashiki that covered the top half of his body and was embroidered with gold.

"Welcome to my humble abode," he said. Addressing Brooke, he added, "It is such a pleasure to meet you, Major Grant, given your notoriety." She shook his hand and was surprised at how smooth and small it was compared to her own. Now facing Khalid, Owiti said, "And you, sir, are?"

"Khalid."

"Ah, a Saudi, are you not? Undoubtedly from the Ministry of Foreign Affairs," he replied with a smirk. "You have come a long way to speak to me but before we discuss whatever business has brought you here, some refreshments are in order."

Owiti tapped on his ever present iPad and by the time the three of them had returned to their seats, two doors hidden in the room's painted walls opened and six women appeared carrying gold-plated trays.

"Are you a food connoisseur, Major Grant?" Owiti asked. "Or as you Americans like to call it, 'a foodie'?"

"Strictly a meat and mashed sweet potatoes girl from Tulsa, Oklahoma. Although when I was on the diplomatic circuit, I did enjoy both British and French cuisine."

Owiti began laughing loudly. "Major Grant, yes, French cuisine, but British cuisine? I don't believe there is such a thing, is there?"

Khalid also smiled.

"I consider myself an expert on African dishes," their host continued, "and you will find few in this country who can discriminate between what is original African food and what was brought by invaders. In the first century it was the Phoenicians who brought sausages, followed by the Carthaginians, who introduced wheat. The Arabs in the seventh century introduced spices, such as saffron, cinnamon, and also brought rice, oranges, and domestic pigs from their forays into China. And let us not forget the Brits who introduced sheep, cattle, and goats. In Somalia, the homeland of my mother, you can see the influence of the Italians who introduced pasta."

Obviously enjoying his lecture, he continued. "Outsiders' religions also came into play. No pork." He paused and said, "Tell me, Major Grant, do you consider yourself an African American or just an American?"

"I think of myself as an American who happens to be black since I have no direct ties to Africa."

"But your parents, surely they came from Africa on slave ships. Have you never traced your roots and wondered where your ancestors were stolen from?"

"No. In my parents' house, race was not seen as a way of defining anyone. It was what was inside one's heart that defined them."

"Come now, don't be naïve."

"Oh, I'm not naïve. I fully understand that in America today race always plays a factor in whatever happens and it always will. But in my family, well, except for one uncle, it never was widely discussed."

Owiti shook his head suggesting disbelief. "A discussion best saved for a future date. Now, let me tell you about what I have prepared for your palates."

Pointing with an index finger, Owiti said, "On that tray is *echicha*, a dish made from cassava, pigeon pea, and palm oil. On the tray being carried next to it is *fufu*, boiled starchy vegetables, in this instance, yams, pounded into dough served with dipping sauce. Then we have *isi ewu*, a traditional eastern Nigeria dish made with a goat's head. There's also *Kelewele*, which is fried plantains seasoned with spices and *Moin moin*, a steamed bean pudding made from a mixture of washed and peeled black-eyed beans, onions, and fresh ground peppers. Please, help yourselves."

"What will you be choosing?" Brooke asked.

"Me?" Owiti replied. "Since you mentioned French cooking, I will be having my staff bring me *Coquilles Saint-Jacques* served on shells. You haven't really tasted scallops until you have them. I will leave the African dishes entirely for you two."

He grinned, revealing his crooked row of bottom teeth and the gap between his front teeth and said, "I didn't say that I enjoyed African dishes. I simply offered them to you."

"Do you play this game with all of your guests?" Khalid asked.

Owiti clapped his hands and the women carrying the trays left the room as quietly and quickly as they had arrived. "I only play such games with guests who were not invited. Do you take me for a fool, Khalid, if that is your actual name? Look around this room. Do you think a fool so easily becomes the richest man in Africa? You did not come here to learn about African cuisine. My time is valuable and it is the only item a wealthy man cannot buy. You have come to accuse me of colluding with a known terrorist, have you not? Tell me what evidence you have that makes you believe such a lie."

"You want to play it blunt, huh?" Brooke asked. "Okay, we have a witness who will testify that you have been and are in direct contact with the Falcon."

"And does this witness have a name? Or should we play a guessing game?"

"The name doesn't matter," Brooke said.

"But it does, my dear. It certainly does, because the word of a criminal is not considered as believable as that of an innocent man."

"Al Arabic correspondent Ebio Kattan," Khalid replied, startling Brooke. She hadn't thought he'd be so forthcoming this quickly. "Would you like to watch a video of her talking about how she slept with you in return for you arranging her interview with the Falcon?"

Owiti laughed. "I employ the best attorneys in the world. What do you Americans like to call them, 'dream teams'? Ebio Kattan is an opportunist and a liar. Even one of my attorneys' lowest educated clerks will be able to obliterate that woman on a witness stand if either of your governments dared to file charges against me."

"She says you are planning to make millions because of the Falcon's threats against U.S. cities," Brooke said.

"Threats that the Falcon disclosed on Ms. Kattan's network. Threats that anyone in the financial world might attempt to use to their advantage, assuming he succeeds in destroying three U.S. cities. Is guessing whether the price of gold will go up or down a crime now?"

Clearly, nothing they were saying was rattling him.

Brooke said, "What about the 'special package' from North Korea?"

For the first time, Brooke saw a glint of surprise in his eyes, but it lasted only a half second.

"We have spoken enough about this foolishness," Owiti declared. "A sand storm is brewing, so it would be both inhospitable and inhumane to turn you out tonight. You may spend the night but for security reasons, which I am certain you understand, I must insist on your bedroom doors being locked until morning. Or you can leave with your flight crew right now and try to find lodging in El Wak since it is unsafe to fly, but I must warn you this is a lawless area and I would not be able to guarantee your safety if you choose to leave this compound."

"And you will guarantee it if we say?" Brooke asked skeptically.

"Major Grant," he replied in a sad voice. "I am an internationally known businessman, not some back street murderer. Do your countries know you are here? Of course they do and I have no wish to harm you or incur the wrath of the mighty United States and its ally, the kingdom of Saudi Arabia. Yes, I will guarantee your personal safety tonight and even have my staff feed you breakfast in the morning. What should it be: pancakes, eggs and sausage, or African food?"

"I believe it would be wise for us to accept your invitation," Khalid said.

The chief butler appeared and escorted them from the grand main room. They were greeted in the hallway by armed guards and directed down different hallways. Brooke's room resembled an expensive hotel suite, but one with bars on the windows and a security camera in one corner. Once inside, she tried the door and found it bolted tight. She had brought along more suitable clothing than the blue denim jeans and shirt that she had been wearing on the flight and had assumed that she would change before meeting Owiti. But he hadn't given either of them a chance, so she washed her face, brushed her teeth, hung a Washington Nationals T-shirt over the security camera, took a shower, and got into her pajamas and went to bed.

They had learned nothing from Owiti, except that he liked French cooking.

CHAPTER THIRTY-FOUR

As soon as Owiti's two houseguests were escorted from the main domed room, he retreated to his private hideaway with its computerized control board and array of security cameras. He watched Major Brooke Grant and Khalid be locked into their separate rooms for the night and smirked when Brooke covered the lens in her bedroom.

He now realized he'd made an error in mentioning a "special package" to Ebio Kattan while bedding her. The question was how to fix the pillow talk problem. His first impulse was to tamper with his guests' older Chinese aircraft so it would fail and crash when it took flight in the morning. But that would only further incriminate him since his guests had revealed Kattan's confession had been videotaped. Clearly, they had no idea where the "special package" or the Destroyer were. Otherwise, they would not have come to speak with him. They would have gone to intercept the nuclear bomb and Hakim Farouk.

Tracking the cargo ship that had transported the bomb from North Korea would be impossible. Merchant vessels were not obligated to report their locations once they entered international waters, and although the International Convention for Safety of Life at Seas, known as SOLAS, required cargo carriers to remain in defined shipping lanes, ships were known to take shortcuts when navigating across the Pacific from port to port. There were more than 46,000 merchant vessels in the world at sea on any given day and those were the ones whose owners actually had registered them. Owiti knew of dozens of African-based cargo ships that had been reported as having been scrapped but actually still were being used. The more he thought about it, the more relaxed and confident Owiti became. North Korea certainly wasn't going to hand over any records that revealed what ships had arrived and exited its ports and even if U.S. intelligence had been monitoring all of its docks, it would be a crapshoot to identify which ship might have been carrying the "special package." If the CIA or some other intelligence service focused on ships registered to Owiti, they might be able to pare down the list. But the African billionaire owned five different merchant marine shipping companies in Africa, which, at any given time, had more than a hundred cargo ships transporting goods by sea. Even if his enemies had identified each of his ships, they still would not have found the *Sea Voyager* because it was registered to a shell company in Denmark, which operated under what was called a "flag of convenience," namely Liberia. It would take days of digging through files in two different continents to trace its ownership to Owiti.

The only real evidence against him was his pillow talk but his attorney could argue that their client was merely trying to impress an overly anxious reporter eager for a scoop.

When Owiti saw the lights go out in the guest rooms being used by Khalid and Brooke, he became bored and decided to retire to his master suite where his wife was waiting.

"We will have sex tonight," he announced when he entered their bedchamber. "Go wash." After she disappeared into a master suite bathroom that was exclusively hers, he used his iPad to send a request to Mostafa.

I require the two Kenyan girls who work in the kitchen, he texted. What are their names?

Mercy and Faith, Mostafa replied.

Yes, the tall skinny one and the one with big breasts.

This was not the first time Mostafa had been ordered to escort girls to Owiti's bedroom. Both came because they knew they faced a beating or worse if they refused.

Mostafa unlocked the door to what was the second most secure room inside the mansion after Owiti's electronic man cave. The

1,600-square-foot bedroom was soundproof because its walls were constructed of three-foot-thick reinforced concrete with two-inch-thick solid steel plates lining the interior walls covered with paneling from Australia called *Buloke*, nicknamed ironwood, considered the hardest wood in the world. The German-manufactured, armored steel door was bullet resistant and had seventeen bolts that extended deep into the walls around it when locked. Owiti's suite served double duty as both a luxurious boudoir and an impregnable safe room. Only Owiti and Mostafa knew the codes necessary to open and close its only door. Owiti didn't even trust his wife with the combination of the electronic lock nor had he approved her fingerprint to be added to the scanner. She was his prisoner, always answerable either to him or Mostafa.

Once inside the suite's foyer, Mostafa told Faith and Mercy to enter the bedroom, remove their clothing, and wait in Owiti's massive bed. The security chief then departed, closing and locking the door behind him.

Owiti was in his bathroom brushing his crooked teeth and spraying on cologne when he heard the naked girls talking to his wife in the oversized bed. Suddenly, they became strangely quiet.

He expected to find them waiting for him when he entered, but instead he saw them staring in the opposite direction. He followed their eyes to a woman holding a pistol. She turned and pointed her weapon at him.

"Who are you?" he demanded. "How did you get in here?"

The woman lowered her aim so a red dot from the handgun's laser sight was now pointed at his right upper thigh. She fired and a .22-caliber slug ripped into his leg, causing him to yelp in pain and grab the wound with both hands. Owiti's iPad, which had a panic button app, was on a nightstand next to his bed and he started toward it, but before he could take a second step, the woman fired another round. This one shattered his left kneecap, causing him to crash onto the marble floor. Owiti's wife screamed but covered her mouth with the red silk sheet that she was holding in front of her. Faith and Mercy pressed against her, terrified. With both of his legs wounded, Owiti pushed himself into a sitting position by pressing his hands against the floor.

"What do you want?" he grimaced.

"I ask, you answer. Where is the nuclear bomb you bought for the Falcon?"

"Who are you?"

She moved her handgun and fired a third round using its laser sight. It hit his right shoulder joint, splintering it, causing him to again cry out in pain.

"It might interest you to know I am firing a Beretta twenty-two-caliber semi-automatic," she said calmly. "At this close range, the bullets will penetrate and shatter bones and joints, but not necessarily kill you until I fire into a vital organ. That means we can play this little game of questions and answers for quite some time. I have plenty of rounds and you have plenty of bones."

She moved another step toward him so she now was less than six feet away. She pointed the red laser dot onto his exposed genitals and said, "What do you value more, your loyalty to the Falcon or your manhood?"

Owiti glared. He was supporting himself in a sitting position completely with his left arm. He clenched his jaw.

She shifted the red dot to his left shoulder blade and fired, causing him to fall backward, striking his head on the marble floor. Each of his four limbs now had broken bones. He was unable to move.

"Now, back to your manhood," she said, moving a foot closer and readjusting her sight.

"If you kill me, you will never find the bomb," he groaned.

"Let's make a deal," she offered. "Your life in return for the information I require."

"You will never make it out of my compound alive."

"I made it in, didn't I?"

"I could lie to you. Tell you anything."

"If you do, I will track you down and we will play this game all over again. Apparently, you still don't understand the seriousness of your current situation."

The female intruder turned and looked at the bed some twelve feet away from her. Without issuing the slightest warning, she fired three times, striking his wife, Mercy, and Faith all in the foreheads, which were fatal shots even with a .22-caliber round.

He gasped.

"No matter where you go," she said, returning her attention to him, "I will find you, and as you can see, I will show no mercy. But if you tell me the truth, I will let you live and you can get yourself a new wife and servants. You can hire bounty hunters, if you wish, to track me down and have your revenge. With all of your billions, you *might* be able to find me. You decide. Does a game of cat and mouse appeal to you or should I continue shooting parts of you until you either die or tell me what I need to know? After your manhood, we can start on your hands and elbows. There are two hundred and six bones in the body and anatomy was one of my favorite subjects."

Owiti was in tremendous pain. He relented. "The nuclear bomb was shipped from the North Korean port of Ranson on a cargo ship called the *Sea Voyager* bound for Jakarta. The Destroyer—Hakim Farouk—now has it."

"Are he and the bomb still there?"

"I believe so. I'm not sure."

"And the Falcon, where is he hiding?"

"I have no idea. We communicate over the computer."

She waved her pistol at his genitals.

"It's the truth," he said, begging. The pain from his shattered bones was so horrific he was moments from passing out. "I've done what you asked," he muttered. "Now please, please take my iPad. There's an app that will summon my personal doctor who travels with me. Just touch it and go."

"None of your wounds are life-threatening. You could survive each of them." She stepped toward the iPad but then stopped. She had been toying with him. "No one helps a terrorist buy a nuclear bomb and lives."

"You can't murder me. I'm a billionaire. You want money. Just name your price."

She pointed her pistol at his forehead and fired.

CHAPTER THIRTY-FIVE

Owiti's private compound
Near the Somalia/Kenya border

Still haunted by her recurring nightmare about her wedding, Brooke Grant was only half asleep when she heard the door to the guest room opening. She bolted up into a sitting position and instinctively reached to her right, where she normally kept her Beretta M9 pistol on a nightstand before realizing it wasn't there.

"Get up!" Ammon Mostafa ordered. "Assemble your things."

She glanced at her watch. It had been four hours since she and Khalid had met with Owiti in the main room.

"Hurry," he said, turning his back to her so she could dress. Khalid was waiting in the hallway with his bags.

"No speaking," Mostafa ordered. He led them down several un-guarded hallways and out a side door where a Land Rover was waiting with its engine running.

"You get in the front seat," he said to Khalid as he hurried around the vehicle to the driver's side. Because of its tinted windows, Brooke couldn't see inside the vehicle, but when she opened the rear door, she discovered their two aircraft pilots and the flight attendant already seated on the second and third seats. They rode in complete silence along the driveway to the sentries on duty, who saw Mostafa driving and immediately opened the front gate.

"What's going on?" Brooke asked quietly.

"Quiet," Mostafa said. "If you value your life."

When they reached the airfield, Mostafa stepped from behind the wheel and drew his sidearm, a chrome-plated Desert Eagle .50-caliber handgun.

"Everyone out of the vehicle. Now!" he commanded. "Bring your belongings and form a line facing the aircraft." He followed behind them.

"I'm not going to get shot without fighting," Brooke whispered to Khalid as they exited the Land Rover.

"Shut up and do what you're told."

She didn't know why, but he seemed unusually calm for being in such a tense situation.

The two sentries guarding the Chinese-made Y-12 aircraft ran forward to assist Mostafa, who was now positioned behind Brooke, Khalid, and the three-member flight crew. As ordered, they were facing the airplane.

As the two sentries moved into position behind the prisoners, Mostafa took a step back and called out, "Raise your hands above your heads and lock your fingers together."

Again, Brooke whispered, "We should have taken him before we got here. Now there are three of them. I'm not going to be—"

"Don't do anything, you fool," the flight attendant standing next to her snapped. "Play along."

Play along? Brooke thought.

By this point, the security guards were unslinging their AK-47s. They were now positioned in between Mostafa and the five prisoners.

The next sounds were two of the loudest gunshots that Brooke had ever heard. She turned her head and saw Mostafa standing over his two sentries. He'd shot both in the back of their heads.

"Go now!" he ordered.

All of them bolted for the aircraft, but as the pilots were starting its engine and Khalid and Brooke were buckling their seat belts, Brooke looked outside and saw the flight attendant handing Mostafa a large duffel bag. She then hurried back into the plane.

"What just happened?" Brooke asked Khalid as they took flight. "We haven't learned anything from Umoja Owiti. We're not done here."

Khalid gave her one of the smug looks that she so despised. "Yes, we are. You and I were Trojan horses."

Because of the engine noise, Brooke wasn't certain that she'd heard him correctly. *Trojan horses? What could that possibly mean?*

The flight attendant appeared from the back of the airplane but she had changed into camouflage fatigues, boots, and a tan T-shirt.

"You can call me Esther," she said to Brooke. "I'm your third KTB team member."

"She's Mossad," Khalid explained. "So are the pilots."

The plane leveled off and the engine noise lessened.

"It was your voice on the flash drive—the woman who interrogated Ebio Kattan," Brooke said. She was slowly piecing together what was happening.

"While Owiti was paying attention to you, I managed to leave my guest quarters and with help from Mostafa get into Owiti's bedroom."

"That bag I saw you give Mostafa?"

"Fifteen million in cash and a new Spanish passport," she replied.

"What did you learn?" Khalid asked her.

"The nuclear bomb and Hakim Farouk are in Jakarta. Owiti didn't know where the Falcon is hiding. They only communicated by computer."

"How did you get him to talk?"

Khalid chuckled.

"I've had a tiring night," Esther said.

She shut her eyes, leaving Brooke to wonder what had made the African billionaire decide to cooperate.

PART FOUR

—⚏—

A PACT WITH THE DEVIL

"The Devil pulls the strings which make us dance..."

—Charles Baudelaire

CHAPTER THIRTY-SIX

Traveling North
Interstate 95

S omeone will leak the story," a clearly nervous Fatimi Olol warned.

"We're finished debating this," Representative Rudy Adeogo said. "It's too late anyway. Too many know: the Justice Department, the U.S. attorney, the defense attorneys appointed to represent Al-Kader, the sheriff who oversees the jail, and Al-Kader."

"Even if none of them tip off the media, you can still be subpoenaed to testify by either side about any private conversations you might have with him."

Adeogo glanced outside the car as they ascended the overpasses along the edge of Baltimore that would take them across the Patapsco River. To their left was downtown, with its Camden Yards, the home field of the Baltimore Orioles, and the Inner Harbor, with its National Aquarium. Adeogo had taken Dheeh and Cassy to the aquarium, where his daughter had squealed when she was permitted to touch a stingray and jellyfish. She had squeezed his hand tightly when they walked down a spiral stairway with thick glass walls behind which were sharks, circling them. That aquarium trip had been one of the most enjoyable in his marriage. It was before Dheeh had learned about his affair. At first, Adeogo had felt tremendously guilty for having cheated on his wife but as time passed, he'd gradually shifted the blame onto her. Theirs was an arranged marriage and Dheeh had never been as affectionate as he'd wished.

"I asked why Al-Kader wasn't in the Baltimore jail," Olol said, interrupting his thoughts. "Guess what they told me?"

"They didn't want to stir up protests."

"Who would protest? He's been accused of helping murder a president. Every Muslim I know is embarrassed because of him. Some have stopped wearing their hijabs for fear of being attacked."

He noticed she was wearing a sky blue one. Why had she never married? He found her striking. His parents had told him that in Somalia it was not uncommon for girls to be married after their first menstrual cycle and if they were not married before their twentieth birthday, everyone assumed there was something wrong with them. Olol had been born in Minneapolis and was Americanized, so he assumed she was unfazed that she was in her early thirties and didn't have a husband. *But why? She spent so much time with him, perhaps she didn't have time for a boyfriend,* he thought.

"A young FBI agent told me," she said, "that Al-Kader is not in the Baltimore jail because the facility is notoriously corrupt. He said there was a gang. What did he call it? Oh, the Black Guerrilla Family that started in the sixties in California prisons as part of the black power movement. Now it's a bunch of criminals who have literally run the Baltimore jail for years."

"What does that term actually mean? 'Running the jail.' Did the prisoners lock up the guards to keep them from escaping?"

He was trying to make a joke, but she didn't laugh.

"The FBI agent said one BGF leader—that's what he called them, the BGFs—got four female guards pregnant. He was having sex with them in his cell. He even had them bringing drugs for him to sell to other inmates. This agent told me they had this case where they arrested eighty guards and prisoners in another Baltimore prison where the BGF was in control. If these BGF criminals are so clever, think what they could have done if they'd applied themselves to an honest job."

"Like being in Congress."

She shot him a confused look.

"A joke," he said ruefully, adding, "Sometimes I think of Congress as me being in jail. I accomplished more when I was working as a community organizer in Cedar-Riverside."

"Planting gardens where torn down buildings once stood? You were elected because your predecessor was a crook and the other candidate had sex with an underage girl. We need someone who is as honest as our representative."

Honest? he silently wondered. *How honest was he?*

"You know how difficult it is for a freshman congressman to accomplish anything meaningful?" he asked her. "You must bow down to more senior members and to your political party. You spend all your time raising money, which I hate doing."

"You're just stressed out. Everyone is right now. The bombing and now the Falcon saying he's going to destroy three cities with his nuclear sword."

"Ironically, the Falcon is accomplishing his goals, unlike me. He's causing people to not trust each other, especially anyone who looks different or doesn't practice the same religion."

"He's getting help from Al-Kader," she grumbled. "He's the stereotype of exactly what those who hate us believe a Muslim terrorist looks like, which is why having you visit him is political sui—"

He interrupted, not wanting to hear another lecture. "How far are we from Elkton?"

"Not too much farther. This FBI agent told me a Navy traitor in the 1980s who got his brother, son, and best friend to spy for the Russians was held in this same jail rather than in Baltimore."

"This FBI agent seems to have told you a lot."

"He was flirting with me. Trying to impress me. I've read studies where women who are attractive and men who are handsome are treated better."

He thought about telling her that he thought she was beautiful, but he changed the subject instead.

"What else did he tell you about Elkton?"

"Him? Nothing else. But I read about it on Wikipedia. It has about six thousand houses and nearly everyone who lives in them is white. No Muslims."

"Another reason why they put Al-Kader there."

The GPS took them directly to the jail on the outskirts of Elkton.

"Thank you, Warden, for letting me come here," Adeogo said, after they passed through a security gate and entered the jail's lobby.

"Actually, I prefer the title 'Director.' I don't use 'warden' because of its pejorative nature. We're not here to judge the people under our supervision."

"Are words really that important in a jail?" Olol asked.

"It's all about respect. If you treat people with respect, they will treat you with respect."

"Respect?" Olol said. "How do you treat a criminal with respect?"

"Let me give you an example. The folks who work for me are addressed as correctional officers. If you call them guards, it's insulting."

"I'm not sure I understand the difference," Adeogo said.

"Calling them a guard is like calling a highly skilled teacher a babysitter."

"What do you call the inmates?" Olol asked. "Guests? Clients?"

"No, we call them prisoners or detainees. They aren't convicts until they're convicted and many are here awaiting trial, like your Imam cleric. They don't like the term 'inmates' because it makes them sound like they're being held in a mental asylum. Words are important inside the walls."

Addressing Adeogo, the director said, "Your press secretary might want to head into town to have lunch. She's not going to be permitted any further."

Olol looked disappointed, but Adeogo said, "I'm certain she will find Elkton interesting."

"Will the congressman's conversation be recorded?" Olol asked. "And, if so, who will receive copies?"

"We actually had a discussion with federal prosecutors about that," the director replied. "Representative Adeogo, you are not part of the legal defense team or the prosecution team. You are not an attorney. But the U.S. attorney said we should allow you to speak privately to Al-Kader in the jail's attorney/client room without recording or videotaping your session, as a courtesy because you're a member of Congress. Naturally, you will have to go through normal security checks and we can't allow cell phones and other restricted items once you pass through the sally port."

"What's a sally port?" Olol asked.

"A sally port is how we keep prisoners from escaping. It's a door, then an open space, and another second door. These two doors are never opened at the same time so there is always a door separating those inside from the free world."

Again addressing Adeogo, the director said, "Congressman, if you follow me, we'll get you through security and squared away for your interview with the prisoner Al-Kader."

Adeogo handed Olol the two cell phones that he carried and emptied his pockets, keeping only his driver's license with his photo ID. He'd been told it would be kept by the correctional officer in the control booth so the congressman could be positively identified when it was time for him to exit the jail's interior.

The interview room where he was taken was about fifteen feet by twelve feet and contained four stools placed around a square steel table. All five were bolted to the floor. Adeogo entered through one door while Al-Kader was brought through an opposite one. Dressed in an orange jumpsuit, the Imam shuffled between the two guards accompanying him. They seated Al-Kader and attached his handcuffed wrists to an eight-inch-long piece of chain bolted to the table. They left his legs shackled.

Adeogo had been told Al-Kader was in his late sixties, but he appeared to be at least seventy years old. He was bone thin and his salt-and-pepper beard couldn't conceal the creases in his face, especially the wrinkles around his eyes. Al-Kader was pale and without any type of head covering; Adeogo noticed for the first time that the religious teacher was balding.

"Have you come to beat me?" Al-Kader asked.

"Have you been beaten here?"

"Yes. But only on the Friday night of my arrest and then it was a Saudi who struck me several times when we were left alone in a room.

He was skilled and didn't do any permanent damage. He stopped when he realized he would learn nothing from me."

"I will talk to Director Grainger about it," Adeogo said. "That sort of behavior is not acceptable."

Al-Kader shrugged. "Talk if you wish, but it will be my word against his and I assume the director sent him to question me. Now, if you want my help, you must help me with a small favor. I am entitled to have a copy of *The Holy Quran*. The guards said I'm being denied one because I might corrupt other prisoners with it, even though that is an impossibility. I'm in total isolation and have no contact with any other prisoners. I can only corrupt myself."

"I will speak to the sheriff as soon as we're done."

Al-Kader sized up the congressman. He'd recognized him from photos in the newspaper, but it was more than that. He was comparing his looks to those of his youngest brother, Abdul Hafeez.

"You look like Abdul," he said.

"His name was George."

Al-Kader smiled. "Yes, I remember him telling me. Your parents named him after George Washington. Ironic, I'd say."

"Not until he fell under your spell."

"Ah, so you have come to see the devil. You have come to learn how I radicalized your innocent little brother. You have come because you wish to blame me for filling him with hatred toward the West and turning him into what Americans describe as a psychopathic monster."

Al-Kader paused and rubbed his hands together because his fingers were cold and sore and massaging them helped. "My dear congressman, you will be disappointed because your brother was not filled with hatred and he was not some radical Islamic terrorist. He was a proud Muslim and I did nothing but open his eyes to a deeper truth."

"Your truth."

"There are no 'your truths' or 'my truths.' There is only truth."

"Let me guess, the only truth is what you believe and only you can define truth."

"Do you believe in gravity? There is no denying it. The same is true about truth and the only truth is Allah's truth and it is true regardless of whether or not you care to acknowledge it, just as if you were to deny gravity, it would still be gravity."

"I didn't come to argue with you about our religion."

"Then you will not be able to understand your brother. Everyone assumes young men are radicalized because I possess some Svengali power over them that brainwashes innocents to kill as if they are mindless robots, when it is Muslims such as you who are the shallow robots. You proclaim you believe in Islam without knowing what Islam is. Without true commitment."

Adeogo didn't want to engage in a religious argument with the Imam because he knew Al-Kader had studied the Holy Quran much more closely than he ever had. Yet it seemed Al-Kader was intent on dragging him into one. The congressman decided to ground his comments in how he felt, making it more difficult for the Imam to criticize since everyone was entitled to express their own feelings, or so he thought.

"I feel Islam is a religion of peace. That is what I accept."

"You accept?" the Imam said in an incredulous voice. "That you accept?" he repeated. "What Allah tells us is not for *you* to accept or reject, any more than a thirsty newborn can reject its mother's milk. You submit to Allah or you die. I simply opened your younger brother's eyes not only about our faith and but also about how the corrupt West has been trying to slaughter us Muslims for centuries."

"The Holy Crusades were a long time ago," Adeogo replied.

"I am not speaking about those ancient days. Do you know why there is so much turmoil in our native lands? It is because Allah is punishing us for allowing the West to turn Muslim against Muslim."

"And when did the West supposedly do this?"

"Have you never heard of the Sykes-Picot document, a secret agreement between the French and English in 1916 with their Russian allies?"

"Actually, I haven't."

"This is because you were educated in Minneapolis and teachers there care nothing about Arab history," Al-Kader declared. "For six centuries, the Turks in the Ottoman Empire controlled the lands around the Mediterranean basin where east and west meet and Arabs lived in harmony. My ancestors roamed the lands without borders and were treated well by their Turkish brothers. This was because Arabs lived under Sharia law and there was no need for borders and no need for man-made governments."

"I came to discuss my brother, not get a history lesson."

"If you don't care to listen, then leave."

Adeogo released a loud sigh and said, "I'm listening."

"In the First World War, the French, Great Britain, and Russia convinced Arabs to kill their fellow Muslim Turkish brothers. They turned Muslim against Muslim and when the West won the war, how did they reward their Arab allies?"

Without waiting for an answer, he said, "They secretly carved up all Arab lands. They created countries where none had been before—Jordan and Iraq. They did not put Arabs in charge, nor did they care about their individual and religious differences. They installed puppets and treated all Arab people as primitive colonists. They replaced Sharia law with man-made laws. They even spoke to Zionists about giving them land, Arab land."

Adeogo assumed that the sooner Al-Kader finished his lecture the quicker he could pose questions about his brother, so he didn't argue or interrupt.

Continuing, Al-Kader said, "The West gave the Jews Israel after World War Two even though the Arab people had nothing to do with the alleged genocide committed by the Germans. We had European Jews moving into our lands and arrogantly acting as if we were the invaders. That is the true history never told in the West."

Contempt was building in the Imam's eyes as he continued speaking. "Would you like to learn another reason why we hate the West? *Hypocrisy*. It was the United States and Britain that overthrew the democratically elected leader of Iran after he nationalized British-owned oil companies. The West installed their puppet, the Shah of Iran. You Americans talk about democracy but only when it doesn't interfere with your economic goals. You claim we are radical Islamic terrorists who hold women in contempt and bondage. Yet, you support the Saudis, a country that does not tolerate public worship by followers of religions other than Islam, including Muslim minorities, such as Shiites. It forbids women from obtaining a passport, marrying, or traveling without the approval of a male guardian. Hypocrites! I explained to your younger brother that hypocrisy is denying your own sins out of convenience. When your brother began seeing how the West abuses Arabs and how it speaks out of both sides of its mouth, the scales began to fall from his eyes."

"Policies change depending on who is the president and what is happening in the Middle East that might impact U.S. interests," Adeogo said. "The Saudis are helping us keep the peace."

"Hypocrisy. This is because men are easily corrupted and politics corrupts absolutely every man absolutely. You are corrupt. This is why Sharia law must be the law all men everywhere follow. Otherwise, there will be no peace, no harmony. You say you are a Muslim but you put government before your God when there is no need for any governments. The Holy Quran has all of the answers and those answers are Sharia law."

"I'd like to speak to you now specifically about my brother."

"We are speaking about what he learned. Do you know who brought him to us in Minnesota?"

"I suppose you will tell me it was Allah."

"No, it was not Allah. It was your own father. Your younger brother was a troublemaker who had joined a gang. Whites and blacks did not befriend him because of his Somali heritage. Your heritage. Your parents asked us to help save him. When I began teaching him how to read the Quran, he quit a gang. I began convincing him his life mattered to Allah and he was Allah's servant. He became like a child being offered sweets. Once he tasted one, he wanted more and more."

"What you instructed him in poisoned his mind. Your interpretations of Islam turned a beautiful religion based on love into one filled with rage and revenge."

"I taught him nothing. He asked questions. I answered them with the truth that you are too blind to see," Al-Kader said. "At first your brother was drawn to *salaf*. He believed the purest form of Islam was practiced by the Prophet Mohammad's earliest followers who spread the word immediately after his death in AD 532. He devoted himself to *da'wah* hoping to spread the Islamic faith and he rejected all violence. He spoke of love and respect, but after studying Scriptures, he realized violence was justified whenever Islam came under attack by Christians. This is why he decided to return to Somalia and join Al-Shabaab, because it was fighting the U.S.'s surrogates there, the Christian Ethiopians and other Christian invaders from African countries. It was there when he learned our struggle is a never-ending war. Have you said the *shahada*?"

"Yes," Adeogo replied. "What Muslim isn't familiar with it?"

"Then say it."

Adeogo hated being manipulated but he did as the Imam demanded.

"'There is no god but Allah and Mohammad is His messenger.' But I feel Allah is simply another name for what the Christians say is their God and the Jews say is their God. There are many paths that direct us to the same destination and we must respect other religions and not force everyone to accept Islam."

"You're a fool. Your younger brother made the same nonsensical arguments until I questioned his logic. Is it not true the Christians proclaim Jesus as the son of God? Do they not believe there is the trinity—the Father, Son, and the Holy Ghost? This is blasphemy based on the *shahada*, which teaches us there is only one God and he is Allah, not three gods. That is idolatry. Do you understand the meaning of *shirk*?"

"*Shirk* is associating some lesser being with Allah, saying Allah has a son or that Allah takes on any human form."

"The Quran says, 'To set up partners with Allah is to devise a sin most heinous indeed.' It prescribes that the penalty for committing *shirk* is death and that is the only acceptable penalty. A Christian who believes in Jesus commits *shirk* and therefore is condemned to death. There is no way to live in harmony with a Christian if you are a righteous follower of Mohammad."

"I don't accept that and what of the Jews?" Adeogo asked. "They do not believe Jesus was the son of God."

"What does the second line of the *shahada* teach—'Mohammad is the messenger of God.' But the Jews make a claim in public that no other religion makes. They believe God talked directly to them. Their Torah says every Jewish man, woman, and child alive—about three million people—heard God speak to them at Mount Sinai. They claim this proves they are God's chosen people because he talked directly to them. But Mohammad is Allah's messenger and his only messenger. God did not talk to the Jews. God chose Mohammad to speak for him. This is what your brother learned from reading the Quran and why he understood to accept other religions is *shirk* and blasphemy. There can be only one."

"I have listened patiently to your religious teachings. Now I shall tell you what I think of you. Your extremism and intolerance are nothing but narcissism. You use your knowledge of Quranic texts to suit your arguments but you do not put our faith in your heart and hold it dear. If anyone disagrees, you condemn them. You make your view the only permissible one and in doing that you have defiled Allah because you are putting your interpretation of the Holy Quran above the Prophet's own words. I might not have your vast knowledge, but like all young Muslim men, I studied the Quran and my father made me memorize much of it. You quote Scriptures but have forgotten that the Prophet himself warned, 'Beware of extremism in religion, for it destroyed those before you.'"

"You dare quote Scriptures to me?"

"You talk about hypocrisy but you pick and choose your Scriptures to fit your own narrow-minded totalitarian beliefs. Chapter one hundred nine of the Quran says, 'Say you, O disbelievers! I worship not what you worship. And nor you worship what I worship. And I shall not worship what you worshipped. And nor you shall worship what I worship. For you, your religion, and for me my religion.' There is nothing in that verse that says Mohammad declared we must destroy anyone who disagrees with us. You and the Falcon have hijacked Islam with your false teachings."

"Because you can quote a single Scripture or two, you believe you have a deeper understanding of Islam than I do."

Without warning, Al-Kader spit into his face.

Congressman Adeogo rose from the table. "You filled my brother's head with lies wrapped in your corrupt teachings. I will not ask for the Holy Quran to be given to you. The thought of having you touch it sickens me."

He called an officer and exited it, leaving Al-Kader sitting, chained to the table.

Adeogo found Fatima Olol waiting patiently in the car parking lot outside the jail.

"Did you find the answers about your brother?" she asked.

"I was a fool coming here."

CHAPTER THIRTY-SEVEN

Oval Office
The White House

CIA Director Payton Grainger heard the whooshing sound of the Sikorsky Sea King helicopter long before he spotted it in the evening darkness. As the lights of *Marine One* passed between the Washington Monument and White House on its way to the South Lawn, Grainger steadied himself knowing that the approaching blades would cause a blast of air. President Wyatt Bowie Austin was returning from Camp David, where he'd been meeting with governors from states with the nation's fifteen largest cities. They'd been discussing the Falcon's tri-city bombing threat.

"Mr. Director, you look like you were born tired and have suffered a relapse," Austin joked as he'd exited the helicopter.

The president's personal assistant was waiting at the Oval Office doorway with a steaming cup of hot chocolate spiked with a taste of bourbon, which Austin insisted helped him sleep at night.

"Payton, you want something to drink?" the president asked as he took a seat on the sofa, rather than behind his desk, and promptly placed the heels of his boots onto the coffee table between it and two overstuffed chairs positioned at the edges of the carpet bearing the presidential seal.

"No thank you, Mr. President."

"You know what kind of boots these are?" Austin asked as he admired his handmade foot apparel. "That's genuine elephant hide and the Texan who made them is so famous he's got a two-year waiting list. He knew I was the vice president when I placed my order and I thought I would jump the line, but he made me wait three years just to prove he didn't give a damn. That really tickled me."

Grainger felt an obligation to smile but he was in too serious of a mood to laugh outright.

The president took a sip of his drink and then said, "Okay, let's get serious. What have you got for me?"

"Our KTB team learned the nuclear bomb was delivered to a terrorist in Jakarta, Indonesia. It was shipped there from North Korea on a cargo ship owned by Umoja Owiti, the African billionaire."

"Where's the bomb now?"

"We're not certain. We've learned from Indonesian authorities that Owiti's ship arrived about ten days ago."

"Could have come and gone," the president noted. "Where's your KTB team?"

"Following the trail. En route to Indonesia to see what it can learn."

"Let's hope the bomb and this terrorist are still there."

The president raised his boots off the table and placed them on the floor. He leaned forward. "Start at the beginning. How'd you find out the bomb was in Jakarta?"

"Our first clue came from Ebio Kattan."

"That Al Arabic reporter? The one who interviewed that son of a bitch?"

"Yes, sir. The Mossad picked her up in Dubai and interrogated her and she fingered Owiti as her go-between with the Falcon, helping her set up her interview."

"Picked her up, huh? Is that a polite way of saying the Mossad worked her over?"

"I didn't ask," Grainger said.

"Smart. Go ahead, what happened next?"

"As soon as it was confirmed Umoja Owiti was involved, the KTB team flew to Owiti's compound in Kenya. A Mossad agent joined them there. They were able to learn from Owiti that the nuclear bomb had been transported from Rason, North Korea, to Jakarta on one of his cargo ships. It was picked up there by a terrorist called 'the Destroyer.' His real name is Hakim Farouk."

"Why do I recognize that name?"

"Because it was in one of your daily intelligence briefing reports. He made the bomb that killed President Allworth."

"Now you're telling me this murderer has the Falcon's nuclear bomb?"

"Yes, sir."

President Austin was quiet for a moment, thinking. "This billionaire in Africa tell the KTB team anything else useful? Does he know where the Falcon is hiding?"

"No, sir. Owiti contacted him only by computer."

"And you believe him? Listen, Grainger, if the Mossad can abduct a television reporter, then we sure as hell can snatch up this billionaire and bring him here for a more intense period of questioning."

"Sir, Mr. Owiti succumbed when he was being questioned by the KTB team."

President Austin did not look displeased. "Can any of this be traced back to us?"

"No, the Mossad staged it to appear that Owiti's chief bodyguard was embezzling money and went on a killing rampage. There'll be no record of our people even being there."

"Good, good. I've always admired how the Mossad acts. Top-notch group. When do you expect the KTB team to reach Jakarta?"

"Within the next twenty-four hours."

"This is progress, but it doesn't change the fact that there's a terrorist running around with a nuclear bomb."

"Yes, sir."

"You mentioned earlier that he also might be making dirty bombs because he spoke about destroying three cities, not just one. Anything new on that?"

"No, sir."

"Get me some answers, Director," the president said.

Their discussion had caused another question to pop into his head. "You were worried about Major Grant being a team player. Sounds like she's fitting right in."

"Major Grant hasn't played any role in any of the rough stuff so far. It's our Saudi and Mossad friends who have been handling that."

"Does she still worry you?"

"A bit, but she wants vengeance against the man who made the bomb and she now knows he's got a nuclear bomb. So far, I've not gotten any complaints from her about the tactics being used."

"Anything else, Grainger?"

"Yes, sir, there are a few other matters I need to discuss with you."

"Let's hear 'em."

"The Imam Al-Kader had a visitor today in the Maryland jail where he is being held. It was Representative Rudy Adeogo from Minnesota. He wasn't there long. I've been told Al-Kader spit in his face after they'd talked for about ten minutes."

"Spit in the congressman's face?" the president repeated, clearly surprised.

"Yes, sir."

"What the hell was that all about?"

"You will recall Representative Adeogo's youngest brother was a terrorist named Abdul Hafeez. The congressman apparently wanted to learn how the Imam radicalized his little brother."

"Probably offered him an extra virgin," the president quietly remarked in a disgusted tone.

"I thought you would want to know about their meeting," Grainger replied. "There's one more item we should discuss that involves the congressman."

Grainger handed the president the manila envelope that Brooke Grant had given him about Mary Margaret Delaney's death.

Austin pulled out its contents. "What am I looking at here?" he asked impatiently.

"Major Grant brought this envelope to me before she left for Africa. The police reports and photos are about the suspicious death of Washington lobbyist Mary Margaret Delaney, who you'll recall worked against you and President Allworth in both of your presidential campaigns."

"I remember her. Tough broad. I was surprised when she offed herself on the G. W. Parkway. Struck me as strange."

"Sir, you need to take a look at two photos from that packet that were taken by a D.C. traffic camera. The first photo captured an image of Mary Margaret Delaney driving through a red light on the same night her body was found. The second shows a car following her through that same traffic light."

The president sorted through the papers until he found the two pictures that Grainger had cited. "I'll be double damned," he said when he examined them closely. "That's Omar Nader, the head of the OIN, in the car chasing her, isn't it?"

"Yes, and the man with him is a Saudi intelligence agent. He's currently on loan to us."

"For what purpose?"

"He's a member of the KTB team. To put it bluntly, he's an assassin."

"A Saudi assassin, huh?" The president paused while he considered what he'd just learned and then said, "Are you implying that Omar Nader and this Saudi killer played a role in Delaney's alleged suicide?"

"Major Brooke Grant thinks so. She's also showed these photos to Representative Adeogo and he admitted that Delaney was trying to blackmail him, apparently at the request of Omar Nader."

"Now let me get this straight. Omar Nader was using Mary Margaret Delaney to blackmail Representative Adeogo?"

"Yes, without getting too deep into the weeds, Nader found out that Adeogo's youngest brother was a terrorist—this was before the congressman held a press conference admitting it. Nader shared that information with Delaney, who then tried to blackmail Adeogo—to make him do whatever Nader and the OIN wanted."

"Adeogo fessing up on his own spoiled that little plan."

"Yes, sir."

"So you think Nader and this Saudi killer decided to eliminate Delaney to keep her from telling the world that Nader and the OIN were going after a fellow Muslim, that about it?"

"Yes, sir, that's Major Grant's theory."

"What a tangled web we weave," the president recited.

"Mr. President," Grainger said, "if I may, let me remind you that Omar Nader does not have diplomatic immunity. What you have in your hands is all circumstantial evidence and most likely never would hold up in a court, but he could be arrested and charged with being an accomplice to a murder."

"Omar Nader has been running around calling me a bigot and accusing me of spreading Islamophobia," the president said, now fully understanding the importance of what Director Grainger had shared with him. "Karma. You know what they say."

CHAPTER THIRTY-EIGHT

The Phoenix Tower
Dubai, UAE

Ebio Kattan learned about African billionaire Umoja Owiti being found dead in his Kenyan mansion by watching her television while she was sequestered inside her bedroom.

On that same newscast, a Dubai police spokesman said no one had any idea what had happened to Kattan, since she had disappeared after broadcasting her exclusive interview with the Falcon.

Filthy and smelly, she sat on the edge of her bed and decided it was time for her to come out of hiding. She retrieved the same dirty clothing that she'd been wearing when she'd been abducted.

Time for some alterations.

Grasping her black bra, she began pulling on the left shoulder strap until its plastic ring snapped. She slipped on her bra but left the torn strap dangling uselessly. Next up was her Armani floral silk satin blouse. Looking in the mirror, she ripped the top of the blouse loose, as if she had been attacked.

Now it was the most difficult part of her ruse. The Mossad had tormented her with loud noises, brilliant lights, cold and hot air, and dousing her with water. That was not shocking enough. She would need more sympathy.

Opening her portable computer, she typed in: At what temperature does human skin burn?

An applied heat of 131°F causes second-degree burns on exposed skin. Pain receptors overload and become numb at a temperature of 140°F. At 162°F, human tissue is destroyed on contact.

Next she typed: Scarring because of burns.

Second Degree Burns: Both the epidermis and the layer underneath, the dermis, are damaged. Second-degree burns are classified into two types: superficial partial thickness or deep partial thickness burns. Superficial partial thickness burns are characterized by local redness and blisters. The burn takes around three weeks to heal. There is generally no scarring, but the pigmentation of the burned area may change. A deep partial thickness burn is characterized by pain and whiteness in the area of the burn. This type of burn leaves a scar.

Kattan decided on a scar.

Reaching into the top drawer of her bathroom vanity, she removed a curling iron that she had purchased in Paris but rarely used, having replaced it with a flat iron. The older gold-plated titanium rod could be set from 0 to 400 degrees Fahrenheit. Kattan pressed the setting switch and watched its digital numbers race upward until it reached 132 degrees. Placing the curling rod on the bathroom's tile floor, she filled a cup with water and gulped down four 200-milligram Advil tablets.

Kattan squeezed her eyes shut, took a deep breath, and stepped on the curling iron, pressing the center of her left foot against the hot metal. She counted out in hurried puffs, "One, two, three," before removing it.

The pain was so intense that she began gasping for air. She placed both of her hands on top of the bathroom vanity and raised her burned foot up behind her. She wasn't done.

Kattan lowered her now burned left foot to the tile and gingerly stood on her tiptoes. Supporting her weight with her arms on the vanity and tiptoes, she thrust the center of her right foot onto the curling rod, burning her sole.

When she pulled it away, she slowly lowered herself to the floor and began to sob. She could smell her burned flesh on the curling rod. Reaching over, she grabbed its handle and pulled its cord from the wall plug. For more than an hour, she remained sitting on the floor crying. When she finally regained her courage, she crawled on her knees to her bed and swallowed a 1 mg dose of Xanax. It helped, but she wanted something more. She needed to wait until dusk for the burns to fully blister. From her nightstand, she retrieved a bottle of Ambien, a sedative used to treat insomnia, and poured out a 10 mg pill. Between the ibuprofen, Xanax, and Ambien, Kattan blacked out.

It was dusk when she awakened. Before burning her feet, she had placed a blue burqa and face veil on the edge of her king-size bed. She slipped it over her torn and filthy Western clothes. It took her several minutes to crawl from her bedroom on her knees to her apartment's front door. Reaching up, she grabbed the doorknob with both hands and used it to pull herself up—first to her knees, and finally to her now badly blistered feet. She ducked under the police tape still draped across her doorway, hobbled out into the hall, and into the elevator. From there, she slipped across the lobby concealed in her burqa, exiting to the rear of her apartment building. There were three large metal trash containers located next to a delivery door. She hid behind one out of sight and shed the burqa.

Now ready for her grand performance, she limped onto the sidewalk and when she saw a car approaching, she collapsed and slowly waved her arm, signaling that she was in distress.

The car came to a hurried stop and Kattan watched as a man and woman scrambled from inside it.

"What happened?" the man asked, looking at her tear-stained face.

"Her feet have been burned!" the woman exclaimed.

"Help me please!" Kattan pleaded. "The hospital."

"I know who this is," the woman said. "The television reporter."

Kattan nodded. "Ebio Kattan from Al Arabic news."

The man placed his arms under her, gently lifting her as the woman opened the back of their four-door Mercedes-Benz.

"You're very lucky," the woman said once they were in the car. "My husband is a doctor."

"We're going to Dubai Hospital on Al Khaleej Street," he said.

As he drove, he pressed a button on his steering wheel and via Bluetooth told his cell phone to call the emergency room. When he'd finished, he glanced in the rearview mirror and said, "I'm an internist, but we have an excellent emergency room. Please, tell us what happened to you."

"I was kidnapped, tortured," she said in a tormented voice. "Please, please, I have no family here. Can you call my television producer? He will meet me at the hospital. I can tell you the number."

The driver called Al Arabic and by the time that Kattan arrived at Dubai Hospital, her producer and a camera operator were waiting outside the entrance along with two members of the hospital medical staff.

As she was lifted from the backseat and placed on a gurney, Kattan screamed in pain.

The cameraman carefully recorded her anguish.

CHAPTER THIRTY-NINE

En route to Jakarta
39,000 feet above the Indian Ocean

Khalid had been the first to board the Boeing 737 Ethiopian Airlines jet at the Addis Ababa Bole International Airport for the flight to Soekarno–Hatta International Airport in Jakarta with a stopover in Dubai. He had chosen a first-class aisle seat in the fourth row on the right side of the aircraft so he could inspect each of the 125 other passengers as they boarded.

Major Brooke Grant settled into her seat two rows up from Khalid on the opposite side of the jet a few minutes later. Meanwhile, Esther from the Mossad waited until she was the last passenger to board, slipping quietly next to Brooke. She preferred not being seen by others on the aircraft.

They repeated this same boarding procedure after their layover in Dubai. It had been twenty hours since their hurried departure from Owiti's estate. When Brooke turned on her portable computer and connected to the jet's Wi-Fi, she discovered for the first time that African billionaire Umoja Owiti had been murdered along with three women, his butler, and two security guards.

Khalid and Esther had avoided answering Brooke's questions about the events that had transpired at the El Wak compound. The fast-breaking stories explained that Kenyan officials suspected Owiti's chief of security had committed seven murders and destroyed recordings from the security cameras on the estate.

Brooke nudged Esther and nodded at the computer screen. "You might wish to read this," she whispered.

"Not interested," Esther replied without glancing up from a movie playing on her iPad.

"This is your handiwork, isn't it?" Brooke asked.

Esther paused her movie, removed the earbud from her left ear, and turned to directly face Brooke in her window seat.

"We needed critical information," Esther said in a flat tone. "You two failed. I didn't."

She returned the earpiece and restarted her movie.

Brooke felt physically ill. She leaned back and closed her eyes. She still was sleeping only a few hours per night because of her nightmares and felt constantly tired. Unexpectedly, the sound of the jet speeding through the air lulled her into a deep sleep.

Esther glanced at Brooke. She had read the Mossad's thick files on both Brooke and Khalid before joining the KTB team. This was not the first time that Esther had accepted an assignment such as this, but because of Brooke's reaction, Esther correctly assumed her American counterpart was a newbie to such deadly tactics. Esther had read that Brooke was known to have fatally wounded at least three men, but that was when they were attacking her. She had never shot anyone in cold blood.

Esther wondered, *Did Brooke's uneasiness stem from America's old Wild West culture that fostered the idea that good guys in white hats never shot anyone who was unarmed or in their backs and always let the bad guy in a black hat have a six-shooter and draw first?*

Esther had watched dozens of such movies with her father. He had been a great fan of John Wayne Westerns. *Perhaps it was Brooke's religious upbringing that made her feel queasy,* Esther thought. It was documented in the Mossad's background file.

As the daughter of a fundamentalist Baptist minister, Brooke undoubtedly had been taught a New Testament tenant about nonviolence, "turning the other cheek" in the face of your enemies, and forgiveness rather than the Old Testament scripture about taking "an eye for an eye."

Esther wasn't certain what sort of information the CIA had collected about her, but she doubted Brooke had been informed that her new KTB team member also had been reared in a deeply religious family.

When she was twelve, Esther had quizzed her local rabbi about the Scripture in Exodus 21:24 that read, "an eye for an eye, a tooth for a tooth, a hand for a hand, a foot for a foot; a burn for a burn, a wound for a wound, a bruise for a bruise."

Her rabbi understood the reason for her question. A Palestinian had rammed his truck into a class of Jewish schoolchildren in the West Bank of Jerusalem, killing two of Esther's classmates. By chance, she had been ill that morning and had stayed at home. The attack had taken place near the settlement of Ofra, where her parents lived. Immediately after it, Israeli forces had killed four potential assailants.

"My child," the rabbi had lectured her, "this Scripture truly sounds like one must be punished in the exact way in which they offended, but the Talmudic sages tell us this verse was never meant to be taken literally in Jewish law. It simply means if someone does an injustice, they are indebted to the individual who they have harmed and owe them compensation. If someone kills your cow, he owes you a cow."

"But what if it is a human life, not a cow," the unrelenting Esther had asked.

"In Leviticus twenty-two we read, 'You shall not desecrate my holy name, that I may be sanctified in the midst of the people of Israel. I am the Lord who sanctifies you.' Do you know what this means, child?" he'd asked.

"Yes, Teacher. If you do a good act as a Jew or a bad act, it either glorifies God or desecrates God. What any single one of us does reflects on all of us and on God. You must never desecrate God."

"Very good. You have learned your lessons well."

"But you haven't answered my question, Rabbi. Is it right to kill someone?"

"Killing is forbidden and a desecration of Torah and of God," he'd replied. "But the Torah and rabbinic interpretations are quite clear. It is forbidden—unless it is in self-defense and even then, it must be a last resort. But your life is precious to God, so you are ethically commanded by God to protect yourself."

"God expects us to protect ourselves by killing others?"

"God doesn't want you to do it, he *demands* it, because otherwise you are demeaning your own life. If someone comes to kill you, you must stop him and kill him if necessary. It is not only permitted, but it is also required."

Esther suspected there was a fundamental difference in how she and Brooke justified killing. Esther had never known of a time when someone was not trying to murder her. She had been told of the threats since childbirth. Every Jew living in the West Bank had been a target. She had seen it for herself. During her final year in high school, she had kept score in a notebook. That year, Palestinians had killed forty-two Israelis and two visiting tourists. Israeli forces had killed two hundred forty-two Palestinians. The Palestinians said the violence came from decades of Israeli rule in territory that the Jews had stolen from them. The Israelis said the bloodshed was fueled by a Palestinian campaign to murder all Jews.

Although Esther had never been to America, she assumed Brooke had not grown up being told that she was a target. She had not been reared to be wary of everyone whom she met. Brooke was an African American and therefore a descendant of slaves, yet Esther assumed the woman sitting next to her had not been terrified as a child of being dragged outside and lynched. For as long as Esther could remember, she had been told stories about how her uncles and aunts had been led into gas chambers. Every night on television, there was footage of rioting Arabs declaring that they would destroy Israel.

Esther shared another painful connection with her KTB teammate. Her mother also had been killed by terrorists—a suicide bombing at the local market. It was sometime after Esther first joined the military and was recruited by the Mossad that she stopped worrying about the morality of what she was being asked to do. By that time, she had rid herself of any guilt. She remembered her first kill but she also remembered that she had felt nothing especially troubling about it or those that followed. Those deaths were borne of pragmatism. She was not committing murder because those she killed wanted her dead.

She turned her head into the aisle to check on Khalid, who nodded when their eyes met.

The Mossad file held much less information about Khalid, whose actual birth name was Saad Khan. While he claimed to be a member of the General Intelligence Directorate, he actually worked for the Mabahith, the Saudi's secret police that oversaw domestic security and counterintelligence. He was born to poor parents in rural Jizan, a neglected province, which he had fled at age fifteen. A relative who was friends with an influential family in Riyadh had gotten Khalid enrolled in a technical high school run by the Ministry of Defense, which put him in line for the military, but he was caught violating Sharia law—the file didn't say which of its strict tenants—and was expelled. It was then the Mabahith secretly recruited him and, ironically, initially assigned him to work as a religious police officer arresting and punishing anyone who violated the kingdom's strict Sharia religious teachings.

Esther knew that those violations could be as simple as a woman speaking to a man without permission of her guardian. Exactly how Khalid had moved up the Mabahith ladder was unknown, but at some point, he had been accused of torturing a British subject who had fled Riyadh. The Englishman had been arrested for "unethical behavior" as a college professor for "encouraging acts of disorder and discord" against the royal family. The teacher's crime: He had strayed from the textbook that he had been issued and had allowed the class to discuss the value of a free press rather than the Saudi press, which required all media to promote "education that inspires national unity." A student had reported him to the religious police for not adhering to the mandatory curriculum.

"I was totally confused when they arrested me and demanded that I sign a confession," the professor later told a London magazine. "I had no idea of what I was supposed to confess to. I tried to ask them. This man named Khalid responded by hitting me with a pickax handle. He beat me all over my body. He brought in a huge twenty-two stone

Saudi to sit on me while he beat the soles of my feet. He forced a metal rod between my knees and hoisted me upside down, and beat me on my exposed buttocks. It was excruciating. The only time he broke off was when he went to pray."

At night, the Englishman said Khalid chained him standing up to a steel door facing bright lights and the moment he looked as though he had fallen asleep, a guard came in and prodded him or hit with a stick to wake him up. The next day, Khalid was there again, ready with his pickax handles. The professor signed a confession and spent two years in a Saudi prison before he was deported.

Esther had found one quote by the Englishman of special interest.

"I said I was innocent, but I quickly learned that innocence to the Saudis is not the same as innocence in the West. The innocent, by the definition given in the Quran, is a term that describes strict Muslims. The Quran explicitly goes into detail about what makes a Muslim not innocent. If you believe in other religions or are atheist, you are not innocent. If you are unclean or eat banned foods, you are not innocent. If you do not abide by the sexual rules laid out in the Quran, you are not innocent. If you do not do your duty of prayer, fasting, and mosque attending, you are not innocent. I was told that because I was an infidel, it was impossible for me to ever be innocent."

According to the Mossad file, Khalid had moved from being an interrogator to becoming a "ghost." He did not have a family and became so proficient at killing he currently worked directly for the head of the Mabahith, a member of the royal family. The Mossad suspected Khalid had been personally responsible for three dozen killings, including at least two prominent Israelis.

When her Mossad superiors had told Esther that she would be working with Khalid, she had questioned why Israel would form an alliance with a Mabahith killer.

She had been given a one-word explanation: Iran.

Her superiors explained that Iran was the most destabilizing factor in the region and there was a power struggle currently under way happening between the Saudis and the Iranians. "While neither is a friend of Israel, the Saudis—pressured by the United States—are more likely to let us live in peace with our Arab neighbors than the Iranians," Esther had been told.

Her superior officers had explained that to the outside world the fighting between the House of Saud and Iran appeared to be because of religious differences. When the Prophet Mohammad unexpectedly died in his wife's house, he had urged reconciliation among his Muslim brothers. But in the battle for succession, two different groups had emerged: the Sunnis and Shias.

Esther knew that 85 percent of the 1.6 billion Muslims in the world were Sunnis and although only 1 percent of them lived in Saudi Arabia, the House of Saud considered itself the seat of Muslim power and its official voice, much to the irritation of other Muslim nations. The much smaller Shia bloc was led by Iran and other Shia bloc nations along the Shia Crescent—the axis of Lebanon, Azerbaijan, and Iraq, as well as Bahrain.

To the outside world, the Saudis and Iran were engaged in a centuries-old battle between Sunnis and Shiites, but Esther's supervisors had said that view was a smoke screen. The fighting was not about religion. It was about dominance. The Iranians wanted the Saudi's oil reserves, and its leaders in Tehran were being backed by Russia. The Saudis were supported by the United States and seen as a stabilizing force in the region. Why did the Americans care? Because they, too, wanted Saudi oil.

The conflict between the House of Saud and the Iranian leaders had been a fairly even match in recent times. But the Saudi family, which had a net worth of some $1.3 trillion, had been badly rattled by the so-called Arab Spring revolts in 2011 and calls for more democratic rule spreading via social media across their kingdom. Iran had quietly supported efforts to undermine the House of Saud by encouraging democratic reforms on social media—not because Iran believed in a freer society, but because it wanted to topple the monarchy.

Iran was backing radical Islamic terrorism because it wanted to drive the United States out of the Middle East. The Saudis needed the United States to keep their kingdom in power. Israel needed the United States to keep its Arab neighbors from destroying it. The

United States needed help from the Saudis and Israelis to find the nuclear bomb, Hakim Farouk, and the Falcon.

Everyone on the KTB had a reason to cooperate. What Esther wondered, as she returned to her iPad, was how many check marks would Khalid receive on the list if she compared his personality to that of a psychopath and whether her other partner, Major Brooke Grant, was strong enough to kill either Hakim Farouk or the Falcon in cold blood if given a chance.

CHAPTER FORTY

Tacoma Park neighborhood
Washington, D.C.

Representative Rudy Adeogo was exhausted when he returned from visiting Mohammad Al-Kader, and as he turned onto the block where he lived in northwest Washington, he became frustrated. There wasn't a single open parking spot on the street, even though it was not yet 9:00 p.m.

As he drove by his two-story house, he noticed a light shining from his daughter's second-story bedroom. He found a place to park on a nearby street and as he was walking up the sidewalk toward his front door, his suspicions were confirmed.

"Daddy! We're home!" his twelve year-old daughter, Cassy, declared as she burst through the front door and ran outside to hug him. He glanced up into the doorway where his wife, Dheeh, was waiting. She had not told him they were returning from Minneapolis.

When Cassy released her grip, he took her tiny hand and climbed the steps up and nodded awkwardly at his wife. "If I'd known you were coming home, I would have been here to greet you."

He bent forward to kiss her, but she turned her lips away so he pecked her cheek as they entered their rented home.

"Daddy," Cassy said, "Mommy has found out where Jennifer is. It's a hospital with horses—but for people, not horses, and she's gotten me permission to see her. Will you go with us?"

Adeogo was surprised. In the past, Dheeh would never have taken it upon herself to arrange such an outing without first clearing it with him. Since learning about his affair with Mary Margaret Delaney,

Dheeh had not only pulled back emotionally but she had also shown more confidence and independence.

"Major Grant is traveling overseas," Dheeh said, "but she notified me by email about Jennifer before she left the country and asked if I would periodically check on her since Jennifer and Cassy are close friends. She told me the names of Jennifer's doctors to ensure we would be allowed to visit. They can accommodate us tomorrow."

Dheeh placed her palm on Cassy's small shoulder and said to their daughter, "Remember, your friend Jennifer has not been well. After the wedding bombing, she stopped talking. It may be difficult when you see her."

"I know all about it," Cassy replied. "She told me once about her make-believe world with unicorns and beautiful rainbows where no one hurts her. She goes there when it's dangerous. But she'll talk to me. I'm so excited, I'm not sure I'll be able to sleep tonight."

Dheeh said, "If your father can't drive us, we will call for an Uber."

"No," Adeogo replied, "I will clear my morning schedule. I want to be there to support both of you and to see Jennifer."

While Cassy got ready for bed, Adeogo and Dheeh went into the kitchen, where she served him a plate of *kashaato*, his favorite coconut-based Somali dessert. In between bites, he told her about his conversation with Al-Kader.

"I don't know why you feel it is incumbent on you to understand your younger brother and how he was radicalized," Dheeh said when he finished. "If you wish to feel guilty, you have another matter better suited for you to focus on."

She cleared his plate and went upstairs to bed without further explanation, leaving him downstairs, where he disappeared into his office for several hours to answer emails.

It was a beautiful spring morning when they left the district, driving west toward the town of Clifton, a picturesque Virginia village with a former Texaco station that had been turned into a popular eatery adjacent to railroad tracks. The Happy Riders Horse Farm's white-fenced acres were located a few miles beyond Main Street, down a two-lane blacktop road that rose and fell as it curved through the trees. A stone house built in the early 1800s and later made modern with several additions rose from a cleared bluff overlooking several horse barns. As Adeogo drove along its winding driveway, Cassy peered through the passenger seat window searching for Jennifer among the young riders in a nearby grassy field.

"I don't see her," she complained.

"We need to check in first before we go looking," Dheeh said.

Adeogo parked and the three of them entered the main house, where they were greeted by a receptionist, who recognized Adeogo and immediately picked up her desk phone.

"Dr. Cummings, the congressman and his family are here," she announced.

A door to her left opened and Dr. Cecil Cummings and Dr. George Jacks came out to welcome them. Dr. Jacks explained that he was continuing to oversee Jennifer's recovery even though he was based at the Champion Mental Hospital in Falls Church while Dr. Cummings was in charge of the horse therapy ranch. Once everyone was seated comfortably inside Dr. Cummings's office, he said, "Let me explain a bit about equine-assisted therapy—or EAT, as we call it."

Cassy smiled at the acronym but caught herself from laughing.

"Primarily, we work with disabled persons with special needs to help them develop better balance, coordination, strength, and sensorimotor system skills."

"While EAT has been proven to help individuals with physical problems," his colleague, Dr. Jacks, said, "the idea that working with horses can help someone overcome a serious mental disorder is rather controversial because there have been no definitive studies that document whether or not EAT can improve cognitive function."

"Why then did you suggest Jennifer come here?" Adeogo asked Dr. Jacks.

"Because her decision to withdraw into her imaginary world appears to have been voluntary on her part and she seems to have a natural affinity for horses. I believe having her care for a horse, having to feed and groom it, will help provide a nonthreatening bridge for her to cross back from her make-believe world to reality."

"Is Jennifer better? Is she talking?" Cassy asked.

Dr. Cummings looked at the preteen and said in a comforting voice, "Your friend still isn't talking but she's not been here that long and it generally takes a month for residents to feel at home. She's outside grooming one of our favorite horses here. The horse is an older gelding named Soupy."

"That's a funny name for a horse." Cassy giggled.

"Jennifer has not ridden Soupy yet even though our therapists are encouraging her to so," Dr. Cummings continued. "We saddle Soupy every morning before Jennifer goes out in the stables to feed him. The horse in the stall next to Soupy is Midnight and we thought that Miss Cassy here might want to ride Midnight this morning. She's fed and saddled and ready to go."

"Can I, Mommy? PLEEAASSEEE?"

"Where is Jennifer now?" Dheeh asked.

"She's in the main stable tending to Soupy," Dr. Cummings replied.

"Can I go now?" Cassy asked, growing impatient.

"First," said Dr. Cummings, "we'll need your parents to sign some waivers but once that's done, I'll direct you to the stable. Do you think you can follow some basic instructions?"

"Of course," Cassy replied indignantly. "I'm not a child."

"We believe it would be best if you simply walk out to the barn by yourself and say hello to Jennifer," Dr. Jacks said. "Don't ask her a bunch of questions. Just walk in as if you saw her yesterday."

"Midnight is next to Soupy," Dr. Cummings said. "Can you get on a horse by yourself?"

Cassy shot him a preteen "duh" look.

"We'll take that for a yes," Dr. Jacks said, smiling. "Once you mount Midnight, you can say something like, 'Jennifer, how would you—'"

"I call her Jenn when we're together," Cassy said, interrupting.

"Okay, good. Say something such as, 'Jenn, I'm going riding. Do you want to ride Soupy?'"

"What should our daughter do if Jennifer doesn't reply?" Dheeh asked.

"I'm glad you asked because this is important. We can't force Jennifer or scare her."

"She wouldn't be afraid of me!" Cassy snapped.

"Jennifer has been through a horrible traumatic experience so we can't browbeat her into participating in anything and risk further traumatizing her."

"What does 'browbeat' mean?" Cassy asked.

"It's an old-fashioned term," Dheeh said, before realizing that she might have just insulted Dr. Jacks, who appeared to be in his seventies.

"It means forcing someone to do something they don't want to do," Adeogo explained, joining their conversation, "like your mother does every night when you don't want to do your homework."

"It's boring."

"Back to Jennifer, or Jenn, as you like to call her," Dr. Jacks said. "Don't tell her that she has to join you. Just get on Midnight and ride out of the barn. That's it."

"I'm sure the doctors won't mind," Adeogo said, "if you ride Midnight for a while even if Jennifer doesn't come out of the barn on Soupy."

"That's right, Congressman. In fact, it might be best, Cassy, if you rode for fifteen minutes or so to see if Jennifer will join you. If she doesn't, then you can ride Midnight back into the stable and one of our handlers will take care of her."

"I know how to take care of a horse after a ride," Cassy said.

"She's been riding for several years at her private school," Dheeh explained. "They require them to groom their own horses."

Addressing Cassy, Dr. Cummings said, "Do you have any questions for either of us, young lady, about Jennifer or Midnight?"

"Nope! I'm ready to go riding."

The five of them walked from the main house along a gravel path to a chest-high wooden fence, where Drs. Cummings and Jacks stopped. "Your parents, Dr. Jacks, and I will stay here," Dr. Cummings told Cassy, "while you go through this gate down to that big red stable in the center, between the two smaller ones. That's where you'll find Jennifer, Soupy, and Midnight. Remember what Dr. Jacks told you."

Cassy bolted toward the stables. "Slow down," Dheeh hollered. "Walk, don't run."

Cassy immediately slowed her pace.

The adults stood in a row along the fence: Adeogo, Dheeh, Dr. Jacks, and Dr. Cummings watching the stable door. A few minutes later, Cassy came riding outside on Midnight and expertly directed the horse to an arena adjacent to the stables. Everyone watched the stable door, hoping that Jennifer would appear next. A minute passed and then another.

Dr. Jacks's cell phone rang. He turned away from them to answer it and when he finished his conversation, he checked his watch and said, "It's been about ten minutes and I need to get back to the hospital, so I'm going to leave you now." He exchanged pleasantries with Adeogo and Dheeh and then said to Dr. Cummings, "Cecil, please call me with an update later today after you have time to observe Jennifer and assess the situation."

Dr. Cummings stayed another five minutes before he, too, received a phone call and walked back to the main house, leaving Adeogo and Dheeh at the fence watching their daughter riding in a giant circle about thirty yards from where they were standing.

"Our daughter's beautiful," Adeogo said as he watched Cassy ask Midnight to pick up the pace. "She's growing up so fast."

"She's always in a hurry," Dheeh said. "She always wants to go here or there, never stop."

Adeogo reached over and took his wife's hand. She did not pull it away. Holding hands, they watched Cassy, who suddenly stopped Midnight and began waving one hand in the air at them, pointing.

They followed her extended hand to the stable door. Jennifer was emerging from it, riding Soupy. She joined Cassy, and the two friends began riding alongside each other, quietly enjoying their mounts.

CHAPTER FORTY-ONE

Soekarno–Hatta International Airport
Outskirts of Jakarta, Indonesia

The deputy chief of BIN (Badan Intelijen Negara)—the Indonesian State Intelligence Agency—was waiting for Brooke, Esther, and Khalid as they walked into the terminal from their Ethiopian Airlines flight.

"No need to go through customs," he announced. "The general is waiting outside. My men will take your bags to hotel."

"I have one checked bag and I'd like it brought directly to me," Brooke replied. When she had boarded a commercial jet to Jakarta, she'd been required to check her gym bag because it contained her Beretta.

"No worry. My men will get but hurry now. Director Sinaga outside. He very important man. Must go."

They fell in behind the rushed deputy and two of his aides, as the group cut a swath through the logjammed airport. All three BIN men were wearing identical black suits with dark sunglasses. Parked outside, a black Mercedes-Benz S600 sedan was waiting with its engine running. Former Indonesian general Sinaga, the BIN's politically appointed director who went by only one name, welcomed them from the comfortable rear seat of the Mercedes while his deputy and the others scurried into a BMW X5 SUV parked directly in front of their boss's armored luxury car with its blinkers flashing.

"I believe you will be very satisfied with our work here," Director Sinaga proclaimed as they pulled away from the airport. Although the highway was divided and their side of the road had three individual lanes, the drivers around them paid no attention to the white hash marks painted on the asphalt. The vehicles weaved, sometimes four abreast, between one another in a constant stream with motorcycles and bicycles forming one giant snake of humanity pouring into Jakarta.

"I've arranged for a full briefing at our headquarters," Director Sinaga said. He was a plump man with a menacing pencil-thin mustache and heavy jowls.

"This is most gracious of you *Bapak* Sinaga," Khalid said, using the Indonesian equivalent of the word *sir* to address the director.

"You've been to Jakarta before?" the director asked.

"I've read about your customs and culture, but this is my first visit," Khalid replied.

"As you know, Director," Brooke said, "we are in a bit of a hurry, so perhaps you can answer a few questions now. We've been told that the *Sea Voyager* cargo ship came to your port from North Korea about ten or eleven days ago. Have you been able to locate records that show when it arrived?"

Sinaga waved his right hand dismissively in the air. "At briefing all will be explained." Glancing outside, he added, "I was governor of Jakarta before I became a general. Do you see how magnificent our city is? It was I who created our public transit and emptied the streets of beggars."

Brooke half listened in frustration as Sinaga continued to blabber about his career as a public servant extraordinaire. The two vehicles eventually reached Pejaten in South Jakarta, where the Sukarno–Hatta State Intelligence Complex was located, a mixture of a dozen buildings, including a pistol range and living quarters for senior BIN officials.

As they pulled to a stop in front of the main building, Sinaga said, "Our facility is named after our first president, Sukarno, and first prime minister, Mohammad Hatta, but many foreigners rush through our country without taking time to learn about us. They are always in a hurry wanting answers."

Brooke assumed his snide comment was directed toward her but she didn't care. He was wasting precious time and they hadn't flown from Africa here for an Indonesian history lesson.

He led them inside to a waiting elevator that took them up several floors to a glass-enclosed conference room with panoramic views of the city. A half dozen BIN officials were waiting, along with plates of rice with chicken filling wrapped in green banana leaves served with tea. After what seemed to Brooke to be an intolerable waste of time, the director rose from the head seat at the large conference table.

"My deputy will now brief you on the important and significant steps we have undertaken to find the nuclear bomb that you are seeking as well as the criminal who has brought it into our great country."

He sat down and his deputy stood with a clicker in his hand. Several grainy photos appeared on a large wall monitor as room-darkening shades descended.

"This foreigner entered our airport thirteen days ago on passport issued to Fares Rahal, but he give fake name. This man be Hakim Farouk," the deputy director explained in his broken English.

Brooke studied Farouk's passport photo. He was traveling under a different name from the one he has used when he fled the United States. He'd called himself Saleem Antar then. This passport had a newer photograph and it is what caught her attention.

Farouk was handsome with softer features than she had imagined for someone who had earned the nickname "the Destroyer." There was softness to his dark eyes that certainly didn't match the rage burning in his heart. His skin was almond colored and his black eyebrows were thinner than many Arab men's, as if they had been plucked. In this photo, his beard was neatly trimmed.

"The day after he come here," the deputy director continued, "two murders happened with a knife." Crime photos of two victims edged with blood flashed onto the monitor. "Both work at Istiqlal Mosque. The younger man, he tour guide there and the older gentleman, he an Imam. Autopsy show both men dead with throats slashed by a knife."

"That's Hakim Farouk's trademark," Khalid volunteered. He glanced at Esther because it was the Mossad who had first informed his service of Farouk's signature habit. "At least that is what our friends in Israel intelligence have told us," he added.

Esther remained stone faced and silent.

"Do you know where Farouk is now?" Brooke asked, trying to speed up the briefing.

The deputy looked at Director Sinaga, who replied, "Major Grant, please let my deputy tell you in chronological order what we have done to assist the United States."

His reply answered Brooke's question. If they had Farouk or knew where he was hiding, they would have already told them.

"Where was Farouk staying in Jakarta when he committed these murders?" Khalid asked.

"We not know where he was in Jakarta but discovered four days ago where he hide out," the deputy replied. He explained that the local police in Bandung had called the BIN after several stray dogs had gathered outside the door of a rented warehouse. The ragged animals were bothering other renters in nearby units. "The police, they go for look inside."

A series of photographs flashed across the screen in rapid order. They showed the interior of the rented unit, a wooden shipping container in one corner of the main room, and the bloated body of a man wrapped in heavy plastic stuffed inside that container.

"The smell inside this warehouse, it stink so bad the dogs come to it," he explained.

"How do you know Farouk was involved in this warehouse killing?" Khalid asked.

"Excellent detective work under Director Sinaga's leadership confirm he do it," the deputy said, nodding in respect to Sinaga.

Brooke had a sarcastic thought. *The fact that the victim left wrapped in plastic had been murdered with a knife and stuffed into a wooden box with North Korean markings on it must have helped.*

"We identify the dead man as a Jakarta day worker. His name Kevin Wahid. We show his photograph to other day laborers who knows him. They say he be on job with his Suzuki Carry Truck several days and no come back for more work."

The deputy director paused for a moment to take a sip of hot tea for his voice, which was beginning to sound scratchy, before glancing at Sinaga, who nodded for him to continue.

"Inside warehouse we find body but no bomb. These pictures taken by security camera at warehouse gate. The footage showed everyone who entered and left. Here two men come in Toyota truck."

Another telltale clue. The camera showed both the dead man's faces and Farouk's. Continuing, the deputy said, "Only one man leave in same truck four days ago only it painted different color. Red. Look at truck back. Now four boxes being carried, not big one."

"Four boxes rather than one," Khalid repeated, shooting both Esther and Brooke a confused look. "Were you able to track his truck?"

Another image appeared on the monitor.

"Here be photo of truck driving into Port of Tanjung Priok four days ago. He leave truck in parking lot. Four boxes no longer on truck when it be found. No sign of him. We think he and four boxes leave Jakarta four days ago on ships."

"Any idea where Farouk and those four containers went four days ago?" Brooke asked.

The deputy again looked at his boss.

Director Sinaga said, "My men are currently at the port looking at security films. You must understand our port is the busiest in our island nation with seventy-six berths and twenty terminals. In the past four days, we have had more than a hundred ships of all sizes pass through it."

Esther, who had not uttered a word earlier, said, "Director Sinaga, information that was forwarded to you identified the African billionaire Umoja Owiti as the individual responsible for transporting a nuclear bomb from North Korea into your county. Have your men zeroed in on the cargo ships he and his companies own that have been entering or leaving your port in the past four days?"

Sinaga looked to his deputy to reply. But the deputy had lowered his eyes and was staring at the table, a clear indication that no one at the BIN had thought of the Umoja Owiti connection.

Esther said, "I'd like to be taken to the port to examine the records and also study the security tapes. The *Sea Voyager* sailed under a Liberian flag. I have a list of Owiti's companies and shell firms that he used."

Sinaga said, "That would be most helpful in identifying where Farouk and the containers have gone."

Khalid spoke next. "While my colleague is at the port, I'd like to travel to Bandung to examine where the body was found. Hakim Farouk was working on something in the warehouse there."

The deputy looked at his boss, Sinaga, who nodded his approval.

"I'll go to Bandung with you," Brooke volunteered.

"Very well, then," Sinaga declared, standing to leave. Speaking to his deputy, he said, "I will trust you to make the appropriate accommodations and report back to me later today."

"Mr. Director," Brooke said, stopping him, "if I may, I have a question. How long does it generally take for a cargo ship to sail from Jakarta to the United States' West Coast?"

Sinaga nodded at his deputy for an answer. "Between twenty to forty days, depending on how many stops it makes first," the deputy announced. "I check it myself."

Sinaga waved his hand toward an aide, who walked to where Brooke, Esther, and Khalid were seated and handed each of them a cell phone.

"These phones are for your use on our island," Sinaga explained. "Service is spotty in Bandung and oftentimes it is difficult to place a call through cell phones with service from other countries, so if you need our assistance, we will place those calls for you."

Yes, Brooke thought, *and having each of us carry a cell phone will enable the BIN to keep track of where we are at all times and also monitor any calls we make.*

Two vehicles were waiting outside. The deputy said he would escort Brooke and Khalid in the BMW X5 to Bandung while a smaller Mercedes and the deputy's assistant would drive Esther to the docks.

"Excuse me, your men haven't brought me my checked bag," Brooke said. She wanted her Beretta from it.

"They already take to hotel. You get it later there. Opposite direction from where we go. Now we go."

Brooke was not happy, but she didn't want to delay anyone.

When the SUV that she and Khalid were riding in reached the city limits, the driver switched on the flashing blue and white lights positioned in the BMW's front grill, a move that would keep them from being stopped by police officers seeking bribes en route to Bandung. But, Brooke discovered, the lights seemed to mean nothing to the other vehicles on the roadway. No one moved out of their path. More than two hours later, they arrived at the warehouse.

The deputy BIN director walked inside, but Khalid touched Brooke's arm, stopping her. Removing his watch, he aimed its stem through the open warehouse door and scanned the room.

"Some sort of secret spy gadget?" she asked.

"Checking for radiation."

"I didn't know you had any expertise in this area."

"You don't send someone who doesn't know how to build a clock to repair one, do you?"

He checked his watch dial. "There is no radioactive residue showing. It's safe for us to go inside."

Brooke entered the warehouse's main room and immediately gagged. Even though the corpse had been removed, the overpowering odor lingered.

The stench didn't appear to bother Khalid, who went directly into the warehouse office where Hakim Farouk had left several cardboard boxes filled with an assortment of wires, tools, and electrical and electronic bits and pieces. After methodically searching through the boxes, he noticed a light brown sliver of something on the dirty concrete floor. Bending down, he inspected it closely.

"Find any clues?" Brooke asked, joining him. She had been checking the main room while intermittently going outside to catch her breath.

"Yes, several, including this," he answered, holding up the sliver of material that he'd picked up from the floor.

Brooke recognized it. "C-4 plastic explosive."

"From the discarded wiring and supplies, I'm fairly certain he was building some sort of sophisticated detonators using C-4."

"Let's step back for a minute," Brooke said. "Farouk came to this warehouse with a single nuclear bomb and he left with four smaller boxes on the back of the truck. Is it possible he took that bomb apart?"

"Unlikely. Why would he? Besides, there is no radioactive residue here indicating he did anything with any toxic radiological chemicals. I think he built three detonators and just kept the nuke as it is."

"How do you know he built detonators? He could have built three bombs using just C-4?"

"Yes, but the Falcon said he would destroy three cities," Khalid replied. "The three containers that we saw on that truck in the security video couldn't have held enough C-4 to destroy a city. Plus, he mentioned a 'nuclear sword,' which would imply that some sort of radioactive matter is involved."

Brooke and Khalid had become so focused on their detective work that neither seemed to notice the oppressive heat and the flies buzzing around them. Neither spoke for several moments as they processed what they had learned.

"What is a detonator for?" Brooke asked rhetorically, breaking the silence. "We know he went to the docks with four boxes on his truck. We know he is used to improvising, using what supplies are available to him. What if he put each of those three C-4 detonators onto three ships that were *already* transporting bags of ammonium nitrate fertilizer? Would that set off an explosion large enough to do considerable damage to a city?"

"If the ship was carrying large amounts of fertilizer or other explosives, the C-4 would spark an explosive reaction turning the ship's cargo into a huge bomb," Khalid said. "But the Falcon said he would *destroy* three cities with a 'nuclear sword.' Not simply set off bombs in them."

"There's the answer," Brooke said. "He has placed the detonators on ships loaded both with explosives and some form of radioactive matter. Oh my God! That's how he's creating his 'nuclear sword.' That's how he's creating three dirty bombs."

"A radioactive sword," Khalid said, correcting her. "Not a nuclear one but deadly just the same. In theory, he would turn three ships into dirty bombs. The detonators would spark a chain reaction explosion that would blow radioactive particles into the air where they could be spread for miles."

They now were thinking the same thoughts.

"That would qualify for destroying an entire city," Brooke said.

"Three cities means Farouk would have to place his detonators on three different ships."

"Three detonators, three ships, aimed at three American seaports with both explosives in their cargos and radioactive materials," Brooke said. "That's got to be it. If we can identify which ships heading to the United States are carrying both explosives and radioactives, then we'll know where his dirty bombs are located."

"What about his nuclear bomb?" Khalid asked. "He left the warehouse with four boxes. That bomb has to be in one of them."

"You're correct. The Falcon actually is going to attack four cities—three with dirty bombs and then a nuclear explosion in a fourth that would kill millions."

"Which means we might be looking for a fourth mystery ship," Khalid said. "How will we find it?"

Before Brooke could react, the Indonesian deputy director rushed into the warehouse. "We go now!" he exclaimed in a clearly panicked voice.

"Why? What's happening?" Brooke asked. "Is it Farouk? Have you found him?"

"No, riots in streets. Not safe!"

They rushed behind him outside and into the waiting BMW. As they were driving away from the warehouse, the cell phone that Brooke had been given began ringing. It was Sinaga.

"Major Grant, you must return immediately to Jakarta and go directly to the airport. I cannot guarantee your personal safety now that your face is all over the news and social media."

CHAPTER FORTY-TWO

Dubai Hospital
Al Khaleej Street, Dubai

Ebio Kattan insisted that doctors in the emergency room leave her alone once they attached the various monitors and an IV. She refused to allow them to immediately treat the painful burns on her feet.

"Are you ready to go live?" she asked her producer while a nurse propped a pillow at the end of the hospital bed for Kattan to lean back on.

The satellite truck parked outside forwarded the images of Kattan to Al Arabic headquarters, where they were matched on a split screen with Al Arabic's most popular anchor, Azim Basher. Regularly scheduled programs were put on hold as the network began its live broadcast from the hospital.

Kattan had never appeared on television without a hijab and light makeup and Basher was visibly surprised when he saw her disheveled appearance and pained expression.

"We are so grateful you are safe and back with us since you disappeared on the same night that you broadcast an exclusive interview on our network with the Falcon," Basher announced. "Where have you been?"

"I was kidnapped by five men while walking to my car in the Al Arabic parking lot here in Dubai," she said in rushed breaths meant to highlight how much pain she was in. The camera slowly pulled back from a tight shot of her face so viewers could see her from the waist up and recognize that she was in a hospital bed.

"They restrained me, covered my face with a hood, and forced me into a van. When we got to a building, I was taken into a dark room and made to strip naked. When I refused, they tore my clothing." Tears began forming in her eyes.

During the next several minutes, Kattan accurately described how she had endured flashing strobe lights, loud sounds, temperatures that switched between hot and cold, and being doused with buckets of cold water.

"I had never been so humiliated or treated so harshly."

"These were men torturing you?" Basher asked.

"No, the men waited outside. It was two women who were interrogating me. They kept demanding I tell them how I had contacted the Falcon for my interview. I explained that I couldn't tell them because I am a journalist. That made them even angrier. I lost track of time. I thought I was going mad. Finally, I told them that I couldn't help them because I was wearing a hood when I was taken to meet with the Falcon. I didn't know where I was taken. I begged them to stop. To release me."

"Surely after you explained this to them, they let you go and stopped this torture," Basher said.

"No," she replied, her voice beginning to tremble. "They accused me of lying. They threatened to have men sexually abuse me if I did not cooperate. But what could I tell them? I knew nothing."

Kattan began to cry. From off camera, her producer handed her a tissue, which she used to wipe her eyes.

"These two women torturing you," Basher said, "they understood that you are an award-winning and highly respected television correspondent for the largest network in the Arab world and yet they threatened you with sexual abuse?"

Mustering her courage, Kattan nodded and said, "They were torturing me because I was a known figure. They said I was using my celebrity status to support the Falcon and his followers by interviewing him. They said I was promoting terrorism against the West. I pleaded with them to understand that as a journalist, I was simply doing my job in reporting what he said, but they slapped me and said

I was his mouthpiece and I deserved to be abused." Once again, she paused to wipe her eyes and sniffle. She grimaced in pain. "This is when they said they were going to punish me."

"Punish you?" Basher asked. "That was their words?"

"Yes, because I had dared to talk to the Falcon. They only wanted the West's side presented on the news so they were going to punish me for interviewing him and allowing him to deliver his threats."

"But the West, especially the United States, should be grateful to you for broadcasting the Falcon's threats because you warned them he is planning to destroy three American cities. It's been widely reported that he has at least one nuclear bomb. Without you, the West would not have known this."

"They had no logic to what they were doing. Only hatred."

"What happened next?"

"The two women brought four men into the room where I was being held against my will, completely naked. I was terrified these men would assault and disgrace me." She stopped, unable for a moment to continue because she was so distraught with emotion.

"Take your time," Basher said.

"Each man grabbed one of my limbs. One seized my right arm. One my left arm. One held my right ankle and one held my left ankle. I could not move. I was trembling in fear and completely helpless and vulnerable."

The cameraman slowly pulled back the camera, exposing more of Kattan under the covers in her hospital bed as she continued describing her torture.

"I became delirious and started screaming but they refused to show me mercy. One of the women showed me a curling iron. She pressed it against the bottom of my right foot. I screamed in agony and she laughed at me. They all did and then the other woman began to laugh and encouraged her by saying, 'Do both feet. Teach her what happens to collaborators who help terrorists. She's just another radical Islamist terrorist. All these Muslims are terrorists.'"

"This woman accused all Muslims of being terrorists?"

"Yes, even though I was screaming, I heard exactly what she said."

"And did she burn your other foot?" Basher asked.

At that moment, the cameraman lowered the lens, revealing both of Kattan's badly burned bare feet. Her smooth tan skin was blood-red where the iron had touched and there were black spots of dead skin clearly visible. The image was disgusting to watch, yet capti-vating as the cameraman kept the burn marks in focus for several moments before he finally returned for a close up of Kattan's an-guished face.

Her riveting account was a mixture of truth and fabrication that she had rehearsed so many times that no one watching would have possi-bly doubted her story.

"All I wanted to do was my job as a journalist and because of that, I was tortured, threatened with assault, and punished by having my feet burned."

"Are you afraid of these people?" Basher asked her.

"Wouldn't you be? I am terrified but I believe the only way to pre-vent them from kidnapping me again is to expose them. I believe those of us in the Muslim world must have the courage to speak out when we are physically assaulted."

"You are a true hero, Ebio," Basher said. "You are brave, a great journalist and a fighter. Now let me ask you, these two women, what can you tell us about them?"

"One was muscular and clearly a soldier of some sort. I had never seen her, but she was wearing a tiny gold necklace and when she bent down to torture me, I saw a Star of David attached to it."

"She was Jewish, then? Most likely a Mossad agent," Basher said, leading her on.

"Yes, yes, I believe she was," Kattan said. Her face was now covered with perspiration. The monitor attached to her showed her blood pres-sure rising. Off camera, the voice of an emergency room doctor could be heard arguing with the Al Arabic producer, telling him that he needed to end the telecast and let Kattan be treated.

"And the other woman who tortured you?" Basher asked in a rushed voice.

"Yes," said Kattan, "I recognized her. I knew her. I was shocked she would treat me with such hatred." Her voice was coming out in puffs now between clenched teeth because of the pain.

"What is her name?" Basher said. "Please tell us, who was this friend who betrayed your trust and tortured you?"

"Major Brooke Grant," Kattan said. "She was the woman who said all Muslims are terrorists. She is the one who laughed while burning my feet."

Kattan passed out. Her eyes closed. Her head slumped to the side. A doctor and nurse could be seen rushing to her bedside.

"Get these cameras out of here!" the doctor yelled.

The network's screen switched only to Basher's face. "We must let the doctors do their best to heal our dear and beloved colleague, Ebio Kattan." He was becoming emotional. His voice cracked. "Who will hold these two women who did this—this unidentified Mossad agent and Major Brooke Grant—accountable?" he asked.

At that moment, a photograph of Brooke Grant appeared on the screen. The caption read: "American torturer."

"Our station is filing a formal complaint with the U.S. government, demanding that Major Grant be punished," he declared.

In the hospital room, a doctor gave Kattan a strong sedative. Before she drifted off, her producer whispered in her ear that her interview had drawn the biggest audience in the network's history, surpassing even her exclusive one with the Falcon.

Ebio Kattan was convinced that her earlier stories had made Brooke Grant a superhero. This one would destroy her.

Twelve minutes after Kattan's live broadcast, a woman who identified herself on Facebook as Carolyn Newcomer posted a message about how an elderly Muslim man had been brought by the police into a Maryland suburban hospital emergency room outside Baltimore where she worked as a nurse.

"His face was a bloody mess of broken bones and missing teeth. I was amazed he was alive," she wrote. "They said he had been in a car accident, but I didn't believe them based on his wounds. Working in the ER, I've seen lots of car accident injuries and I've also seen lots of bar fight injuries. This man had been beaten. It was clear they didn't want anyone to be left alone with this patient. However, when the doctor took them out of the room to speak privately to them, this poor man grabbed my hand and said in a low voice: 'Don't let them kill me!' The name on his chart was Bob Smith but I knew it wasn't his actual name because he was an older Arab gentleman and I had seen him on television. He whispered and I couldn't hear him so I lowered my head and he said, 'I'm Mohammad Al-Kader. They beat me. They're going to kill me.' I didn't know what to do so I said, 'You'll be fine. This is America.' Then he said, 'I'm innocent. They're going to make me confess.' I didn't know what to think and the police were about to come back in and I was getting afraid and that's when I noticed tears in this old man's eyes and he said something really strange. He told me these men had urinated and defecated on his core-ran."

Carolyn Newcomer's Facebook post was instantaneously posted on an Internet site identified as the International Muslim Post News, which corrected her spelling of the "core-ran" to Quran. The website published stories in both English and Arabic and it added a photo of the Imam Mohammad Al-Kader under the headline: JAILED MUSLIM CLERIC BEATEN, NEAR DEATH—HOLY QURAN DESECRATED. As part of the article, the news site reposted the cell phone video of Al-Kader being forcibly taken from his study in the Great Mosque of Allah in Maryland by men dressed in all black wielding plastic shields, batons, and other riot gear.

Within an hour, that site's news account had amassed more than 10 million views and thousands of shares as it spread at bulletlike speed across social media in the Arab world. News about Al-Kader's beating and the desecration of the Holy Quran was paired with Ebio Kattan's disturbing account of how Major Brooke Grant had burned the newscaster's feet with a curling iron and called all Muslims terrorists.

But it was the desecration of the Holy Quran that most outraged the Muslim world.

CHAPTER FORTY-THREE

Situation Room
The White House

President Wyatt Bowie Austin's eyes darted between the six flat-panel display televisions inside the briefing room of the Situation Room in the White House's West Wing. Each screen showed demonstrations sparked by the Facebook post describing the beating of Imam Mohammad Al-Kader, desecration of the Holy Quran, and burning of Correspondent Ebio Kattan's feet.

In Kuala Lumpur, Malaysia, thousands gathered on the streets shouting, "Go to hell, America!" as they burned U.S. and Israeli flags outside the U.S. embassy. On another monitor, some five thousand marchers in Dhaka, Bangladesh, spat on, kicked, and burned an image of President Austin dressed in a cowboy hat and his trademark boots. In the Lebanese capital of Beirut, a protester declared, "We will cut off the feet that desecrated the Quran!" In the Sudan, thousands gathered outside the American embassy in Khartoum, where they used shoes and slippers to beat two straw dolls representing Austin and Brooke Grant. The situation in Islamabad was more violent. Some six thousand Pakistanis were throwing stones and battling local riot police. But the images that most concerned the president and his assembled national security team were on the monitor relaying live footage from Jakarta where Indonesian police were holding back a mob threatening to climb or topple the ten-foot-tall iron fencing that encircled the U.S. embassy grounds.

"The Indonesian president is sending troops to reinforce the police," President Austin's national security advisor Stephen Jacobs announced.

"The Marine guards are destroying documents and moving the ambassador into an embassy safe room in case the perimeter is breached. The Indonesian president has promised us that his troops will protect our people."

"Based on what we are watching, it sure doesn't look that way," President Austin replied.

"As you know, Mr. President, security is the responsibility of the host government," Jacobs explained. "If there's going to be an escalation in violence, we'll have to depend on the locals to handle it. We can't have the embassy Marine guard firing into an angry mob. It would be disastrous."

"You got an evacuation plan?" Austin asked.

"Our closest base is in Darwin, an Australian port city. We have some three thousand Marines stationed there and I'm sending in a FAST team from Japan, but that's more than seven hours away," Jacobs replied, referring to a Fleet Antiterrorism Security Team composed of Marines specially trained to rescue Americans pinned in hostile environments. Our best chance is the USS *John Paul Jones*, a Wasp-class amphibious assault ship, doing maneuvers at sea and less than two hours from Jakarta. I've already diverted it to Indonesia."

"What's it capable of doing in a situation such as this?" Austin asked.

"Plenty. The ship has four V-22 Osprey tiltrotor aircraft, eight Sea Knight helicopters, and four Sea Stallion choppers for transport along with four Bell Iroquois utility helicopters," Jacobs replied. "Even though the Marines onboard are not part of a FAST team, they're Marines."

"Then they're fully capable of flying into Jakarta and getting our people out via rooftop if necessary," the president replied. "I want those aircraft in the sky as soon as they can take off."

"Yes, sir. We've had a prickly relationship with the Indonesian president and his military because of his country's history of human rights abuse but I don't think he or his generals will object."

"Remind him that this is a rescue mission," Director Grainger said, "not an invasion."

"Mr. President," Jacobs said, "there's some other steps we can take to ease world tensions. Our technical people have investigated the original Facebook post that reportedly describes Mohammad Al-Kader being taken to a hospital for treatment. There is no Carolyn Newcomer who works as an ER nurse and the International Muslim Post News is a fictional news site created to make the fake story seem legitimate."

CIA Director Grainger joined the conversation. "This fake news was written specifically to stir up Muslim protests and anti-American hatred."

"Who's behind it?"

"It appears the SAVAK."

"First the Iranians help the North Koreans design a nuclear bomb and now this," Austin snarled. "We made a mistake not teaching them a lesson when Jimmy Carter was running things and they took our people hostage in Tehran. I'm not going to allow that to happen here."

"Facebook has agreed to remove the fake Newcomer post," Jacobs reported, "and the *New York Times* and *Washington Post* are posting stories about us identifying the International Muslim Post News as a fake news site."

"Nobody in the Arab world will believe that," Austin retorted. "In their countries, their newspapers are nothing but shills for the government; besides, we got this Al Arabic correspondent telling the world that Major Brooke Grant tortured her with a curling iron."

"Major Grant was in the United States when Ebio Kattan was abducted," Director Grainger volunteered. "She was burying her aunt and uncle. Unfortunately, she's overseas right now so we can't put her on television, but we can release the funeral information to the media and prove that Ebio Kattan is clearly a liar. General Frank Grant's funeral was widely covered by the networks."

"That's an excellent idea," the president said. "There's got to be footage of Major Grant at her aunt's and uncle's funerals, proving she couldn't have been torturing this fake news correspondent."

National Security Director Jacobs entered the conversation by asking Director Grainger, "Do you believe the Mossad abducted and tortured that woman?"

Grainger knew the Mossad had nabbed Kattan because the Israeli intelligence service had done it at his request as part of the KTB team's investigation. He didn't want to admit that, so he did what skilled lawyers always do when dodging a question. He answered with one of his own. "If this reporter isn't telling the truth about Major Grant, why should we trust her claims about the Mossad?"

"Let's focus on the immediate," President Austin said. "What would happen if we put Al-Kader on national television as proof nobody beat him?"

"That's an idea well worth pursuing," Grainger replied with enthusiasm. "Live footage would show he hasn't been tortured. The only risk is we don't know what Al-Kader will say. He might claim we are forcing him to talk."

"What we need is independent collaboration along with footage showing Al-Kader is healthy," said Jacobs. "Someone with credibility. What if we asked the Saudi ambassador? His eyewitness account would go a long way."

"A brilliant idea," President Austin replied. Turning to an aide, he said, "Call the jail and tell them to get Al-Kader ready for visitors and notify the ambassador. If necessary, I will speak to him in person." His assistant left the room.

"There's another security matter we need to resolve," Jacobs said, "and that's your personal security. The Falcon already has demonstrated that he can explode a bomb in Washington and kill a sitting president. We can't afford to have a repeat of that. I'd like to suggest that you move out of the White House to a more secure facility. We have several alternatives where your safety would be—"

"Not in your lifetime," President Austin said, cutting him short. "I'm not about to go stick my head in some hole and cower because this little Arab bug wants to crawl up my pant leg. What kind of message do you think that would send the American public—especially the folks here in Washington—if I were to go into hiding?"

"But, sir," Jacobs said. "If something did happen to you, that would be an even worse message. Washington has to be high on his target list and he has a nuclear bomb."

"I'm not running away. But it might be a good time for the new vice president to go on a mission to visit out NATO allies, to assure them that while we have lost President Allworth, we're still in operation and we're determined to track down and destroy our enemies."

His eyes returned to the screen showing the police trying to hold back protesters in Jakarta. Soldiers with rifles had started to arrive. He was about to make a comment when his aide, who he'd sent to call the jail, rejoined them and whispered in his ear.

"Are you joking?" the president demanded in an angry voice. "Tell everyone what you just told me."

"The Imam Al-Kader told jail officials he will not speak to anyone except for Representative Adeogo," the aide said.

"Since when does a prisoner decide who he'll meet with?" the president declared. "Tell those guards to pull his ass out of that cell."

"Sir," Director Grainger said, "that might be exactly what he wants. A scuffle so that he does end up with bruises."

"If we do what he asks," Jacobs added, "he might be more willing to help us."

The president thought for a moment. He didn't like the idea of meeting a demand by a radical Islamist, but what Grainger and Jacobs were saying made sense. "Okay, let's see if Representative Adeogo is willing to go see the Imam. But I still want the Saudi ambassador going up there, too, to put eyes on him. Meanwhile, I want the press secretary to squash this fake news about Major Grant burning this reporter's feet and most of all, I want helicopters flying into Jakarta to get our people out!"

His eyes returned to the monitor where the crowds around the U.S. embassy in Jakarta were swelling by the second. "I'm not going to have another Mogadishu and Benghazi fiasco—not on my watch."

CHAPTER FORTY-FOUR

Outskirts
Jakarta, Indonesia

Not safe driving to U.S. embassy," the deputy BIN director informed Brooke and Khalid as they entered the city's outer limits.

"We can drive to my embassy," Khalid volunteered. "Major Grant will be safe there. Or, perhaps, your BIN headquarters."

"No," the deputy said. "Her picture all over news. She tortured famous TV correspondent. Your embassy says she no come there either. Not safe at BIN. No one want her."

"I didn't torture anyone!" Brooke exclaimed.

"Woman on TV. She say you burnt her feet with curling iron. Other Americans desecrate Holy Quran. Not good for you to be here. Everyone angry."

"What reporter says I burned her?"

"Al Arabic. Very famous woman. No can go to embassy."

Brooke knew instantly that he was referring to Ebio Kattan. *But why would she lie?*

"Then drive us to the Port of Tanjung Priok where our colleague, Esther, is going through shipping manifests," Brooke said.

The deputy called Director Sinaga on his cell phone.

"Director Sinaga say too dangerous to drive in this car. People see you very bad. You got hijab?"

"No. And I don't have a scarf either."

"Director Sinaga, he tell me put you in taxi and send to port. No trouble. I tell driver take you long way. No problem."

"You're throwing us out?" Brooke said, stunned.

"We'll go together," Khalid said.

The deputy BIN director ordered the driver to pull over and hailed a taxi. After they slid into the cab's backseat, Khalid said, "I'm calling my embassy. I'm pretty sure we can get you inside there safely."

He dialed a number on the cell phone the BIN had given him but there was no connection.

"Phone's dead. The BIN is trying to distance itself from us," he warned.

The driver turned up the volume on an English-speaking radio station whose reporter was describing what was happening outside the U.S. embassy, where a crowd of more than a thousand protesters had gathered.

Brooke noticed the cabdriver glancing at her in the rearview mirror. She needed her Beretta and silently cursed at herself for not insisting earlier that the BIN deputy bring it to her.

As promised, the driver stayed clear of the center of the city where the demonstration was happening. Most of Jakarta's residents were staying inside their homes, afraid to go outside. It had been four hours since Ebio Kattan's hospital interview in Dubai had aired in Jakarta, followed by the fake stories about Al-Kader and the desecration of the Holy Quran, giving time for everyone on the island to have heard the news.

"Lookey, lookey," the cabdriver said, poking a finger up into the black sky as he drove. Brooke followed his finger to the blinking lights coming from a covey of Navy rescue helicopters inbound for the U.S. embassy. He turned up the radio just as the station's reporter was breathlessly describing how the helicopters were evacuating the embassy staff from its rooftop.

"The Jakarta police and soldiers are losing control," the reporter announced. "I see a protester burning an American flag." On the radio you could hear demonstrators gathered around the reporter yelling, "Death to America!"

"Someone has flipped over a car and set it on fire," the reporter warned. "It looks like the last U.S. helicopter is leaving."

As they continued listening, the reporter described how the police and soldiers had begun abandoning their posts because the embassy was vacated. Within minutes, the mob pushed so hard against the ten-foot fence that pieces of it were knocked to the ground. The crowd burst through, scrambling across the manicured lawn to the embassy, where they began pounding on the doors and windows. Someone got inside.

"I can see fires being started," the reporter said. "Someone on the roof of the embassy is waving the black jihadist flag." He was silent for a moment and then added, "Ladies and gentlemen, I've just been told by my producers that large groups are assembling at the Istiqlal Mosque to protect it after a report on social media that a U.S. warship is going to shell it. Fires have been started at both the Jakarta Cathedral and the Immanuel Church near the mosque. I've been told Muslims and Christians are both going there to protect these places of worship. Fistfights are being reported. Please, please stay in your homes. It is not safe on the streets."

Inside the cab, Brooke said, "This is insanity. The United States isn't going to shell a Muslim mosque."

Her comment caused the taxi driver to nervously glance at her in his rearview mirror. He knew from her speech that she was an American.

About a mile from the seaport's main entrance, the driver turned onto a one-lane street being blocked by about thirty men making their way toward the mosque. They were armed with baseball bats.

The driver beeped his horn and the group began to separate to allow him to pass but when the taxi slowed, one of the men spotted Brooke in the backseat wearing Western clothing and no hijab. He yelled to his friends that foreigners were in the cab. The taxi driver panicked and accelerated, forcing the men in front of him to leap sideways to avoid being hit. Already agitated, the men began chasing the cab, throwing rocks as they tried to overcome it. Scared he would be pulled out of his taxi and beaten, the driver stopped about two hundred yards from the port's entrance.

"Out!" he yelled, looking back at the men, some forty yards behind him.

"Let's go!" Khalid said, glancing over his shoulder as he pushed open the passenger door.

Brooke did the same and they began running side by side toward the gated port entrance.

By the time the mob chasing them reached the cab, its driver was yelling, "She's an American. The woman running."

His words saved himself from a beating as the men quickened their pace darting after Brooke and Khalid. Two of the men were much faster runners than the others and just before Khalid and Brooke reached the port's security booth, one of them leaped at Brooke. His arms wrapped around her waist and slid down her ankles, knocking her forward into the asphalt. She immediately twisted onto her back and began kicking, trying to free her legs, striking him in the face with her shoe heel. He released his hold and rolled sideways to avoid another blow to his head. But his partner was instantly on top of her, pinning down her right arm, driving his knee against her chest, knocking the wind out of her. She was trapped and he was raising his fist to slug her.

From the corner of her eye, Brooke saw Khalid come flying back to help her. He grabbed the man on top of her and with adrenaline-fueled strength, he lifted him by his throat with his left arm, clutching the man's windpipe, forcing him to open his mouth wide to gasp for air. In that split second, Khalid's right arm shot up from his side and he shoved the barrel of a small pistol into the man's mouth, pulling the trigger. A pop and the dead man dropped onto the street.

The other fast-footed attacker who had tackled Brooke rushed Khalid, who calmly raised his pistol and fired a round directly into the man's forehead, killing him too.

Khalid waved his small handgun in the air so the others dashing toward them could see he was armed. This caused them to stop fifteen feet away. The face of the second dead man was covered with blood, but the first attacker, who had been shot inside the mouth, looked as if he were merely sleeping. The small-caliber bullet had not penetrated the rear of the man's skull and with his mouth closed, there was no blood.

"Get to the security booth! Now!" Khalid ordered as Brooke lifted herself off the pavement and began running toward the guardhouse, where two uniformed port security guards were watching. Khalid calmly walked backward with his eyes and his gun aimed at the mob.

As soon as Khalid entered the glass-fronted guardhouse, he tucked his pistol into his pocket. By then, Brooke had explained that the BIN had sent them to find Esther, who'd arrived hours earlier. The nervous guards immediately opened an iron gate adjacent to the booth, allowing Khalid and Brooke to enter the port compound, which was surrounded by a tall chain-link fence.

The men who had chased them gathered around their fallen friends. "They killed both of them!" one declared. Mistakenly assuming that Khalid was from the United States, he yelled, "Kill the Americans!"

His cry reenergized the crowd as it burst forward to the gatehouse where the two port authority guards were waiting. Both decided it was safer to open the iron entry gate rather than get embroiled in a melee.

Brooke and Khalid found Esther exiting the harbor master's main building about three hundred yards from the port entrance.

"I have the records," she told them.

Glancing back, Khalid could see the men coming after them.

"I've been trying to call you," Esther said, "but these BIN phones stopped working."

"The U.S. embassy has been evacuated. It's on fire," Brooke said. "You don't have an embassy here, do you?"

"No, Indonesia isn't too fond of Jews," Esther replied. "But I heard the radio reports and managed to use a landline inside to call for help. A U.S. Navy ship is sending a rescue boat to Pier Sixteen for us."

"We need to hurry," Khalid said nervously, nodding in the direction of the approaching men.

"This way," Esther hollered as she sprinted about fifty yards before turning to her right onto Pier Sixteen, which stuck like a long index finger from the shoreline into the ocean. They bolted down the pier until they reached its end.

"Now what?" Brooke asked. "We're cornered."

Khalid drew his pistol and fired, striking one of the threatening men in his leg, causing him to fall forward onto his hands. The .22-caliber pistol that Khalid was firing barely made a sound but the man's screams caused those around him to slow their pace.

A blinding spotlight suddenly illuminated the pier, causing the pursuing men to shield their eyes as they glanced upward at an approaching Seahawk helicopter. Searching the ocean behind them, Brooke spotted a Naval Special Warfare Rigid Inflatable Boat racing toward them. The spotlight caused their pursuers to stop about twenty yards from them, but now they began moving forward slowly with their baseball bats raised and ready to strike.

The Marines on the helicopter were under orders not to fire at any civilians on the ground unless first fired upon. Roping down from the pier would only endanger more lives. Brooke, Khalid, and Esther had only one option.

"Jump!" Esther screamed as she leaped from the pier. She dropped a good thirty feet before her feet hit the choppy seawater.

"Go!" Khalid called to Brooke.

Crossing her arms over her chest, Brooke stepped from the edge, falling faster than she had imagined, striking the seawater and immediately sinking below its waves. Feeling a sense of panic, she began frantically swimming upward. She reached the surface, gulping for air just as Khalid splashed into the sea near her. She treaded water and looked upward at the dock. She could hear the sound of flash bang grenades fired from the helicopter onto the pier to confuse and disorient the attackers. Next came canisters of tear gas turning the spotlighted pier gray with fog.

The men on the pier coughed, spit, and began running back toward the city.

As she bobbed in the water, Brooke felt a hand grab her. A Marine from the rescue craft grabbed her shoulder. He'd leaped into the water to help guide her safely to the boat.

Within moments, the seacraft was racing back to the USS *John Paul Jones*. Brooke stared at Jakarta behind them. She could see licks of light reflected off the glass skyscrapers, a testament to the burning

U.S. embassy. A second set of flames could be seen where the Jakarta Cathedral and Immanuel Church were on fire next to the Istiqlal Mosque.

"We're lucky we escaped," Khalid said.

"I didn't know you were carrying a pistol," Brooke replied. "How did you get it onboard our commercial flight?"

"There are ways," he said. "My little popgun is not very loud and has little stopping power but at a close distance it's deadly enough."

"Shooting someone in the mouth is about as close as you can get," she replied.

"Even a tiny slug fired up into the brain is fatal, but a louder gun would have been more effective at keeping those men back."

Brooke had seen the damage before that a .22 short round could inflict when fired at an upward angle into the roof of a mouth. That is exactly how the Washington lobbyist Mary Margaret Delaney had "committed suicide."

CHAPTER FORTY-FIVE

"I wasn't certain you would come," Imam Mohammad Al-Kader said in a calm voice as he sat chained to the steel table where they previously had met.

"President Austin personally asked me; otherwise I wouldn't," Representative Rudy Adeogo replied. "As surely you know, the president wants the Saudi ambassador to speak to you personally about your treatment in jail."

Al-Kader smiled. "Ah, yes, I had to sign a release form saying I would agree to accept both of you as visitors. Rather incredible, isn't it? A prisoner accused of sedition and attempting to overthrow the U.S. government still has the right to refuse visitors when he is in a jail."

"You are an American citizen even if you don't act like one."

"I became a U.S. citizen out of practicality, but I have never believed in your country's corrupt principles nor in your so-called democracy. I am an Arab in my heart and you are a fool if you believe you can change our ways."

"And why is that?" Adeogo asked.

"Because the Arab world has a long established history of family, tribe, and religious sects that overshadow any wish for democratic unification. We don't want and, more importantly, we don't need your American democracy."

"I don't agree. I believe every person wishes to live free, wishes to better himself and his family, wishes to live in peace with his neighbors and wishes the best for his fellow man. These are the principles that have made America great."

"Nonsense," Al-Kader replied. "Remember where you are sitting and who you are talking to—a man in chains whose crime is speaking the truth."

"You are in chains because you conspired to overthrow the United States."

"I am in chains because your people do not want to obey the truth."

"And what truth is that?" Adeogo asked. He didn't want to be drawn into a political debate, but he couldn't help himself as he sat across from the self-pious Imam.

"You talk about American values and democracy," Al-Kader said. "But your form of democracy only works if people have respect for the law and in the Arab world, people do not trust in the rule of law. There are no judges who cannot be bribed, no police who cannot be paid for a few dollars to look the other way. This is why your attempts to establish a democracy in the Arab world will never succeed."

Adeogo had expected a less coherent rant. Curious, he asked, "Then what will work?"

"There are two choices and only two. A strongman can establish peace and stability in the Middle East. Look at Egypt under Mubarak, Libya under Gaddafi, and Iraq under Saddam."

"They were oppressors."

"Yes, but so are the leaders in Saudi Arabia and the other Arab nations that are your allies. There is only one way to end the rule of strongmen," the Imam explained. "And that is Sharia law. It is our best hope for uniting all Arabs and ultimately for achieving freedom from tyranny, because it is based on the will of Allah, not man."

"I agree that respect for the law is essential to preventing oppression," Adeogo said thoughtfully. "But I believe in the people's right to draft their own laws. I do not believe in forcing anyone to accept a single faith, especially your narrow interpretation of Islam. I believe there is goodness in every person and that democracy, true democracy, is the bedrock of freedom."

Although his hands were cuffed, Al-Kader managed to clap them, mocking the congressman. "By their nature, men are evil," he said. "Goodness does not triumph over evil. If it did there would be no need for laws, for leaders, not even for Allah."

Quickening his speech to prevent Adeogo from interrupting him, Al-Kader continued: "The United States is trying to re-create itself in the Middle East. It is attempting to force its values and principles onto the rest of the world. But what is the United States? It is a country less than three hundred years old. The great Roman Empire lasted fifteen hundred years. Do you know the two things that destroyed it? It became a republic with a form of democracy, rather than being run by Caesar, a strongman who controlled with military might. The second cause for its demise was Christianity. Yes, a religion that challenged the existing beliefs—a religion that people respected more than a dictator or the rule of Roman law. This is the power of religion. And ours is the only true religion."

"I don't accept your explanation of why Rome fell anymore than I accept your claim that democracies can't exist in the Middle East or your beliefs that different religions cannot co-exist. While the United States is less than three hundred years old, it is the refinement of man's thinking over centuries. It is an example of what generations have strived to achieve."

Al-Kader shook his head, indicating disgust. "Do you not realize there soon will be more followers of Allah on this planet than any other religion? You cannot stop what Allah wishes and what Allah wishes is blind obedience to Sharia law."

Adeogo had heard enough from the Imam. It was time for the congressman to get to the reason for their meeting. "You claim to be a religious man," he said. "A man who preaches great truths, so let's now discover if you really do respect and tell the truth. The Saudi ambassador is waiting outside. Tell him the truth about how you have been treated by this country that you so belittle."

"I have no intention of actually talking to anyone but you," Al-Kader declared. "He may come into this jail but I will not utter one word to him."

"Not even to stop the violence happening in Muslim countries? Happening in the Arab world?"

"Why would I want to help stop demonstrations against a nation punishing me for speaking the truth inside my mosque? Let them burn every American embassy."

"You care nothing for the truth; otherwise you would show the world that you have not been mistreated, you have not been beaten and the Holy Quran was not desecrated in front of you, because you were never given a copy of it," Adeogo said, rising from the table. "I do not consider you a religious man. You care nothing that innocent people are being hurt and dying because of false rumors and lies."

Al-Kader shrugged. The scolding he'd just received hadn't changed any of his thinking nor touched his heart. Just the same, he said, "Sit down, Congressman. I summoned you because I require you to deliver a message to the president for me. A message that I can entrust only to you."

"Me?" Adeogo replied, still standing. "You spit in my face. You and I are not friends and I have no interest in helping the Imam who radicalized my youngest brother."

"I understand but you are still the only man whom I can trust."

"You trust me, a man who has every reason to despise you?"

"I trust you to deliver the president a message."

"Tell it to the Saudi ambassador."

"He is a politician who answers to the royal family. He is like a stick floating on the ocean, bobbing up and down, going this way and that, depending upon the desires of his masters. He acts as if he is a friend to the Christians and to the Jews instead of revealing his true feelings. I spit in your face. He spits in the faces of all Americans behind their backs and laughs at their naiveté. You are a Muslim who truly believes everyone is good and must coexist. You do not wear a mask in this human pageant. It must be you who speaks directly to the president about my offer. Not the Saudi ambassador."

"What do you possibly have to offer the president?"

"I will tell him where the Falcon is hiding."

A look of disbelief crossed Adeogo's face. "You are willing to tell the president of the United States where the Falcon is hiding in return for . . . what exactly?"

"My release from this prison. I will also surrender my American citizenship and all of the rights that come with it. I will gladly leave this nation never to return, and, most important of all, I want a written promise from President Austin that he will not order his people to kill me."

"Anything else?" Adeogo asked sarcastically.

"Yes. The government has a twenty-five-million-dollar reward on the Falcon's head. I will expect it."

Adeogo laughed. "You want the president of the United States to set you free, pay you twenty-five million in blood money, and relocate you to some foreign land where you can spend the rest of your life continuing to spew hatred? Are you not on the same side as the Falcon? Do you not share his radical beliefs? Why would you want to help us?"

"My reasons are none of your concern, nor should they be of the president's."

"You are serious, aren't you?" Adeogo asked, still puzzled.

"Will you deliver my offer to him?" the Imam repeated.

Adeogo glanced at the older man chained to the table and tried, without success, to guess the game he was playing. "Yes, I will take your offer to the president but I want a sign of good faith. Not for the president but for me personally. If you want me to be your messenger, then you must speak to the delegation that is waiting. No, wait, I want more than that from you. I will ask the jail director here to allow them to use their camera phones to stream video of you publicly stating that you were never harmed, never tortured, and the Holy Quran was not desecrated. If you do that, I will play the negotiator between you and the Oval Office."

"Then invite the ambassador inside. I will tell him exactly what you demand and in return, I will expect you to tell President Austin that I am willing to present him with the Falcon's head."

CHAPTER FORTY-SIX

Aboard the USS John Paul Jones
Off the Indonesian coast

Inside the hull of the Wasp-class amphibious assault ship, Brooke, Khalid, and the ship's commander, Captain Douglas Torrey, gathered around a computer screen where Esther was pulling data from a flash drive. It contained the names of cargo ships leaving the Port of Tanjung Priok on the day Hakim Farouk and his wooden boxes disappeared.

"None of the boxes Farouk brought to the Jakarta port was very big, so I assume they would be packed into larger metal shipping containers on the docks at some point," Esther said. "Captain Torrey, can you tell me the actual size of a standard shipping container that gets loaded on a cargo ship?"

"Containers originally were twenty feet long, eight feet tall, and eight feet wide," Captain Torrey answered. "The acronym for them is TEU, which stands for 'twenty-foot equivalent units.' But as ships became larger, so did TEUs. Today most TEUs are forty feet long, or twice the size of original units."

"Thinking like a terrorist, it seems to me Hakim Farouk has two options," Khalid said. "He can place his detonators into TEUs and locate them near other containers carrying explosives and radioactive materials, turning the entire ship into a giant dirty bomb. Or he could slip one of his detonators into a forty-foot-long standard TEU and pack it with explosives and boxes of radioactive materials—making that single TEU a dirty bomb."

"To create a single dirty bomb inside a TEU," Captain Torrey said, "he'd have to have help from workers in Jakarta who were packing each TEU with cargo for transport."

"That wouldn't have been too difficult," Esther replied. "A few thousand dollars in bribes would get inspectors to look the other way and a few hundred dollars would get dockworkers to pack a TEU with both explosives and radioactive materials."

"If Farouk did the latter," Brooke said, following Khalid's logic, "a single TEU could arrive at a U.S. seaport, be unloaded from a cargo ship, and put on a rail car or attached to a semitrailer. It could be transported anywhere inside the country. A semitruck could drive it directly into Manhattan or Denver or some other major city."

"If I were a terrorist, I would detonate a dirty bomb while it's still on a cargo ship," Captain Torrey interjected. "You could combine it with other explosives on the ship, causing much more damage."

"Wouldn't being stored deep inside a ship's cargo hold restrict most of the blast and prevent radioactive matter from escaping and causing harm?" Brooke asked.

"Modern-day container ships are designed to carry their TEUs stacked high on their decks, not down below them," the captain explained. "I'm guessing the top deck is where Hakim Farouk would place his dirty bombs."

"Stacking them high on the deck would help spread contaminants into the air," Esther agreed.

"How many TEUs can one of these container ships carry?" Brooke asked.

"It depends on the size of the ship," Captain Torrey replied. "The small 'feeder' ships carry about a thousand TEUs while the largest can carry more than nineteen thousand TEUs."

"Nineteen thousand?" Brooke said, clearly surprised by that high number. "Okay, tell me how many tons of goods can each one of those nineteen thousand TEU containers hold?"

"A twenty-foot container can be filled with about thirty tons," the captain answered. "Also, for stabilization at sea, TEUs often are not individually strapped down on a deck but are bundled together and strapped down as one bigger unit."

"Which is exactly what Hakim Farouk would want—one of his C-4 detonators hidden inside a container that was strapped together with other TEUs carrying explosives and radioactive materials," Khalid replied.

"That could create a huge bomb," Brooke said in a fearful voice.

"Here's a comparison for you," Captain Torrey volunteered. "The so-called Mother of All Bombs is considered the largest non-nuclear bomb the United States has in its arsenal. It has a blast yield of about *eleven tons* of TNT."

No one spoke for a moment as each considered how destructive a blast could be on a ship that was carrying thirty tons of explosives in dozens or even hundreds of TEUs, plus radioactive materials.

Focusing on her computer, Esther said, "There were twenty-two ships either directly owned or under the control of companies with a connection to Umoja Owiti that left the Tanjung Priok port during the time period when Farouk would have delivered his boxes. Cargo manifests show that ten of them were traveling to the United States and all of them are transporting explosives in the form of ammonium nitrate emulsion chemical products. Mostly fertilizer."

"We know Farouk built three C-4 detonators. That means he's loaded them on three of the ten vessels traveling to America," Khalid said.

"How about radioactive materials?" Brooke asked. "Does that narrow it down? Are there records showing which of the ten ships are carrying radioactive matter?"

"We can't tell from the manifests. I did an extensive computer match at the harbormaster's office and discovered an Owiti-owned company has been bringing cesium-137 into Jakarta over several months, supposedly for delivery to a manufacturer of medical devices. I suspect it's a dummy firm. But there are no manifests that show cesium-137 ever leaving Indonesia on any cargo ships. Obviously, someone helped Farouk get the cesium-137 onto the three ships that we need to find."

"So much for Indonesia carefully monitoring radioactive materials," Brooke noted dryly. "What ports are the ten ships sailing to?"

"Six are destined for the West Coast and the other four are traveling through the Panama Canal into the Gulf, where they are heading to Houston, New Orleans, Norfolk, and New York," Esther replied. "The six sailing to the West Coast are scheduled to arrive at Los Angeles, Long Beach, Oakland, Seattle, and Tacoma."

"That's only five West Coast destinations."

"Two are going the same place—Los Angeles."

"What about the nuclear bomb?" Brooke asked. "Did you find anything suspicious in the port records that might help us identify which ship it is on?"

"Nothing useful. But let's think this through," Esther said. "There's no evidence Farouk left the Jakarta port, which would imply he and the fourth box from his truck—the one containing the nuclear bomb—boarded a ship coming to America. I believe he's traveling on the same vessel that's transporting the nuclear bomb. At this stage of the game, he wouldn't want to risk letting it out of his sight."

"Hitching a ride on a cargo ship is popular for someone without much cash because it's cheaper than a cruise line," Captain Torrey said. "There are no casinos, swimming pools, or nightclubs."

"We might be able to determine where the nuclear bomb is by looking at those passenger lists," Esther said. "If we find him, we'll find the nuclear bomb."

"How many passengers are on the ten ships heading to the United States?" Khalid asked.

"A total of twenty-six—all males. At least eighteen of them had Muslim-sounding names."

"You're profiling," Khalid replied, smirking.

"Can I assume you've already checked Farouk's aliases?" Brooke asked.

"I did and there weren't any on the passenger lists. Clearly, he's using a completely new name and traveling under a new passport."

"Farouk is a loner," Brooke replied. "Did you find any passengers traveling alone?"

"That's a good observation," Esther said. "But, no, all of the passengers were traveling with at least one other person."

"I need to tell Washington about the ten ships," Brooke said. "The Navy will need to intercept them before they can get anywhere close to our shorelines."

"I'll arrange a secure line for you," Captain Torrey said. "Meanwhile, I'll have two officers escort Esther and Khalid to the officer's mess." Addressing them, he added, "I'm sure you'll understand we can't have foreign intelligence officers on our ship unescorted."

Khalid and Esther left with two crew members, while Captain Torrey led Brooke toward a secure communication area. As they were walking, Brooke summarized, "We have ten ships somewhere in the Pacific and we know three of them are carrying dirty bombs. We know the nuclear bomb is also on a ship. How easy will it be to find four ships? The Pacific is a big, big ocean."

"Locating Owiti's ships will not be as difficult as you might imagine, even if they deviate from international shipping lanes and try to sneak close to our coasts. After World War Two, our government created a string of underwater listening posts around the world to track Soviet submarines. The system was called SOSUS, an acronym for 'sound surveillance system' and some of those listening devices were so sensitive they could not only detect the presence of submarines but also Soviet four-engine bombers flying overhead because the tips of the long propellers caused a sonic boom that reached beneath the surface of the ocean, transmitting a sonic shock that was picked up by the hydrophones."

"A listening system that could hear the ships coming from any direction."

"Theoretically, but a Navy traitor divulged our SOSUS system to the Soviet Union during the Cold War, which prompted them to launch a counter-campaign where they sent their naval ships to destroy the hydrophones. They got some, but not most, of them."

"So there are gaps in the system?"

"Most of the SOSUS grid in the Pacific is still operational but our technology has improved since the Cold War and we now have satellites we can use to locate ships coming into our territorial waters."

"We still won't know which of the ships are carrying cesium-137 and the nuclear bomb," she said.

"Finding the ships with cesium-137 may not be as problematic as you think," Captain Torrey replied. "You are aware of our drone capabilities in the air. Why would you assume we don't have that same drone capability underwater?"

"Underwater drones can detect cesium-137 even if it is sealed in lead on a ship?"

"Major Grant," the captain replied with a smile, "don't ever underestimate the brilliance of U.S. military technology."

"If that's the case, we can identify the three ships before they reach our waters and intercept them. Can the drones pinpoint a nuclear bomb?"

"Sadly, no. We won't have any idea which of the ten ships coming to America it will be on, unless you can use the passenger lists to identify Farouk," Captain Torrey said.

Once in the ship's communication center, Brooke was able to speak directly to Director Grainger, who listened carefully before commenting.

"I want you, Esther and Khalid, to leave immediately for Los Angeles," he said. "Have the captain fly you to Australia, where we'll have a private jet waiting. While the Navy is determining which three ships are carrying cesium-137, you need to concentrate on locating Farouk and the nuclear bomb."

"Yes, the fourth ship."

"Major Grant," he said, "you can't assume Farouk put it on a fourth ship. It might be on one of the same ships as the three carrying dirty bombs."

"Why would he do that?" she asked.

"Several reasons come to mind, but here is the most obvious. Farouk will want all of his bombs to be detonated on the same day, so he will need them on three different ships that reach the United States on the same day."

"I'm not following you. Why must the ships reach the United States on the same day?"

"Farouk doesn't know we're on to his plan. He's got to be thinking about simultaneous explosions because if one dirty bomb exploded in a U.S. seaport, he knows we would immediately close down all of our seaports. We'd stop all incoming cargo ships for inspection outside our borders before they came anywhere near our shores."

"You're right," Brooke said. "It's the same reason why terrorists attacked four targets simultaneously on nine-eleven. They had to all strike on the same day before we set up airport screening."

"Farouk doesn't just want one dirty bomb to get into America. He wants to hit us with three on the same day and, quite frankly, I think he plans to detonate the nuclear bomb on that same day too. The ultimate grand finale. In addition to investigating each passenger, look to see which of those ten ships are scheduled to arrive in a U.S. port on the same day."

As they ended their call, Brooke was impressed with Director Grainger's quick grasp of the situation. Suggesting the KTB team focus on the passenger lists was obvious. They had already thought of that. But looking to see which ships would be arriving in ports on the same day was a stroke of brilliance. That is how they would find the nuclear bomb. She felt certain of it.

Brooke found Khalid and Esther in the officer's dining room and quickly explained what Director Grainger had suggested. A few moments later, Esther excused herself, leaving Brooke with Khalid.

"In all this confusion," she said, "I didn't have time to thank you, Khalid, for saving my life when we were running to the pier."

"We are teammates, are we not?" he said. "I protect your back and you protect mine. Now, when do we leave for L.A.? I've never been there."

Brooke smiled but wondered if that was a lie, just as he'd lied about never being in Washington, D.C., before.

CHAPTER FORTY-SEVEN

Somewhere over the Pacific
En route to Los Angeles

The Gulfstream G650 private jet whisked Brooke, Khalid, and Esther from Australia to the United States. It was registered to a CIA shell company based in Las Vegas, and at a travel speed of eight hundred miles per hour, it was the fastest nonmilitary private jet available. Cruising at 51,000 feet in order to avoid airline traffic congestion and adverse weather, the KTB team focused on passenger lists. It was a frustrating process because Esther's flash drive contained only the names of each traveler and a passport number. In flight, there wasn't much they could do to research the men's backgrounds.

They did discover that five men with Muslim names had boarded a cargo vessel named the *Blue Neptune* and it was carrying several hundred tons of explosives en route to Los Angeles. It seemed a likely suspect.

Esther's flash drive records also did not have a complete list of the ships' arrival schedules. The KTB team would have to get that information after their flight landed.

Director Grainger had arranged for their jet to land at Naval Base Ventura County, formerly called Point Mugu, which President Ronald Reagan had used for visits to his Santa Barbara ranch while serving in the White House and where his casket had been brought home from Washington, D.C., after lying in state in the Capitol Rotunda.

About an hour before landing, Esther slipped into the comfortable seat next to Brooke.

"With everything that was happening in Jakarta, I don't think you have actually seen these videos circulating on social media about you," Esther explained as she handed Brooke an iPad.

The YouTube footage on the screen showed Al Arabic correspondent Ebio Kattan in her hospital room describing how she had been tortured by two women.

"One was muscular and clearly a soldier of some sort. I had never seen her, but she was wearing a tiny gold necklace and when she bent down to torture me, I saw a Star of David attached to it."

"She was Jewish, then? Most likely a Mossad agent?"

"Yes, yes, I believe she was."

"And the other woman who tortured you?"

"Yes, I recognized her. I knew her. I was shocked she would treat me with such hatred."

"What is her name? Please tell us who was this friend who betrayed your trust and tortured you?"

"Major Brooke Grant. She was the woman who said all Muslims are terrorists. She is the one who laughed while burning my feet."

Brooke did a double take. "She's lying! I didn't have anything to do with her interrogation and I certainly didn't burn her feet with a curling iron."

"You don't have to convince me that you're innocent. Remember, I was in charge of her interrogation. The U.S. media already has proven her story is a lie. They have released video of you attending funerals for your aunt and uncle at the same time when Ebio Kattan said you were torturing her. The head of the Al Arabic network has issued a statement saying it is further investigating Ebio Kattan's story while she is still recovering from her burns."

Brooke stared down at the iPad, which she'd paused on a picture of Kattan's singed feet. "Did you do this to her?" she asked.

"I subjected her to loud noises and flashing lights to disorient her, stripped her naked to make her feel helpless and vulnerable, and doused her with water while changing the room temperature. All that is true, but I never threatened to have her sexually assaulted and I didn't burn her feet with a curling iron."

"Then who did?"

"My guess is Ebio Kattan burned her own feet. That's the only logical explanation."

"But why?"

"Ratings and sympathy. Look, Arabs already hate us Jews, so blaming the Mossad for burning her feet is not international news. Blaming the United States and especially you makes it much more important. Plus, it turns you from a victim of Islamic violence at your wedding into someone who deserves to be punished for claiming all Muslims are terrorists. To many of her viewers, she's just justified the Washington bombing."

Esther retrieved the iPad from Brooke, explaining, "Here's another video you need to watch."

The next YouTube video showed Imam Mohammad Al-Kader seated inside a jail handcuffed and chained to a steel table.

"My fellow Muslim brothers and sisters," he said in a robotic tone. "In the name of Allah, the most holy and beloved, and in the name of his messenger, Mohammad, the blessed chosen one, I ask you to stop rioting. The Americans have not tortured me and our beloved and sacred Quran has not been desecrated in front of me."

Al-Kader continued talking but his words were drowned out by a voice-over in Arabic and then English repeating the sentence:

"The Americans have not tortured me and our beloved and sacred Quran has not been desecrated in front of me."

Esther said, "The Iranians were behind the false reports about Al-Kader being beaten."

"I'm glad he cleared the air."

"It hardly matters. Arabs will not change their minds. They will assume he was forced to say what he said. This is because they want to believe the lies. The more important question for us is why did Al-Kader make such a statement?"

"My government wouldn't force him to say those words."

"Then he must have some other motive. Some scheme in mind."

"Isn't it possible he simply wanted to do the right thing and end the unnecessary violence?" Brooke asked.

"Don't be naïve. Do you think an Imam who has preached hatred against the United Sates suddenly is concerned because Muslims are burning U.S. embassies?"

"He could be. He's a religious man."

"He's a killer who cloaks himself in piety."

"You shot three innocent women in Umoja Owiti's bed," Brooke said, clearly speaking before thinking about the words passing through her lips.

Taking back her iPad, Esther said, "I shot those women because our escape plan was based on blaming Ammon Mostafa, the security chief, for Owiti's death. If I had let them live, they would have identified me, and Kenyan officials would have known that Khalid, me, and you were there. Instead of judging me, you should be grateful."

Standing from her seat, she added, "Never compare me again to Al-Kader. He is a killer who breaks into your house and murders you in your sleep. I am the one who stops him. If you do not understand this difference, you are blind and foolish." Still irritated, she started to walk away but stopped for a final parting shot. "Ebio Kattan lied about you. She put your life in danger. If you want someone to judge, judge her. The Falcon murdered your future husband, your family, a president, and three hundred wedding guests. If you want someone to judge, judge him. And when you are done, look in the mirror and judge yourself. But never judge me again." She sat in a seat away from Brooke.

Khalid appeared just in time to hear Esther's parting comments. He approached Brooke armed with coffee.

"Me delivering you coffee has become cliché," he said, handing her a cup. Nodding at Esther, he asked, "Trouble in paradise?"

"I'm afraid I've offended our colleague."

"Israelis are easily offended."

"And Muslim men are always sweet talkers."

He sat down next to her in the same seat where Esther had been sitting moments earlier and said, "Not all Muslim men—as you learned in Jakarta when that mob was chasing you."

"Khalid," she said, "there's something I need to tell you. It's something I've been holding back but I feel compelled to say, especially now because you saved my life in Jakarta. I don't want to deceive you."

He read the concern on her face and put down his cup.

"What's so serious, Major?"

"I know you were involved in the murder of Mary Margaret Delaney," she blurted out. "I know you lied about never having been in Washington, D.C."

"If you are accusing me of being a liar and a murderer," he said in an eerily calm voice, "you should be polite enough to tell me who this person was."

"A lobbyist, a red-haired, white woman who worked in Washington, D.C. Her body was found in her BMW parked on the George Washington Parkway. Remember her now?"

"What makes you believe I was somehow involved in this woman's death?"

"Don't be coy. She was shot in the roof of her mouth with a .22-caliber handgun—the same way you shot that man who tackled me in front of the port entrance. You held him in the air and jammed your gun into his mouth and fired."

"And I am the only individual on this planet who owns a small-caliber pistol? You are describing a coincidence. Is it not possible that this woman shot herself in her mouth because she was vain and didn't wish to spoil her looks?"

"I've seen photos of you and Omar Nader riding through an intersection directly behind her car a few minutes before her death. You were chasing her."

"A man rides down the street on a bicycle and is struck by a speeding car. If he had arrived at that intersection a few seconds earlier or later, he would have been spared. Mr. Nader and I happened to race through the same red light as a depressed woman who is on her way to end her own life. You see something sinister. I see a mere coincidence of timing."

Khalid picked up his coffee and took a sip. "Why are you mentioning this woman's death now? What purpose does it achieve?"

"Truthfully, I'm not certain. You rescued me and for that I am grateful, but this woman did not commit suicide and I felt it was important for me to tell you that I know that. If for no other reason than for her reputation."

"Her reputation? You think this matters to a dead woman?"

"What did she do to Omar Nader or the Saudi government to deserve being murdered?"

"Major Grant, you are a very judgmental person. Americans always believe actions need to be explained and justified."

"Murder certainly should be."

"If I asked you, 'Major Grant, have you ever committed a murder?' you would be offended. Self-defense is not murder, you would tell me. This is how you live with your actions."

"What do you tell yourself?"

"Sometimes people need to die, so you kill them. There is no point in demanding to know why. If you need some justification to ease your conscience, then you can create one. I don't. Hakim Farouk and the Falcon defend their actions by quoting the Holy Quran. You kill in self-defense. Esther sees some greater good in the deaths she causes. A fly buzzing around your head disturbs your meal. You swat it. Your rationalizations are irrelevant to the fly. You do it because you can. That is what I do and I sleep well at night."

"You should know Director Grainger has photographs of you and Omar Nader in a car chasing Delaney on the night she died. You have diplomatic immunity, but Mr. Nader doesn't. He could be arrested and charged."

Khalid grunted. "Will you accuse a man as important as him with such flimsy evidence and for what reason? When it comes to relations between our country and your own, this woman was insignificant."

He picked up the remainder of his coffee and said, "Now you have offended us both. Jew and Muslim. We'll be landing very soon, Major Grant. Forgive me if I choose to sit in a different seat."

CHAPTER FORTY-EIGHT

Ebio Kattan's apartment
Dubai, United Arab Emirates

It took Ebio Kattan several moments to respond to the knock on her door. She had not yet fully mastered the crutches she needed to walk.

Before answering, she peered through the security peephole and when she saw the two men waiting in the hallway, she felt an instant sensation of dread.

Dildar Seif was the chairman of the Al Arabic television network and one of the most powerful men in Dubai. But it was his companion who she feared more. Yash Tahan was a high-ranking prosecutor in Dubai's criminal court system. Quickly slipping on a hijab that she kept by the door, she unbolted the lock and forced a modest smile.

"Gentlemen," she said quietly. "Please come inside. May I offer you some refreshments? Tea? Coffee?"

"No," Chairman Seif answered in an already angry voice.

"I have tea," she repeated.

Customs dictated that an Arab host was required to offer refreshments at least three times to any guest who visited them. The guest should decline at least twice before finally accepting. Yet, the Al Arabic network chairman felt no need to abide by this long-held tradition.

"You came on my network and said you were tortured," Chairman Seif declared. "You said you were abducted, threatened with sexual abuse, and had your feet burned." He seemed to be spitting each word from his mouth as if it were venom. "You said a female Mossad agent and the American soldier Brooke Grant did this to you."

"Do you deny making these claims?" Prosecutor Tahan asked.

Kattan was keenly aware of what she had said and the videos posted on social media that contradicted her charges against Brooke Grant.

"Chairman Seif and Prosecutor Tahan," she replied, "I was in shock and confused about Major Grant when I was taken to the hospital. Only minutes before I had been found wandering delirious on a sidewalk outside this very building."

"You are aware," Prosecutor Tahan replied, "that under federal law number 3 of 1987, defamation constitutes a *criminal* act and is subject to the penalties specified under Chapter Six—Crimes Perpetrated Against Reputation: Libel, Abuse, and Disclose of Secrets, Articles 371 to 380."

Lowering her eyes, she said in a self-deprecating voice, "Chairman Seif and Prosecutor Tahan, you have seen evidence of my torture. No one can deny I was abducted and abused. Nor can they deny my feet were badly burned, causing me tremendous pain and suffering."

"The U.S. ambassador has lodged a formal complaint about your accusations against Major Grant and has provided irrefutable evidence that she did not participate in any alleged abuse," the prosecutor responded.

"If I misspoke about Major Grant, I will welcome the opportunity to apologize on the air for this case of mistaken identity because of my delirium, but that doesn't change that I was abducted and tortured."

"I have no intention of ever allowing you on the Al Arabic network again," Chairman Seif declared, joining their conversation. "By lying, you have harmed our credibility with viewers and helped spark riots and demonstrations against the United States. I have come here this morning to fire you and tell you that no self-respecting television network will ever employ you again. Your career as a journalist is finished."

Kattan couldn't believe what he'd just told her. She knew of other correspondents who had embellished stories and even fictionalized reports to make them more sensational. She suspected there had to be some deeper reason why she was being treated so harshly.

Prosecutor Tahan said, "Having you appear on television would only embarrass our nation for a second time."

"Please, gentlemen, can we sit down and discuss this rationally?" she asked. It was not only the pain from her burns that was making her feel queasy. She hobbled to a kitchen table. Both men followed and everyone watched Prosecutor Tahan remove a multipaged legal document from his briefcase after they sat down.

"This is a personal statement prepared for your signature," he said. "It is a personal apology from you to Major Brooke Grant and also to the U.S. government. In it, you are admitting your error and stating that neither Major Grant nor any other U.S. citizen was involved in your abduction and torture. We have given you a logical explanation that will help Al Arabic and our country appear less culpable. It states that you misspoke while you were under the influence of a strong sedative, which caused you to hallucinate and falsely accuse Major Grant of calling all Muslims terrorists and burning your feet."

He handed the thick document to her along with his Montblanc pen. Continuing, he said, "*Your* statement further explains that this sedative—a neuromuscular blocking agent—was given to you before you arrived at the hospital, a requirement necessary because of the hospital's records and the many doctors and nurses who treated you. This drug was administered by the doctor who found you on the sidewalk and drove you there. We have attached notarized depositions from him and his wife about this sedative being injected into you. This explanation will be our official explanation and will be conveyed to the U.S. ambassador along with your personal apology and your decision to voluntarily end your career as a journalist."

Chairman Seif said, "Al Arabic will release a written copy of this statement to be read on the air. We will explain that you have resigned to focus on regaining your physical health."

"Is there no other way?" she pleaded.

"No!" the prosecutor said harshly.

"And if I do not sign?" she asked.

"You will be prosecuted and sentenced to a minimum of ten years of confinement."

What choice do I have? Kattan picked up her pen and signed her name on the legal paperwork without bothering to read it.

"This is only the first step," Prosecutor Tahan continued. "You need to leave Dubai within seven days. You are being expelled. All but five thousand U.S. dollars in your personal accounts will be surrendered to the government as a penalty. If you do not leave the country or if you decide to protest the financial consequences of your actions, you will be judged under Sharia law, which will condemn you to a minimum of eighty lashes in public plus possible other physical penalties, including amputations."

Kattan wished she could turn back time. If she'd not accused Major Brooke Grant of torturing her, none of this would be happening.

"I was abducted and I was tortured, and you both know it," she said, tears flowing down her face. "I am a victim. I am a victim."

"Repeating it does not change anything. Because you lied about part of your story, no one knows what other parts of your story are true," Prosecutor Tahan said. There was not the slightest hint of mercy or understanding in his voice. "What we do know is you defamed an American who survived a bomb attack on her wedding day that killed a U.S. president. You have embarrassed the entire Arab world by accusing her of being an enemy of peace-loving Muslims."

Kattan slid both the pen and document across the table to him. She was still trying to understand the harshness of what was happening.

"I have signed a document acknowledging my mistake and an apology but, Mr. Prosecutor, these penalties are extreme. Is there not some way for me to be politically rehabilitated?"

"The punishment is what certain U.S. officials have requested," Tahan disclosed, "and what the highest of levels have approved. There is no appeal and there will be no leniency."

Certain U.S. officials, she thought. *Clearly the CIA.*

With a contemptuous look, Al Arabic Chairman Seif said, "As smart as you are, how could you be so naïve? Consider yourself lucky that you are not in jail. Everyone knows Al Arabic serves as the voice of our government. Everyone knows our nation hosts more U.S. Navy ships in our ports than any other in the world except for the United States. We have been close allies for more than forty years with the Americans and yet you accused them."

Continuing, Prosecutor Tahan said, "Our friends in Saudi intelligence tell us you provided information to the Mossad."

Everyone at the kitchen table knew the UAE did not recognize Israel as a nation or have diplomatic relations with it. Israel was considered a terrorist state by the UAE government and helping them put Kattan at risk of being accused of a crime much worse than defaming Major Brooke Grant. Treason was punishable by death.

"The Falcon and his followers will be coming after you for helping the Israelis, and so will the Mossad for accusing them," Chairman Seif warned.

Prosecutor Tahan added, "The Jews were able to abduct you from the parking garage of a secure Al Arabic studio. This is why it is best you leave Dubai. We do not need this trouble."

The two men stood. "Remember, seven days," Tahan said, "or you will be tried under Sharia law." They left her apartment without waiting for her to escort them to the door.

The once confident Kattan, winner of the most coveted beauty award in the Arab world, an internationally respected journalist, and the most recognized face on Al Arabic, sat at her table alone and afraid. An antimicrobial dressing made of soft silicone that released silver into the open wounds on her feet needed to be changed, but she was afraid to return to the hospital. She was afraid to leave her apartment. Where would she go? Without a job? With only $5,000?

One lie had ended her career, robbed her of her money, stripped her of respect, and made her a woman who would always have to keep one eye looking behind her.

All she could think about at that moment was how much more she hated Major Brooke Grant.

CHAPTER FORTY-NINE

Oval Office
The White House
Washington, D.C.

Representative Rudy Adeogo was waiting outside the Oval Office wearing a polka-dotted blue and white necktie.

Dheeh had bought it for him after she saw a popular television show host wearing one and she'd insisted he wear it. Adeogo now regretted appeasing her. He felt self-conscious.

Trying to make her happy was part of his effort to rebuild their still troubled relationship, but a more subdued tie would have been more appropriate for a presidential meeting. In Washington, how one dressed sent a message just as clearly as how one spoke, which was why most everyone dressed conservatively, or, compared to fashionable New Yorkers, rather drably. To do other than the norm was to risk not being taken seriously.

But a polka-dotted tie?

Adeogo had started feeling uneasy about his neckwear the moment the Secret Service granted him access into the White House grounds. With each second waiting for the president his self-doubt grew.

CIA director Payton Grainger appeared from the Oval Office with an outstretched hand.

"Representative Adeogo," he said warmly. "The president is ready to see you now. We just finished our talk. He's asked me to stick around for yours."

Adeogo noticed Grainger was wearing a solid blue tie.

"If the president has requested you being here, I am happy to oblige," Adeogo replied.

"I understand you have a personal message from this terrorist Mohammad Al-Kader for the president," Grainger said as they entered the Oval Office.

Before Adeogo could reply, he heard the president's booming voice.

"Glad you've come to brief me, Congressman," he declared, rising from behind his desk.

The president noticed Adeogo surveying his surroundings.

"First time in the Oval Office?" the president asked.

"Yes, sir, Mr. President."

"A lot of history has been made in this room and nearly everything in here has a story behind it. Take this, for example," he said, walking from behind his desk and running his palm over its top. "When I moved in here, I was told there were six desks I could choose from and each had its own history. My predecessor used the Resolute desk—a gift from Queen Victoria built with actual timbers from an English exploration ship that sank in the Arctic. Quite a story, isn't it?"

"Yes, indeed, Mr. President."

"I chose a different desk. This desk. It's called the Theodore Roosevelt desk. I figured good old Teddy had more in common with me than some English queen. If you pull out the desk drawer, you'll see the signatures of Truman, Eisenhower, and Richard Nixon because it's a tradition for presidents and vice presidents to sign their desks. The last one to sign this one was Vice President Dick Cheney."

He crossed the room to where two sofas faced each other at the edges of a carpet bearing the presidential seal and motioned for Adeogo and Grainger to sit on the couch opposite of him.

"Now, let's talk about Al-Kader," President Austin said. "First, let me thank you for going to see him and getting him to appear on television. That was important to quieting the disturbances. But tell me, why did he want to meet specifically with you?"

"As you know," Adeogo explained, "my youngest brother was radicalized by him. I believe that is why." Adeogo glanced first at the president's face and then Grainger's. "I trust you and Director Grainger understand that my religious beliefs have nothing in common with what Al-Kader teaches or believes. His interpretations are a total corruption of our faith."

"Al-Kader gave you a message for me," the president said.

"Mr. President, Al-Kader wants to cut a deal. He says he can tell you where you can capture the Falcon."

"He claims to know where the Falcon is currently hiding?" Grainger said in a surprised voice.

"How could an Imam sitting in a Maryland jail know that?" President Austin asked. "And why would he be willing to betray him?"

"I have no idea. He said he will tell you the exact location."

"We're supposed to just take his word and release him from jail?" President Austin asked.

"No, sir, he understands he will remain in jail until you catch or kill the Falcon. Only then will he expect you to release him."

"And what does he expect in return?" Grainger asked.

"First, of course, is his unconditional freedom. All charges dropped. No new charges filed. Second, a French passport with a new name."

"He's asking us to put him into some sort of international witness protection program?" Grainger asked. "Does he really believe the French will take him?"

"He's asked to leave our country immediately after the Falcon is caught or killed. He wants to fly on a commercial airline—a first-class ticket to Paris. He expects the twenty-five-million-dollar reward for the Falcon deposited into a bank account there."

"Is that all?" the president asked sarcastically.

"Actually, there is another condition. He wants you—as president—to sign a legal contract that states the U.S. government will not track him down and murder him and he wants me to hold on to it."

"He wants to use you as an insurance policy, if I understand what you are saying," the president said.

"Yes, if the CIA or any other U.S. intelligence service were to go after him and harm him, he would expect me to make the president's letter public. To reveal the contract between you and how it had been violated."

"Al-Kader thinks he's a very clever man," the president said.

"A man facing a lifetime in jail has plenty of time to think," Grainger said.

"The Imam told me the United States will never find the Falcon without his help," Adeogo warned.

"It's a lot to ask," President Austin said. "As you said, this is the same Imam who radicalized your brother and, apparently, the suicide bomber who murdered our president and three hundred wedding guests."

"I agree," Adeogo replied. "I promised him that I would deliver his message. I will be happy to tell him that you have no interest accepting his offer."

"Mr. President," Grainger said, "we might want to discuss this a bit more before rejecting it. We're talking about locating and terminating a worldwide terrorist who has claimed credit for assassinating a sitting U.S. president. We're talking about a radical Islamic terrorist who is threatening to destroy three major cities and also has a nuclear bomb. Taking him prisoner or killing him would send a very powerful message to the world, just as eliminating Osama bin Laden did."

"What about blowback?" the president asked. "Al-Kader was arrested on prime-time television. Our case against him is solid. One hundred percent. He can't just disappear without the courts and the media demanding to know why."

"Sir, no case is a hundred percent. He's been charged with seditious conspiracy and that can be a difficult accusation to prove, especially against a religious leader, even with testimony by an informant and tape recordings," Grainger replied. "Let's also not forget that most Americans believe they have a right to say whatever they want, when they want, and how they want. Plus, if there is a trial, we must remember that it was my agency that initially recruited, trained, and sent him to Afghanistan to fight. We also helped him become a U.S. citizen."

"Director Grainger, the mood in our country is such that we could put the Prophet Mohammad himself on trial and get a conviction in an American courtroom," the president said, adding, "I mean no offense, Representative Adeogo."

"I understand," Adeogo said. "This is a frightening time to be a Muslim in America."

"It will only get worse if the Falcon destroys three cities and sets off a nuclear bomb," Grainger argued. "Mr. President, we need to ask ourselves if brokering a discreet deal with Al-Kader, who is a relatively small fish, is worth catching the biggest fish right now."

"I don't want to put my name on any piece of paper that could show up later and reveal I cut a deal with him."

"Representative Adeogo," Grainger said, "could you convince him to accept a letter from me, rather than the president? And would he agree to keep this so-called insurance letter completely confidential if we kept our end of the bargain?"

"I can certainly present that."

"What keeps Al-Kader from disclosing it as soon as he is released?" the president asked.

"He would not want the Arab world to know he betrayed the Falcon," Grainger said.

"True. Still, we can't turn Al-Kader loose in France with twenty-five million and have him reappear and start preaching about the need to impose Sharia law."

"The president has a point," Grainger said. "Al-Kader needs to agree to disappear. Vanish. Is he willing to do that?"

"I'll ask him."

"Tell him if he shows up anywhere in the world in a mosque preaching, we will come after him," President Austin said.

Addressing Adeogo, Grainger asked, "Could this be *taqiyya*?"

"Ah, the claim it is permissible for Muslims to lie to nonbelievers in order to advance the cause of Islam and defeat their enemies," Adeogo said. "I don't know."

"Did he give you any indication why he is willing to help us track down the Falcon?"

Adeogo shook his head.

President Austin stood from the sofa and said, "Director Grainger and I will discuss this and get back to you. Again, thank you for bringing this to our attention."

"Before I go, Mr. President," Adeogo said, "there's something else I need to tell you and Director Grainger. It's about Major Brooke Grant."

Adeogo looked hesitant for a moment and then said, "Major Grant came to me with evidence that suggests Mary Margaret Delaney, a Washington lobbyist whose body was found in her parked BMW on the George Washington Parkway, did not commit suicide. Major Grant believes Omar Nader and another Saudi might have killed her."

"Yes," said Grainger. "She brought her evidence to me and I am taking the proper steps to ensure it is fully investigated. As you are aware, Omar Nader is a powerful and well-respected Arab leader. We can't rush an investigation of this sensitivity."

"Yes, yes, I understand," Adeogo said. "I wanted you to know that I personally agree with Major Grant. I believe Omar Nader had this woman murdered."

"Thank you again," President Austin said as he began walking the congressman toward the Oval Office's exit. "I'll have Director Grainger keep you posted on the investigation of Omar Nader."

"Thank you, sir," Adeogo replied, "and thank you for telling me a bit about the Oval Office and its history."

"Glad to," President Austin said, adding, "I like your tie. Haven't seen many polka-dotted ones being worn around this town."

Adeogo couldn't tell if the president was being sincere. "My wife bought it for me," he replied. "I'll tell her you complimented me on it."

"Please do."

President Austin moved immediately to his desk after Adeogo left.

"Tell me your thoughts," he said to Grainger.

"Killing the Falcon is more important than sending this Imam to prison for life."

Grainger thought for a moment and then added, "Mr. President, I believe I have thought of a way that this could be a win-win for us. A way to outfox Al-Kader and also deal with the troublesome Omar Nader."

PART FIVE

—ᵚᵚ—

BEHEADING THE HYDRA

"Would he not have grown tired and weary of marshalling and arming his forces, weary of his sieges and pursuits amid unnumbered revolts, desertions, and riots of subject peoples...as if he were cutting off the heads of a hydra which ever grew again in renewed wars among these faithless and conspiring peoples?"

—Plutarch, Roman citizen and Greek
biographer writing about Alexander
the Great's fourth-century BC attempt
to control modern-day Afghanistan

CHAPTER FIFTY

Aboard an Owiti-owned container ship
International waters, Pacific Ocean

Giovanni Capo, a portly Italian who'd spent most of his fifty-two years at sea, was clearly upset when he approached his close friend, Jesús Alvarez, the chief officer, inside the ship's bridge castle.

"He's doing it again," Capo announced in a tone laced with disgust.

Alvarez, a scholarly-looking Puerto Rican with thick glasses, glanced up from the gauges, switches, and dials on the bridge control panel positioned before him.

"Joe, there's nothing wrong with a man praying," he said.

"I get that. Hell, I pray each time we reach a new port that I'll meet the woman of my dreams."

"You mean a woman of the night," Alvarez smirked.

"*L'amore è cieco*," Capo replied. "Praying, it's okay by me, but praying five times a day and him repeating the same words over and over while chanting Allah Allah Allah—it's giving me the creeps."

"We've worked alongside Muslims for years. We're owned by a Turkish company, remember?"

"Yeah, but we never had a Muslim doing all this praying and being all monklike. He's starting trouble."

"Trouble? What trouble?"

"Before he came aboard, we didn't have no one falling down on their knees praying to Allah unless we was caught in a typhoon or Jules poisoned us with his cooking. And just so you know, our cook, he ain't none pleased with this Muslim passenger showing up in his galley."

Capo paused to catch his breath before continuing, "You do realize Jules—he's a Jew, right?"

"I'm not one to pay attention to another man's religious beliefs," Alvarez answered.

"Neither am I, until this here passenger came aboard, and come to think of it, when was the last time we carted around a passenger? This here ain't no luxury liner."

Capo was right. The accommodations onboard their ship were barren. Except for a tiny gym, hot tub, and sauna, there were no niceties, although the food was excellent—even better than on cruise liners. Men who worked hard deserved to eat well and Jules made certain they did.

"You just don't show up at a Jakarta port and catch a ride," Capo complained. "Not unless the captain was shorthanded, which we weren't. And this guy ain't working. He spends all day alone in his cabin, unless he's eating by himself or he's up on the deck praying. I don't like it. Yesterday, two crew members, fellas you and me known for years, they got down and prayed with him. Like chickens in a row. Allah this, Allah that."

"There were supposed to be two of them as passengers," Alvarez said.

"You're right. The other passenger signed up, brought his gear on board, and then disappeared when it was time to leave Jakarta. The captain left his stuff behind. It's another sign, I tell you, that something ain't right. Maybe our passenger did something to him."

"What? Why are you so riled up?"

"Because," Capo said, lowering his voice, "you heard about this terrorist who's going to destroy three U.S. cities. It's been all over the news."

"And the Americans said it wasn't true. He ain't got three nuclear bombs."

"I don't care. How do you think that terrorist is going to pull off something like that? My point is you could slip a nuclear bomb into one of these shipping containers and sail it right into a harbor."

Capo pointed through the front bridge's windows toward the bow where rows of cargo containers were stacked like a pyramid, with the tallest rising five containers high with descending rows on either side. It was just about dusk and the setting sun made the rainbow colors of the containers look like a scrambled Rubik's Cube.

"You ever seen a nuclear bomb?" Alvarez asked.

"Hell no, except in movies."

"And you think our Muslim passenger just strolled into some Indonesian market and bought one and then slipped it onboard our ship?"

"I'm just saying it could happen."

"Well, just 'cause he's an Arab don't mean he's a terrorist and can smuggle a bomb aboard. You're being prejudiced."

"I don't trust him. I'm going down to search through his personal stuff while he's praying."

"That's one of the stupidest ideas you've ever had."

Capo chuckled. "Actually, I already checked his cabin."

"What? You broke into his quarters?"

"I went to see what he was hiding."

"And what'd you find?"

"Two changes of clothes, a book, and a cell phone. Along with one photograph in his book. A picture of a woman and young girl."

"No nuclear bomb tucked under his pillow?"

"Laugh if you want, but I still don't like it. Allah this and Allah that. If the captain is charging him for passage, he should start charging him double for bringing Allah along with him."

"Capo, you need to tend to your charts and radio checks and stop worrying just because we got a Muslim passenger praying and keeping to himself. Besides, even if there was a nuclear bomb in our cargo, we're out in the middle of the Pacific. Who you gonna call?"

"The U.S. Navy."

"And tell them what? We got a Arab Muslim praying on our ship and Joe Capo thinks he snuck on a nuclear bomb with him?"

For the next several hours, the two men worked quietly at their posts, until the captain replaced Alvarez on the bridge. As the first officer was descending to his quarters, he decided to duck into the ship's combination gym, hot tub, and sauna room. He stripped, tucked his clothes into a locker, removed his glasses, grabbed a towel, and entered the small wood-lined chamber.

"Oh," he said. "I'm usually alone at this hour." Without his glasses, it took him a moment to recognize the man sitting across from him.

Hakim Farouk nodded politely.

Alvarez sucked in a deep breath and shut his eyes. He was exhausted. He blew the hot air from his mouth.

Farouk watched him in silence.

"How do you like our ship?" Alvarez asked. "Pretty boring if you're not a member of the crew, huh?"

"All men should, and I quote, 'Beware of two features: boredom and laziness. If you are bored, you shall be not patient with a right, and if you are lazy, you shall not carry out a right.'"

"What's that from?"

"A Muslim saying."

"Just the same our ship doesn't have many comforts. No cell phones. No cable television. No Internet. No swimming pool. No women. Not to mention seasickness, given we ride in water a bit rougher than them stabilized cruise boats. And you're the only passenger. Hey, did you know the other man who signed up in Jakarta?"

"No, I did not know there was another passenger until I boarded the ship and the captain told me."

"He got here before you. I thought maybe you were friends or you might have bumped into each other since you were assigned adjoining quarters."

Farouk didn't react and that irritated Alvarez. He thought it rude and also considered it a challenge. He felt obligated to make this passenger say more.

"How you passing your time?" he asked.

"I read. I meditate. I pray. I like solitude and especially the quiet."

"Oh yeah. I'm a reader too. Generally a few pages each night. Helps me get to sleep. I like the older stuff. Louis L'Amour. Now, he could write. People think he only wrote Westerns, but he worked on a freighter and wrote about ships too. You ever read any of his books?"

"No," Farouk said. "I'm unfamiliar with him. I only need one book."

"One book? That's all? The same one? No offense, but you must either be a slow reader or it must be one hell of a good book."

"The Holy Quran," Farouk replied, "it contains all a man needs to read and learn."

CHAPTER FIFTY-ONE

Camp Pendleton
Oceanside, California

*R*un. *Run. She was with Jennifer. Clutching her hand. Hurry. Hurry. He was coming. Too late. The sound. The blast. The shock from the explosion threw them forward. No! No! She'd lost her grip on Jennifer's hand. They were separated. She could see her falling into a black hole. Jennifer looking up at her, helpless, terrified. Out of reach. She was disappearing now into the darkness. Stop! Stop! She reached as far as she could for her daughter's hand but Jennifer was gone. Now she felt his presence. He was there. Laughing. Coming for her. Laughing because Jennifer was gone. Laughing because she was helpless. She could see his silhouette in the flames behind him, hear his breathing, and smell his foul breath. He swung his arm. A flash. The glint of steel. A knife.*

Major Brooke Grant screamed and shot up in her bed, panting, drenched with sweat. It was the same nightmare. The one she'd had each night since the bombing at her wedding. Each night. Every night.

There was no point trying to go back to sleep. She was too rattled to shut her eyes. Too old to believe in bogeymen and yet this one was real. She checked her watch. A few minutes after 5:00 a.m. She left her bed, slipped on running apparel, and went outside. Still dark, but with enough lights for her to make her way along the blacktop. Slow and then faster, faster, and faster until she had to stop before her lungs burst. By the time she returned, the sun was rising—5:45 a.m. Time to shower. Time to be awake.

Stripping, Brooke stepped inside the stall and turned on the water.

Without thinking, she opened her lips and let some slosh into her mouth before quickly realizing what she'd done.

She'd been warned not to drink water from any faucet in the Camp Pendleton quarters. Something about chemicals from firefighting foam used during training exercises contaminating the ground water.

She leaned her head against the wall of the shower and began spitting. Brooke Grant was determined she would not cry. Not even in her shower. Not even alone.

After landing at Naval Base Ventura County, the KTB team had each been offered base quarters. Only Brooke had accepted. Khalid and Esther had chosen to stay in nearby hotels. None of them wanted to spend any more time than necessary with the other at the secure base workspace they'd been provided.

Grabbing a towel as she stepped from the shower, Brooke checked her watch and noted that it was nearly 9:30 a.m. EST. She called Dr. George Jacks's personal cell.

"Major Grant," he said after the second ring. "I was expecting your morning call. You checking to see if I'm at the hospital?"

"Are you?" she replied.

"Nope, still stuck in traffic on the beltway."

"How's Jennifer?"

"Nothing new to report since you called me yesterday morning. As I said, she's gotten comfortable riding Soupy with her friend Cassy Adeogo, whose mother brings her out to the ranch each afternoon after school, but Jennifer is still not talking to Cassy or anyone else. I warned you this is going to take time, certainly more than a few weeks."

Brooke hesitated. Had it been just weeks since the wedding bomb attack? So much had happened that she'd thought it had been much longer.

"When I return to Washington, I must see her. I'm not waiting anymore. I'm taking her home with me."

"Major Grant," he replied in a firm voice, "I'm going to the horse therapy ranch this afternoon to speak with Dr. Cummings about her progress and I will get back to you, but obviously, if you want to go see her and take her home, I am not going to stop you. Do you know when that might be?"

"Soon, I hope. Very soon."

"We've been over this before, Major Grant. You feel guilty because you're not here, but trust me, Jennifer is completely unaware of how much time it has been since she's seen you. It's like someone with Alzheimer's. One day flows seamlessly into the next as they move in and out of reality."

"How can you be so certain?"

"Because she wasn't startled or surprised when Cassy appeared. Your ward—"

"Daughter," Brooke said, correcting him.

"Jennifer is still lost in a world of her own making where time doesn't matter."

"It does to me."

"I'm pulling into the hospital parking lot right now," he said. "I need to end this call. Just let me know when you will be returning to Washington so we can talk in person about gradually reducing Jennifer's time at the therapy ranch."

Brooke wasn't certain she believed he really was at his office, but she had no choice.

"I'll call tomorrow to learn how she is doing," Brooke said, ending their conversation.

As she hurriedly dressed, Brooke couldn't get Jennifer off her mind. Dr. Jacks was right. She did feel guilty about not being home. She missed her and couldn't understand how it was possible that Jennifer didn't feel that same sense of loss and yearning.

Since arriving at Camp Pendleton four days ago, she'd fallen into a routine. Up for a morning run, a protein shake for breakfast and one slice of toasted wheat bread. Shower, dress, call Dr. Jacks, and then report to the secure office. After her criticism of Khalid and Esther on the jet ride to California, they had worked begrudgingly together with long, awkward silences. She and Esther had spent most of their time on computers or making international calls trying to glean more information about the twenty-six passengers aboard the ten ships en route to the United States.

Only one passenger had been an American. The rest had come from Indonesia, India, or third-world countries; the majority of them had boarded before reaching Jakarta during stops in other ports.

It was a tedious assignment. Many of the men appeared to be vagabonds. Many came from countries with no centralized passport control or police computer systems or, if they did have them, those in charge weren't inclined to share information.

At the suggestion of Director Grainger, Esther had checked the ten ships' arrival dates and had discovered that none of the vessels was scheduled to reach a U.S. port on the same day.

That had been a frustrating discovery for the team.

While they'd been busy, Khalid had rarely shown his face. He'd preferred to work at the Saudi consulate in Los Angeles, explaining it was easier for him to keep in touch with his GID counterparts, although both Esther and Brooke were convinced Khalid was a Mabahith "fixer" and lacked any real computer or research skills.

With each passing day, Brooke became more restless. Why was it taking so long to find the three ships carrying radioactive materials? The process had sounded so straightforward when it had been first explained. Between satellites, SOSUS, and underwater drones capable of detecting radioactivity, it was supposed to be a snap. That is what she'd been told by Captain Torrey.

Tick tock, tick tock.

On this particular morning, Brooke didn't see either Esther or Khalid when she arrived in their shared office and was just as happy they weren't there. She telephoned Langley. Nothing new to report, she was told. Hanging up, she typed in a series of passwords until the secure computer file that she was working on appeared on her screen.

In addition to the research she'd been doing, Brooke had busied herself gathering every shred of information that she could about the two men she was now pursuing.

She'd discovered Hakim Farouk had learned his bomb-making

skills from reading old manuals used at the so-called airport camp, or the Al Farouq training grounds near Kandahar, Afghanistan. In 1998, the United States attacked that Al-Qaeda facility with cruise missiles in retaliation for jihadist bombings at the U.S. embassies in Tanzania and Nairobi. Those two embassy bombings had introduced Osama bin Laden and Al-Qaeda to the world. For many, they'd marked the start of the United States being drawn into its ongoing fight against radical Islamists.

The first time Western intelligence had heard Hakim Farouk's name was after the September 17, 2008, attack on the U.S. embassy in Sana'a, Yemen's capital, when five bombs were detonated during an attempt to breach security walls outside the embassy in a fierce twenty-minute gun battle. An informant claimed Farouk had built all five bombs.

A psychologist at Langley had done a profile of Farouk and had determined that he fit a common profile for radical Islamic terrorists:

Farouk is a man who is angry, alienated, and feels disenfranchised. He does not believe the current political system can be changed from within. He is convinced that engaging in violence against the state is not immoral but is justified. He associates with others sympathetic to his cause and believes that by participating in a movement he will receive such social and psychological rewards such as camaraderie, a higher sense of self, and a larger purpose in his life. In his particular case, he has zeroed in on the United States, Christians, and Jews as the target of his aggression and the embodiment of evil, injustice, and immorality.

A Mossad profiler had issued a slightly different analysis:

Hakim Farouk's actions, especially random murders, suggest the emergence of a psychopathic personality disorder that manifests itself in a lack of ability to feel love or empathy. An underlying cause for his violence could be a misguided attempt by himself to test his capacity to feel another's pain and, by feeling it, regain some personal humanity or prove to himself that he is immune to actual feelings of empathy. Some event in his life may have caused him permanent psychological impairment and an inability to connect with others out of fear.

Brooke read and reread the final sentences of the Mossad evaluation. In one of her first conversations with Khalid, he'd said Farouk had been an illegitimate baby discarded at an orphanage in Oman, where he had been treated cruelly. That story would explain a lack of empathy for others. The other story was that Farouk was from Yemen and had lost his wife, Ayeesha, and daughter, Leyia, when an American missile killed them.

Either way, Farouk had some tragedy in his life that attracted him to murder—either in an attempt to regain his personal humanity or to reveal he was immune to actual feelings for others.

What troubled Brooke was that she, too, had suffered tremendous loss in her life. There was no doubt that she loved Jennifer but she wondered if the losses she'd endured had created a metaphorical scab on her heart. There was a time in her life when the strained relationship with her two KTB colleagues would have nagged at her. But it didn't.

Why had she felt so compelled to criticize both of them for their cavalier attitudes about taking a life?

She kept reassuring herself that she could never become the cold-blooded killers that they were. She was better than them.

Was she?

Brooke thought about the Nietzsche quote: *"He who fights with monsters should look to it that he himself does not become a monster. And if you gaze long into an abyss, the abyss also gazes into you."*

She pushed those thoughts aside and instead moved on to her file about the Falcon.

The first mention of the Falcon had been recorded by Jennifer's father, Gunter Conner, when he'd been stationed by the agency in Cairo. He'd recruited an Egyptian source code-named Ra, after the sun god. It had been Ra who'd mentioned that a new jihadist leader was emerging or, as Conner's original reports quoted, "He appeared from the desert. Some say Yemen, others Somalia. A few said Egypt. He came from nowhere but soon he was everywhere."

According to Ra, this emerging figure had helped plan the 1997 attack on sixty-two people at Deir el-Bahri, a popular tourist attraction near Luxor. Six gunmen armed with automatic weapons and knives had trapped tourists inside the Temple of Hatshepsut and slaughtered them during a horrific forty-five-minute rampage. Women had been mutilated with machetes. A note praising Allah had been found later tucked inside a disemboweled body. Among the dead were a five-year-old British boy and Japanese honeymooners.

Ra was responsible for creating the Falcon moniker by telling Conner that the mysterious, always masked jihadist was "like a falcon who flies high above us. He sees and acts but is not seen..."

Eight years after the Luxor attack, the masked jihadist had made his first YouTube appearance during which he had given a long soliloquy attacking the United States for interfering in Middle Eastern affairs and calling for all Muslims to unite.

The Falcon had disappeared after that but had resurfaced nearly a decade later when he was seen on another YouTube video beheading a Somalia "blasphemer" and then five years later in a video shot on a beach where he'd decapitated six Christians near Misrata, Libya.

By Brooke's estimates, the Falcon was at least in his fifties and yet he seemed as agile as a much younger man and still filled with hatred.

Her cell phone rang.

"We're a go!" CIA Director Grainger said.

CHAPTER FIFTY-TWO

Aboard the USS Freedom
Off the coast of Seattle, Washington

Major Brooke Grant hit the jackpot.

The Navy had finally identified three ships carrying cesium-137 plus explosives. If they were lucky, Hakim Farouk and the North Korean nuclear bomb would also be on one of those three ships. If not, the Navy would have to intercept the other seven ships while they still were in the Pacific.

Stopping the three ships was now the KTB's priority and Brooke was eager to get to it.

Director Grainger had assigned each KTB team member a specific ship. After a briefing at Camp Pendleton, they'd been driven to naval aircraft that had taken each of them to a different amphibious command ship in the Pacific that was being used as a staging area. Brooke, Esther, and Khalid would be responsible for boarding each ship after it was under the Navy's control to determine if Hakim Farouk was a passenger.

The trio's parting had not included any emotional good-byes. After their briefing, they'd simply gone their separate ways with not as much as a handshake or cheery "Good luck!"

The U.S. Navy had taken only forty hours to identify which of the three container ships were carrying deadly radioactive matter. But the White House, the Pentagon, and top intelligence officials had chosen not to rush what the Navy technically called an "opposed boarding" of each vessel.

Instead, the Navy had not approached the ships but had allowed them to continue sailing across the Pacific while it had assembled its most experienced VBSS (visit, board, search, and seizure) special-ops personnel and brought them to the West Coast, where they'd spent a day familiarizing themselves with container ships similar to the three suspected vessels.

Brooke had been given first choice of the three ships, followed by Esther, and finally Khalid.

She had chosen the *Blue Neptune* because it was en route to the Los Angeles harbor and was one of the largest container ships in the entire Pacific—longer than the Empire State Building, wider than the width of a football field, and as tall as a twenty-story building. It was carrying 21,000 TEUs, including 800 TEUs that each were filled with thirty tons of explosive materials. That meant Farouk's dirty bomb would be surrounded by 24,000 tons of explosives packed around radioactive matter. Plus, six men with Muslim names had boarded it in Jakarta.

Los Angeles also was the tenth busiest port in the United States, and once the *Blue Neptune* entered its harbor, the container ship would be less than twenty miles from downtown L.A., a metropolitan city of just under 4 million people.

Brooke didn't understand why Esther had selected the *Bella Francis*, which at 850 feet in length was the smallest of the three. It was carrying a total of only 925 TEUs and less than a single ton of explosive materials to New Orleans where the bulk of its cargo would be loaded onto barges, which would then undergo a 445-mile trip along rivers to the most unlikely of places—Oklahoma.

Even though Brooke had been born in Tulsa, she hadn't realized the Tulsa Port of Catoosa was one of the largest inland ports in the nation—thanks to federal pork barrel projects that had made the Arkansas River navigable.

Khalid had been assigned to the *Carrie Morton*, the second largest of the three container vessels. At 1,200 feet long, it was carrying 14,101 TEUs, mostly filled with electronics, clothing, furniture, and sporting goods for the likes of Target, Best Buy, and Amazon. But it was also carrying twenty-three tons of explosives into the Seattle seaport.

From the Marine Corps Air Station at Camp Pendleton, Brooke had flown directly to the USS *Freedom* amphibious assault ship where she'd been hustled into a preattack briefing.

"We're not certain if the captains of these three vessels are even aware they're carrying radioactive materials," Captain George Baker explained. "We can't take any chances. We must assume they know their ships are carrying bombs and also assume the crew and possibly passengers are hostiles ready to fight."

Brooke deduced that Khalid and Esther were being given nearly identical briefings onboard the *Carrie Morton* and *Bella Francis.*

"Given the danger of having a captain or crew member detonate a radioactive explosive device upon learning his ship is going to be boarded, we must rely on stealth. We will not be requesting permission to board the *Blue Neptune* as is customary under maritime law."

Continuing, Captain Baker methodically reviewed the sequence of events for the "opposed boarding" of the *Blue Neptune*. The launching of an aircraft capable of using electronic countermeasures to block all of the *Blue Neptune's* communication equipment would be the first step. This would prevent its captain from warning the other two ships, if they were colluding. The countermeasures also would jam the ship's radar, sonar, and other detection systems that could alert a captain to approaching naval boarding vessels and aircraft.

"The suspected bomb maker," Captain Baker continued, "has a history of using cell phones to jolt a detonation charge. Unfortunately, turning a cell phone into a trigger has become so easy that brainy kids use them to detonate fireworks on the Fourth of July. Our jamming equipment will block all cell phone signals, including satellite phone calls, but as an added precaution, all three of the suspected ships will be boarded before they enter cell phone service areas along our coasts. These precautions should render any cell phone detonators useless."

As soon as Captain Baker concluded his briefing, she raised her hand. She noticed no one else in the room had a question.

"Are there other ways one of these dirty bombs could be detonated?"

"We're not certain how sophisticated the detonators are. Generally, there are three ways. The first is the already mentioned cell phone detonation. The second would be by hand, meaning someone would have to physically enter the TEU where the device is being stored and manually fire a detonator. The third would be some sort of exterior explosion that could cause the dirty bomb to explode and release its radioactive materials."

"By 'explosion' you mean a terrorist firing an RPG into a container?"

"That certainly could do the trick, depending on how Hakim Farouk has jerry-rigged his detonators. This explains why we must take charge of the *Blue Neptune* quickly, before he or any hostiles on-board can act."

Captain Baker introduced the Marine VBSS team leader in charge of the actual boarding and he explained the primary assault would be done aerially with sea support as backup. The mission would begin predawn this morning when the highly automated ship's seventeen crew members were sleeping. His briefing was short and mostly intended for Brooke, since the VBSS team already had been drilled repeatedly about their respective duties.

An hour after the briefing ended, a Navy aircraft took flight to jam the ability of the *Blue Neptune*, which was some ten nautical miles away, to communicate with the outside world. Moments later, a pair of Super Hornet jet fighters took flight. Armed with precision-guided bombs, the Hornets also were equipped with six-barrel Gatling-style rotary cannons. They flew high enough above the *Blue Neptune* so the ship's crew couldn't see them.

From the USS *Freedom*'s control room, Brooke watched as VBSS trained SEALs boarded two HH-60H Sea Hawk helicopters on the deck with muffled engines for Special-Ops missions. After lifting off, the choppers flew precariously close to the ocean waves as they made their approach toward the gigantic container ship's stern.

Cameras on the Sea Hawks and worn on each of the Special-Ops SEALs relayed what was happening to Captain Baker and Brooke inside the USS *Freedom*'s communications room.

"Ever seen a VBSS, Major Grant?" Captain Baker asked.

"No, sir."

"Stealth is the key. Surprise them. Get aboard and take control before anyone can react. The bridge and the bridge castle's upper decks
are always the first target, but obviously, we must take charge of the
quarters, engine room, and communications and fire controls."

In addition to visuals, Brooke could hear the SEAL leader speaking
to his fellow VBSS teammates. The initial boarding force would
fast rope down from the helicopters onto the deck while operators
aboard high-tech, high-speed, and low-profile surface combatant craft
launched earlier would arrive alongside the *Blue Neptune* for interdic-
tion support.

As Brooke watched, the *Blue Neptune* slowly came into focus as seen
from the helicopters as they skated just above the ocean waves. Within
minutes, the first helicopter popped above the ship's fantail, where it
hovered some forty feet above its deck.

The first SEAL slipped down the heavy rope unchallenged. The
next was ten feet behind him, carefully spaced to allow three Marines
to descend on the fast rope in rapid fire. The six soldiers who reached
the deck first formed a protective semicircle, dropping on one knee
with their M4 carbines shouldered and ready to fire.

The team was deploying so quickly Brooke began to feel confident
the *Blue Neptune* would be under Navy control before its crew realized
what was happening. That is when she heard the rapid popping of
AK-47 assault rifles. The rounds came from at least a dozen men
hiding inside the seven-story-tall bridge castle and another eight positioned on the *Blue Neptune's* deck.

Three of the six SEALs who'd fast roped down were hit, and another
was fatally wounded midway down the rope and fell. At that moment, two terrorists appeared on the deck with shoulder-fired rocket-
propelled grenades. Puffs of white smoke spit from the rear of their
tubes when the RPG-7s were fired at the hovering helicopter. Each
grenade struck its mark. One exploded in the helicopter's cockpit, the
other its tail. The RPGs exploded with a brilliant flash in the predawn
light. Amid the huge yellow bursts of flame, the Sea Hawk aircraft
came crashing down onto the deck, killing two Marines below it.

The second Sea Hawk rose upward, giving it higher ground as a Marine fired a Gauss-16A minigun through the open chopper's side door at the terrorists below hiding on the *Blue Neptune*'s deck. One of the terrorists was blown overboard when hit by the powerful rapid-fired rounds; another was ripped into pieces at the same time as he was pulling the trigger of an RPG aimed at the helicopter. He collapsed while firing and the grenade flew low and sideways into a TEU only a few feet away, causing a fire that ignited two of his fellow terrorists who were near it. They ran screaming in flames across the deck before collapsing.

The terrorists firing from the deck and those hiding behind port-holes in the *Blue Neptune*'s bridge castle were making it impossible for any SEALs to fast rope down under such intense fire from the second Sea Hawk.

"They were ready for a fight," Captain Baker said bitterly as he watched the monitors in the USS *Freedom*'s communications room. "And there's a hell of a lot more of them than seventeen crew members."

"They must have been standing watch twenty-four-seven ever since they left Jakarta," Brooke suggested.

Captain Baker ordered the second Sea Hawk to back away from the *Blue Neptune*'s deck before it suffered the same fate as the first. As it was retreating, an RPG fired from a porthole midway up the bridge castle barely missed the chopper's cockpit.

An eerie calm seemed to settle over the container ship. Brooke imagined the captain and crew cheering inside the bridge, thinking they had driven away the Marines. Several terrorists hurried to extinguish the fires on the deck while others searched for any of the SEALs who had fast roped down and possibly survived the mayhem.

It was in this moment that the two Super Hornet multirole fighters came swooping down from 20,000 feet, their twin engines spitting fire behind them as they approached the ship's bow. They were a fearsome sight of America's superior firepower. It would have taken a miracle for an RPG fired from the deck to hit one of the lightning-fast Super Hornets that appeared so dramatically the terrorists on the *Blue*

Neptune deck seemed more mesmerized by their approach than terrified.

The first pilot unleashed a barrage from his jet's Gatling-style
20-mm M61 rotary cannons capable of firing six thousand rounds per
minute. The slugs were precisely aimed at the top floor bridge's windows and the bridge castle's lower decks to avoid possibly hitting
any TEU that might contain combustible materials or explosives. The
rounds riddled the flat-faced structure with fist-sized holes and killed
anyone within their trajectory.

The second fighter jet fired its rounds seconds later, further pock-
marking the steel walls of the rectangular building.

The Super Hornets pulled up after strafing the front of the cargo
ship as if they were in an aerial acrobatic show, vanishing momentarily
into the breaking morning sky before circling downward with another
fierce thunderclap of 20-mm rounds. This time, they approached from
the stern, peppering the opposite side of the bridge castle with such
intensity that it would have been impossible for an average-sized human standing behind its steel walls to survive.

The Super Hornets vanished as quickly as they had descended and
the second Sea Hawk helicopter reappeared. Its human cargo of SEALs
fast roped down while its gunner fired .50-caliber rounds at any terrorist who dared show himself.

The boarding team fanned out across the deck, driving the remain-
ing terrorists into the ship's bridge and lower cargo hold. As soon as
the ship's deck was secure, the SEALs tossed pilot ladders over the
Blue Neptune's side to the waiting fast boats that had brought rein-
forcements.

More than thirty SEALs swarmed onto the ship but only a
carefully selected handful entered the bridge castle and steps descending into the cargo hold. In teams of six, they systematically
made their way first up to the bridge and then down to lower decks
armed with M4s, 9 mm pistols, concussion grenades, and plastic
hand ties. On the bridge, they found the mortally wounded captain
lying near a black jihadist flag that had been tacked onto the wall.
It appeared the ship's captain had been forced at gunpoint to pilot

the ship, given that an armed dead terrorist was positioned near his body.

"I count twelve dead in the bridge castle," the team leader radioed to Captain Baker, who was monitoring the assault from the USS *Freedom*. "At least twice that many were shooting at us, plus those on the deck. We'll give you a body count after we sweep the ship."

"Judging from that black flag and the AK-47s, this ship was on a suicide mission," Brooke remarked into a headset. "Have you secured the dirty bomb?"

"We believe it's stacked high near the bow. We're searching for it now and should find it by the time you arrive."

A helicopter was landing on the USS *Freedom*'s deck but Brooke had to wait momentarily, standing at attention, as the bodies of dead and wounded SEALs were being unloaded.

By the time she reached the *Blue Neptune*, the ship had been searched and secured. Seventeen men with their hands tied behind their backs were waiting for her in a straight line on the main deck. The first told her that all seventeen survivors were crew members and explained that heavily armed terrorists had commandeered the *Blue Neptune* shortly after it left Jakarta. They'd had help from the six passengers who had come aboard in the Indonesian port. Rather than surrender, every terrorist on the vessel had been killed exchanging gunfire with the SEALs.

After taking time to interview each of the crew members, Brooke turned her attention to the dead terrorists whose bodies had been displayed on the deck. A Marine assigned to help her photographed each corpse and collected DNA samples for further identification.

"Did you find your bomb maker?" Captain Baker asked impatiently through the headset under her combat helmet.

"No, but two of these bodies have been burned beyond recognition and one of the terrorists was blown off the deck during the fighting. Hakim Farouk could have been one of them."

As soon as she was finished with her assignment, Brooke asked, "What's the status of disarming the dirty bomb?"

"The bomb disposal and radioactive team are dealing with that,"

Captain Baker replied. "Once it is disarmed, they can begin searching the containers for your missing nuke."

"I want to look at the dirty bomb's detonator," she said.

"All in good time, Major," Captain Baker replied.

Brooke made her way to the bow, where she spotted a number of SEALs centered near one stack of TEUs. When she reached them, she was stopped by the SEAL boarding team's leader. Some thirty feet away, four men in heavy bomb disposal suits and masks were inspecting a rusty red TEU marked PROPERTY OF SEA TRIDENT SHIPPING.

"Welcome, Major," the squad leader said. "Figured you'd end up here based on your reputation for always being in the most dangerous places."

"Sea Trident Shipping is a company owned by Umoja Owiti," she said.

"Who's he?"

"One of the masterminds of this entire dirty bomb campaign," she responded. "What's the status?"

"Still checking for booby traps and triggers. We don't want to blow us all to hell."

He shot Brooke a grin and added, "Don't worry. You can be damn sure these are the best of the best."

"They'd better be. I don't have to remind you what the captain said at the briefing."

"Right, Major, we've got some eight hundred shipping containers around us all packed with explosives and somewhere is a large amount of cesium-137. That's why everyone is taking it slow and easy."

Captain Baker overheard their conversation aboard the USS *Freedom* and spoke to Brooke through her earpiece. "Major, I thought I specifically told you to wait until I gave you the all clear."

"With all due respect, sir, your exact words were 'all in good time,' which I interpreted to mean that it was a good time for me to move forward."

The squad leader listening to their exchange winced at her flimsy explanation.

Captain Baker controlled his anger. He was well aware that

Brooke's uncle had been the former chairman of the joint chiefs of staff and that Brooke was answering directly to CIA Director Grainger. He decided to not chastise her for her impertinence.

"*Allahu Akbar!*" a man yelled. "*Allahu Akbar!*"

Seemingly from nowhere, a terrorist wearing a vest wrapped with explosives and holding what Brooke assumed was a detonator bolted toward the bomb disposal unit outside the Sea Trident container.

"Don't let him blow himself—" Brooke shouted.

But her sentence was drowned out by the sounds of the squad leader standing next to her and another SEAL firing their 9 mm pistols. All four of their slugs hit the charging man's torso, stopping him.

For a moment, no one moved or spoke. Then slowly, Brooke and the squad leader began walking toward the fatally wounded terrorist.

"Where the hell did he come from?" a furious Captain Baker demanded over the headsets.

"Not sure, Captain," the SEAL leader replied. "This area had been swept."

The leader of the bomb squad began waving his hand at Brooke and the squad leader, a signal for them to keep away. One of his experts bent down to examine the terrorist and disarm his suicide vest. After he finished, he walked to where Brooke and the SEAL squad leader were waiting.

"We all should be dead right now," he announced, holding up a wire and switch. "This Jimmy Jihad pushed the detonation switch before he was shot. We should have been blown up." Nodding at the switch in his hand, he explained, "Lucky for us, he left his suicide vest in the salt air. This switch malfunctioned because it was corroded."

CHAPTER FIFTY-THREE

Boarding of the Carrie Morton
Pacific Ocean en route to Seattle

The first moment the captain of the northwestern bound container ship, *Carrie Morton*, realized his vessel was being boarded was when a SEAL burst into the bridge with his pistol drawn.

"You are being boarded by the United States Navy," the SEAL declared, sticking to the script that had been given him by his superior officer. "We have reason to believe the *Carrie Morton* contains illegal cargo. We are taking charge of your vessel to undertake a search. The *Carrie Morton* will remain under our control until this search is completed to our satisfaction. Do you understand?"

The captain raised his hands above his head and answered, "You'll get no fight from us. What cargo are you seeking? Drugs?" The rest of the crew members on the bridge raised their hands too.

During the next two hours, the SEALs cautiously made their way through the ship. They rousted the passengers and the crew members who were sleeping and took them to the top deck in plastic tie handcuffs. No one would be freed until his identity was confirmed. No one resisted and it appeared no radical Islamic fighters were onboard. As the explosive and radioactive specialists swarmed over the TEUs, Saudi intelligence agent Khalid interviewed each detainee in search of the elusive Hakim Farouk. He was not among them.

CIA Director Payton Grainger, who was monitoring the search from a command post in Washington, ordered Khalid to reinterrogate each man to ensure everyone on the vessel had been accounted for and positively identified. Grainger already had told the SEAL leader conducting the search to look for TEUs marked with SEA TRIDENT SHIPPING on their sides.

"A terrorist was hiding on the *Blue Neptune* wearing a suicide vest and he almost cost the life of everyone on that ship," Grainger warned Khalid.

The Saudi agent repeated his duties and reported that Hakim Farouk was definitely not onboard.

"Keep the *Carrie Morton* at its current location well away from Seattle and await further orders," the SEAL leader was told.

It took another hour for them to find Farouk's dirty bomb stacked amid the other TEUs. It was inside a Sea Trident Shipping container, identical to the one found on the *Blue Neptune*. The only difference was that a single TEU contained all three ingredients for making a dirty bomb—a detonator, explosives, and cesium-137, neatly packed inside a forty-foot-long unit.

In Washington, Director Grainger conferred with Brooke about what they'd learned from boarding both ships.

"Farouk clearly intended for the *Blue Neptune* to be detonated when it entered the Los Angeles seaport," Grainger said. "It had the most explosives, the most radioactive materials, and it was being protected by and under the control of the jihadists."

"I agree," Brooke replied. "It was a suicide mission and even though one terrorist was blown overboard during the boarding and two were burned beyond recognition, I don't believe Farouk was traveling on the *Blue Neptune* because a search showed it wasn't carrying the nuclear bomb."

Grainger replied, "Let's move on to the *Carrie Morton*. There were no terrorists on it, no Hakim Farouk, no nuclear bomb. Its captain didn't have any idea he was transporting a dirty bomb."

"The explosives, radioactive material, and detonator were all found in a single container too," Brooke said.

"I don't believe Seattle was the target. I think the container was supposed to be unloaded and sent by truck or rail elsewhere."

"A traveling dirty bomb," Brooke said.

"Which brings us to the *Bella Francis*. Let's review what you and Esther learned about it."

"It is carrying radioactive materials plus a small amount of explosives. Not many at all. It's bound for New Orleans, where it will drop off most of its TEUs. Those containers are supposed to be unloaded onto barges and taken up rivers to the Port of Catoosa outside Tulsa, Oklahoma."

"Can you get on a computer? I want you to check something about the three ships."

Several minutes later, she said, "Okay, yes, I've pulled up all the records that Esther was working with."

"You and Esther checked to see when the three ships were scheduled to arrive at their respective seaports, didn't you?"

"Esther is the one who checked. She said they were arriving on different days so we focused mainly on the passengers after that."

Grainger thought for a moment and then said, "We now know the *Blue Neptune* was going to be exploded when it reached Los Angeles. What date was that?"

Brooke checked. "The last Monday in May." She hesitated and then she and Grainger said at the same time, "Memorial Day."

"Quick," he said, "now that we know the dirty bomb on the *Carrie Morton* wasn't meant to be exploded in Seattle, see where it was supposed to be taken and when it was scheduled to get there."

Khalid had given Director Grainger the serial number of the Sea Trident Shipping container that contained the bomb. Grainger told it to Brooke, who entered it into the computer.

"It was being sent by truck to Chicago," she replied excitedly. "And it was supposed to arrive on Memorial Day."

Both of them understood instantly that Director Grainger's theory about simultaneous explosions on the same day had been correct. *When the three ships were arriving in port didn't matter.* It was the date when *their cargos* were being delivered that did.

Brooke immediately called up information about the *Bella Francis*. A check of its delivery records confirmed it.

"The cargo on the *Bella Francis* is scheduled to be dropped off in

New Orleans and loaded on barges for delivery to the Port of Catoosa on Memorial Day," she said. "It all fits."

"I'm guessing those barges heading to Tulsa will be filled with explosives," Grainger said. "That would make the dirty bomb on the ship big enough to do significant damage by spreading radioactive materials over northeastern Oklahoma."

Having called up the delivery schedule, Brooke spotted something else about the *Bella Francis*.

"Director Grainger," she said in a suspicious voice, "the *Bella Francis*'s next port of call after stopping in New Orleans is New York Harbor."

"Quick. When is it scheduled to arrive there?"

It took Brooke a moment to check. "It is scheduled to arrive—oh my God—on *Memorial Day*!"

The CIA director took no satisfaction in realizing that his initial theory was correct. Three dirty bombs would be exploded on a single day. Their targets: Los Angeles, Chicago, and Tulsa, proving that the Falcon could strike any region of the nation. That same day, the nuclear bomb would go off in New York's harbor. Four cities in a single day.

"Sir," Brooke said in a solemn voice, "I don't think Esther missed any of this. That's why she chose the *Bella Francis* even though it looked like the least likely of the three ships. I think she figured this out and just didn't tell us. When is the Navy boarding the *Bella Francis*?"

CHAPTER FIFTY-FOUR

Aboard the USS Vigilant, *staging ship*
Off the Panamanian coast

"You knew, didn't you?" Director Grainger asked over a secure phone line. "You knew the cargo delivery dates were all on Memorial Day."

"My people have been dealing with these terrorists for a long, long time," she replied. "I suspected the *Bella Francis* because its final port of call was New York City. I didn't think the Falcon or Farouk would waste a nuclear bomb on any city but the international capital of the world."

"You should have shared your theory," he said.

"For what purpose? All it would have changed is that Brooke Grant would have been sent to board the *Bella Francis*. In all honesty, who do you think is better prepared if Hakim Farouk is on it?"

She had a point. Esther and Khalid were both highly trained killers. Brooke was a former military attaché who'd been forced to kill. There was a difference in Grainger's mind.

"Now, I have a question for you," Esther said. "When will your Navy SEALs finally board the *Bella Francis*?"

"Be patient," he replied, ending their call.

Grainger had never felt so frustrated. The *Bella Francis* had not been boarded because a sudden and unexpected storm had swept up the Panamanian coastline at the same time the *Blue Neptune* and the *Carrie Morton* were being commandeered by SEALs.

Meteorologists predicted the storm could last several days, which meant the *Bella Francis* would continue traveling unchecked toward the Gulf of Panama.

Grainger had been arguing with four-star admiral Dexter Kowalski for three days about sending in the SEALs.

"We need to seize it while it's still in international waters regardless of the weather," he'd warned.

But Admiral Kowalski had reminded him that the Pacific Ocean was larger than any ship and that during World War Two, a typhoon had sunk three destroyers and damaged nine other warships. This was no typhoon, but waves breaking against the container ship and strong winds made boarding the *Bella Francis* impractical. Weather forecasters predicted the storm would lessen in another thirty hours. They had no choice but to hang on.

Four days after the other two ships had been boarded, the weather cleared and Admiral Kowalski decided to green-light a VBSS SEAL team boarding.

Finally.

Major Brooke Grant had pleaded with Director Grainger to let her join Esther on the USS *Vigilant* but he had refused. The amphibious assault ship had been caught in the same violent storm as the *Bella Francis*, making getting Brooke there risky. It would be up to Esther to find Hakim Farouk and both the dirty bomb and the nuclear bomb.

Director Grainger and Admiral Kowalski monitored the boarding from inside a Pentagon situation room with images sent via satellite from cameras on the helicopters and SEALs, just as had been done during the earlier two boardings.

The procedure would be identical. A communication jamming aircraft would take flight, followed by a pair of SuperCobras and two HH-60H Sea Hawk helicopters transporting SEALs from the USS *Vigilant*.

"Hopefully there won't be any jihadists onboard," Admiral Kowalski said.

"All it will take is one," Grainger replied. "If Hakim Farouk is on the ship, he'll blow it up. We must get to him first."

The *Bella Francis* was still far enough away from the Panamanian shoreline to not cause substantial damage, although it would kill everyone onboard.

"Your SEALs need to find Hakim Farouk quickly," Grainger said, nervously repeating the obvious.

As they watched, the first Sea Hawk arrived at the ship and rose upward from the ocean above the stern. Grainger and Admiral Kowalski braced themselves for the worst. SEALs immediately began fast roping to the deck. Grainger and Kowalski each stared intently at the Pentagon monitors.

Not a single shot or RPG was fired.

The views on the Pentagon multiple screens from cameras attached to each soldier's helmet showed the SEALs hustling up a metal staircase inside the bridge castle.

No one opposed them. Within minutes, they burst through the bridge's door with guns ready.

"Who are you?" an alarmed captain demanded.

"U.S. Navy," the lead officer declared, reciting the same monologue that had been issued to each SEAL squad leader.

The captain shot his first mate a puzzled look.

"Put your hands behind your backs," the SEAL squad leader barked as his men readied plastic ties to bind the crew members' wrists.

"Did you say you were seizing the *Bella Francis*?" the captain asked calmly.

"Yes, your ship, the *Bella Francis*."

"I believe you and the U.S. Navy have made a terrible error," the captain replied. "This is not the *Bella Francis*. My ship is the *Bella Francishco*."

The captain nodded his head downward toward a bronze plaque on the bridge's control panel that bore the ship's name—*Bella Francishco*.

"Free the captain and confirm the ship's name," Admiral Kowalski ordered through his headset from the Pentagon.

"Sir, I'll have no idea if the paperwork he shows me is legitimate."

"That's why you're wearing helmet cams, son. We'll check records here too."

"What the hell is happening?" Grainger demanded. "Did we just board the wrong ship?"

Within a half hour, the puzzle was solved.

"During the storm," Admiral Kowalski explained, "the *Bella Francis* and the *Bella Francishco* passed close to each other and those responsible for tracking the *Bella Francis* mistakenly began trailing the wrong container ship."

"For god's sake, aren't they different sizes?" Grainger complained.

"It was a one-in-a-million coincidence. Not only did the ships have similar names, but they are also twin ships. Both built in Hamburg, Germany, within two years of each other. Both sold to Italian shipping companies and both traveling through international waters along courses that happened to bring them into close proximity when the storm hit and obstructed our tracking operation."

Grainger cursed under his breath and asked, "Then where in the hell is the *Bella Francis*?"

"We've located it in the Gulf of Panama approaching the Bridge of the Americas," Admiral Kowalski replied.

"At the mouth of the canal?"

"Yes," Admiral Kowalski replied sheepishly. "I've arranged a briefing."

One of his aides filled in Grainger. The director didn't like what he heard. Ships approaching the canal on the Pacific side first passed under the Bridge of the Americas at Balboa Harbor near Panama City before they reached the Miraflores Locks. These locks lifted vessels to a higher level where the ship next entered the Pedro Miguel Locks. The two locks formed only a small portion of the canal cut-through. The majority of the crossing was spent navigating through a man-made lake and passageways created when the canal was constructed.

"There are more than a million Panamanians living in Panama City, which is only three or four miles from where the ship is currently traveling," the briefer said.

Grainger was enraged. "Your people screwed up," he told Admiral Kowalski. "I'm leaving it up to you to alert the president."

Within an hour, Admiral Kowalski, the other members of the joint chiefs of staff, Director Grainger, and senior intelligence officials had gathered inside the White House's situation room.

A visibly angry President Austin entered the underground complex and began demanding answers as he was walking toward his chair at the conference table. "Admiral, did you have someone on duty who couldn't find his ass with both hands stuck in his back pockets?" he asked.

"It was a freak occurrence, Mr. President," Admiral Kowalski said, defending his men's actions. "There was a violent storm and—"

Taking his seat, President Austin waved a dismissive hand toward the admiral. "That's the past. We now have a container ship entering the Panama Canal zone with a terrorist onboard armed with both a dirty bomb and a nuclear weapon. Has the Panamanian government been told?"

"No, sir," Director Grainger replied.

"Explain all of this to me once again, Director Grainger, so we can be a hundred percent certain what we are dealing with," the president said.

The director signaled an aide, who dimmed the lights and a chart appeared on a large monitor. "Here's the complete timetable," Grainger began. "We know the North Koreans sold a nuclear bomb to the Falcon that was shipped from the Ranson port to Jakarta where Hakim Farouk is waiting."

Everyone was following along on the chart.

"Farouk takes that bomb to Bandung with him and this is when we make our first wrong assumption. We initially thought he was dismantling it to make three dirty bombs. Instead, he leaves it untouched and builds three detonators. He loads those detonators on three U.S.-bound ships that are already carrying both explosives and radioactive materials. Our underwater drones detect the cesium-137. This is how we know what three ships are carrying dirty bombs. But at this point, we still don't know what he's done with the nuclear bomb."

Grainger glanced at President Austin, who was paying close attention to the chart. The president had already been thoroughly briefed on this but apparently wanted everyone in the situation room to hear it, given the imminent danger the nuclear bomb posed.

"The key to understanding Farouk's plan became clear when we boarded the *Blue Neptune*. He had made it into a giant dirty bomb that would arrive in port on Memorial Day. Next we boarded the *Carrie Morton* and learned the dirty bomb on it was scheduled to be delivered by truck to Chicago on Memorial Day. Which brings us to the *Bella Francis*. Its radioactive material and a small amount of explosives were scheduled to be unloaded in New Orleans and placed on slow-moving barges with other explosives on a nearly five-hundred-mile trip up navigable rivers for delivery to Tulsa, which they would reach on Memorial Day. Meanwhile, the *Bella Francis* would continue up the East Coast to New York Harbor, where it would reach its final destination on Memorial Day."

"Amazing," President Austin said. "Three dirty bombs and a nuclear bomb all ready to be detonated on Memorial Day when we are honoring our military heroes who have died. How in the hell did these terrorists work out such complicated timing?"

"With help from African billionaire Umoja Owiti, who owns the ships and the shipping containers."

No one spoke while President Austin rapped his right fingers hard against the conference table. "Can we board the *Bella Francis* while it is in the canal zone?" he asked.

"Yes," Admiral Kowalski said, "with permission from the Panamanian government."

"But if Hakim Farouk panics and detonates a nuclear bomb," Grainger warned, "millions will die and the canal will be destroyed and contaminated for decades."

"My SEALs can capture or kill him before he can react," Admiral Kowalski said defensively.

President Austin gave him a skeptical glance. "You lost an entire damn ship while it was at sea, Admiral."

"What happens if we don't do anything?" Director Grainger asked. "What if we allow the *Bella Francis* to continue through the canal and then board it after it enters the Caribbean and is, say, off the coast of Honduras or Nicaragua? Fewer people would be at risk."

"What if the canal zone is his actual target?" President Austin asked.

"The Falcon said he would attack three U.S. cities. He wants to embarrass us, not Panama. Destroying the canal zone would greatly harm shipping, which would further alienate him from countries that use the canal to transport oil and other goods from the Middle East. I believe New York City has always been his primary target. It's our most populated metropolitan area and hitting it again after the nine-eleven attacks would show that despite all of the security efforts, we are still vulnerable."

"How long does it take a ship to pass through the canal zone?" the president said.

"Between twelve to twenty-four hours," Admiral Kowalski replied.

President Austin thought for a moment before speaking. "Hakim Farouk has been isolated while crossing the Pacific. No communication. Now that he's in the canal zone, he'll have access to the Internet and also will be able to use his cell phone. If he discovers the *Carrie Morton* and *Blue Neptune* have been boarded and seized in the middle of the Pacific and their bombs disarmed, he'll know we're on to him and possibly blow up the *Bella Francis* smack dab in the middle of Panama."

"Sir," Admiral Kowalski replied, "both the *Carrie Morton* and the *Blue Neptune* are being held in international waters. They are literally hundreds of miles away from land out in the Pacific Ocean and the men on those ships have been prevented by SEALs from sending any messages. We have Marines guarding and holding each vessel right where it was boarded. It's highly unlikely Hakim Farouk will know we have seized control of those two ships. In fact, I'd venture it is close to impossible. No one in the world knows we've commandeered them."

"All we need is twenty-four hours," Director Grainger said. "By then the *Bella Francis* will have passed through the canal."

President Austin rapped his fingers even harder against the conference room table, as if he were pounding on a piano keyboard with his right hand.

"What's your decision, Mr. President?" Grainger asked. "Shall we warn the Panamanian president and attempt to board the *Bella Francis* or let the container ship continue through the canal unmolested and board it once it's on the Atlantic side?"

"My advice would be—" Admiral Kowalski started to offer, but he was cut off by President Austin.

"If your people had done their jobs, we wouldn't be in this mess. I'm not going to inform the Panamanian government. But I am going to pray to God for help that this cargo ship makes it through the canal zone without that nuclear bomb being detonated."

Rising from his chair, President Austin leaned forward and spoke directly to Admiral Kowalski. "This is a hell of a risk we're taking. You just make damn sure word about the *Carrie Morton* and *Blue Neptune* doesn't leak out during the next twenty-four hours, Admiral."

CHAPTER FIFTY-FIVE

CIA Headquarters
Langley, Virginia

Director Payton Grainger's executive assistant said an emergency call was on a secure line.

"Mr. Director, I understand you're in a bit of a crisis," Yossi Bar-Lev, the director of the Mossad, said.

"Which one?" Grainger replied, trying to sound nonchalant. He didn't know how much Bar-Lev had learned and wasn't about to volunteer any clues.

"Esther told me your Navy lost track of the *Bella Francis*, a ship that is transporting both a dirty bomb and a nuclear one through the Panama Canal zone," Bar-Lev replied. "She was supposed to board it to identify Hakim Farouk but is still awaiting your orders while waiting on the USS *Vigilant*."

"Isn't she supposed to be reporting to me?" Grainger bristled.

"Let's not play games," the Mossad director answered. "We have known each other far too long. She is on loan to you. You don't own her loyalty."

"She is on loan, which means Esther needs to follow *my* orders. Her job is to positively identify Hakim Farouk, nothing more."

"My friend, why are you squandering the many talents of a highly skilled Mossad operative?" Bar-Lev replied. "Was it not Esther who found a way to penetrate the African billionaire Umoja Owiti's security? Was it not her who first identified the *Bella Francis* as the ship that Hakim Farouk has chosen to attack New York City?"

Grainger didn't reply. He was irked that Esther had told Bar-Lev everything.

"My friend," Bar-Lev continued, "might I suggest you have Esther board the *Bella Francis* at an opportune time and dispose of this terrorist rather than sending in the Marines and Panamanian forces, which risks scaring him. Has she not demonstrated that she is very good at what she does?"

"You seem to be overlooking a few things. Esther is a woman and there are no women on the *Bella Francis*. If she is seen, Hakim Farouk would instantly suspect her, even if she posed as an inspector. Secondly, the ship is moving through the canal during daylight hours, so she couldn't sneak aboard at night."

"Is that all? For her, those are easily overcome. She is one of my most resourceful operatives."

"There were armed terrorists hiding on the *Blue Neptune*. For someone even as talented as Esther that could present problems if the ship is under the control of jihadists. Our government can't risk it and *neither* should the Mossad."

"Director Grainger, I would not think of having Esther interfere with your plans. But you owe me this. What is your plan?"

Grainger thought for a moment and then said, "To permit the *Bella Francis* to sail through the Canal Zone unmolested and take the appropriate action when it's in the Atlantic."

"A risky venture, at least for the Panamanians, who I can assume know nothing about a container ship carrying two bombs through their territory. Let me ask you. Do you intend to keep Esther twiddling her thumbs in the Pacific?"

"No, once the *Bella Francis* crosses through the canal zone, I'll need her to identify Hakim Farouk. But that is her *only* task at this moment."

"A suggestion, my friend. She must cross from the Pacific to reach the Atlantic. Correct?" He chuckled good-naturedly. "What possible harm can come from flying her into Panama and arranging for her to observe the *Bella Francis* as it makes its passageway through the canal? Perhaps posing as a dockworker or tourist. She could get video of the

Bella Francis that could reveal if Hakim Farouk is, indeed, onboard that vessel, as you suspect. Or if there are others like him on the ship."

Grainger considered the offer. "What you are proposing makes sense," he said, "but I want to remind you, our government does not want Esther boarding that ship to kill Hakim Farouk. Is that clear? Do I have your word? Do not get involved in this. Let that ship pass undisturbed through the canal. That is just not me talking; it is what President Austin has decided."

"Relax," Bar-Lev said. "She will be told by you and by me not to board the ship without your permission but, my friend, please know that we will not stand with you if Hakim Farouk explodes his bombs in the canal zone. Your country will have to take full blame for not intercepting that ship."

"I understand. Esther is on loan. She is not a scapegoat."

"Shalom, my friend, and good luck."

Grainger sat quietly at his desk while his mind raced. He had played the game of chess for as long as he could remember. His father had taught him the basics at age six. Over the years, he'd learned that in a tactical chess game that included sacrificial attacks and many forced moves, it was possible for an accomplished player to think as many as ten or even fifteen moves ahead.

Calling on those skills now, he spent the next hour making arrangements and then he began calling the three members of the KTB team. His first call was to Khalid, who was still waiting for orders on a naval staging ship in the northwest Pacific outside Seattle.

Khalid was in a foul mood. "I've been seasick for days on this stinking tub. I hope you are calling to get me off this boat."

"That's exactly why I am calling," Grainger replied. "I've arranged for a plane to return you to Washington. I require your special skills. I will explain once you get here."

"What about the Jewish Mossad agent and your own Major Brooke Grant?" he asked.

"They'll be busy with other assignments unrelated to your task. I am breaking up the KTB team. You will not be seeing either of them again."

Khalid did not seem disappointed by the news.

The next call went to Major Brooke Grant, who was still aboard the USS *Freedom*, a hundred miles off the California coast.

"I am arranging for you to return to Washington, D.C., immediately," Grainger said.

"But what about the nuclear bomb on the *Bella Francis*?" she asked in an alarmed voice. "What about Hakim Farouk?"

"We have that situation under control. I need you for a new assignment."

"What could be more important than stopping a nuclear bomb attack?"

"Major Grant, must you always challenge my decisions?" he replied. "I need you to go on a Special-Ops mission after the Falcon."

The mere mention of the master terrorist's name ended her urge to argue. "You know where he's hiding?" she asked as a dozen thoughts filled her mind.

"Save your questions for my personal briefing when you get back."

"You can't get me to Washington quick enough."

Director Grainger's next call was to Esther on the USS *Vigilant* off the Panamanian coast.

"I just spoke to your boss," Grainger said in a voice peppered with irritation. "I would prefer you speaking to me before you contact him in the future."

Esther didn't reply. She saw no reason to defend herself.

Grainger said, "Director Bar-Lev and I have agreed that you will NOT, I repeat will NOT, attempt to board the *Bella Francis* as it moves through the canal zone. However, I am arranging for you to fly into Panama for intel purposes *only*. We need to confirm Hakim Farouk is on the *Bella Francis* and whether or not he is alone or has armed jihadists with him. But again, you are NOT to take any action against him or the vessel."

"I understand," Esther replied, "but quite frankly I don't agree. If Farouk is foolish enough to appear on deck, a good sniper could terminate him and I am a very good sniper."

"And if another terrorist is onboard, he would detonate the bombs.

No, we do it my way or you're on a flight to Tel Aviv," Grainger said firmly.

"I understand."

"I've arranged for a helicopter to fly you into Panama, where you will be taken to the Pedro Miguel Locks. The *Bella Francis* will be raised to the same level there as Gatun Lake, which it must cross before entering another set of locks to be lowered to the Atlantic Ocean."

"And what would you have me do once I get to these locks?"

"Tourists are not allowed on the docks. The closest you can get is a hundred yards away in an observation deck and parking lot. Fortunately the Pedro Miguel Locks handle two ships at a time side by side. My people are arranging for you to board an American cruise ship that will be alongside the *Bella Francis* when both are in the locks. You will blend in with tourists taking photos and have a clear view of everyone on the deck of the *Bella Francis*."

"You are a clever man, Mr. Director," Esther said. "I suspect you will have one of your men accompany me on this cruise ship. We will be posing, no doubt, as a happy couple just watching how the canal docks raise and lower ships, just like other tourists."

"That's the plan."

"It's also a way for you to make certain I have a babysitter, giving me no opportunity to kill Hakim Farouk on my own."

"The thought that you might try something like that did cross my mind even though Director Bar-Lev has assured me that you will do as ordered. Expect to leave within the hour."

Having spoken to all three members of his original KTB team, Director Grainger had one more chess piece to move into place. Perhaps the most critical in his entire scheme.

"Representative Adeogo," Grainger said, when the congressman answered his call. "I've just spoken to President Austin and he has authorized me to accompany you to Elkton, Maryland, to meet personally with the Imam Mohammad Al-Kader and make him an offer."

"I must say, I am surprised," Adeogo replied.

"Sedition is different from committing actual acts of terrorism," Grainger replied. "The President puts a higher price on the Falcon than the Imam and if Al-Kader can tell us where he is, we are willing to negotiate."

"He doesn't want to negotiate. He has given you a list of demands."

"I'm well aware of Al-Kader's demands and we are willing to comply with almost all of them. Time is of the essence so I'd like to visit him with you as quickly as you are free. I'm having the legal paperwork drawn up as we speak."

"Let me check my schedule," Adeogo replied, "and have my assistant call you."

"Let's not involve any assistants. Just you and me. What we are doing is a high-priority, national security issue that you will be bound by law not to disclose. That's how the president wants it."

"Trust me, Mr. Director," Adeogo answered. "I have no interest in wanting any of this negotiating made public."

CHAPTER FIFTY-SIX

Tocumen International Airport
Panama City, Panama

*A*t least they sent me a handsome American, Esther thought.

After passage of the Torrijos-Carter Treaties, which transferred the Panama Canal to the Panamanian government in 1997, the United States had closed all of its military bases on the isle. Consequently, Esther had flown from the USS *Vigilant* to a commercial airfield. As she walked across a tarmac to a waiting Robinson R44 four-seat helicopter, she sized up the tall American waiting for her. He was dressed in khaki Bermuda shorts, a dark blue Tommy Bahama shirt decorated with light blue flowers, sandals, mirrored sunglasses, and a New York Yankees ball cap. From the size of his biceps and calf muscles, she guessed he was a Marine, probably Special Ops. She put him in his early thirties.

Esther extended her hand and they exchanged firm grips.

"Terry McGill," he said, smiling.

"Esther," she answered.

He cracked a smile and she saw that he had gold crowns on two premolars on his left and a slight scar that corresponded with them on his cheek. Part of her training was to notice such things.

"Esther, huh," he said as they boarded the chopper. "You intel types really think giving a fake or only first name protects your identity nowadays with facial recognition software and all the other high-tech gizmos out there?"

Gizmos. She'd not heard that word used for a long time and only by much older men from Southern states.

"You're a SEAL, not CIA," she replied. "Probably Mississippi?"

"Oohrah, ma'am. But no. Alabama."

"Close enough. If we're supposed to be playing the roles of lovers on a cruise, you'd better drop the *ma'am*."

He grinned again.

"Oh," he continued, "here's some clothes. They said you'd be wearing military fatigues." He handed her a shopping bag that contained a similar outfit to his—khaki shorts, a pink and white paisley swim tee, and sandals. She didn't bother to ask how the CIA knew her size.

"I'll turn my head," he offered.

"Suit yourself," she replied as she began slipping out of her military wear in the back of the helicopter next to him. As she was pulling her camo T-shirt over her head, momentarily covering her eyes, he stole a glance and noticed several pockmarks on her abdomen. Bullet wounds.

"How much you bench press?" he asked as he handed her a pair of mirrored sunglasses that matched his.

"I weigh a hundred and twenty pounds," she replied. "I bench around one hundred and eighty." That put her near the top of women her size when it came to lifting weights. "And you?"

"One eighty-five weight and a bit over three hundred on a good day."

"Since we're sharing such personal information," she said, "how'd you get those gold crowns and scar?"

"Rifle butt. Guy didn't like my answers and I didn't like his questions."

"Now that we've covered the stuff every dating couple needs to know," she quipped, "tell me your plan."

He handed her a bulky Nikon digital camera with a long leather strap.

"I'm just here to keep you company. Decoration. We'll land on a cruise ship called *The Getaway*. It enters the locks at the same time as the *Bella Francis* container ship. We stand out on a deck and you record everything you see. That Nikon sends it directly to wherever it is supposed to be sent. Then we catch a ride off the ship and we both go on to live happily ever after."

"Those are your only orders?" she asked.

"Oh," he said, grinning, "I'm not supposed to let you out of my sight. Hopefully you're not planning on trying to give me the slip."

"Don't worry, Washington was very clear about what I can and can't do."

"Then we should have an interesting day, maybe slip in a few beers or shots of tequila after you send off the video. Could be fun spending some time on that cruise ship, relaxing together."

They both felt the ninety-degree heat as soon as they stepped from the helicopter onto *The Getaway*, a sparkling white, fifteen-deck cruise ship. Their aerial arrival appeared to stir little interest among the two thousand passengers sunning themselves or engaging in the luxury cruise line's other amenities. No one hurried to see who they were.

"I was sent to welcome you aboard," one of the captain's officers greeted them, "and then leave you alone until you wish to depart. So welcome aboard. Just ask for Andy Fuller if you need anything and one of our crew will find me."

"Before you leave," Esther said, "when will we be entering the Pedro Miguel Lock?"

"Rather quickly," he said. "There's less than two miles between the Miraflores Locks, which we've already passed through, and the Pedro Miguel Locks, which will float us up to the same level as Gatun Lake."

Although the Pacific and Atlantic were both at sea level, he explained, the Isthmus of Panama was not flat. The locks took ships to Gatun Lake, which was eighty-five feet above sea level. That man-made lake was twenty-one miles long and made up the majority of the forty-eight mile crossing.

"Can ships heading to the Atlantic and those traveling the opposite way to the Pacific be in the same lock at the same time?"

"Yes and no," Fuller replied. He was clearly enjoying sharing his expertise. Continuing, he explained that all of the locks have two lanes that allow multiple ships to pass through at the same time, but they cannot handle large vessels going opposite directions so in the day-time, the locks switch directions every six hours and priority is given to larger ships. At night, smaller ships can go in opposite directions.

"Between thirty-five and forty ships a day go through the canal," he said, "so it's a busy place and no one gets through without paying a toll. A fellow who swam the canal even got charged."

Pointing to his right, he said, "We'll be going through the locks at the same time as the *Bella Francis*, that container ship over there."

"How's that work?" Esther asked.

"Both of us have to wait for canal pilots to take control of our ships," he said. "They're the only ones allowed to guide a ship into the locks. They can't have a captain ram into one of the docks and it's tricky lining up a ship because, as you will see, there isn't a lot of extra room on the port or starboard. Once we get into the lock, everyone onboard just takes it easy while the mules pull us into the correct position."

"Mules?" Esther repeated.

"It's a term from the past when mules actually did pull ships into each lock. Now the mules are little rail track vehicles made by Mitsubishi." He glanced at his watch and said, "I wish we were going through with another cruise ship. That's always fun for passengers because you're almost close enough to reach out and touch hands."

"I'm certain we won't be disappointed," Esther replied.

Esther and her fake Marine lover watched the *Bella Francis* as it came nearer to them and the Pedro Miguel Locks.

"I'd like to get as high up on this cruise liner as I can to start," she announced, all business. "I'll need you to count the number of crew that you see. There should be twenty-two according to the ship's log and that's all."

The helipad was at the bow of the cruise liner on its main deck in a roped off area. They hurried from it and listened to piped in Caribbean steel drum music being played on the elevator that raised them to the top deck just under the bridge. By this time, *The Getaway* already had entered the lock and was being pulled forward by mules. The *Bella Francis* was only a few minutes behind as the ground canal crew worked expertly to attach its mule lines.

Esther and McGill found an open spot along the ship's rails where dozens of passengers already had gathered.

"I'm surprised this cruise ship doesn't turn on its side with everyone running over here to look at the *Bella Francis*," McGill joked.

"It's good we're not the only ones gawking," Esther replied.

McGill joined her in surveying the *Bella Francis* as its crew came outside to wave to cruise line passengers.

"With the pilot and mules running things, I'm assuming it's break time," McGill said as he began counting the crew onboard the container ship, most of whom had lighted cigarettes. He raised his right hand and pointed at each man as he counted him.

"Put down your hand!" Esther snapped. "Don't call attention to us."

She was slowly sliding her camera from the ship's bow to its stern, pausing to focus its massive telephoto lens on every man aboard the *Bella Francis*. She was conscious that the images she was taking were being sent via satellite to Langley, where analysts were poring over them. Reaching into her pant pocket, she inserted a tiny flesh-colored device that looked like a hearing aide into her ear. She could now hear directions from the CIA, primarily Director Grainger, who was in the monitoring room.

"The audio on the Nikon you're using isn't working," Grainger told her. "We can't hear a word of what is being said but the video stream is sending clear pictures to us. If you spot Farouk, point your camera directly at McGill's face. That will be your signal to us that he's on the cargo carrier. Now nod your camera up and down to indicate you understand my instructions."

Esther, who could hear Grainger perfectly, did as she was instructed.

"I keep losing track because the crew is moving around," McGill complained, "but I've counted twenty-one men several times. I'm going to assume the captain stays on the bridge even when he's not in control, which means the only visible men on that ship are crew members."

Suddenly there was a commotion on the container ship. All of the men on it ran to the side closest to *The Getaway* and began hollering and cheering.

"There's why," Esther said, nodding to her left.

One of the men on the container ship had held up a crudely drawn sign that featured what were supposed to be women's breasts and the initials "SUYT" on it. A young woman in a skimpy swimsuit standing some fifty feet from Esther and McGill obliged by lifting up her top.

A cruise line attendant hurried to her and asked her to cover herself.

"Classy," Esther said, clearly disgusted.

"Hey, those guys on the container ship have been at sea for a long time."

"Maybe they should stay there."

Apparently, another woman on a lower deck raised her blouse and the frazzled cruise line employee rushed down nearby steps to confront her.

It was then that Esther spotted a lone figure emerging from the *Bella Francis* bridge castle carrying a rolled up bundle under his arm. Unlike the others on the container ship who were urging women on the cruise liner to go topless, this figure moved to the opposite side of the container ship away from the commotion.

Esther realized the sun had nearly set behind them. *He's getting ready for prayer time*, she thought. *That's got to be him.*

She extended her telephoto lens as far as possible, causing the image of the man to become a mass of blurry pixels. Frustrated, she leaned forward as if another foot would make a difference in the image's quality.

It has to be Hakim Farouk, she told herself. As she watched, the man positioned his prayer mat toward Mecca, got down onto his knees, and began bowing, touching his forehead to the steel deck. A horn sounded, indicating that the two ships had been raised to the proper level for them to be pulled free of the locks. Surely, she thought, Director Grainger would realize from the images that she was transmitting that this man was Hakim Farouk, the Destroyer, the maker of bombs. In that split second, she turned her lens away from the praying man and pointed it directly at McGill's face, the agreed upon signal that Esther had identified Farouk.

"Oh, honey, let me do that," she heard a woman say over her shoulder. "Don't you want to be in the same photo with your sweetheart?"

An older woman with dyed black hair that was much too dark for her age was standing behind Esther with a man who must have been her husband.

"Let me take a photo with that big honking camera of yours and then you can take a shot of Harvey and me," the woman volunteered, smiling as she reached out to take Esther's Nikon.

"That's very kind of you, ma'am," McGill said, stepping between the woman and Esther, "but my girlfriend is sensitive about who uses her camera. I just got it for her. Let me take a photo of you two first."

"Why, you are a gentleman indeed," the woman said as Esther stepped out of the way so the older couple could slide up next to the ship's rail. She handed McGill her cell phone and said to her husband, "Harvey, is my hair okay?"

"Beautiful as always, my dear!"

"Oh, you're such a charmer," she giggled. "Been married nearly forty years and he's still sweet on me."

McGill held up the cell phone and said, "Now smile!"

"Please take two or three," the woman said. "Sometimes I close my eyes even when there's no flash. Just nervous, I guess."

He did as told and returned the cell phone to her.

"Thank you, young man," she said. Glancing around, she asked, "Where did your girlfriend run off to? I was going to offer to take a photo on my cell phone and email it to you. My grandkids taught me how to do it and it's really simple. I wouldn't have touched her camera."

McGill was instantly annoyed as he searched to his right, left, and then behind him.

Esther was gone.

CHAPTER FIFTY-SEVEN

Gatun Lake
Panama Canal

S ailors called it the *Order of the Ditch*.

Four members of the *Bella Francis*'s crew had never passed through the Panama Canal and the ship's captain decided his men would have a special late-night celebration after exiting the Pedro Miguel Locks.

Their real initiation would happen after their vessel completed the crossing and entered the Atlantic when the newbies would be doused with beer to commemorate their acceptance into the Order.

But the captain had decided to reward his crew early because of their actions during the treacherous Pacific storm that had plummeted the ship. Many of his men had risked their lives by going outside during the pounding waves and rain to ensure cargo containers were securely lashed in place. It was time to reward them.

The men took turns leaving their duty posts during the evening to visit the galley where Jules the cook had prepared dozens of specialty desserts served with bottles of premium beer.

Hakim Farouk had no interest in socializing with the crew but he'd overheard one of them mentioning the cook had baked a tray of *Bint al-Sahn*—a Yemeni delicacy prepared from white flour, eggs, and yeast and dipped in a honey and butter mixture. Apparently the captain had grown fond of it while piloting in the Mediterranean and had asked the Jewish cook to prepare it. Farouk had few indulgences but *Bint al-Sahn* was one of them.

As he entered the galley, he saw the boisterous crew members clustered around the tables drinking alcohol. He quietly welcomed the day the *Bella Francis* would sail into New York harbor and he would blow them to hell. There were five Muslim crew members in the room who had joined him on occasion to pray. Yet not one of them prayed the required five times per day and as Farouk took a seat alone at a corner table, he noticed every Muslim except him was drinking alcohol, which he considered a sacrilege.

The *Bint al-Sahn* tasted sweet in his mouth.

Farouk sensed someone was watching him and when he glanced up from his dessert, he recognized the crew member who'd shared a sauna with him. He was Jesús Alvarez, the ship's second highest-ranking officer.

Alvarez arrived at his table with two beers.

"Join me?" he asked, offering a bottle.

"It is forbidden."

Alvarez glanced at the other Muslims in the room and said, "They must disagree but suit yourself. I'll finish both since I'm off duty."

Farouk forced a smile.

"What you eating?" Alvarez asked.

"It is a Yemeni dessert. You should try some."

"I just might after I finish these beers. What'd you think of them locks? Pretty amazing how they lifted our ship. Been through them many times and am impressed every time."

"A true engineering marvel."

"Yep, good old Yankee willpower. You know the French tried to build the canal but gave up. That's when good old Teddy Roosevelt took charge and got the damn thing done in about twelve years. The entire story is in one of the books that I just finished. Bet you didn't know that more than fifty-five hundred men died working on what we're traveling on right now. I got the book in my gear if you decide to read something other than the Quran."

Farouk didn't want to chat with Alvarez and felt his attitude was both condescending and arrogant. He hoped his unwanted guest would leave, but Alvarez didn't appear to be in a hurry. After several uncomfortable silent minutes, Farouk gave in. "Your name is Alvarez. That's not a typical American name."

"It is where I'm from. My father was a Mexican and my mother was a Texan. She threw a big hissy fit when he insisted my first name be Jesús because she wanted me to have a more common name—such as David, Bob, Bill, or what not—but my old man refused to give in and if you know anything about Texas women and how headstrong they can be, then you know how much more bullheaded he was than her." He laughed at his own description of his parents.

Another uncomfortable moment passed as Alvarez finished his beer and started on the second bottle.

"Remind me again why you asked to join us in Jakarta," Alvarez said.

"Solitude and cheap passage to New York."

"People are scared sometimes of deeply religious Muslims because of all the stuff going on."

"Are you frightened of me?"

"No, and I didn't mean to offend. But you got to admit, your sudden appearance in Jakarta was a bit unusual for most of us. The captain said he got a message from our owner telling him to take you and your cargo aboard no questions asked. And then there was the other guy who was supposed to come aboard and simply disappeared."

"People are always scared of what they do not know. In America, Muslims are a minority and minorities are always treated badly. As a mixed breed, you should know this."

"Mixed breed?" Alvarez repeated, lifting an eyebrow. "I'll let that pass but it's not a term I'd suggest you throw around unless you're looking for a fight."

"I didn't realize it was insulting."

"Truth is, you might have a point about being treated differently. When I was in high school, the guidance counselor told me all I could hope for was working at a Taco Bell someday. That's why I signed up for the Navy. Did time in the first Gulf War and came back to work as a merchant marine."

"The first Gulf War," Farouk said. "You have been to Iraq?"

"No, I never put foot on dry land. Served on a battleship during Operation Desert Storm when old Saddam tried to take over Kuwait. Had his eye on the Saudis, too, until we kicked his ass. Tell me, you're from Yemen, right? Isn't that what you told me? What'd you think of Saddam and that mess in Iraq?"

Farouk intentionally appeared nonchalant. He had no intention of revealing his true feelings to this stranger. "Politics is not something that concerns me."

"Part of me thinks the United States should just pull out of the whole damn Middle East and if those people want to kill themselves, then let them do it."

"Those people?"

"Sorry. Guess it's my turn to apologize."

Farouk wasn't certain if Alvarez was being sincere or duplicitous. Regardless, Alvarez stood to leave even though he'd only finished half of his second beer. He paused when he spotted his pal Giovanni Capo hurrying toward him carrying an iPad.

"Jesús, you got to see this!" Capo exclaimed. "It's the most incredible YouTube video I've seen." He looked around the room at the others and hollered, "Hey, everyone. Come look at what I got."

"This isn't some freak porno, is it?" Alvarez loudly declared. "One of your sicko shows."

"Nope, it's a video of an actual U.S. Navy attack on a container ship, I kid you not. It's mind-blowing!"

Farouk, who had planned to slip away, suddenly moved closer to Capo so he could have an unobstructed view of the iPad's screen. At least seven other men clustered around Alvarez and Capo to watch.

A helicopter could be seen in the video, hovering above the container ship's stern as U.S. Marines fast roped down. Although there was no sound, it was clear gunfire erupted and two RPGs could be seen destroying the helicopter, which came crashing down in flames onto the deck.

"Oh my God!" a crew member exclaimed. "Is this real?"

"It gets better," Capo declared. "Keep watching."

Within seconds, two U.S. fighter jets appeared, swooping from the sky and firing into the container ship's tall bridge castle, prompting a chorus of expletives from the men watching.

"Them fighters are Navy Super Hornets," Alvarez said as the video continued. "Saw them in the Gulf War. Them's twenty-millimeter rounds tearing up that bridge. Trust me, every one of those crew members got torn to shreds."

"Why would the Navy attack a merchant ship?" someone asked.

"It's a fake video that some kid in his underwear posted," said another.

"It's got to be footage from a new movie, Capo. It didn't really happen. It's a Hollywood trailer, you moron," a crew member standing next to him jeered.

"Who posted it?" Alvarez asked.

"It showed up on a Russian website ten minutes ago," Capo explained. "It apparently was taken by one of their subs that just happened to see it through a periscope."

"That sub was most likely shadowing whatever Navy ship those fighter jets came from," Alvarez said. "That's what they do."

"Bet it's fake. Didn't really happen," a crew member said.

"What container ship is it?" Alvarez asked.

Capo touched the screen to pause it. "*Blue Neptune* is painted on its bow."

"Our captain hasn't gotten any official communications about a container ship by that name being boarded by the U.S. Navy and we sure as hell haven't heard anything about a merchant ship being shot up by jet fighters like that," Alvarez said. "If this is real, the captain needs to see this. C'mon, Joe, bring it with you up to the bridge."

As Alvarez and Capo exited the galley, Hakim Farouk also slipped out into the hallway. He knew what he needed to do. It would be only a matter of time before the captain realized the *Blue Neptune* had been in Jakarta at the same time as the *Bella Francis*. It would be only a matter of time before the Western media would begin showing the footage and documenting that it was real. And it would be only a matter of time before the captain and crew deduced the reason for such a violent attack was tied to terrorism and the Falcon's threat to attack three U.S. cities with nuclear weapons.

Hurrying to his quarters, he tucked his copy of the Holy Quran under this arm and picked up his cell phone.

Because the *Bella Francis* was in Panama, his cell phone showed there was service.

CHAPTER FIFTY-EIGHT

Gatun Lake
Panama Canal Zone

The fireball from the ten-kiloton nuclear bomb hidden inside a Sea Trident Shipping container scorched and destroyed everything within 656 feet of what had been the *Bella Francis*.

Hakim Farouk detonated the nuclear bomb while the ship was waiting its turn to enter the Gatun Locks, three sets of locks, laid end to end, that lowered eastbound ships to the Atlantic Ocean.

The bomb was not nearly as powerful as nuclear bombs created during the Cold War, the most deadly being a 50-megaton Soviet bomb that had the blasting power of 50 million tons of TNT. In fact, when North Korea exploded its first 10-kiloton bomb underground in 2013, U.S. intelligence agencies weren't even certain a nuclear explosion had happened.

Now the world would witness firsthand the damage the bomb could inflict.

Six miles away in the coastal town of Colon, known as Panama's second city, the foundations of the city's historic buildings crumbled, walls collapsed, windows were shattered, and many of the town's hundred thousand residents saw the telltale mushroom cloud and heard the loud boom that came with a nuclear explosion.

The closest village to the blast site was Gatun, which had thrived when the canal was being built in the early 1900s, but in recent years had become a virtual ghost town. It literally vanished from the burnt ground. Its three hundred residents, mostly canal employees, were incinerated along with their whitewashed wooden houses built on stilts.

The biggest loss of lives happened on four cruise ships. One was *The Getaway* that was only a hundred yards away from the *Bella Francis* when the bomb was detonated. It and another cruise ship had been waiting for their turn to enter the locks and be lowered ninety-six feet to the Atlantic. The nuclear blast reduced the two cruise ships to melted jigsaw puzzle–size pieces and incinerated everyone onboard. Those two ships accounted for seven thousand deaths.

The other two cruise liners nearby had already entered the first canal lock. They were side by side waiting to be lowered to the ocean, a process that took two hours and required ships to step down through three locks. Everyone aboard those cruise liners also perished as their vessels were blown backward in the locks by the initial blast wave. The ships' broken shells resembled giant metallic snowflakes cascading down onto the two lower locks behind and below them. Incredibly, those two locks did not burst despite thousands of tons of water from Gatun Lake that now gushed from the busted upper-most one, turning the canal into a giant spigot. Another six thousand deaths were added to the toll from deaths on those two cruise ships, and there were more to come.

Construction workers had poured some 1,820,000 cubic meters of concrete into enormous steel forms to create the three-step lock system. Despite that thickness, the interior walls of the canal's up-permost lock crumbled, with huge chunks of it being blown away. Pushed by the now-contaminated water, those concrete pieces cata-pulted from the blast site, flying over the two canal locks below before crashing down to crush whatever was beneath them.

Less than three miles from the blast site, the man-made earthen, hydroelectric Gatun Dam built to stem the Chagres River and create the 345,000-acre man-made lake gave way, releasing its hold on much of the lake's 4.2 million acres of water, which surged downward toward the sea with tsunami force, destroying everything in its path. Trees were uprooted, animals drowned, houses busted into pieces, and their residents buried in the mixture of water, sludge, and debris.

The racing water shooting from the busted uppermost lock swept toward the Atlantic with tremendous force, destroying the former

U.S. Fort Davis military base before reaching Limon Bay. The plunging water and air blast from the nuclear explosion caused a swell so strong it overflowed Colon's docks miles away even though the city was not in the initial blast zone.

While fires raged along the Gatun Lake's shoreline, a fifteen-mile-per-hour wind spread radioactive fallout. It traveled airborne along Panama's seacoast, contaminating a forty-mile swath of villages from Colon to Cacique and extending out into the sea for another thirty miles. The mortality rate for those exposed to radiation would be 70 percent and that wasn't counting future cancer deaths, which would be in the thousands.

The immediate worry was that the two lower locks might not hold, causing hysterical radio reports in Panama that all of Gatun Lake would be drained, becoming a radioactive moonscape crater.

Ninety-nine percent of all container ships in the world passed through the Panama Canal. No longer. It would be unusable for an unknown number of years because of radiation.

Nearly nine thousand miles away from the blast, the Falcon sat on the floor of a remote Afghan house watching news reports on a computer via a satellite hookup. He was becoming angrier with each passing moment. His valuable nuclear bomb had been detonated on a Panamanian lake far away from its intended New York City target.

President Wyatt Austin appeared on television within hours after the blast to announce that a radical Islamic terrorist was responsible for the destruction.

"We believe a Yemeni-born terrorist named Hakim Farouk detonated the nuclear device in Panama. We further believe he is the man who made the bomb that exploded in Washington, killing President Sally Allworth."

The president revealed that the U.S. Navy had intercepted two other container ships—the *Blue Neptune* and the *Carrie Morton*—that also had been carrying bombs built by Farouk.

"These ships were en route to Los Angeles and Seattle," he said. "We should be proud that our military and intelligence services were able to prevent them from reaching our West Coast. At the same time, we join the world in mourning the loss of so many lives in Panama, including the deaths of hundreds of Americans who were aboard cruise ships on vacations.

"We suspect the radical Islamic terrorist aboard the *Bella Francis* did not intend for the canal zone to be his actual target, given that he exploded the bomb in a sparsely populated area. The cargo ship's final port of call was New York Harbor, which is where we believe he intended to explode the nuclear device. We will never know what led him to detonate the bomb in Panama."

The United States would immediately begin sending financial aid to Panama. In addition, President Austin said he would ask Congress to increase spending on Homeland Security specifically to better safeguard the nation's costal ports.

"Every day some six million containers are unloaded from cargo vessels in U.S. ports," he said. "We have twelve thousand miles of coastline to protect."

There was no mention in his carefully worded statement about how a storm had kept the U.S. Navy from intercepting the *Bella Francis* while it was still in international waters or how the Marines had boarded the wrong ship.

Having assured the American people that its government was being ever watchful, President Austin began to lay blame.

"With assistance from our allies, we have traced this nuclear bomb to North Korea, which built it with assistance from Iran and its scientists. The civilized nations of the world cannot tolerate such incomprehensible behavior from these two rogue nations."

He said the United States was in the process of scheduling a meeting with other "freedom loving" nations.

"We will determine an appropriate response for this crime against all of humanity. I promise you, it will be swift and it will be severe," he said, "and I can further promise the American people and the civilized world that the United States will use all of its might and power to find those responsible for these barbaric acts. The jihadist coward who hides his face behind a black mask because he is a weakling will be punished. It may take time, but he will be found and he, along with his accomplices, will be held accountable before us and before God for the atrocities that he has committed."

When the president finished his speech, the Falcon switched off his computer, ending his viewing session. It was time for him to burrow in deep and disappear, at least for a while.

CHAPTER FIFTY-NINE

County Correctional Facility
Elkton, Maryland

Mohammad Al-Kader's eyes were filled with contempt as he sat opposite the metal table in the jail's attorney-client meeting room, glaring at the man responsible for him being abducted from the safety of his Maryland mosque and charged with seditious conspiracy.

CIA Director Payton Grainger did not flinch.

It bothered him not at all that the Imam who had preached strict adherence of Sharia law and was responsible for assisting in the murder of a U.S. president despised him.

Neither man had met previously. All they knew about the other was what they had read and heard from others. And yet both despised the other and saw him as a mortal enemy.

Between them sat Representative Rudy Adeogo, the go-between, a role that he'd not sought, not wanted, but had been cast in by the series of unfortunate events that had brought the three of them together on this rainy evening.

"The nuclear bomb in Panama," Al-Kader began. "I assume you have evidence to back up your president's claim it was the handiwork of my Muslim brother the Falcon?"

Grainger had played too many of these games to be deceived.

Al-Kader knew the Falcon was responsible. He didn't need to hear CIA confirmation. His question was the Imam's way of posturing their conversation by reminding Grainger that the United States had not been able to prevent the Falcon from detonating a nuclear bomb.

It was a way for Al-Kader to cast himself—federal prisoner number 14634-129—not as a supplicant, but as a superior in their negotiations.

Grainger didn't bother to answer; instead he plucked an 8-by-10 grainy photograph from his briefcase and slid it across the cold metal surface to where Al-Kader's handcuffed wrists were chained to the table. The Mossad's Esther had taken the image from the deck of *The Getaway* cruise liner. It showed Hakim Farouk kneeling in prayer on the *Bella Francis*'s deck.

Al-Kader made no effort to pick up the photograph or study it. Instead, he glanced down briefly before returning his eyes to Grainger's.

"You were close, Mr. Director," he said, "but apparently not close enough."

"Two of our people died getting that photo. Can you confirm his name?"

"Hakim Farouk, known by some as 'the Destroyer' for his bomb-making skills, but anyone who watched your president's speech after the nuclear bomb explosion could provide that information."

"But not everyone knows him personally. You have met him, haven't you?"

"Yes, many years ago. He was a faithful servant of Allah, blessed be his holy name. We read, 'For a man once asked Mohammad, "which of men is the best?" Mohammad replies that it is the man who is always ready for battle and flies into it seeking death at places where it can be expected.' Hakim was such a man. You Americans murdered his wife and child."

"He didn't have a family. He lied about them."

"Are you so certain?"

"It no longer matters now because he is dead. Let's talk about your demands in exchange for information," Grainger said, shifting his weight on the uncomfortable metal stool that he was perched on. He dropped a thick stack of legal papers on the table, causing a loud bang.

"Primary among them is your immediate release from jail, the dropping of all federal charges pending against you, your deportation from the United States, and a promise by our government to not arrest, harass, or harm you in the future."

"The documents should say 'not kill me,'" Al-Kader replied.

Grainger flipped to a clause on the tenth page. "Read it for yourself. It's in there, all spelled out. The U.S. government 'will not kill you or seek to harm you.' Shall we move on?"

Without waiting for Al-Kader to answer, Grainger said, "In addition to what's already been mentioned, there is the issuance of a French passport under a different name, plus a first-class ticket on a commercial airline to Paris, where you have asked for a flat to be rented for one month."

"And does that document clarify my obligations?"

"Yes, it says you will not engage in any acts of terrorism and if you do, then your actions nullify our agreement. Rest assured, we will come after you."

"I am not a terrorist," Al-Kader replied. "I am a servant of Allah whose commands I preach."

"And yet, somehow you claim to know where the Falcon, who is clearly a radical Islamic terrorist, is hiding," Grainger retorted.

The Imam turned his attention to Representative Adeogo. "Have you read these legal forms?"

"I am not a lawyer and if I were, I would not be *your* lawyer nor are we friends," he replied. "I'm not certain why you have involved me in this arrangement."

"Let me ask you a question, Congressman Adeogo. How do you strike a bargain with a snake? The answer is simple. You cannot make a bargain with a snake because a snake is what a snake is. You must make a bargain with the man who can control the snake."

"Then you have made a terrible error in your judgment," Adeogo said. "I certainly don't control the president of the United States or the director of the Central Intelligence Agency."

Al-Kader returned his gaze to Grainger and said, "The director of the CIA is a liar and deceiver. He will betray me as soon as he learns what information I have to offer. He will violate these legal papers without giving the matter a moment of his thought. But you, Mr.

Congressman, are a fellow Muslim. A member of the House of Representatives. Your U.S. Constitution provides for 'checks and balances.' And that is what I am instituting here. If the president or Director Grainger betrays me, I believe you will do the right thing and expose them with these legal documents."

"Why should I?" Adeogo asked. "Your false teachings have brought nothing but murder and suffering in the Arab world and to me personally."

"Are you not familiar with what is called the twenty-first of the greater sins?"

"The breaking of a promise."

"Yes, we are taught 'those who break the covenant of Allah after its confirmation and cut asunder that which Allah has ordered to be joined and make mischief in the land; upon them shall be curse and they shall have the evil of the abode.' If you will not keep your word to me, I believe you will keep it to Allah. You will not violate the twenty-first of the great sins. And I will demand that you swear to me before Allah that you will keep your promise to me."

Eager to be done with this, Grainger moved on. "We have agreed to pay you twenty-five million by wire transfer into a French bank but only if the Falcon is captured or killed because of what you tell us."

"I will require another twenty million in U.S. currency and I want those additional funds wired to a bank in Kuwait. Now that Hakim Farouk destroyed your precious Panama Canal, my information is worth more."

Adeogo was surprised by Al-Kader's audacity, but Grainger didn't blink.

"We are prepared to offer you a total of thirty million U.S.," the CIA director said.

"Thirty-five, with the additional ten going to my sister in Kuwait City."

"Agreed," Grainger said. "Thirty-five million in total." He removed an ink pen from his Navy blazer, opened the contract, wrote the new $35 million payment figure in the margins of the corresponding clause, initialed it, and signed and dated the document's final page. Bending down, he removed a duplicate copy from his case and did the same. When finished, he pushed both stacks to Al-Kader and said, "Your turn."

"Did your president sign this contract as I demanded?"

"No. I signed it. Take it or leave it."

"I will not agree unless President Austin signs this covenant. What does your president have to fear? As long as he abides by its terms, no one will ever know that his name is on this document."

"I guess we can't make a deal," Grainger said, picking up the two contracts and standing. "Your last chance for freedom is about to walk out the door."

Al-Kader remained stoic.

Representative Adeogo stood, assuming their meeting was over, but Grainger hesitated and then sat back down. He'd been bluffing. From his briefcase he produced an entirely new set of documents. He corrected the financial paragraphs and flipped to the last page.

Signed in bold letters was "Wyatt Bowie Austin, President, the United States."

Adeogo was stunned.

Al-Kader picked up the ink pen but said, "I have two more requests before I sign, but they are for the congressman, not you. The first is that you accompany me to Paris when I am released from this jail."

"Paris? Me! Why?"

"The obvious. To ensure I arrive there without an 'accident.'"

Grainger said, "The agency will pick up the tab, Congressman."

"What's your other request?" Adeogo asked.

"I've already mentioned it. You must swear to me before Allah that you will take my copy of this agreement, and if the president, Director Grainger, or your government violates it, you will make it public."

Adeogo hesitated. Grainger said, "Go ahead, give him your word, promise him, so he will sign this damn thing and we can get on with this."

Adeogo said, "I promise I will keep my word to you."

Al-Kader scratched his name on both copies, sliding one toward Grainger and the other to Adeogo.

"Why are you doing this?" Adeogo asked Al-Kader.

"The reasons are known to me and no one else should be concerned," Al-Kader said in a smug voice.

"Where is the Falcon?" Grainger asked.

"Because of the murder of President Sally Allworth and the destruction of the Panama Canal, no country will give him shelter, not even the Iranians or North Koreans. That means his normal network of hiding places is unavailable. It leaves him no choice but to take shelter in a cave in the great White Mountains that separate Afghanistan and Pakistan."

"Do you think you can play the president and me as fools?" Grainger said in a terse voice. "My government fell for all that nonsense about the Tora Bora caverns with two thousand fighters hiding in them years ago but not now."

"You bombed the wrong cave. There was no huge Tora Bora cavern but there is a cave in the White Mountains and that is where the Falcon will go to hide. He will go there because it is the only place he can go."

"Okay, tell me about this secret cave," Grainger said, clearly unconvinced.

"You will find it in Lor Koh, a mountain southeast of the city of Farah in western Afghanistan. When the Mujahedeen were fighting the Soviets, they renamed it Sharafat Koh, which means 'Honor Mountain' but the Afghan communists called it 'Mordar Koh,' which means 'Filthy Mountain.'"

"Never heard of it," Adeogo said.

"I have," Grainger replied. "We built a base at the Farah airport while we still had troops there."

"You should remember it for another reason, Mr. Director," Al-Kader replied.

"I don't have any idea what the two of you are talking about," Representative Adeogo interjected.

"In 2009, Farah was the scene of violent protests against the United States," Grainger explained as he glared at Al-Kader. "Three villages had been struck by B-1 bombers and the locals claimed nearly one hundred and fifty civilians died. Four protesters yelling 'Death to America' were killed by police during riots."

Al-Kader interrupted. "Just so you hear the entire truth, Congressman, you must know this was not simply an air raid by a few U.S. aircraft. It was a demonstration of your famous 'shock and awe,' the destruction of three villages literally reduced to sand. Only bomb craters where people's dwellings once were. Tell him who was killed."

Grainger frowned. He did not like being used.

"I see I must tell the truth," Al-Kader said when it became clear Grainger wasn't going to answer. "Ninety-three of those who died were children. Only twenty-two were adults. Farah was once a thriving city with more than a hundred thousand residents. Now there are less than half that number living there. It once was a fortress constructed by Alexander the Great. Now it is a pitiful place of much suffering."

Al-Kader continued. "Do you know what happened to many of those villagers whose homes were destroyed and children were slaughtered by your bombers?"

"No, but I'm sure you're going to tell me," Grainger replied.

"At least twenty of them traveled from where their village had once been to Honor Mountain. It is a magnificent peak more than twelve hundred meters above the desert and there are many canyons in it where our ancestors—the very first humans—lived and left their marks on cave walls. All of these homeless wanderers decided to live on the mountain and they are bound together by a passionate hatred toward all outsiders, but especially Americans. They are a tribal people, uneducated, but sworn in their allegiance to the Falcon. They will honor that promise to their death."

Al-Kader twisted on the metal stool underneath him. There was no support for his back and with his wrists secured to the center of the square table, he'd been forced to lean forward the entire time they had been talking. He was growing weary.

"Mr. Director, we are done for the night. Tomorrow, send your people with detailed maps of Honor Mountain. I will show them where the Falcon is hiding. But I am done speaking to you forever." He glanced at his copy of the signed contract and then at Representative Adeogo. "You have given me your word. You have promised me before Allah."

"I'll put it in my safe-deposit box," Adeogo replied with disgust. "I only wish this was the last time that you and I would have to meet."

"Once we get to Paris, you will be free of me," Al-Kader said.

The Imam hollered and waved at a correctional officer who was standing outside the closed door but could keep track of what was happening by glancing through an eye-level reinforced window into the room.

"My visitors are done here," he announced as soon as an officer entered the room.

Director Grainger and Representative Adeogo were soon outside in the crisp evening air. They had ridden to Elkton from CIA headquarters in a helicopter and both settled into its backseats for the return trip to Langley, slipping on headsets so they could communicate.

"Has this been a gigantic waste of time? Some sick game the Imam is playing?" Adeogo asked.

"That's the same question the president is going to ask me. I will be sending our most senior polygrapher to test Al-Kader tomorrow but if he is telling the truth, we'll need to move quickly. The only reason Al-Kader knows where the Falcon has gone to hide is because the terrorist is scared and has retreated to his safest refuge. Eventually, he will reappear with some new attack plan."

"How long do you think he will remain hidden?"

"The Falcon thrives on attention and he has to be disappointed his nuclear bomb was exploded in Panama instead of New York City. He also must be frustrated that we intercepted the other two bombs. His primary financial backer is dead. He needs to find some other source in addition to Iran."

"Who'd he lose?"

"An African billionaire named Umoja Owiti."

"Ah, I read about his murder. His bodyguard killed him and three women in Owiti's own bedroom." He hesitated and looked at Director Grainger. "At least that is what the papers said. The bodyguard escaped and has never been caught."

If he was expecting Grainger to tell him more than what the media had reported, he was disappointed.

"Like I said," Grainger said, skipping over Owiti's death, "our profilers believe the Falcon is not going to be off the grid for long, so this could be our best shot at killing him."

"I don't understand why Al-Kader told us about the cave?" Adeogo said. "I don't believe he did it for money or simply to get out of jail. He has to have some other motive."

"Everyone always has an ulterior motive. If you are lucky, you figure it out before it comes back and bites you."

"Hidden motives. Including you?"

"Everyone."

The director nodded at the copy of Al-Kader's contract that the congressman was holding on his lap.

"Will you give me that document? Now that's he's agreed to cooperate, I'd like to destroy it along with my copy."

Adeogo looked surprised. "I gave Al-Kader my word as a fellow Muslim before Allah."

"You gave your word to a man who radicalized your younger brother and assisted in the murder of our president. You owe him nothing."

"Yes, but I owe Allah everything. I am not a radical, but I am a believer and my faith is an important part of my life."

"Congressman, I know about your personal problems with your wife, Dheeh, and what caused them. I think you might have broken more important promises than the one you just made to a terrorist."

Grainger's words cut him to the quick.

"I did not ask to be part of these negotiations, Director Grainger," he said in a quiet and thoughtful voice. "You played a role in dragging me into it and now you feel free to chastise me for my failings in my personal relationship with my wife. What you might not have considered is that I have learned a lesson from my personal struggles about keeping promises. I have no intention of giving this contract to you and I expect both you and the president to honor it."

"You are making a poor choice when it comes to redeeming yourself," Grainger replied.

The pilot interrupted to tell them they would be landing at Langley in less than ten minutes.

Grainger said, "Major Brooke Grant is flying in tomorrow from the Pacific Coast. If Al-Kader is telling the truth, I am planning on sending her with the team that goes after the Falcon."

"She deserves to be there."

"We need her help in identifying him. She's the only American who's ever spoken directly to him. Before we land, there is something else I want to tell you. Major Grant and you both talked to me about the police reports and photographs that suggest Omar Nader committed a murder."

"Yes, the traffic light pictures of Omar Nader and another man chasing after Mary Margaret Delaney on the night she died. Major Grant and I do not believe it was a suicide."

"I've spoken to the Justice Department and the attorney general and federal prosecutors in Virginia where the death happened do not believe there is sufficient evidence to proceed with a murder investigation against Omar Nader and his driver."

"I am truly sorry to hear that."

"I'm not finished. I reached out to my counterpart in Riyadh and Omar Nader is being recalled to Saudi Arabia tomorrow morning and I expect him to be resigning from his executive director position at the OIN soon thereafter. The other man in question will be leaving the United States too."

As they began their descent, Adeogo wondered what "hidden motive" Director Grainger had in arranging Omar Nader's recall and resignation.

CHAPTER SIXTY

Secret U.S. military staging camp
Outside Farah, Afghanistan

U.S. Navy SEAL Michael Gold wasn't given a choice.

He didn't like being told Major Brooke Grant would be joining his handpicked CIA team of twenty seasoned Special-Ops fighters going after the Falcon in the White Mountains. But her participation had been ordered directly by CIA Director Grainger. This was why he was currently sitting across from Brooke at a portable table inside a sand-colored tent giving her a one-on-one briefing.

"For the past ten days, we've had a series of drones flying over our target nonstop at fifty thousand feet to keep them from being seen or heard on the ground. The Falcon has chosen an extremely difficult cave for us to assault."

Tucked high in a canyon on Honor Mountain, the cave's entrance could be reached only by walking along a cliff-hugging trail that was just wide enough for one person. It zigzagged nearly a thousand feet up the rock face of a sheer cliff that rose at an eighty-five-foot angle between two snowcapped ridges. At the base of the V-shaped canyon were openings to dozens of additional caves, some created by nature and others by men. The drone surveillance revealed this bottom rung of caves contained a labyrinth of connecting passageways, like tiny fingers, with no ceilings. It was as if Mother Nature had used her fingernails to scratch down deeply into the base of the crevice, creating several lines of natural foxholes. These crooked walkways and caves made a frontal assault foolhardy.

According to the intel provided Gold, there could be as many as fifty hardened fighters loyal to the Falcon living in these lower caves. Anyone attempting to reach the trail leading to the entrance of the Falcon's lair would first have to defeat them.

"If you managed to reach the trail, you would be completely in the open while climbing up it to his cave's entrance," Gold explained. "A sniper could pick you off one at a time. Like shooting those little duck targets at an amusement park side show."

Trying to enter the cave by rappelling downward would be equally as treacherous because its actual opening was in a section of the cliff's sheer wall protected by an overhang, as if some angry, mythical giant had smashed a fist into the rock, creating an indentation. Again, anyone climbing downward would be easy prey for snipers.

Brooke knew the intel had come directly from Mohammad Al-Kader, one of the few men the Falcon trusted enough to have allowed him to visit his cave hideout. Gold clearly did not know the source and for a moment, Brooke wondered how he would react if told he and his men were about to risk their lives on information from a radical Islamic Imam who had contributed indirectly to the murder of a former U.S. president.

"Just for argument's sake, let's say we actually fought our way up to that cave entrance or rappelled down and entered it," Gold said. "We've been told that the cave's entryway goes another twenty yards back before it opens into a large chamber with about a dozen rooms, each approximately ten feet square and tall enough for an average man to stand in. This is where the Falcon's personal bodyguards live."

After his SEALs got through the bodyguards, they would have to go even deeper in the cave. At some point, water had created a series of caverns and tunnels inside the mountain. In one of these caverns was a three-foot-tall tunnel that had to be crawled through to reach yet another opening where the Falcon lived.

"This freak has burrowed himself so deep inside the mountain, we'd have a better chance of breaking into NORAD than going inside after him."

"Can you kill him with a bunker buster?" Brooke asked.

"That was everyone's first thought. Just bomb the hell out of the mountain."

Gold explained that a guided missile could be directed into the mouth of the Falcon's cave and it would kill everyone near its entrance. But the experts agreed that such a tactic would only destroy the entrance, not necessarily kill him.

"They even talked about using a thermobaric weapon but again, we would simply be closing the mouse's front door," Gold explained.

"Burying the Falcon alive sounds like a good alternative to me," Brooke replied.

"Yes, it would, Major, but intel tells us he has an escape route out of his living quarters." Gold produced a second map. It showed satellite imagery of Honor Mountain's many canyons. Using his finger as a pointer, he indicated a spot marked with a tiny X. "Right here, at this location, is where the cave's entrance is located and where the fighters loyal to the Falcon live at its base. But intel says his escape route is an exit more than two miles away." He slid his finger across to a different canyon.

"Are you telling me that his men dug a two-mile-long escape tunnel for him?"

"Nope, nature did, and that's his Achilles' heel."

Gold tossed several aerial photos taken by the drones onto the tabletop. They showed different angles of this second canyon exit, through which the Falcon would emerge. Brooke inspected the photos closely and didn't see any obvious cave openings. The photos showed a narrow canyon with a less steep incline. About fifty yards from the ravine's base was a ledge where rocks appeared to have fallen and been caught as part of some long-ago landslide.

"Major, look really close at these rocks," Gold said, handing her a close-up of the ledge. "Notice anything?"

Brooke inspected the photo. "Yes, at first I thought these rocks were just a haphazard collection of stones, but there are six separate piles of them."

"Bingo. To tell you the truth, none of us realized the significance of those six piles until one morning when we got lucky."

He handed her another aerial photograph that showed six women in burqas, each emerging, as if by magic, from the six mounds of rocks.

Before she could ask a question, he produced yet another photograph that showed the six women walking in a single file down the canyon slope to its bottom.

"We followed these women for about twenty minutes and discovered they were meeting a truck on a nearby road," he continued to explain. "They were buying supplies that they carried back up the canyon to those six piles of rocks. That's when we finally got it. Those aren't piles of rocks that just happened to get caught on that ledge during a rockslide. They're camouflage, strategically placed in front of six caves where those women live."

"When I was a kid," Brooke said, "my family took me on a vacation to New Mexico where we visited the Gila Cliff Dwellings National Park."

"Never been there," Gold said.

"Ancient people hid in the cliffs above a river and eventually built their houses into the cliff face. If an enemy came, they were on high ground and they could pull up their ladders or ropes. I was only seven, so I don't remember much more except that when you looked, you couldn't necessarily see the houses from a distance because they blended into the mountain."

"It's what primitive people do," Gold said. "They use natural cover to their advantage, but that's not all we noticed after we realized what we were looking at. These six women followed each other footstep to footstep in single file and their route was circuitous—several steps one way, then a sharp left, a few more and a right, up and down and sideways. We thought initially they were trying to cover their tracks."

"Mines," Brooke said. "IEDs."

Gold was impressed. "That's right. The Soviets left behind tons of unexploded ordinance and if someone goes charging up that slope toward those six piles of rocks on that ledge, there's a good chance they're going to get blown up."

"Which of these six caves is part of the Falcon's escape route?" she asked. "All of them or just one?"

"Intel says only one of them contains his escape tunnel but this is where we have a problem."

"A problem?" she quipped. "It strikes me we already have a ton of problems."

"You're right. Our intel falls short because whoever our source is, the last time he was there, only five stone caves dwellings existed and he said the escape tunnel exited into the center one."

"Let's figure this out," Brooke said, picking up a sheet of paper from the table. She drew four Xs and a single E.

"These four Xs and the E represent the five original cave entrances," she explained. "The E is the cave with the escape tunnel inside it."

Gold looked at her drawing.

X-X-E-X-X.

"Okay, so what's your point, Major?"

Beneath that line, she drew a second one, only this time she added an 0 to the right side: X-X-E-X-X-0.

"The 0 is the newest mound of rocks, assuming it was built in front of a cave to the right of the other five caves."

Under that line she drew another line with the 0 reversed, on the left side. "Here's what it would look like if the new cave is on the opposite end," she explained.

Gold looked at the sheet, which now contained three lines.

X-X-E-X-X
X-X-E-X-X-0
0-X-X-E-X-X

"The escape tunnel has to be either in the third or fourth cave, depending on which side they built the new sixth mound," Brooke explained.

"Clever. The other mounds can't contain the exit," Gold said.

"What's your plan?" she asked.

"We don't know how extensive the underground maze is inside

the mountain. It was created millions of years ago by water," Gold said. "There's no point in us going inside after him. We could wander around for weeks. Our only choice is to force the mouse to come to us."

"Two questions," Brooke said. "Actually, I have three. Let's start with how are you going to force him to use his emergency exit?"

"That's an easy one. We going to fire a missile directly into his cave's front door and then fire a second one, completely sealing off that entrance. Next, we'll keep the fighters at the bottom of the canyon pinned down in their caves with missiles fired by our drones. This attack will make it appear that we intend to launch a full frontal assault."

"Make him panic and run," she said. "Which brings me to my second question. If you're going to shut his front door, why not just blast those six caves on that ledge with missiles too? Sealing in both his front door and the back door."

"Because we don't know what the labyrinth inside that mountain looks like. There could be some other way out. Some tunnel or cave we don't know about. We want him to come out of his escape exit, not some alternative. That's when we'll have him. What's your third question?"

"You've scared him. You've sealed the front door. You know where he will be exiting. Can I assume you will be waiting at the base of that canyon for him to appear—that's when you catch him?"

"That would be the most logical, but we don't do logical. We don't know how many of his supporters are with him inside the mountain and might be fleeing with him. Will one fighter coming out or dozens? What if he exits into the safety of one of those mounds and stays there without coming down into the canyon? We can't afford to sit at the bottom of the ravine waiting for him to appear. We have to be waiting when he pops his head out of that escape tunnel."

"And just how do you intend to do that?"

"We're going to scale the slope without getting blown up by the IEDs. We're going to sneak into the two caves, one of which has a tunnel in it. And we're going to capture or kill him when he appears."

"Just so I understand this plan of yours," Brooke said in a skeptical voice. "You and your men are going to march up a slope littered with IEDs and land mines, seize control of two caves where there could be enemy combatants, and surprise the Falcon when he pops out? That's your plan?"

"Yes."

"At night. Walking through a minefield?"

"That's the plan."

"That's suicide. How are you going to get up to the ledge at night without detonating an IED or mine?"

"Advanced technology, Major. Computer imagining and digital re-creation," Gold said. "You use GPS or Waze when you're stateside to navigate, right? We will use the same basic philosophy here. We have mapped those six women's footsteps individually and used a computer to plot each one's exact steps to identify where we can safely walk as we climb the slope to the ledge. Just like following directions from a GPS."

Brooke was dumbstruck. "Do you know how many times my GPS has told me to take a wrong turn?" she asked.

"Major, they don't ask us to do easy. They call us to do the impossible. Now, where would you like to be when we embrace the suck?"

"At the tip of the spear."

CHAPTER SIXTY-ONE

On the canyon floor beneath the six caves
Honor Mountain, Afghanistan

They'd chosen a moonless night, so dark it was impossible to see the outline of someone directly in front of you until they appeared like a fish suddenly rising from the ocean depths.

Brooke hated using night-vision goggles. The eerie green glow made everything surreal. But tonight they were essential, especially the cutting-edge version she was now wearing. It had a tiny square in its upper right lens that would use GPS to guide her safely up a path through the IEDs and leftover Soviet mines to the ledge. Gold had decided to lead, followed by Brooke and four more SEALs walking in single file. They would split into two units after they reached the six camouflaged cave entrances, assuming they made it there. Their success depended on surprising the occupants in two of the caves. Once inside, they would wait for the Falcon.

Gold had positioned the rest of his SEALs along a ridge directly across from the six caves. Their job was to engage any enemy combatants who might emerge from the four caves that didn't contain the escape tunnel. They would also mark the four caves with lasers. If necessary, AGM-114M Hellfire II missiles could be fired into them by drones.

At one point, Brooke had asked why the SEALs simply didn't fast rope down onto the ledge from helicopters rather than risk climbing the booby-trapped slope. Gold had explained that the sound of their blades would awaken combatants inside the caves. No one wanted to risk having an RPG fired into a helicopter as it hovered helpless in the canyon. Rappelling from the mountaintop above the ledge was considered impossible given the deep snow and the treacherous angle of descent.

Brooke thought to herself, *If I live through this, I'm going to seriously consider retirement.* She wondered about Jennifer and in that moment was filled with doubt. She thought: *What am I doing here? I could have waited somewhere safe.* And then she thought about the Falcon. She and Jennifer would never be safe until he was either behind bars for life or dead. She had to be here to make certain one those outcomes happened.

Because intel photos had spotted only six women carrying supplies, CIA and Pentagon analysts didn't believe many combatants were hiding inside the caves. The women weren't toting enough supplies to feed more than a few mouths.

Each of the six caves had been assigned names by Gold for easy identification. He, Brooke, and a third team member nicknamed Slim Jim would take control of Cave Alpha, one of the two caves where the Falcon might appear from an escape tunnel. The other SEALs would secure Cave Bravo, the second possible escape route. They had exactly twenty-two minutes to climb the slope and take control of both caves. That is when two guided missiles would be fired by drones into the mouth of the Falcon's cave entrance in the canyon two miles away.

Gold had told Brooke to become his shadow. He knew she was important to the CIA, the White House, and top Pentagon brass. He didn't want to lose her on his watch.

With Brooke walking directly behind him, Gold checked his watch, gave a hand signal, and took his first step from the canyon base up the heavily mined slope toward the ledge. One misstep by any of them and all six would be seriously wounded or killed.

Even with the GPS guiding their footsteps, it was tricky. The climb required stepping on loose rocks. About halfway up it, Slim Jim's boot hit the edge of a fist-size stone, causing it to tumble down the slope as all of them watched helplessly. Luckily, it didn't detonate any explosives.

"That was damn close," Gold whispered. "Watch your feet."

Except for that mishap, the six reached the ledge without incident. Brooke let out a quick sigh of relief as she followed Gold to the mound of rocks directly in front of Cave Alpha. Slim Jim was behind her. As they suspected, the rocks were a façade. A narrow passageway cut between them and the mountain. They slipped into this narrow opening and walked about ten feet when they reached a wooden door made from rough timbers. There was no lock or handle, just a piece of leather to pull. Gold gently tugged on the heavy door, pulling it toward them but abruptly stopped after opening it only an inch. He'd spotted a trip wire attached to its base. Through his headset, he warned the three SEALs entering Cave Bravo, assuming the door to that cave would also be armed.

The wire led from the door to a Russian MON-50 claymore-shaped antipersonnel device that would have easily killed them. Bending down, he snipped its trip wire. As he did, he felt a strange sense of relief. The occupants inside were depending on the claymore to protect them from intruders rather than owning a dog, which would have sniffed their scent and begun yelping. He guessed there were no dogs because the animals could have accidentally tripped the IEDs and mines buried on the slope.

The door opened outward easily now, allowing them to duck inside a room that Brooke estimated was twelve feet wide, nine feet long, and seven feet tall. She assumed this was the cave's main room. Carpets covered the stone floor. In one corner was a five-foot-tall wooden cabinet made from thick mountain timbers. Except for various jugs and cooking utensils, the room was bare. Dying embers glowed from a hole carved into a corner near a crack where smoke could be vented. The embers gave the room a ghostly feel. There were two long pieces of black fabric hanging along one wall with candlelight flickering from behind their edges. These smaller cutouts from the main room had to be sleeping quarters.

Gold, Brooke, and Slim Jim suddenly felt the ground beneath them tremble and heard the distant sound of explosions. It was the guided missiles being fired into the Falcon's front entrance and the drone strike aimed at the enemy fighters inside the caves at the base of that canyon some two miles away.

A man's fingers appeared on the side of the heavy bedroom curtain less than five feet from where Gold was standing. As the drapery was being swept open, Brooke saw a man emerging armed with an AK-47 assault rifle.

Gold fired his Heckler & Koch MP7 machine pistol equipped with a suppressor. *Pop. Pop.* Two DM11 rounds capable of penetrating body armor zipped through his chest, killing him instantly before hitting the cave's rock walls. His wife, who was lying on the floor in their bed, saw her husband fall. She reached for a second assault rifle next to her but with the curtain now open, Slim Jim saw her and fired. She died where she had been sleeping only minutes before.

Brooke moved toward the other thick bedroom curtain. She didn't sense any movement behind it or hear any talking. With her MP7 pistol drawn, she took a deep breath, steadied her nerves, and peeked behind it.

Two children, whom Brooke guessed were four and five, were curled together asleep on bedding, completely unaware that their parents had just been fatally shot.

Gold looked over his shoulder and removed two disposable plastic handcuffs for the children but Brooke stopped him from entering the room. "They're no threat," she whispered, closing the drapery.

Slim Jim positioned himself at the doorway. He could hear the sounds of Heckler & Koch HK416 rifles being fired outside by his fellow team members from the opposite side of the canyon. Clearly, enemy combatants were emerging from the other four caves. A jihadist fighter appeared at the entrance of Cave Alpha. He called out in Arabic, expecting its occupants to come join him. Instead, Slim Jim fired, killing him. He dropped dead at the entrance of the long passageway leading into the cave.

Gold and Brooke searched the main room, looking under the carpets and shoving the heavy wooden cabinet out from the cave wall. They found nothing suspicious, no openings that could be used as part of an escape route.

Brooke entered the parents' bedroom, first stepping over the dead father and then skirting around his dead wife. Again nothing, except a bed pad, covers, a candle, and a worn copy of the Quran. She couldn't imagine living in such a barren space. It was while Brooke was in the bedroom that she heard a loud boom and her nostrils instantly filled with dust. Hurrying into the main room, she found Gold kneeling over Slim Jim.

"What happened?" she yelled.

"Help me with bandages," Gold said.

An Islamic fighter had tossed a Russian-made RGO hand grenade down the passageway that led to their cave's door, blowing its timbers apart. He'd known intruders were inside because he'd stumbled on the dead jihadist who Slim Jim had shot earlier. Slim Jim had been using the door as a shield, peeking through a crack, when the grenade had shattered it. He was bleeding badly and had two busted legs and a broken arm.

Awakened by the blast, the two children in the second bedroom began screaming from inside the bedroom for their parents, afraid to move.

Although Gold's headset had worked while he was outside the cave's now shattered door, it was useless inside the cave's main room. "I've got to get out there. We may need to abort."

As Gold was moving toward the doorway, four explosions rocked the mountain. They came from AGM-114M Hellfire II missiles fired into the four caves near them. The caves were about ten yards apart and the blasts caused both Brooke and Gold to fall to the floor. Both were grateful that they were deep enough inside the mountain to keep them from being the victims of friendly fire. Clearly, Gold's assault plan was unraveling and there was still no sign of the Falcon.

"I need to get outside," Gold yelled. He hurried out of the doorway into the narrow passageway, leaving Brooke alone in the main room listening to the terrified children in their bedroom sobbing and still screaming for their parents.

Gold's radio worked. "Report," he said into the flesh-colored microphone near his lips.

"Dead Ali Babas but more will be coming," his second-in-command reported from across the ridge. "You got the package yet? Because in minutes, this canyon is going to be crawling with Johnny Jihads."

"There's no escape tunnel in our cave. Slim Jim is wounded. Major Grant is still inside."

Gold called the three SEALs who had taken control of Cave Bravo, the other likely escape route for the Falcon.

"We found us a hole, just waiting for the mouse to—"

His sentence was cut short when Gold heard through his earpiece a man screaming *Allahu Akbar* followed by an explosion.

"Suicide vest," Gold deduced, speaking into his microphone. "I'm going from Cave Alpha to Cave Bravo to assist and assess. DO NOT SHOOT ME. Copy?"

"Got you, Chief. We'll keep them off your back," came the reply from the team on the opposite ridge.

Gold slowly stepped from Cave Alpha.

"We see you," his second-in-command confirmed as Gold now ran toward Cave Bravo to check on the victims of the suspected suicide vest blast.

Gold found the cave's layout identical. A narrow passageway behind a rock façade led into Cave Bravo. His three SEALs were dead along with the remains of a suicide bomber. Their bodies were positioned around a two-foot hole in the cave's main room that apparently had been hidden behind a thick rug. Obviously, it was the Falcon's escape exit but he was nowhere in sight.

Back in Cave Alpha, Brooke was kneeling on the stone floor, administering first aid to Slim Jim, when she heard the two screaming girls in the bedroom suddenly become quiet. She sensed there was someone else in the cave.

She swung around fast and rolled on her abdomen across the floor. Her quick movement saved her from a bullet that nearly grazed her head. Obviously, there were two escape holes, one in Cave Alpha and one in Cave Bravo.

She saw him. The Falcon, dressed in his trademark all black garb, including his hooded ski mask with a slit for his eyes. He had crawled from a hole in the girls' unchecked bedroom and was holding both of the children before him, using them as a human shield.

Brooke scooted across the floor behind the five-foot-tall wooden cabinet that she and Gold had moved earlier when looking for his escape exit.

The Falcon fired another round from his pistol, hitting and killing Slim Jim.

Even though the only light that he could use was coming from a lone candle on the floor of the girl's bedroom, it was bright enough from the fire embers that he had seen Brooke's face. Kneeling down behind the two crying girls made it impossible for Brooke to shoot him.

He called out in English: "Major Grant, at last!"

"You don't have a chance. Let the girls go. Surrender."

He laughed loudly. "It would appear you are the one who is at a clear disadvantage." He began firing into the wooden chest, hoping his rounds would penetrate it and kill her.

Pinned between the huge chest and wall, she considered her options. Khalid would have shot the girls and the Falcon. She could almost hear him whispering to her, "Their lives are nothing. Save yourself." Next she heard Esther. "Shoot. If they die, it is God's will and serves a higher purpose."

Unsure what to do, she hesitated as the Falcon fired again into the wooden cabinet, this time sending a slug within inches of her.

Although Gold was unaware what was unfolding in Cave Alpha, he decided to throw two grenades into the escape hole inside Cave Bravo. One was hurled to his left and the other to his right to kill any future suicide vest–wearing jihadists who might emerge from the escape route.

The grenade heaved down the tunnel in the direction of Cave Alpha where Brooke and the Falcon were at a standoff exploded. It blew a big gap in the bedroom wall, sending shards of stone flying into the main room, pelting the Falcon and further traumatizing the two girls he was using as a shield.

They panicked and burst free from the Falcon's grasp, bolting toward their parents' bedroom in complete fright, not yet realizing what awaited them there.

Exposed now, the Falcon blasted away at the wooden cabinet, emptying the clip in his semi-automatic. He needed to reload and reached for a replacement clip.

Seeing her chance, Brooke slid from behind the cabinet and began shooting. A round struck his left hip, shattering the joint, causing him to collapse. As he crumpled face-first onto the floor, both his pistol and ammunition flew from his fingers.

She had him. Helpless. Lying facedown in front of her.

Brooke dashed over and planted her right knee directly on his back, pinning him in place. She pressed the barrel of her weapon against the side of his skull.

Kill him! Pull the trigger!

She hesitated. She had to look at his face. With her left hand, she jerked the black ski mask from his head and instantly wished that she had left it in place.

She had envisioned a monster beneath the black covering, some grotesque face of pure evil. Instead, she saw a thirtysomething, rather handsome man, no different from any Arab graduate student attending a U.S. university. Evil wore an ordinary face.

Thirty years old. Way too young to have been one of the architects of the 1997 terrorist attack at Deir el-Bahari. But it was the voice she'd heard when they'd spoke on the phone in Somalia after Brooke had foiled a bombing in Mogadishu.

"How many of you have there been?" she demanded.

He smirked. "I'm the second. You killed the first several years ago in a drone attack."

She heard someone call her name, coming up behind her. It was Gold. "You got the bastard. Kill him while I drag Slim Jim outside. I've called in helicopters to get us out of here."

In her mind, Brooke saw herself squeezing the trigger. She saw the Falcon's brains being blow apart onto the cave floor. She saw the blood and she realized it was her duty to shoot. He had shown the people who she'd loved no mercy. Pull the trigger and the nightmare would be over. He would be gone from her life forever.

But she hesitated.

Gold noticed. "I'll do it," he volunteered, walking toward her and the Falcon.

"Wait," she said. "Don't you get it? They'll just replace him with another Falcon. If we take him prisoner, we can use voiceprints to prove it's him."

Gold was unconvinced.

"Saving him isn't mercy," she said. "The world needs to know we have him. We can interrogate him. I can't just kill him in cold blood."

Gold leaned down and smashed the butt of his pistol into the Falcon's face, busting his nose, causing him to cry out in pain.

"Do what you want," he said, attaching plastic cuffs to the Falcon's wrists behind his back.

"I've got to get Slim Jim out of here before we all die. The Black Hawks are loading up. But my men go up first and if RPGs start showing up, he's getting a slug in the head from me and a shove over the ledge into the land mines."

Gold walked over to Slim Jim and lifted his dead friend's body onto his shoulders. As he walked through the doorway to the helicopters hovering outside, he called back, "Make up your mind, Major!"

"I knew you wouldn't do it." The Falcon smirked. "You are weak. I will kill Jennifer and then I will kill you—just as I promised. Allah has condemned you and that bitch you call your daughter. I will take my time when I come for her. Hers will not be an easy death."

Gold was sending Slim Jim's body up to the helicopter when Brooke emerged from the passageway by herself.

"Where's the Falcon?" he asked.

"I've got photos of his corpse and a DNA sample. They'll have to do."

CHAPTER SIXTY-TWO

Above the Atlantic Ocean
En route to Paris, France

Mohammad Al-Kader was unrecognizable.

Gone was his salt-and-peppered beard, his long hair, and the flowing robes of an Imam. He was now dressed in tailored light blue shirt and dark gray Armani suit. He was traveling under a French passport with a new name and was seated inside a commercial jet's first-class compartment. It had rows of open-top "cubicle" seating. Two comfortable seats capable of being reclined into beds were arranged side by side with a waist-high partition between them and a window that could be raised or lowered for privacy.

In the cubicle next to Al-Kader, Representative Rudy Adeogo was reading the *Washington Gazette*'s front-page account of the Falcon's death inside an Afghanistan cave hidden deep in the White Mountains. The paper quoted Major Brooke Grant recounting how the radical Islamic terrorist had been fatally shot during an intense firefight after he had cowardly tried to use two children as human shields. There was no mention in the story about how the Falcon's wrists had been tied together when she'd executed him.

Earlier, Adeogo had read a sidebar that reported the Justice Department had dropped its charges of seditious conspiracy against Al-Kader. Prosecutors had decided to forgo a trial because prosecuting the Imam would have exposed the identity of highly valued informants, the paper noted. Instead, it had stripped the Imam of his U.S. citizenship and deported him to an unnamed nation.

Folding the newspaper and slipping it into a meshed storage shelf next to his seat, Adeogo watched Al-Kader enjoying a meal of lamb and rice that had been brought to him by a flight attendant. The Imam disgusted him.

"Don't be angry," Al-Kader said, sensing the congressman's contempt. "I kept my end of the agreement. Have you kept your promise to me?"

"Yes, your copy of the agreement is my safe-deposit box."

Al-Kader cut another juicy slice of lamb and said, "Congressman, there is only one man who expects that agreement to be honored—and that is you."

Al-Kader pressed a button that raised the fogged glass barrier between them, leaving Adeogo to wonder about his comment.

It was nearly six o'clock in the morning when the Boeing 787 touched down at Europe's second-busiest airport. A flight attendant approached and said, "You two gentlemen have been invited to deplane first. Welcome to La Ville-Lumière. Please enjoy your stay."

Al-Kader and Representative Adeogo were walking up the jet bridge when two men in dark suits with flesh-colored earpieces appeared.

"Excuse me, Representative Adeogo," one said, completely ignoring Al-Kader. "My name is John. We're from the U.S. embassy. Please come with us."

"I promised to stay with this man until we reached a Paris flat that's been rented for him. A car should be waiting for us after we clear immigration and customs," Adeogo explained.

"There's been a change in plans, sir," John politely replied. "Your life is in danger."

"What will happen if I don't comply?" Adeogo asked suspiciously.

"Please, Congressman, this is for your own safety and protection," John said. "We don't want to make a scene, but if necessary, we've been authorized by Director Grainger to detain you physically." He opened his jacket, revealing a pair of handcuffs in a leather pouch attached to his belt.

"The director of the CIA has told you to physically restrain a member of Congress?" Adeogo asked, becoming irked.

"There's been a reported threat to your life," John said. "There's a return flight boarding for Washington Dulles in a few minutes that the three of us are booked on."

"There is no threat. This is an abduction!" Adeogo replied indignantly.

Al-Kader watched Representative Adeogo being led away.

Inside the terminal, Adeogo had one of the two men on either side, escorting him through the terminal. As they walked, Adeogo noticed an Arab man hurry past. He recognized the man's face, but couldn't immediately place him.

Within thirty minutes, Adeogo was sitting in another first-class cabin in a commercial jet taking off on an eight-hour return flight to Dulles Airport along with the two escorts Grainger had sent. When they landed, a flight attendant invited the three of them to be the first to deplane. His escorts walked him through passport control and customs without stopping. He spotted a government-issued car waiting curbside outside the airport with two SUVs parked nearby.

John opened the rear passenger door of the sedan for Adeogo.

"Welcome home, Congressman," Director Grainger said. "Please join me."

"Will you handcuff me if I don't?" Adeogo asked bitterly. "How dare you threaten and abduct a United States congressman. I'm going to report this to the House and hold a news conference."

"Please ride with me for a while. There are reasons why you might want to reconsider," Director Grainger replied in a calm voice. "No handcuffs, I promise."

Adeogo slid down next to him in the rear seat.

"Congressman, we received information from a credible source that Al-Kader's network intended to kidnap you once the two of you exited the airport."

Adeogo couldn't tell if he was lying or the threat had been real.

"If we had not intervened," Grainger continued, "you'd be sitting somewhere in Paris with a black hood over your head."

Grainger sounded convincing but then deception was part of his job description.

As the car began driving away from the terminal, Adeogo suddenly realized the identity of the Arab man who'd hurried past him in the Paris airport terminal. It was the same Arab who'd been driving the car with Omar Nader in pursuit of Mary Margaret Delaney on the night that she'd died. It was Khalid, the Saudi "fixer."

"You're responsible for all of this, aren't you?" Adeogo said, making it clear that it was not a question but an accusation. "The president and you promised not to kill Al-Kader so you've gotten the Saudis to do it."

Grainger didn't respond. He waited to see if the congressman would figure out all of the chesslike moves that had been made.

Adeogo's mind was racing. "You used the evidence that Major Brooke Grant and I gave you, didn't you? The police reports and photos. You used them to force Omar Nader, the head of the OIN, to resign and leave the country. You threatened to charge him with murdering Mary Margaret Delaney and then offered him a deal. A way out. His resignation and an assignment for Khalid, a killing."

It was all coming into focus now.

"Is the president in on this too?" Adeogo asked.

Grainger said, "The president was not particularly fond of Omar Nader. The White House is happy that Nader is choosing to resign."

"Does President Austin know you sent a Saudi assassin to kill Al-Kader?"

"Representative Adeogo," Grainger said, "I have no idea about the whereabouts of the Imam. I've been told by the French that he made it through customs and immigration in Paris, but has not yet arrived at the flat that was rented for him. Nor has he gone to the bank to claim his reward."

"He's dead, then. Your plan worked."

"I have no confirmation of that," Grainger said coldly. "As far as I know, he has disappeared on his own, but why should you care?"

"Because I made him a promise."

"Would you like to hear my theory for why he betrayed the Falcon?" Grainger asked. "It wasn't because he'd stopped backing terrorism or abandoned his call for Sharia law. He betrayed the Falcon so he could return to the Middle East and claim leadership of these terrorist groups for himself. He revealed where the Falcon was hiding because he knew we would kill the Falcon, creating an opening for him to fill."

"I don't know if what you are saying is true or simply an illusion that you are spinning. But you're forgetting the contract the president signed with Al-Kader—the one in my safe-deposit box."

"As far as I know, the president never signed any such document. I doubt the president would have signed any agreement with a known terrorist."

"I saw his name on the agreement. I was there. I have a copy in my bank safe-deposit box."

"Are you certain of that, Congressman?"

Adeogo read between the lines. "Director Grainger, if you broke into my safe-deposit box and destroyed that contract, I will expose you and demand that you be prosecuted."

Grainger slipped his hand inside the Navy blue blazer that he was wearing and removed a single sheet of paper.

"Before you make any more threats, you should read this," he said.

He handed Adeogo the presidential pardon signed by President Austin, forgiving any illegal acts that Director Grainger had committed in his pursuit of the terrorist known as the Falcon.

"Congressman, cooperating with Imam Al-Kader was the only way we could locate the Falcon and make our nation and the world safer. But the United States couldn't simply allow Al-Kader to walk away free and reward him with thirty-five million dollars. He was indirectly responsible for murdering our president. Remember, it was Al-Kader who radicalized your brother and turned him into a terrorist. All of us did what needed to be done, but you are mistaken if you think I can allow a contract to surface between the president and a terrorist. Your copy of that document has been destroyed, just as mine has been. And I would suggest that you focus on why all of this was necessary and simply forget about your promise to Al-Kader. Forget for the good of all of us and for the good of the country."

They had reached Adeogo's neighborhood in Takoma Park and were approaching his house.

"I genuinely like you," Grainger told Adeogo. "You are a good man and we need people such as you in Congress. But you must understand that in our fight against terrorism, there is no simple black-and-white world anymore of right and wrong. All lines blur now. When you go into your house tonight, you need to ask yourself only one question— are you and your family safer because Al-Kader and the Falcon are dead? If the answer is yes, then you should be happy when you wake up in the morning. I did not manipulate you. I gave you the opportunity to be an American patriot. You should be proud of what you have done. Good night, Congressman."

CHAPTER SIXTY-THREE

Three weeks later
Happy Riders Horse Farm
Clifton, Virginia

J ennifer is so, so happy now that you are home," Dheeh Adeogo gushed.

She and Brooke were standing with their arms resting on the top rail of a white fence watching their daughters leisurely riding Soupy and Midnight along a well-worn circular path.

It was a warm Friday afternoon with a clear blue sky. Both girls were dressed in tan breeches, tall black riding boots, crisp white blouses, and English riding helmets. The picturesque image could have been photographed for a Virginia tourist brochure.

"Dr. Jacks had me worried," Brooke said. "He was afraid Jennifer would backslide when she saw me."

"Doctors," Dheeh puffed. "What do they really know about the power of a mother's love? I always knew Jennifer would embrace you the moment you came home."

"It was the happiest day of my life. I came directly here from the airport and she was outside riding. She slipped off her horse and ran to me. We both started crying and neither of us wanted to let go."

The two mothers enjoyed a moment of silence watching their daughters ride.

"They are so full of joy and also mischief at this age," Dheeh said. "It is quite remarkable given what both of our daughters have experienced."

"A pair of resilient BFFs."

"I'm sorry Jennifer still does not talk," Dheeh said sadly.

"We've developed a sort of Jennifer sign language that gets us by."

"Oh, I know. Cassy understands her. They use it when they don't want me to know what they are plotting."

Brooke laughed and said, "Would you let Cassy spend the night with us since there's no school tomorrow? Jennifer would love it."

"What a delightful idea. I'm certain Cassy will be excited as well." Lowering her voice to a whisper, she confided, "It will be good for Rudy and me too."

"I haven't wanted to intrude. Are things better?"

"Actually, I have been dying to tell you. We've decided to have another child even though Cassy will be so much older. I've always wanted another baby and Rudy has agreed to try."

Brooke hugged Dheeh and said, "I'm so thrilled for you."

"I must ask you to please not tell anyone, especially Cassy," Dheeh cautioned. "We want to wait until I become pregnant. Maybe tonight will be that night!" Dheeh covered her mouth with her hand to hide her embarrassment at being so brash.

Jennifer and Cassy arrived at the fence where their mothers were whispering and dismounted.

"We're not supposed to race, but we were sort of doing that," Cassy boasted. "I think Midnight is much faster."

"How would you like to spend the night at our house tonight, Cassy?" Brooke asked.

"Oh, Mother, can I please?" she begged Dheeh.

"You should ask Jennifer if she wants to invite you?"

Cassy looked at Jennifer, whose entire face was one huge smile. She rapidly nodded.

"She does!" Cassy interpreted. The two girls grabbed hands and began jumping up and down in excitement.

"Calm yourselves," Dheeh said. "You must first tend to the horses."

"To celebrate, why don't we can get ice cream on the way home?" Brooke suggested.

"Before dinner?" Dheeh asked skeptically.

"There's a popular saying," Brooke replied. "'Eat dessert first.'"

On their ride home, they stopped at a Clifton ice cream parlor where Cassy chose two dips of double chocolate and ordered two scoops of vanilla mixed with cookies for Jennifer. The girls sat outside on a park bench next to a life-size statue of a Jersey cow and licked their cones.

It was shortly after 6:00 p.m. when they reached the long driveway that led up a hill to Brooke's Victorian farmhouse outside Berryville, Virginia, a rural town best remembered because Confederate colonel John S. Mosby, the famed "Gray Ghost," had raided a Union supply train there during the Civil War and escaped with much needed supplies. Built in 1883, Brooke's green-trimmed, white clapboard house was her retreat from the world. It sat in the center of a clearing on the crest of a hill surrounded by native Virginia pines.

Brooke noticed an unfamiliar black sedan parked near her home's front porch and immediately opened the arm rest storage box between the front bucket seats of her Jaguar XF, where she had stashed a 9 mm Beretta. Checking the rearview mirror, she was relieved Jennifer and Cassy were preoccupied and hadn't noticed her retrieve the handgun.

Brook relaxed as soon as the mystery driver stepped into the open.

"Reverend Taylor," she said as she exited the Jaguar. "What brings you here?"

Cassy and Jennifer raced over to her side.

"Cassy," Brooke said, "this is the Reverend Doctor Thaddeus Taylor. And, Jennifer, you should remember him from going with your aunt Geraldine to church."

"What lovely young ladies," the preacher replied, slightly bowing to them.

"Have you been waiting here long?" Brooke asked him.

"Only about ten minutes. I was writing a note on the back of my business card to leave on your door."

The girls disappeared inside the two-story house while Brooke led Reverend Taylor up the front steps and into the parlor. While her house was from the 1800s, Brooke had decorated it with modern pieces and brightly painted wall colors. Reverend Taylor plopped down in an overstuffed bright green chair while she sat in the only antique in the room—a JFK wooden rocker that had belonged to her aunt Geraldine.

"Everyone at church has been praying for you and wondering how you and little Miss Jennifer are doing," the preacher said. "I also came to see you, because the last time we spoke you were pretty darn angry at God."

"I remember, Pastor. It was a rough time immediately after the bombing and I apologize if I offended you."

"Oh, you didn't offend me. You wanted to know why bad things happened to good people and I'm used to questions like that. It's the answers that are sometimes difficult for us to accept. Tell me, child, do you still blame God for the savagery at your wedding?"

"No, I do not blame God. I blame the man who detonated the bomb. I blame the man who made the bomb. I blame the man who told them to make the bomb. But I do not blame God. You see, Pastor, I've come to accept that everything in my life is a gift from God. From my birth into a loving family, to Jennifer becoming my daughter, and those in my family who are gone now but who I was blessed to have in my life—all of them were gifts to me made possible by him. I have accepted what you told me—that there is evil in this world, that life is truly difficult and suffering is part of our lives. If life were easy, why would we need him? He does not create suffering; the evil in men's hearts do. But it is suffering that bonds us to him."

"That's right, Miss Brooke. I'm so happy you understand this."

"I do have another question." She paused, clearly thinking how she wanted to present it. She decided to be direct. "I committed murder. Can I be forgiven?"

"Brooke," he said softly, "the Ten Commandments give us a list of rules and regulations. Can you name them all?"

"No, Pastor, but I'm certainly aware of the ones I've broken and one of them is 'Thou shalt not kill' and if I'm condemned to hell for what I did, I am prepared for that because he was truly an evil man who destroyed many, many innocent lives."

"Oh my my," he replied softly. "You are quoting the King James Bible. Newer versions say you should not commit murder."

He was silent for a thoughtful moment. "Let me tell you a confession," he said. "I served in Vietnam and I saw my share of killing and, quite frankly, I did my share of killing. Yes, now I am a pastor, but this was before I found the Lord and I'm here to tell you, there is killing and there is killing."

"Is there really a difference?"

"As a society, we have decided someone who defends his or her life is not guilty of murder and someone who kills an enemy in defense of the common good, to stop those who would hurt others—that is not murder either. You said this man you killed was responsible for killing thousands of innocent people. I read the papers. The Falcon and his fellow radical Islamists aren't soldiers fighting in some Holy Crusade. They're butchers of children who wrap themselves in religion to hide the evil they commit. What's happening to you now is that you have come home and have time to ponder it."

"I can still see his face before I shot him. I learned in that cave that when you take another life and you look down at what you have done—that is a loss for you too. A loss of your own humanity. I became as much a savage as the Falcon when I shot him."

"I will not minimize the taking of another person's life, but you must remember that moral ambiguity disappears when it's you facing someone else intent on killing you."

"Yes, Pastor, but I chose to execute him. I could have spared him."

She had not planned on admitting that and she wasn't certain Reverend Taylor fully understood what she was now acknowledging because the newspaper accounts reported the Falcon had died during an exchange of gunfire.

"Miss Brooke," he said quietly. "This is between you and God. Ask for forgiveness. God will grant it because you are not a savage. You are his child. I just mentioned the Ten Commandments. I've always believed God left one out. Maybe he did it on purpose and it might just be the most important commandment of all."

"C'mon, Reverend, aren't keeping Ten Commandments difficult enough without you adding another?"

He slapped his knee with his open palm and laughed loudly. "The biggest sin of all—the one I like to call the eleventh commandment—outshines the others, including, 'Thou shalt not kill' but no one even recognizes it."

"What is it?"

"It's believing you actually know God. People do a lot of noodling about why God did this or why God did that or why God didn't do this or why God didn't do that. Yet in First Corinthians we read: 'For now we see through a glass, darkly; but then face to face: now I know in part; but then shall I know even as also I am known.'"

"I'm confused. What does that mean?"

"It means we don't fully understand God and we never will. These radical Islamists are examples of men who violate the eleventh commandment. They decided they know God so well, so intimately, that they can speak for him—not *about* God but for God. They have created a God in their own image and they've decided if you don't agree with them and do what they say, why, they are going to kill you. These radical Islamic extremists have created a false idol—a God of their own molding—that serves their own arrogant purposes. And that, my child, is real evil. No red costume that kids put on at Halloween with their pointed skulls and dagger tails. It's thinking you are God's sword and executioner, rather than his humble servant."

Standing, he said, "Well that's enough theology for one visit. We just hope to see you and Jennifer in church one of these days and please tell Jennifer to bring along that other little girl."

"Cassy. She's a Muslim."

"Good, they'll enjoy our youth group."

"You just told me about your eleventh commandment—people believing they know more than God does and claim to speak for him. Who can we trust then to speak for God?"

"Miss Grant, no one needs to speak for him. I read one time that all these brilliant linguists and theologians put all of the great religious books into a computer, books like the Holy Bible, the Quran, the Torah, and religious teachings followed by Buddhists and Hindus and you know what they found? The computer spit out one thing that every one of those great books revealed as a divine truth—that you should treat other people like you would want them to treat you."

"The Golden Rule."

"Yes, it really is that simple. If you accept that, I think it's pretty clear to see who is evil. If you feel the need to be forgiven for ending the Falcon's life, then ask God to forgive you. But for what it is worth, we need people willing to stand up to evil." He started to leave but stopped himself at the front doorway.

"Would you mind if we pray before I left?" he asked. "Last time you refused. Too much pain in your heart."

"I'd like that, Reverend. Let me get the girls."

Cassy and Jennifer rushed downstairs as soon as they heard her call for them.

"We want to know if we can have pizza?" Cassy asked.

"Sure, but first Reverend Taylor wants us to hold hands and pray."

"I'm a Muslim," Cassy volunteered.

"Good for you," the minister replied as they formed a circle holding hands.

"Thank you, Lord, for creating each of us and making us different because it would be a boring world if we weren't. Thank you, Lord, for loving us because your love is unconditional and for telling us to love others. Thank you, Lord, for letting us show our love each day to others through our actions, words, and deeds. Amen. Or as my Muslim friends would say, 'Praise be to Allah.'"

When they released hands, he winked at the two girls and said quietly to Brooke, "If only we lived in a world where all of us could accept each other like these two girls do. There's a reason why Jesus said, 'Let the little children come to me, and do not hinder them, for the kingdom of heaven belongs to such as these.'"

As soon as he was gone, Cassy said, "Your preacher prayed a lot about love. Well, Jennifer and I love cheese pizza!"

Brooke dialed a Berryville delivery service and noticed while she was placing her order that Cassy was examining the touch pad by the front door. It was part of the house's elaborate security system. After Brooke finished her call, Cassy said, "Miss Grant, Jennifer showed me

your secret room upstairs. The one with all of the television monitors."

"It's called a safe room. Would you like to see inside it? We haven't
had the entire security system on lately because deer kept tripping
some of the alarms, but let's go upstairs and fire up everything."

The girls scampered upstairs to what appeared to be a closet door
that they'd already opened. Behind it was a reinforced steel door that
led into the safe room. It had a wall of monitors and switches as well
as a telephone that had been connected directly to a private security
company. Brooke had dropped that extra charge from her monthly bill
now that the Falcon was dead. She'd also not been as vigilant about
using all of the elaborate system's early warning signals.

At the control panel, Brooke turned on the monitors and activated
the outside cameras and motion detectors.

"When the pizza delivery comes, you'll see for yourself how this
works," she said. "Meanwhile, let's go back downstairs and you girls
can play some games while I make us a salad."

"Will there be a loud siren when the pizza man comes?" Cassy
asked.

"No," Brooke replied. "I have set the controls so it only buzzes on
my cell phone and then the cameras hidden outside show me who is
approaching." She didn't bother to explain why she had turned off the
loud alarm inside the house. She was worried it would terrify Jennifer
if it sounded.

Brooke handed her cell phone to Cassy to monitor and all of them
went downstairs. The girls had been playing a video game in the living room for about thirty minutes when Brooke's cell phone buzzed
and the two girls hurried into the kitchen to show her the video now
showing on it. The first hidden camera at the driveway showed a pizza
delivery car turning off the main road. About midway up the blacktop
drive, a second camera broadcast an image of the car approaching the
house and a third camera on the porch showed a teenage boy exiting
the vehicle with a pizza box.

Cassy and Jennifer rushed to the front door and opened it before he
could knock, startling him, which delighted both of them. Brooke al-

ready had given Jennifer enough cash for the large cheese pizza and a tip.

"Watching him on your phone was really cool," Cassy said, returning it to her. "I'll tell my dad about it and maybe we can get one."

Eager to return to their video games, both girls gobbled down several slices before hurrying back into the family room, leaving Brooke to clean up the kitchen and bake cookies for dessert. She had never been much of a cook but was trying to improve so she could teach Jennifer.

Brooke had just slid the first sheet of cookie dough into her oven when her phone buzzed on the kitchen counter. She'd forgotten to turn off the motion detectors after the pizza delivery. She looked at the image that flashed on its screen, expecting to see a deer.

It was a man.

Quickly removing her apron, she dashed from the kitchen into the front closet where she kept her Beretta while simultaneously calling to the girls.

"Get your shoes on. We need to go outside."

"But we're just—" Cassy began to protest.

Brooke cut her short with a harsh, "NOW!"

Sensing something was wrong, both of them hurried to the front door, where Brooke was waiting. Cassy saw the pistol.

"We're going to play a game," Brooke said. "Hide-and-seek."

Cassy and Jennifer shot skeptical looks at her. Both were too old to be lied to. Clearly they were in danger.

"Okay," Brooke said. "It's not a game. I need both of you to run as fast as you can from the front door into the woods directly across from us. Stay together and stay hiding in the woods until help arrives."

"Someone bad is here," Cassy said.

"Don't worry. I will protect you."

Brooke touched the security pad by the door, turning off the motion-activated lights at the front of the porch that would have spotlighted the girls as they ran. The security monitor listed the time as 9:11 p.m.

"Ready?" she asked. "I'll be right behind you, promise."

Cassy grabbed Jennifer's hand and felt it trembling. "We can do this, Miss Grant," Cassy said. "Together we're not afraid."

Brooke pulled open the door. "Run!"

The girls flew outside, down the front steps and across the open grassy clearing toward the surrounding trees, the closest being some sixty yards away.

With her Beretta in her right hand, Brooke waited for a few moments. She didn't want to draw attention to the fleeing girls. She checked the image on her cell phone and began running from the house in a different direction from Jennifer and Cassy.

Because she was not used to pressing keys on her phone in her left hand with only her thumb while she was running, she slowed about twenty yards away from her front door and tapped in 9-1-1.

She hit SEND.

Her Victorian farmhouse behind her exploded with a tremendous clap.

The blast wave threw Brooke forward as pieces of splintered wooden boards, glass slivers, and metal fragments flew around her. A plank from the home's siding slammed against her right calf, cracking a bone, causing her to crash face-first into the unmowed grass.

In terrible pain, she glanced to her side and realized the girls were in the tree line out of harm's way. Through gritted teeth, she forced herself to sit and check her leg. The fibula bone was sticking out of her torn pant leg but she was not bleeding profusely. Her beloved farmhouse was burning, illuminating the crest of the hill with a bright orange glow, as if someone had started a huge bonfire.

Her Beretta was gone, having been dropped when she'd been knocked forward by the explosion's shock wave. She needed a weapon.

Reaching to her side, she grabbed a piece of wood that until moments ago had been part of the house's front porch. It was about three feet long, two inches wide and an inch thick. Because of her broken leg, she could not run. She had no choice but to wait.

Brooke had recognized Hakim Farouk the moment his image had appeared on her phone via an outside security camera. She'd seen him placing explosives at the rear of her house. As the Destroyer, that was always his first weapon of choice. Like everyone else, she'd assumed he had died when he'd detonated the nuclear bomb hidden aboard the *Bella Francis* in the Panama Canal. Clearly, he had escaped.

He appeared in the flickering lights and began causally strolling toward her, like a ghost rising from her past. In his right hand, he was holding a knife—his other trademark killing tool.

She took a firm hold on the wooden stake on her lap. There was a nail protruding from its tip, which she would put to good use. But she would have to wait until he was near enough.

He taunted her as he approached.

"It was your own phone that detonated the explosion," he bragged. "I turned it into a detonator with my computer and was hoping you would dial 9-1-1 while still inside. Now your death will be more intimate."

He spotted the wooden club on her lap and stopped out of her reach. She was facing him holding the club in her right hand like a baseball bat while sitting on her buttocks with both of her legs stretched out before her. For a second, there was a standoff and then Farouk darted around and rushed up from behind, making it difficult for her to strike him.

He was much quicker than she'd imagined. She twisted her body in a failed attempt to hit him but he was too fast. He kicked her arm, causing her to lose her grip, knocking the board out of her hand. His right foot came down on top of her right wrist, causing her to scream and pinning it against her thigh. In one smooth motion, he snatched her thick hair with his left hand, jerked her head back, exposing her smooth neck for his knife now poised above her head.

She was helpless and understood that she was about to die.

Thud. Thud.

The sounds were so muffled she barely heard them above the crackling sound of her still burning house.

Farouk's grip on her hair loosened and he toppled onto the grass. Blood was coming from two holes in his chest.

Where? Who?

A solitary figure carrying a rifle walked from the woods.

"I've been following him since he jumped ship in Panama," Esther explained. "How badly are you injured?"

"I thought you were dead! My leg is broken."

The two women could hear the sirens of approaching emergency vehicles from Berryville alerted by the powerful blast and flames.

Cassy and Jennifer came running from the woods. Jennifer reached Brooke first, dropped to her knees, and threw her arms around her.

"Mommy! Mommy!" she gasped. "Did he hurt you?"

"Sweetie!" Brooke exclaimed. "You're talking. You're talking." She kissed her cheek and forehead. "You're talking!"

Cassy bent down, too, joining them in a group hug. "Look!" Cassy exclaimed, pointing toward the driveway where the first fire truck had just reached the crest of the hill. An ambulance was directly behind it.

"Go tell them we're out here," Brooke said. "Mommy's hurt."

Both girls ran toward the approaching emergency vehicles, screaming and waving their hands wildly.

"Thank you, Esther, for saving my life," Brooke said. She glanced at Hakim Farouk's crumpled body lying near her in the grass.

"We're KTB teammates, remember," Esther replied. Slinging her rifle, she walked to Farouk's body, straddling it while holding her cell phone directly over his head. She leaned down close to snap a photograph for her Israeli superiors to verify his death.

Hakim Farouk lunged upward, thrusting his knife into her abdomen before falling back with a thud, a final act of hatred before he died.

Esther stared at the knife sticking into her in total disbelief. She grabbed its hilt with both hands and collapsed next to Farouk.

In a panic, Brooke dragged herself toward Esther.

"Don't die! We're not going to let them beat us!" Brooke cried in a voice filled with exasperation and fear. "We're not going to let them beat us! Not them!"

ACKNOWLEDGMENTS

The authors wish to thank Joe DeSantis for his contributions to the development, writing, and editing of this novel. His political experience and insights were invaluable.

We also are grateful to our agents, Kathy Lubbers and David Vigliano, as well as Kate Hartson, our editor at Center Street, an imprint of Hachette Book Group.

In addition, Newt Gingrich wishes to acknowledge: Steve Hanser, who for forty years taught him to think historically; General Chuck Boyd, who tutored him about national security; Joan Dempsey, whose long career in intelligence has been dedicated to protecting America; Congressman Bob Livingston, who epitomizes excellence as an public servant; Terry Balderson, who sends us a lot of articles that end up informing our books; Barry Casselman and Annette Meeks, who introduced us to the vibrant and exciting Somali community in Minneapolis; daughters, Kathy Lubbers and Jackie Cushman, and their husbands, Paul Lubbers and Jimmy Cushman, who have encouraged all of his adventures; grandchildren, Maggie and Robert Cushman, whose future safety keeps him focused on national security and politics; and his wife, Callista Gingrich, whose companionship and love make it all worthwhile.

Pete Earley wishes to thank: Dan and Karen Amato, Gloria Brown, James Brown, LeRue and Ellen Brown, Bob and Mary Donnell, William Donnell, Amanda Driscoll, John and Susan Driscoll, George and Linda Earley, Paul and Ginger Gural, Lauren and Chris Hurlburt,

Walter and Keran Herrington, Marie Heffelfinger, Michelle Holland, Don and Susan Infeld, Kelly McGraw, Ray and Julie McGraw, Peyton and Libby Mahaffey, Dan Morton, David and Cindy Morton, Richard and Joan Miles, Jay and Barbara Myerson, Bassey Nyambi, Nyambi and Atai Nyambi, Mike Sager, Jay and Elsie Strine, Lynn and LouAnn Smith, and Kendall and Carolyn Starkweather. He also is grateful for the love and support of his wife, Patti Michele Luzi, and his children, Stephen, Kevin, Tony, Kathy, Kyle, Evan, and Traci, and granddaughter Maribella.

NEWT GINGRICH is a former Speaker of the House and 2012 presidential candidate. He is a Fox News contributor and author of 35 books, including 15 *New York Times* bestsellers, most recently the #1 *New York Times* bestseller *Understanding Trump*. Newt and his wife Callista host and produce documentary films.

PETE EARLEY is a former *Washington Post* reporter and author of 16 books, including three *New York Times* bestsellers. He was a finalist for the 2007 Pulitzer Prize and has written extensively about Congress, the White House, the FBI, and the CIA.